THE KISS OF LIFE

I looked at the man again, and jumped a little because his eyes had opened. They were blue, and I
had never seen blue eyes before. He stared at me as
if he did not believe I was there. Then his mouth
moved, and he spoke a gasping word I did not understand. Something strong moved within me, and I
hurried to fetch my water bowl.

I knelt over the bowl, took a big mouthful of water,
then went quickly back to the man and lifted his
head in the crook of my arm. Then I pulled his mouth
open a little, put my lips between his, and gently
squirted water into his mouth. I felt his body twitch,
and he lifted an arm, trying feebly to hold my face
against his as he sucked at my mouth even when the
water was gone.

Also by Madeleine Brent:

THE CAPRICORN STONE

THE LONG MASQUERADE*

A HERITAGE OF SHADOWS*

STORMSWIFT*

*Published by Fawcett Books

GOLDEN URCHIN

Madeleine Brent

FAWCETT CREST • NEW YORK

A Fawcett Crest Book
Published by Ballantine Books
Copyright © 1986 by Madeleine Brent

Library of Congress Catalog Card Number: 86-8959

ISBN 0-449-21389-7

This edition published by arrangement with Doubleday & Company, Inc.

Manufactured in the United States of America

First Ballantine Books Edition: January 1988

ONE

I LAID THE SMALL OBJECT ON THE BACK OF MY WRIST TO STUDY
it. Even though I had now lived many summers, perhaps as
many as could be numbered on three hands, I was still ashamed
of my pale skin and my fiery hair and the spray of tiny brown
spots on my nose and cheeks. Long ago, when I was small, I
had given up putting ashes on my hair to make it black, because
the other girl-children had mocked me worse than before. But I
still had the habit of hiding the palms of my hands as much as
possible, for they remained even paler than the rest of my body
because they had not been darkened by the sun.

The object lying on my wrist was as big as a man's eye, but
perfectly round, like the full moon. It was the color of dark
sand, and no thicker than the edge of the comeback boomerang
the boy-children played with, yet it was hard as stone, and as
strong. I could not bend it. On the face of the strange object
somebody had carved a tiny picture of a sitting-down person
holding a spear with three points. When I looked closely I felt
sure this was a woman, and I laughed because she had a funny
kind of bowl upside down on her head. I turned the object over
and found that almost the whole of the other side carried a carving of a woman's head.

Kneeling beside me, Yuma touched the carving with his finger, then touched my nose, giggling. "Like you, Mitji," he said. "Same funny nose."

I slapped his thigh, but not very hard because Yuma was the person I liked most. Of all our family, and of all the other families in our tribe, Yuma was the only person who had ever given me warmth since I lost my mother when she went away to marry a man in another tribe, three summers before. She would have taken me with her, but the man would not have me. Everybody knew that Manyi was not my true mother and that I was a spirit who had returned from the dead. Other babies were born a milky color but quickly became properly dark-skinned. I had not been born from Manyi's body, but had been reborn through the power of an ancestor-spirit and put in a place for Manyi to find me at a time when her true baby had died. I had heard that a few of our people in other tribes had hair the color of dry grass, but none had a white body like mine, and none had a thin nose and fiery hair.

I had heard, too, that far away where the edge of the world touched the great waters there were many new tribes who had come out of the waters and onto the land. Their skins were white and they wore coverings on their bodies all the year round, but these were not fashioned from possum or kangaroo skins, like the cloaks we wore on cold nights, and they could not have been woven from human hair, like the girdle I wore with its tassel of emu feathers, for no such quantity of human hair could exist.

Sometimes, in secret, I wondered if it might be possible for me to live among one of these tribes. Perhaps they would not be able to tell that I was a spirit returned from the dead, and would think I was one of them. Among my own people I was regarded as a freak. In years gone by, the girl-children had both feared and mocked me, so I had spent most of my time playing with Yuma and other boys. Now that I was older, and had become a woman last summer, the people of our tribe seemed to be even less friendly toward me and I felt an outcast. Mitapuyi, the senior man of our family, together with other elders, had

made known to me that I would not be allowed to marry, nor to
take part in the usual rituals of our people.

Strangely, perhaps because I was not a normal person, I had
no wish to marry and was glad that I had not been put through
the rituals that were performed when a girl became a woman.
But I sometimes dreamed how wonderful it would be to live
among the new tribes from the great waters, who were made
like me and so would never realize that I was a freak.

I looked up from the object on my wrist and said, "I have
seen nothing like this before. What is it, Yuma?"

We were resting in a creekbed, half a morning's walk through
many sandhills from the waterhole where our tribe had been
living since the last new moon, so we were quite alone, but
Yuma still looked carefully about him and lowered his voice as
he said, "It is *mapanpa*. Powerful *mapanpa*, Mitji."

This was in the days when the only tongue I spoke was that
of our people, and I knew nothing of the words I use now, apart
from a ghost-memory of another kind of world in the dreamtime
before I was born. I am speaking now of my own dreamtime,
not the Great Dreamtime, the *tjukurpa* we called it, when the
totem-spirits were creating the world before men and women
were made. I had no memory of words from my own dreamtime, but I have learned much since that day in the gully. When
Yuma spoke of *mapanpa* he meant an object possessing magical
powers, like the secret talismans used by Ulurka, our sorcerer.
My own name, Mitji, meant "white woman." The strange ones
from the great waters, those we had never seen but had been
told about by other tribes when we gathered for a corroboree,
had been given the name *walypala*, meaning "white people."

Yuma reached out and turned the object over so that it again
showed the sitting-down woman with the three-pointed spear.
Then he pointed to some very small signs around the edge of
the little disc. Taking the bone from his nose, he began to scratch
in the dust with the point of it, craning his neck to look at the
tiny marks again and again as he drew them one by one on the

ground. Yuma was a clever artist who made good rock paintings, and he copied the marks well.

ONE PENNY.

He pointed to a small space below the ground where the
woman's feet rested, and carefully copied some more marks that
had been carved there.

1887.

For a while we sat looking at the marks, and they were so
powerful that I felt a shiver go through my body and I tossed
the object from my wrist. Yuma caught it and grinned. "Big
mapanpa," he said. "I will find others and become a greater
sorcerer than Ulurka, to heal sickness and drive away *mamu.*"
The spirits that moved at night were called *mamu*, and were said
to be dangerous, but I had never seen or felt one near me. "I
will carve these signs on my magic bone," Yuma went on, "and
when I point it at my enemies they will die."

I said, "You have not got a magic bone, Yuma."

He smoothed a hand over the dust to wipe out the marks. "I
will get one," he said in a manner so offhand that I looked at
him sharply. "It must be a bone from the chest of a female
kangaroo"—he yawned—"hunted and killed by a woman. This
was shown to me in a dream."

I laughed then. "So that is why you ask me to come to this
place with you every day. You hope we may sight a kangaroo
for me to hunt and kill away from the men, who would not allow
it. You are foolish, Yuma. Woman gathers, man hunts. Woman
finds *ngaru* fruit and seeds and witchetty grubs. She digs for
yams, she collects berries and birds' eggs and nuts. She catches
lizards and frogs and snakes. She does not hunt."

Yuma sniffed and pointed to his weapons lying close beside
him, then to my own. "You are not a true woman, Mitji. You
carry a throwing club and a spear and a spear-thrower. They are
not so heavy as mine, but for three summers now you have taken
small game with them, for I taught you well." He pointed again.
"You carry the boomerang I made for you. It is not so heavy as
mine, but it is a war boomerang, a hunting boomerang, not a

little comeback *kali* that children use in play. No woman carries weapons as you do; therefore you are not a true woman. But the kangaroo will not know this, so you can hunt and kill a female for me; then I will get my magic bone.''

I considered this for a while. It seemed to me that to say I was not a woman because I carried weapons was an upside-down thought. I had a woman's body, I felt like a woman, and I would have acted like one if I had been permitted to do so. But because I was a freak I had been forced to grow up in ways that were different from those of the other girl-children. There was no point in arguing about this with Yuma. He was a man, and if he said that I was not a true woman, then this was the end of the matter. Besides, I would be happy to help him, for he had always been kind to me, especially after Manyi had gone away.

I still missed Manyi. Among our people the women suckled babies for as long as four summers, and Manyi had suckled me for two after finding me in the place where the totem-spirit had created me. My first memory was of being at her breast—my first memory after the dreamtime, that is—and so it was a great sorrow to me when she was sold to another tribe for marriage. I would never forget that Yuma was the one who had given me warmth then, even though at that time he was a boy who had yet to be initiated.

I said, ''The biggest game I have ever brought down was an emu. Perhaps I cannot bring down a kangaroo.''

Yuma picked up my boomerang and pressed his little *mapan-pa* against it, muttering to himself. Then he said, ''I have made some magic to help. You will do it, Mitji.''

I gathered my weapons and stood up. ''First we have to find a female kangaroo. It is more than four moons since our people tasted kangaroo meat, and we have been coming to this place for many days now without finding kangaroo tracks.''

''We will find,'' said Yuma, tucking his *mapanpa* away in the pouch at his belt and restoring the bone to his nose. ''We will find when we go farther, to the place beyond the hill, where the mulga trees grow.''

We set off again, sometimes talking but always looking, looking, looking, to read every tiny sign left by bird or beast. I was as good as most of the boys at seeing where a lizard had scuttled or a falcon had pounced on some small creature, but my nose— my small, straight, funny nose—was almost useless. I could be within a long spear's throw of water under the ground, yet be scarcely able to scent it, and I was deeply ashamed of this.

As we walked I said, "Where did the *mapanpa* come from, Yuma?"

"Katapi, the new wife of Nyiki, brought it with her. It came to her from another woman who married a man of her tribe. The other woman's people are far away and have met with some of the *walypala*." Yuma touched the little pouch at his belt. "This was made by *walypala* magic, Mitji. It is very powerful. You saw the head of the woman carved on it? She is the Elder of Elders among the *walypala*. They have many tribes, and she is the senior person of the senior family of them all."

I almost laughed again. It was clear to me that the new wife of Nyiki had not spoken truly in telling such a story, for it was impossible to have a woman as senior person of a family, and even more impossible that she could be an Elder of Elders, over many tribes. But I did not want to make Yuma unhappy, so I held down my laughter and only said, "What did you give Nyiki in exchange, Yuma?"

Among our people it was impossible to give or receive without something changing hands in exchange. I had made my own spear and spear-thrower, but Yuma had made my boomerang for me, and in exchange I had given him a belt I had plaited from snakeskin. Now he said, "I gave some hair from my sister. Nyiki wanted it so that Katapi could weave a new tassel for his belt."

I was starting to say something else when I saw the faint tracks of a *kurkati*, a kind of lizard. At once I pointed them out to Yuma, and we began to follow them as they wound this way and that between clumps of the pale green spiky grass that spread across the dunes and plains. After a while the tracks became stronger, and then we found the burrow. Yuma jumped on the ground a little way from the hole to block the tunnel, and I dropped to my knees to work quickly with my digging stick. The lizard was no deeper than from my wrist to my elbow, and very soon Yuma was able to catch its tail, pull it out, and kill it with a blow from his throwing club.

It was not a big lizard, weighing no more than a few handfuls of sand, but Yuma was very pleased as he tied it to his belt, for it meant that he would not return to our camp empty-handed from the day's hunting. We went on through the sandhills until we came to a flat place with red rocks and low cliffs rising from the ground amid scrub and mulga trees. Here we had built a *mangu*, a small circle of brush in which we could hide and keep watch for any game coming to the nearby creekbed.

There was water just below the gravel of the creekbed, and together we cleared a small soak-hole we had already dug so that water would gather to give a strong scent and bring game to this spot. We drank well ourselves, then moved downwind to squat in the *mangu*. This was the third day we had come here to hunt, but without success. By good fortune I had found some ripe *kampurarpa* fruit on our way back the first day, and Yuma had caught a carpet snake the second day. Otherwise we would have had nothing to take back to our families.

There were signs that kangaroos used this creekbed, for we could see the round depressions they made in the soil by beating with their tails to crush the scrub and make a sleeping place. But, though we waited till the sun had moved well across the sky, no animal of any kind came near, only birds on the wing, too high to bring down with a throwing club or boomerang.

I could see that Yuma was very sad, and I felt sorry for him. "Do you want to lie with me, Yuma?" I asked. "Perhaps it will make you happy."

He shrugged and looked away. "I cannot lie with one who is not a true woman, Mitji. It would make bad magic, and might take away my manhood."

Among our people, boys and girls quite young would lie together like men and women as part of their playing, but this had not happened with me. The boys were afraid to couple with a freak, and even if they had wanted me I felt no desire for them. Today I had offered to lie with Yuma partly because I wanted to take away his sorrow and partly because I was curious about what happened between a man and a woman in this way. But I had a small glad feeling when he refused me.

Before the sun had gone down we reached the place where our tribe was camped, and the dingoes came yapping and barking to greet us. I had collected a bowl of *wangunu* seeds in the mulga country before returning, and later I had used a thorn to dig some witchetty grubs from holes in the trunk of a tree. I would have liked to give these to some of the small children, but I could not, for this would mean that they or their mothers or fathers would have to make a gift to me in return. Quite often it happened that I felt a wish to do things like this that were strange or wrong or impossible among true people, so I was always being reminded that I was not one of them.

As it was summer, we had not made huts of bark for our camp but had put up brushwood shelters to give daytime shade. I saw that our families would eat well tonight, for some of the men had killed an emu, and the women had set it in a small trench and piled hot embers on the carcass to roast it. Among our people, all food was shared, according to certain rules, among the kin of whoever had hunted or gathered the food. Although I was not a true person, I was still regarded as kin to Aldinga, the father of my mother, Manyi, so I was always given my proper share. Yuma and I divided the lizard, the *wangunu* seeds, and the witchetty grubs between us for our two families. Then Yuma took a young girl called Wytala a little way off to lie with her, and I joined my kinswomen and began to prepare the seeds for grinding.

When this was done I stayed to gossip with them for a while, telling them that Yuma and I had found a place where he hoped to kill a kangaroo, and that we would try again tomorrow. They made fun of me, saying that it must have been my fiery hair that kept the kangaroos away, because they could see it from the distance of a day's march. They spoke in jest, and I was used to being made fun of, but still it made a small heaviness within me, and I found it hard to smile and laugh with them.

After a little while I went out of the camp to practice with my boomerang. Some of the boys were playing with their *kali*, competing to see who could throw one so that it returned closest to a marked spot. I had done well in this when I was younger, until I found that it made the boys angry when I was better than they were. After that, I took care to throw so that I missed the marked spot. It was difficult enough to be Mitji the freak without having the boys dislike me as well. One day they would be men, and elders, with the right to beat me if they so chose.

Mine was a fighting boomerang, not made to return, so each time I threw it at the gum tree I had chosen as a target I had to walk many paces to recover it. Nobody took notice of me while I was doing this. I think our people had come to feel that the strange ways of Mitji were natural to somebody of her strange appearance, and they were not concerned about what I did as long as I bore my fair share of the work and caused no trouble.

Later, when the sun went down, I ate with my kinsfolk, brought water in a wooden bowl from the water hole for the men, then went to sleep under one of the brushwood shelters with Tankai, a girl born in the same summer that Manyi found me, two smaller children, and one of the dingoes at my back for warmth.

Next day I set out again with Yuma for the mulga country. As soon as we had left the camp he said, "You have not told anyone about my *mapanpa*?"

"No, of course not, Yuma. My tongue does not wag."

"Good." He touched the pouch at his belt. "Then I will tell you a magic word. You must never speak it aloud. If you do, you will die. Only I can speak it aloud without dying, but if we say it together inside our heads as we walk, without sound, then it will bring the kangaroo to the creekbed today."

I felt excited but a little frightened to be helping him in such powerful magic, and my voice came small from my mouth as I said, "What is the word?"

He touched a finger to his lips and spoke in a whisper. "It is the name of the woman on the *mapanpa*, the Elder of Elders, over all the *walypala* tribes. It is . . . *Mitjiquin*!"

I almost echoed the word in surprise, for part of it was my own name, but I managed to swallow it without speech. *Mitjiquin*. White-woman-*quin*. I wondered what *quin* might mean but did not dare to ask. As we walked, and rested in the gully, and walked again, I kept speaking the word in my head, as Yuma had told me. I was a little fearful at first, but this slowly passed, and then I began to feel a new fear. If the magic worked and a kangaroo came, would I be able to bring it down and kill it? This was what Yuma needed, and I was very worried that I might fail him.

Mitjiquin . . . mitjiquin . . . mitjiquin . . .

The speaking in our heads did not distract our eyes from their constant task of looking for signs that might lead to food. Once we found tracks of a big lizard, a goanna, but they led toward the place of sunrise, away from the route we were taking, and Yuma said we could not turn aside to hunt it. Each day on this journey we did not follow our own tracks, made before, but traveled a little distance from them to cover new ground that might offer food. On this day we tracked a possum to a hollow tree, and Yuma killed it with his spear. This pleased him very much, for he said it was a sign that his magic was working.

When we reached the creekbed we drank deeply and made sure the soak-hole was filling again with water, then went to hide in our circle of brushwood, not speaking, but saying the magic word in our heads. After the sun had passed the highest point of its daily journey across the sky, we ate some honey ants I had brought with me in a possum-skin bag. Their bellies were swollen with sweet honey, so they made good eating.

It was not long after this that Yuma suddenly lifted his head sharply, and I saw his nostrils twitching. I stopped breathing, to listen better, and heard the faint *thump-thump* that told of a moving kangaroo. In sign language our people used while hunting, Yuma said there was only one creature approaching, and I agreed. Then, as the sound came closer, he signed for me to keep low so that my fiery hair would not show above the brushwood concealing us. I felt angry with myself because I had not thought to put mud or charcoal on my hair in readiness for this moment, but Yuma had not thought of it either.

The thumping stopped no more than a spear-throw away. I caught the scent now, and heard the kangaroo begin to drink from the soak-hole. Very slowly, Yuma rose to peer over the brushwood. Then he signed to me that the moment had come. Strange chills and sweats passed through my body, and I saw my hand shake as I fitted the butt of my spear into the spur of my spear-thrower, then gripped the knob of grassgum at the other end of the thrower. Cautiously, I rose from my squatting position.

It was not a large kangaroo, for as it lifted its head from the soakhole I saw that it stood lower than my shoulder by the width of two hands, and from the blue-gray color of its skin I knew that this was a female. The males were red. A touch of relief eased my anxiety, for it might have been one of the great kangaroos standing twice as tall, and these were very dangerous if attacked.

Moving slowly, aware of Yuma's eyes flicking back and forth from the kangaroo to me, I leaned back, extending my throwing arm, resting the forward part of the spear on the fingers of my other hand. I was in the very act of throwing when the eagle appeared, flying low along the creekbed, great wings beating the air as it swept by, no more than the height of a tall tree above the ground.

The kangaroo was startled, and it jumped as I made my cast. The spear struck home, but in the big part of the hind leg instead of under the foreleg, by the heart. Next moment the creature was jumping away, the spear dragging and hindering its flight at first, but then pulling free. In moments my quarry was well beyond spear-throw. I heard a wail of despair from Yuma, and a pain passed through my body. What I did next was done without thought, as if my ancestor-spirit had suddenly possessed me.

I found I had jumped the brushwood fence and was holding my boomerang, poised to throw. My arm came sweeping forward over my head, and I watched the long curved piece of wood spinning end over end before turning to the horizontal. Yuma was chanting ''Mitjiquin! Mitjiquin!'' This was surely powerful magic, for the boomerang struck hard against the small head of the kangaroo, toppling her to the ground, stunned.

I was already running hard, scooping up my fallen spear with its fire-hardened point, hearing Yuma call out behind me as I ran on. Then I was standing over the creature just as it began to stir, and I drove my spear up between the ribs to its heart. Yuma came up and began dancing round the kangaroo, crowing with delight. I should have felt as he did, for here was meat such as our families had not tasted for several moons, and beyond that I had secured for Yuma the magic bone that would be such a powerful *mapanpa*. But there was an emptiness within me, and I turned away to squat with my back to Yuma as he began to slit open the hide with the sharp stone he carried.

Later we tied the legs of the kangaroo and I helped lift it onto Yuma's shoulders for our return to camp. We stopped for him to rest several times on the journey, but he did not mind having the burden to carry, for he was filled with delight. Not only had he secured the special bone from a female kangaroo slain by a woman, but he would be acclaimed as a fine hunter by our people. We could not tell them that it was I who had made the kill, because this was man's work, and we could not offer any reason for what we had done without revealing the important secret of Yuma's dream and his *mapanpa*.

There was a feast that night, and we all slept with swollen bellies. Next morning Yuma gave me a claw from the kangaroo to hang on a cord round my neck in exchange for the help I had given him. But in the days that followed, he seemed to lose all the warmth he had once shown me. This made a pain in my heart, for I had done nothing to hurt him. It was as if he now felt anger toward me simply because I knew of his *mitjiquin* and his magic bone, but I had not asked him to tell me the secrets of his *mitjiquin*, and it was he who had wanted me to secure the bone for him.

I became very lonely, not having Yuma for my friend, and one day I did a wrong thing that only one who was not a true person would think of doing. I collected some fine fat witchetty grubs, all bigger than my thumb, cooked them lightly, and took them to Yuma. At once he became very angry with me and said I was trying to make him give me some of his magic in exchange. Too late I realized that it would be useless to say the food was a gift, for he would never understand this. So I told him something equally true, that all I wanted from him in exchange was a little warmth.

This made no difference, for he did not believe me and became very threatening, saying that if ever I spoke of the secrets he had told me, he would point the bone at me and I would die. I went away from the camp to be by myself for the rest of that day, sitting in the shade of a big red rock, sometimes weeping a little, sometimes angry, hating the white skin and fiery hair that clothed my spirit, but knowing that these could never be changed.

That night I dreamed I was visiting the land of the *walypala*. All the men and women and children had white skin and red hair like mine, with little brown specks around their small noses. They had coverings like woven hair about their loins and chests, and their camp was filled with huge huts of bark, four paces across and twice as high as a man. When I came to their camp they welcomed me with much outflowing of warmth, giving me juicy meat to eat and coverings to put on my body. I was so happy that tears ran from my eyes, but then I woke to a loneliness that seemed even deeper than before. This was the moment when it came to me that I would go walkabout, a long walkabout, keeping the middle-day sun at my back and the setting sun on my spear-arm side, till at last I found the camp of the *walypala* who had come from the great waters.

I decided that I would not try to deceive them into thinking I was of their own kind. I would explain that I was not a true person but a freak from a blackskin tribe, and I would ask if I might stay with them and learn their ways. Then, if I worked hard at gathering food for them and hunting for them, perhaps I would find some who would be warm toward me, so that I no longer felt alone.

I knew that in less than a moon our people would be moving on toward the middle-day sun to make camp in a new place, three or four days' march away, because most of the food near our present camp had been gathered and eaten. I planned to go walkabout in the opposite direction, and I decided to leave the day before whichever day our elders chose for our move.

There was little preparation for me to make. I had my weapons, a wooden bowl, a digging stick, and a possum-skin bag in which I would carry some smoke-dried pieces of meat. When our people moved, the women usually carried fire-sticks, pieces of smoldering mulga wood, but I would not need one. I could always make fire by using my spear-thrower as a rubbing stick on a piece of soft wood. The most important thing for my walk-about would be water. I would drink a full belly of water before leaving, but the only way I could carry any would be in the bowl on my head, with a piece of twisted grass floating on the water to stop it splashing.

The question of water would not trouble me greatly for the first few days, because in our wanderings through the land belonging to our tribe we had come from the direction in which I would now be going, so I knew where to find the water holes. Once I continued farther away from the middle-day sun, I would be moving through unknown country. Then I would have to find water wherever I could, by digging in a dry riverbed, by draining some from the roots of certain trees, by chewing the purple flowers that held moisture, or by finding some water frogs. These frogs filled their bodies with water and burrowed underground during the dry moons. When I found signs of one I could easily dig it up and squeeze the water out. Then I could cook and eat it.

On the day of my going I left the camp quietly, long before dawn, so that I would be far away before anyone found that I was gone. For as many spear-throws as I could number on two hands I pulled a bundle of long emu feathers after me to spoil my tracks. This would not stop the men finding my sign or following me by scent if they wished, but I did not think anyone would take such trouble. With Manyi gone, and Yuma losing his warmth for me, there was nobody left who would wish to find me. The elders might be angry that I was not there with the other women to carry children and belongings to our next camp, but they would not waste time having me brought back to be beaten for my offense.

For the next four days I walked from sunrise until middle-morning, rested in whatever shade I could find throughout the greatest heat of the day, then walked on again until a little while before sunset. As I walked I did not think about the people I had left, and did not think very much about what would happen when I found the camps of the *walypala*, for it was too hard to make pictures in my mind of how they would be. For most of the time I walked and rested with my mind asleep except for being always alert for signs of food or water.

After those first four days my progress became slower, for now I was in strange country and it was more barren than the country I had left. Despite this, I was never hungry, and was thirsty only three times during the two-hands of days that followed. Sometimes at night, alone as I had never been before, I was afraid that the *mamu*, the night spirits, would pounce on me, but by saying "*mitjiquin*" many times in my head I was able to drive them away—or at least to drive my fears away.

There was one night when I dreamed again about the *walypala*, but this time they did not welcome me and give me warmth from their hearts. Instead they beat me with sticks and drove me away from their camp. This dream made me troubled in my mind, but I could only hope that it was a false sign.

In the morning I ate some fruit and the rest of a lizard I had cooked the night before, then went on my way. Before I had walked for more than a small part of the morning, I came suddenly upon a sight that made my heart beat quickly with fear.

I was moving through rock and sandhill country, broken by wide stretches of flat sand, and as I emerged from the low hills onto a desert plain I saw ahead of me a creature shaped like something in a bad dream. It was much bigger than the biggest kangaroo, standing on four long legs, its upcurving neck twice as thick as my body and as long as my digging stick, ending in a small head like a very bad drawing of a kangaroo's head. The body, high above the ground, was covered with short hair and rose in two great lumps along the back.

The animal was no more than three long spear-throws from where I stood, its head low as it chewed at some brown tufts of grass. I gripped my spear nervously, wanting to run and hide but at the same time so filled with wonder at this amazing sight that I had to stand my ground and stare, hoping the creature was not some kind of giant dingo that might tear me to pieces and eat me.

As I stared, the animal lifted its head, looked at me in a cold way, and went on chewing. Then I saw that between the two lumps on its back was what seemed to be a thick pile of skins, and they were fastened there by a girdle of skin that passed under the belly, in much the same way that my girdle was fastened around my waist.

Suddenly a memory came to me. The older men and women of our people always taught children much about the creatures of the world, explaining how they lived, how best to read their tracks and hunt them, and how their skins and bones could be used. One old man, Jabaljari by name, had once scratched on a piece of soft rock the shape of two animals that he said had been brought to the world by the *walypala* tribes. He had seen both in his youth, when he had traveled toward the place of the rising sun for a corroboree.

The first was called *wurpa*. It was many times bigger than a dingo, could run very fast, and the *walypala* used it for pulling heavy burdens along the ground. Also, he said, the *walypala* could sit upon the *wurpa* and go wherever they wished without having to walk. The second animal he scratched on the rock was even bigger than the *wurpa*, and I remembered now that it had a long neck, long legs, and big lumps on its back. Jabaljari had been told that this was called *kamil*. It was an easier word to say than *wurpa*, and much like the word used by the white tribes. *Wurpa* was not like the word used by the white tribes, because in their speech were sounds our people could not make.

I stopped remembering what Jabaljari had said and put all my mind to studying the animal. So this was a *kamil*, and I was seeing it with my own eyes. Excitement began to grow within me. If the *kamil* was used by the *walypala*, then perhaps I was not far from one of their camps. And if they sat on a *wurpa* to travel, then perhaps they also sat on a *kamil* instead of walking. The pile of skins fastened between the lumps seemed to be a place on which to sit, and now I saw that leather ropes hung from a band fastened around the *kamil's* head.

I began to move slowly toward the creature, talking gently in the way I always spoke to our camp dingoes. It showed no sign of being dangerous, and in a little while I was standing quite close to it. Now I saw that the pile of skins was really a very thick piece of hide, thicker than the top of my leg, with another skin on top of it, but the upper skin seemed to be woven from hair of all different colors, some fiery like my own. Again I wondered how the *walypala* could grow so much hair, and I marveled that they had hair of so many colors.

Even though I was taken up with looking at this strange creature, I had noted the shape of its tracks and would always know them again. I had also noted the direction of the tracks. If I followed them back the way they had come, then surely they would lead me to a *walypala* camp, as long as the camp was not too far away. If it was more than two-hands of days' walking, then in the end I might find the tracks too faint to follow, for I was not as skilled in following sign as the true persons of our people.

A spirit moved suddenly within me. I began to say "*mitjiquin, mitjiquin*" inside my head, and moved slowly closer until I was able to gather the strip of hide that hung from the band around the *kamil's* head. "Come," I said aloud but gently. "Let us go and find the *walypala*. If they have lost you, and if I take you back to them, perhaps their hearts will grow warm toward me and they will let me live among them."

Still chewing, the *kamil* gave me another cold look, but when I pulled gently on the strip of hide it turned and began to plod beside me as I set off along the line of tracks it had made across the sandy plain. My heart lifted within me. "It sees me as a *walypala*!" I thought with joy. "It sees my white skin and my fiery hair, and it obeys me as it would obey a true *walypala*!"

When the sun was well risen I stopped to rest until the big heat of the day had passed. There was no shade, and I was about to dig a hole to lie in when the *kamil* settled down on its belly in a way that made me laugh, going down first on its foreknees and then lowering its hindquarters. In this position it gave a good patch of shade in which I could lie down and rest.

Later, before we set off again, I looked at some of the strange things hanging on strips of hide from the *kamil*. There were bags of hide and of strong grass, beautifully made, that were empty now but which my nose told me had once held food. There were things shaped rather like bags, but made of hard material, as hard as Yuma's *mapanpa* with the picture of the *mitjiquin*. The only opening in them was a small hole with a plug of hard-soft stuff filling the hole. When I pulled one of these plugs out I could smell that there had once been water inside, and I thought how clever the *walypala* must be to have such things for carrying water. They were so much better than our wooden bowls, which lost much water to the sun.

The *kamil* also carried a wonderful digging stick with a broad blade of the same stone-hard substance as the water carriers, but even thicker and stronger. Beside this hung two more dig-

ging sticks shaped like a person standing with both arms outstretched and slightly curved. The straight part was of wood,
and I knew this must be the handle. The curved part was of the
hard substance, but as thick as my wrist in the middle, and
pointed like a blunt spear at each end.

There was a big bundle of woven material, very strong and
far too coarse to be human hair. But the strangest thing of all
was an object mostly hidden in a long thin bag of hide. It was
partly of wood, partly of the hard substance, and when I slid it
a little way out of the bag holding it I saw that the hard substance
became round and straight like a thick stick, but perfect and
without blemish. I could not tell if it was solid like a stick, but
judged from the weight that it might be hollow like a reed. It
was greasy to touch, and from it came a smell I had never known
before, a fierce, sharp smell of something burnt. To me it came
as a bad smell, dangerous, and I quickly let the thing slide down
into its bag again.

When I tugged on the *kamil's* head strap it blew bad breath
at me and would not move, but I banged on the ground with my
digging stick and shouted angrily till the creature came to its
feet in the same funny way as it had knelt down. Then it followed
me obediently.

Sometime later, when the sun was no more than its own height
above the horizon, I came upon the first *walypala* I had ever
seen . . . or the first I could ever remember seeing.

TWO

THE MAN WORE COVERINGS OF WOVEN MATERIAL OVER THE whole of his body except for his head and hands. Close to where he lay on the sand was a bowl-shaped thing of soft material with an empty space in it, and I could see at once that this was something he had worn on his head, like the woman in the small picture on Yuma's *mapanpa*.

He had been dead for almost half a day, killed by the sun, his tongue black and swollen. I felt great disappointment as I squatted beside him, studying him. Although his skin was burnt, he was certainly a *walypala*, for when I pushed back the covering of his arm and looked at the skin on the inside, near the elbow, it was pale like my own. Strangely, his front tooth had not been knocked out, which meant that he had never been initiated into manhood.

When I had first seen what the *kamil* carried I had thought the *walypala* must be very clever, but this one had not been at all clever. His cheeks and belly were sunken with hunger, and it was clear that he had not drunk water for more than a day and had drunk very little for several days before. When I looked at the tracks it was easy to see that he had been following the *kamil*, trying to catch it. For how long, I could not tell until I followed the tracks back, but I thought he must have continued walking in the big heat of the day, and this had taken all the water out of his body, so he died.

When I looked back over his tracks for two or three spear-throws I saw that he had fallen to his knees and crawled a little way before his strength went from him. It seemed a very foolish way to die, but I realized that it must have happened because a *walypala* sorcerer had pointed the bone at this man, causing him to bring about his own death. His beard and hair were turning gray, so I guessed he must be an elder of his tribe and I wondered how his *walypala* widows would mourn him. Among our own people the widows mourned for days, gashing their legs and scalps to make the blood run, and often cutting off a finger joint.

I did not want to linger in case the man's spirit was still hovering nearby, waiting to be released by mourning rites unknown to me, but my eye was caught by a pouch of glossy hide at his girdle. After summoning up all my courage, and repeating *"mitjiquin!"* many times in my head for protection, I managed to open the strange fastening of his girdle and pull the pouch away. I was not sure why I did this. Perhaps at the back of my mind was the thought that this man might himself have been a sorcerer and that his pouch, like Yuma's, held some powerful *mapanpa.* If so, then when I found the *walypala* tribe I would have something valuable to offer in exchange for their allowing me to live among them.

In the pouch was a piece of stuff the same shape as the blade of the digging stick on the *kamil*, but little thicker than a leaf. I could see that it had once been as white as a tooth, but most of it was covered with the marks of fingers and the straight edges were ragged and torn. It had been folded twice, and when I opened it I saw that on one side had been drawn many black lines, but they did not make a picture or a pattern.

I felt a wrongness about this *mapanpa*, and was about to throw it aside when some spirit within me made me pause. I decided not to throw it away where the dead man's spirit might be lurking in case it displeased him, but to carry it a good distance first. What remained in the pouch were some small stones, each about as big as a child's tooth. I tipped them onto my palm and found they were the color of yellow sand, but with a kind of shining surface as if they held small parts of the sun. The stones were in some ways similar in substance to the *mapanpa* Yuma had shown me, but when I tried one against my teeth it felt softer.

They were very pretty stones, and I decided they must be good *mapanpa* that I could offer to the *walypala* tribe, so I put them in my possum-skin pouch. The white-leaf thing with the black lines I put back in the glossy hide pouch and tucked this into one of the bags hanging from the *kamil* because I did not want it close to me. I was disappointed because the man was dead, and also because where his hair was not gray it was black, and I had always thought that every *walypala* must have fiery hair like mine. Before leaving him, I found a sharp stone and cut my leg to shed a little blood so that his spirit would know he had been mourned, even though only by a stranger; but it was a very small cut.

I took the *kamil's* head strap and we went on, still following the tracks. I had drunk the last of my water that morning, but was not troubled because ahead I could see a saltmarsh, and I knew there would be fresh water feeding it underground. There would also be water frogs nearby, and ample food to be found among the rocks and sandhills beyond. The dead *walypala* could have found plenty to eat and drink if he had not been cursed by a sorcerer so that his mind was made foolish.

When I scented fresh water we stopped for the night, for the sun had gone and dusk was falling. I had to dig as deep as my arm, but the wonderful digging stick from the *kamil* made it quite easy. I drank a full bowl of water myself, then another, and with my belly filled I waited for more water to seep into the hole so that the *kamil* could drink. When it had done so, the creature lay down as before and closed its eyes. I drove my own digging stick into the ground, tied the head strap to it, then moved away to gather some grass and wood.

The *kamil* opened its eyes to watch as I sawed with the edge of my spear-thrower on a piece of soft wood until there were enough bright embers to cup in a ball of grass and blow to flame. Soon I had a good fire, and when the wood had burnt to hot ashes I cut up the snake I had caught earlier that day and cooked it. Half I put in my bag for the next day, then offered a piece to the *kamil*. It only turned its head away, so I ate all the rest myself.

In the morning I let the *kamil* drink the water hole empty because I wanted to be sure it would not die. For myself I was able to find some water frogs and get enough from them to half fill my bowl. Then I gathered up my weapons, took hold of the *kamil's* head strap, and shouted at him until he got up. Before we reached the sandhills I found a place where *yelka* grew widely, and I dug up many of the tubers because I discovered that the *kamil* liked them. We went on together, eating them as we followed the tracks, and I felt the *kamil* was growing warm toward me. For a while I wondered if I might be able to climb up and ride on its back, but I was afraid that it would go off in the wrong direction once I stopped leading it.

When we reached a broken ridge of red rock I stopped as we passed through a gap between two sloping walls. Rather nervously I took the *walypala* pouch containing the white-leaf *mapanpa* with the black lines on it, and pushed it into a crevice at the level of my shoulder. Then I hurried on again with a feeling of relief. Half a morning later, still following the tracks made by the *kamil* and by the man who had pursued it and died, I came suddenly upon signs that startled me.

Here was a strange tangle of tracks, all in a small area. They had been made by the *kamil* and the dead man . . . and *another* man. I dropped to one knee, studying the sign, and it was not difficult to read a part of what had happened. There had been a struggle of some sort. A man had fallen here, and nearby something glinted by a small rock. I moved to look at it and found beside the rock a piece of something hard and glistening brightly, but shapeless, as if it had been flung against the rock with magic force. When I put my nose to it I found it had the same fierce, sharp, burnt smell that came from the strange long thing of wood and hard-substance carried by the *kamil* in a close-fitting bag.

I looked about me and saw lying on the ground another of the long things, just like the one in the narrow bag on the *kamil*, and now I could see that the part made from the shiny hard-substance, so smooth and so perfectly round, was not solid like a stick but hollow like a giant reed. It seemed to me that the lump of glinting substance by the rock might have come out of the open end of the reedlike tube, and as I knelt there trying to read these signs a sudden thought came to me.

Perhaps the strange long thing with the smell that made me afraid was a magic spear-thrower of the *walypala*, but instead of throwing a spear it threw a small piece of glinting magic substance with such power that when it hit the rock it changed shape as if it had been as soft as *ngaru* fruit. I shook my head in wonder and said, "I wish you could speak, *kamil*, for you live with the *walypala* and you must surely know if this bad-smell thing is a magic thrower of tiny spears."

I stood up, turning my attention to the tracks of the second man. It was he who had fallen, and now I could tell that he had lain where he fell for a while, for the light wind had formed a tiny ridge of sand on that side of his body as he lay. Then he had got to his hands and knees, and crawled away toward . . .

My heart jumped within me, for as my eyes followed the tracks to a low outcrop only a long spear-throw away, I saw a figure huddled in the scanty shade of the rock. He was down-wind from me or I would already have scented him, and he lay very still. I tied the *kamil* to my digging stick and walked toward the man, feeling heavy in my breast, for it seemed that this must be another dead *walypala*. But as I knelt beside him I heard him draw in a breath and saw his eyelids quiver.

He lay on his side with eyes closed. A swollen bruise ran from ear to temple, with a trickle of dried blood where the skin was broken. He wore coverings on his body much like those of the first man I had found, but this one was younger, with hair and beard the color of the bright stones I had taken from the dead *walypala* and put in my pouch. That man had been killed by the sun, and this man was close to death from the same cause. His lips were swollen and cracked, his skin dry, and I knew that the water had been sucked from his body.

Once again I was puzzled, for when I looked about me I saw a hill with a few trees and a patch of pale green grass. It was within easy walking distance and I knew I would find water there, so I could not understand why this man was allowing himself to die.

I said, "Mitji is thinking foolish thoughts, *kamil*. This *walypala* is dying like the other because a sorcerer of his tribe has pointed the bone at him." I turned my head to look at the *kamil*, and my eye caught the tracks again. There had been a struggle. This man had been hit hard on the side of the head, perhaps with the shiny hard-substance of the bad-smell thing. He had lain in sleep for a while, then had come to his senses and crawled into the shade of the rock, but he had not had the strength to go and dig for water. I nodded to myself and said, "Perhaps he is not being killed by magic, *kamil*. And if not, then perhaps it is safe for me to help him."

I looked down at the man again, and jumped a little because his eyes had opened. They were blue, and I had never seen blue eyes before. He stared at me as if he did not believe I was there. Then his mouth moved, and he spoke a gasping word I did not understand. Something strong moved suddenly within me, and I hurried to fetch my water bowl from where I had set it down with my weapons. I wished I could have put water into one of the strange enclosed bowls of the *walypala*, for it would have been easy to let him drink from the small hole, but I could not put the water from my bowl into it without spilling, and I did not want to lose any.

I knelt over the bowl, took a big mouthful of water, then went quickly back to the man and lifted his head in the crook of my arm. Then I pulled his mouth open a little, put my lips between his, and gently squirted water into his mouth. I felt his body twitch, and he lifted an arm, trying feebly to hold my face against his as he sucked at my mouth even when the water was gone.

I pushed him away and said, "Be patient. I will bring you more." I could see that he did not understand, and I was not surprised, for I knew the *walypala* had a different tongue from the tongue I spoke. So I smiled at him to show warmth and used sign language to tell him that I would bring more water. Then I went back to the bowl again, and again, and once more for the last mouthful of it. Each time, as I knelt to squirt the water into his mouth, he no longer tried to clutch me, but lay quietly and allowed me to give him the water carefully, so that no drop was lost.

Speaking and making signs at the same time, I told him that I must go to dig for more water and that I would be gone for as long as it would take the sun to move from there to there. He did not understand, so I pointed to the shadow of the rock and scratched a mark on the ground to show where the shadow would be when I returned.

I was not sure that he understood this, but his eyes were less distant now, and he stared at me most strangely, his gaze wandering again and again to my fiery hair. I made a final sign for him to rest quietly in the shade, then set off with the *kamil* for the distant hillside. It took only as long to get there as for the sun to march the distance between the tips of two spread fingers pointed at the sky, and good fortune was with me when I came to the hill. After I had dug only to the depth of my knee at the foot of a thin gully I came to water that quickly rose up in the hole. First I filled the strange *walypala* bowls, holding each one below the water till all the air had bubbled out and putting in the plug to prevent spilling. When this was done I drank my fill, then let the *kamil* drink.

This was a fine place for food, for I saw the tracks of snakes and lizards and small birds. I found no eggs, and because I was anxious to return to the *walypala* I lingered only long enough to dig out a *goanna* and to collect some fat tree grubs. The sun was coming up to middle-day when I reached the rock where he lay, and at once I took the plug from one of his bowls so that he could put the hole to his mouth and drink. I kept hold of it, ready to take it away, for I could not let him drink too much too quickly.

He did not resist when I took the bowl away, but spoke some words and nodded his head in a way that made me think he was thankful to me for showing him warmth. I led the *kamil* forward and shouted at it until it lay down, giving us more shade. Then I lay down myself beside the man to wait for the big heat of the day to pass. He spoke once or twice, but I did not understand. Then he took my hand, turning it to show the pale palm, and he turned his own arm to show the pale inside skin that was not burnt by the sun. He touched my palm, then his own skin, then my hair, and said two words, not once but several times, very slowly. The first word was like the first part of Yuma's name, but drawn out: *Yuuu.* The second word was like the first part of Wytala's name, but again drawn out: *Wyyyt.*

I guessed that he was saying we had skin of the same color, and I moved my head to signal agreement. I wanted to explain that I had white skin and fiery hair not because I was a *walypala*, like him, but because I was a freak and not a true person at all. This was too difficult to tell in sign language, so instead I sat up and began trying to tell him that we could not move until he was strong. I said that there was much food and water near this place, so I would bring him plenty to eat and drink. Then, in perhaps two days, perhaps three, we could go to find his tribe.

He seemed to understand some of what I was trying to tell him, but I sensed an uneasiness in him as I spoke and made signs. Instead of watching me, he kept not quite looking at me, or else looking very fixedly at my face, as if he did not like to look at the skin of my body. I wondered if this was because I wore no decorative pattern of scars on my shoulders and breasts, as all true women of our people did. I had been forbidden this by the elders, and I had not minded then, for something in my spirit turned me away from the making of scars, but now I felt a little sad that this man, the first *walypala* I had ever known, might turn his eyes away from my body because he thought me ugly without scars.

When I grew tired of talking and making signs we just rested until the sun was moving down the sky toward the earth. Three times I gave the man more to drink, and I could see that already he was recovering from the heat sickness that had killed his friend.

His friend? I recalled that there had been a struggle and looked again at the great bruise on the man's head. It seemed the dead *walypala* had been an enemy rather than a friend, but that was nothing to do with me.

The man was sleeping when I gathered up my weapons, but he woke as I stood up, and spoke in a husky voice. I guessed he was asking what I was about to do, so I made signs that I would go hunting and gathering food, then would fetch more water. He moved his head up and down, which seemed to be his way of saying he understood, and I knelt to give him more to drink before I left. This time, when he had finished, he held my arm for a little while and spoke very slowly and seriously, looking into my eyes and giving my arm a little pat after every few words.

I decided he was giving me thanks for the water, so I smiled at him and said I wanted to be his friend. I wondered if he would think my face ugly when I smiled, because unlike all true persons of our tribe I had not had one of my front teeth knocked out, and had not had the center part of my nose pierced to carry a bone. But the sick *walypala* kept looking at my face as he spoke, so I felt he did not think it ugly like my body.

I stood up and remained still for a little while, saying "*mitjiquin, mitjiquin*" in my head in the hope that the magic word might guide me in my hunting and food gathering. In only the space of a few heartbeats I was swept by awed astonishment, for the spell was answered as a bird with red wattles around its neck, a honey eater, swept down from the sky and lighted on a ridge of rock no more than half a spear-throw away.

I made a gentle movement with my hand to tell the man to

keep still and quiet, then very slowly I took my throwing club and drew my arm back until I was ready to throw. The honey eater dipped its head to pick up some ants crawling on the rock, and in that moment I threw. It was not a perfect throw, but the heavy end of the club caught a wing of the honey eater just as it lifted from the ground. It went tumbling over, fluttering, and I ran very fast to catch it and twist its neck before it could recover.

I was very pleased as I picked up my club and walked back to where the man lay. His eyes were wide as he stared at me, and he moved his head from side to side as if there was something he could not understand. I laid the bird down near him and said, "This is a beginning. Now I will take one of the *walypala* bags hanging on the *kamil*, and I will be gone while the sun moves from there to there. Then I will come back and take the *kamil* to the place of water to fill all the *walypala* bowls, and when I return I will cook food for us to eat." I made signs as I spoke, but I did not think he understood much. However, he nodded his head feebly and closed his eyes, so I thought he must know I would not go away and leave him to die.

I did not use "*mitjiquin*" anymore for fear of exhausting its magic, but still I had much success that day, returning with a bandicoot, witchetty grubs, two snakes, some honey, a bag of tubers, and some nourishing seeds to chew. Also I found water nearer than the distant hillside. I had to dig deeper for it, but with the wonderful digging stick from the *kamil* this took no longer than for the sun to move the width of two closed fingers across the sky.

When I returned, leading the *kamil* and with all the water bowls filled, the man was sitting up with his back to the rock, and he had found strength to crawl out and pick up the strange thing of wood and hard-substance with the bad smoky smell. I asked him what it was, and he tried to tell me with signs and sounds, but I did not understand.

I let him drink as much as he wished now, and then showed him all the food I had brought back with me. His eyes grew wide again, and he pointed to his mouth and patted his belly to tell me he was very hungry. I said, "Soon you will have a full belly," and I began to make a fire, feeling a little strange because the man watched all that I did very closely, as if he had never seen anyone make a fire before. When the wood I had collected was burning well, I added some dried *kamil* dung to it, then found a sharp stone and began to skin the bandicoot.

The man spoke, reached to the back of the strap around his waist, and held out something with a piece of glittering hard-substance set in bone. *"Nyyyf,"* he said slowly. *"Nyyyf."* He ran it carefully along his forearm, and to my amazement the glittering part was so sharp that it cut away a broad strip of the fine hairs growing on his skin.

He handed the *nyyyf* to me with a sign of warning. I began to use it very slowly and carefully, but even so I was able to skin the bandicoot much faster than I had ever done before. When I thought of the digging stick, the strap-fastenings, the *nyyyf*, and the water bowls, I could only marvel at the magic skill of the *walypala* tribe in shaping the hard-substance to whatever form they wished.

I gave back the *nyyyf*, dug a small hole, put some glowing ashes in the bottom, laid the best pieces of the bandicoot on them, and piled more hot ashes on top. I wanted very much to please the *walypala*, so I had chosen the best of the meat for our meal tonight, and now I laid some fine big witchetty grubs on top of the ashes so that we would have something especially tasty to begin with. While they were cooking I plucked the honey eater and asked for the *nyyyf* again to open the bird so that I could draw out part of the insides. When this was done I cut up the snakes before giving back the *nyyyf*.

"When the bandicoot is cooked," I said, "we will cook the rest of the meat so that it will not go bad, and we can eat it tomorrow."

The man replied, and although I did not know what his words meant, I felt that we were understanding each other in a way. When the grubs were cooked to a brown color I took them from the ashes, allowed them to cool a little, then offered them to the

man. For a moment he stared at them with such an uneasy look
that I feared he was about to be angry with me, as Yuma had
been when I tried to make him a gift of some fine grubs. But
then the man took one, closed his eyes tightly, and pushed it
into his mouth, chewing and swallowing very quickly. I was
disappointed that he showed no pleasure, but thankful that he
had not rejected my offering.

When he had finished he drew in a deep breath, then reached
for another and began to chew in the same uneasy but determined way. I would have given them all to him, but by signs he
made me eat three myself. When they were gone we ate some
tubers, and by the time we had finished these the pieces of
bandicoot were cooked. I raked the ashes away, blew on the
meat to cool it, then gave some to the man and kept some for
myself.

As the sun dropped behind the earth we sat side by side with
our backs to the rock, the *kamil* watching us with a lofty air as
we ate our juicy pieces of meat. "Soon you will be strong
again," I said to the man. "Then we will find your people and
ask that they will let me live among them. Because I am not a
true person but a freak, I have been almost alone for all my life,
except for the dreamtime before I was made. It is a cold thing
to be alone, and the heart grows heavy with it. I hope there may
be some among your people who will be warm toward me."

I knew he could not understand any of this, and I did not
understand what he said to me in reply, but I think we both
knew that if we kept trying to talk, then understanding would
grow.

THE NEXT TWO DAYS WERE THE STRANGEST I HAD KNOWN IN
my life, even though far less strange than what was soon to
come. With food and water, the man's strength came quickly
back to him, and by the third morning he was able to walk. The
first thing he did was to open one of the bags carried by the
kamil and take out a body-covering of the kind he wore himself,

making signs for me to put my head through the hole and my arms into the tubes.

I would not do this, even to please the *walypala*, for I could not move quickly or stalk or use my weapons at a moment's notice if I was trapped in such a body-covering. At first he seemed troubled, but then he laughed and put the thing away. Next he wanted us to start traveling at once, and again I would not agree. I did not know how far we might have to go before we found his tribe, and he needed at least one more day to rest and gather strength, even if the *kamil* would carry him.

There was another reason for delay. Rain was coming. I had seen the signs with the rising of the moon, and I could smell it now. Rain of this kind might come to our land only once in three or more summers, but then so much would fall so fast that it might sweep down a gully and beat a man out of his senses, burying him beneath so great a weight of water that he could no longer breathe air, and would die.

At such times the sun would go dark and the black sky would be cracked by huge snakes of light. Creatures of the earth would hide from the fury of the rain, and our people, too, would hide, not only from the storm but from the *mamu* that stalked through the darkness seeking victims. When the rain passed, the desert would become green for a while and there would be flowers of many colors spread over all the earth, but while the rain lasted it was madness to attempt any traveling.

I tried to explain this to the man, and he tried to explain something to me, but I could not grasp his meaning. Then he became angry and seemed to be saying that if I would not go with him he would go alone. I watched him struggle up onto the back of the *kamil*, and then he spoke a word that made it stand up ready to move away. As I watched I felt so unhappy that tears came from my eyes and ran down my face. I did not speak, but the man looked down at me and shouted angrily. Then he made the *kamil* kneel again and climbed wearily down from its back.

I said, "Good! Good! Please do not go. If you go, you may die. A great rain is coming." I took a water bowl from the *kamil*, pulled the plug free, and sprinkled water over my head, pointing to the sky and making great movements with my arms to tell him that a big rain was coming. Then with my digging stick I scratched on the ground a picture of a shelter made of branches and leaves, such as we used against the wind in the cold season, though they were of little use against a great rain. I pointed to the far hillside and said, "I will take the *kamil* and cut branches from the bushes there with your *nyyyf*. We can make a shelter against the rock here, and cover it with pieces of the woven stuff you carry."

I told the whole story a second time, acting out as much of it as I could, and suddenly I saw that understanding had come to the man. He began to talk, and at the same time moved to the *kamil* and took a long bag from where it hung. Once again I could only watch with growing amazement as he unrolled something from within the bag, fastened some sticks together by magic, and began to make such a shelter as I had never dreamed of.

"*Tent,*" he kept saying. "*Tent.*" Then he spoke some other words, and by using gestures he told me how I could help him to make the shelter stand securely. I was clumsy in this, but he did not become angry again, and soon the task was finished. We had the finest shelter in the world ready for us when the rain came, a shelter so magical that I was almost afraid to crawl into it for the first time.

We tethered the *kamil* and took everything from its back to put in the *tent*, which still left room for ourselves. Then I brought out some of yesterday's cold food, and we ate a good meal before sitting down by the rock to wait for the rain. It came a few hours later. Almost from one moment to the next the sky grew dark, one or two huge drops of water fell, and we scarcely had time to go into the *tent* before the sky broke and the rain fell like spears, as many spears as there would be grains of sand in the sandhills.

I knelt at the opening of the *tent*, watching the ground grow dark as it drank the rain, listening to the drumming on the thin walls of the *tent*, marveling that no drop of water came through, but shivering with fear as the snake *mamu* flashed across the blackness, roaring with fury as they tried to break the sky so that it would fall upon us.

I turned to look at the man, and in the gloom I saw that he had taken something from a stiff bag, a strange glistening thing made of the hard-substance, but also with another substance I could see right through to the other side. The man had a tiny twig in his hand. He touched it to his foot-covering, and I gasped with surprise as I saw the tiny twig burst into flame at one end. He put the flame inside the see-through substance, and at once a larger flame took life there so that light filled the *tent* as if from a small sun.

The man hung the small sun from a stick running across the top of the *tent*. "*Lamp*," he said, and pointed. "*Lamp*." I think he could see that I was frightened then, for he moved to sit facing me, took my hands, and spoke very quietly and gently to me. Then he held up one of my hands, pointed to it, and said slowly, "*Haaand*." He looked at me and waited. I guessed what he wanted, and spoke the word as he had spoken it. He nodded, let go of my hands, ran a finger down his arm from shoulder to wrist, and said, "*Aaarm*."

Excitement swept through me as I repeated the word, and I forgot my fears as I realized that the man had begun to teach me the tongue of the *walypala*. Despite the noise of the storm I could hear him clearly as we sat close together in the light of the *lamp* while he gave me my first teaching.

Leg, foot, eyes, nose, mouth. Food and water. Day and night. Sun and moon. Eat, drink, sleep, go, come, wait. Yes. No. Good. Bad. Luke.

Luke was his name, and easy for me to say, but some words were difficult even though I understood their meaning, for there were sounds in the *walypala* tongue that my mouth had never made before. I had to try many times before I could make the first sound of the word *food* and of the word *sun*. Our people did not use these sounds in their speech, and they came strangely to my lips. I did not try to teach Luke any of the tongue I spoke, for he had no need to learn it. The only word I told him was my name, Mitji.

My heart was full of warmth as we talked and made signs to each other, our understanding growing a little with every new word I learned. I would have gone on all day, but there came a time when Luke lifted a hand and said, "Finish now." He gestured. "More another time." I did not quite know those words, but I understood what he was saying, and in the light of the *lamp* I could see that he was very tired.

I told him to lie down, and I put a soft piece of woven stuff under his head for comfort. Luke was a strong man, not a child, but he was tired like a child because he had almost died, and I wanted to do all things to give him rest so that he would quickly be well again. If my breasts had been big, like those of Manyi, my mother, I would have held him with his head on them to sleep, as Manyi had held me when I was very young, but I had not long been a woman and my breasts were still small. Also, I thought Luke did not like my body, since he always looked away from it. I sat cross-legged by his side, took one of his hands to hold in both my own, then began to sing a story that Manyi had sung for me and for her true children, about a great hunter who rescued his wife after she had been carried off by *mamu*.

I sang quietly, so that Luke could just hear me above the sound of the rain on the *tent*, and he lay looking at me for a while with wondering questions in his eyes before the eyelids drooped suddenly and he slept. I sat holding his hand, listening to the storm but no longer afraid, repeating in my mind all the *walypala* words I now knew.

The rain lasted for as long as it would take the sun to march across the sky from my spread thumb to my small finger, then stopped. The darkness passed, the sky became whole again, and the sun marched on unharmed. I could smell steam rising from the wet ground, and I knew there would be many deep puddles among the rocks from which we could fill our water bowls. The tubers would grow fat, the seeds would grow plump, and hunting would be good. Suddenly a new fear struck me. Perhaps Luke would not need me now to find food for him. Perhaps he would not take me to live among his tribe.

I must have pressed his hand in my anxiety, for he stirred and opened his eyes, staring at me in surprise for a moment until his memory returned. As he sat up he put a hand to his heart and spoke my name with some other words. I was trying desperately to think what gift I could offer him in exchange for taking me to his tribe, but I had nothing to give except my digging stick and my weapons, and I felt sure he did not want these things.

Then I remembered something, and I fumbled with the pouch at my girdle, saying, "Wait. Wait." I loosened the pouch and tipped into my hand the glittering yellow stones I had taken from the dead man. Here, surely, were some powerful *mapanpa*. I held them out for Luke to see, then took his hand, put the stones on his palm, and folded his fingers over them. I spoke in a mixture of signs and *walypala* words and my own words, saying, "Here is strong magic I took from the dead *walypala*. I give them to you. In exchange I ask that you let me go with you and live among your people."

I said this in different ways three times, while Luke looked from the stones in his hand to me and back again with a strange expression in his eyes. "Yuuu taaake," I repeated at last, pointing to the stones. Then, "Yuuu taaake me. . . ." I pointed through the opening of the *tent*, "Go *walypala*. . . . " I touched his white skin, then my own. "Go *walypala tent eat-drink-sleep day-night.*"

His hand closed again on the bright stones. Then he beckoned and crawled out of the tent. I followed, and as I stood up he took me by the arm and led me to where the camel lay, surrounded by puddles, its fur heavy with water. Luke pointed to me, to himself, then to the *kamil*. "Yuuu. Me. *Kamil*," he said, and pointed to the distant skyline. "Go——" The last word was new to me. Later, much later, I learned that it was "together."

We left next morning with full bellies and all our water bowls filled. Luke sat on the *kamil* and I walked beside the animal, carrying my weapons. I did not know where the *walypala* tribe was camped, and had intended to continue with the middle-day sun at my back until I reached the great waters, but Luke showed me a very small magic thing with a see-through cover and a thin black stick, like a long thorn. Whichever way he turned the thing, the long thorn always moved to point in the same direction. This *mapanpa* was called "compass," and told him where to go.

I was very happy for the first two days of our going together, for when we rested during the middle-day heat and when we stopped at sunset Luke would tell me new words. He also began to teach me how to say several words together, with small words between. "We stop now. We go now. It is hot. It is very hot. Can you find more water? Can you find food tomorrow? This is a lamp. This is a match. I light the lamp with the match."

Sometimes there were words I could not grasp the meaning of, but after trying for a little while we would laugh and Luke would choose another word for me to learn. Once he asked to see how I threw my boomerang and how I used my spear-thrower. I showed him, using a small bush as a target, and I think he said that he was surprised a woman could use weapons so well. I wanted to explain that I was not a true woman and had grown up playing with the boys of our people, so I had learned to do man-things, not woman-things, but this was a story far too difficult for me to tell with my few words of the *walypala* tongue.

In turn I asked about the strange thing with the bad smoky smell I thought might be his spear-thrower. He frowned as if not quite knowing what to do, but then seemed to make up his mind. First he took the *kamil* a little way off, made it lie down, and tethered it firmly to a broken mulga tree. He came back to me carrying his spear-thrower, then used words and signs to tell me that something would make a very loud noise but I was not to be afraid. He pointed to a rock sticking out of the ground as his target, but it was too far away for any spear to reach. As I watched, he opened a small hole in the spear-thrower, pressed something into it, then put the wooden part to his shoulder and pointed the tube of hard-substance at the rock.

Suddenly there came a noise that made me jump with both feet off the ground and make ready to run. It was like the roar of the sky *mamu* during a storm, but sharper and harder, with the sound all squeezed together. The smoky burning smell was very strong, and came from Luke's spear-thrower. I was frightened, but he came to me and took my hand, speaking quietly, and together we walked many steps until we reached the rock. Then I saw that a piece of it had broken off and shattered into many small fragments, leaving a fresh scar on the rock with a glistening streak on it. On the ground was a shapeless lump of hard-substance. This was the tiny spear he had pressed into the hole in the spear-thrower, but then it had been beautifully shaped, like a pointed finger.

I had guessed something of this when I first found the spear-thrower lying amid tracks showing signs of a scuffle, with Luke lying nearby, but now I had seen the true power of the *walypala* weapon, and it was magic far beyond our greatest sorcerers.

"*Ry-ful*," said Luke, and patted the spear-thrower. "You say, Mitji."

"*Ry-ful*," I echoed warily, and put my hands behind my back so that I would not touch this fearsome thing even by accident.

That night after we had eaten I learned more words before we slept, but in the morning my happiness had gone and I felt very strange. My head carried a pain inside, and my body felt hot and cold at the same time under the skin. I knew the reason, and my heart was like stone within me. Far, far away, Yuma was pointing the bone at me, perhaps aided by Ulurka. Because I had run away, and perhaps because I had used Yuma's *mitji-quin* magic for hunting, they had decided I must die.

It was a bitter thing for me to face. I had found a *walypala*, I had given him my heart-warmth and received from him some heart-warmth in return. He was taking me to live with his tribe, and I was sure he would have spoken well for me there. But now this would never happen. I could feel the death-magic within me, and knew that in fewer days than I could count on one hand, I would die.

As we set off on our journey again that day I tried to think of ways in which I could explain this to Luke, but it was impossible. I did not know enough words. Then it began to trouble me that if I died soon, before bringing Luke safely to his tribe, he might also die. I had seen for myself that he had to rely upon me for finding food and water, so I knew he could not live long without me. No doubt there were people in his tribe whose task it was to hunt and find food and water for others, but Luke was not one of them.

I did not know how many days of travel lay ahead, but I decided we must cover as much ground as possible each day that remained to me. I would hide from Luke the sickness within me until I could walk no longer, for fear he might try to make me rest. If I did this, and tried very hard to keep our water bowls and our food bags filled, then perhaps after I died Luke would live long enough to reach his tribe.

By next morning the sickness had grown, and Luke must have seen something different in me, for he asked questions. Was another great rain coming? Was I sad? Was my body not good? Was I feeling pain?

I managed to smile, and kept saying, "No. No, Luke. My body is good. Strong."

He tried to make me ride on the *kamil* that day, but I would not, for if I did I could easily have missed signs and tracks I needed to help me find food and water.

Next day when I woke I was very frightened, for red spots had appeared all over my body, and this was surely a powerful curse indeed, for I had never known or heard of such a thing before. It was something I could not hide from Luke, and when he saw what had happened to me he became very troubled, putting his hand on my brow, feeling my wrist, and saying many words I could not understand because my mind was spinning and changing shape like dust devils in a wind.

He tried by force to put me on the *kamil*, but I struggled against him and wept and shouted that I could live one more day to find food and water for him. In the end he gave up trying, but then he wanted to walk with me, and I knew we would have to go slowly if he did, so I begged him, with signs and with what words I could remember, to ride on the *kamil*, weeping again and falling to my knees to scoop sand over my head so that he would understand my distress.

At last he climbed on the *kamil* and we set off. There were times that day when my mind moved away into the sky and I walked as if in sleep until it returned, but always it came quickly back if my eyes saw any sign that meant food or water. Soon after we had rested through the middle-day heat I saw birds coming to the ground by a creekbed. This brought my mind back from the sky, and I told Luke he must wait with the *kamil* until I called him.

I walked a long way to the creekbed, going very slowly once I was near, and with my boomerang I brought down a big brown bird that my people called *linuwa*, enough to give Luke food for some days. The birds had been drinking from a damp patch in the creekbed, but after very little work with the digging stick I found water and was able to call Luke by waving my arm. While I plucked and drew out the bad parts of the *linuwa*, Luke filled all our water bowls and gave the *kamil* water to drink before we went on our way again.

My legs were very tired now, and I no longer tried to fight against the death-magic, for I had done all I could. My friend Luke had food and water. He would use it wisely, and if his totem spirits were kind to him he would come safely home to his tribe. I began to hear my own breathing as if it came from another person, and the ground moved under my feet so that I strayed from side to side as I walked. It seemed to me that night was coming long before time, for the world was growing quickly dark. Yet when I lifted my head with a great effort I could see, as if through a cloud of smoke, that the sun was still high above the skyline.

My head dropped and I could see only the sandy ground at my feet. One step, another step, one step, another step, I saw my feet going down on the ground before me, the red spots showing brightly on the skin of my legs, but my feet were going farther away from me and the world was growing darker yet.

I heard Luke call out from somewhere in the sky. Next moment my feet had gone and my knees were on the ground. The world tilted to one side, the ground struck me on the side of my face. Then my spirit sank into a great blackness and was gone.

THREE

How long my spirit was gone I could not tell, but in the time that followed I knew I had not quite died, and knew that this must be because Luke was using *walypala* magic I did not know he possessed in order to fight the death-sickness sent by Yuma.

For most of the time my spirit slept, but sometimes a small piece of my mind emerged from the darkness, as if into a dream-time, a troubled and frightening dreamtime, for I could feel the devils under my skin and in my head, trying to kill me, trying to grip my chest to stop me breathing.

Sometimes when I woke I knew that I was on the *kamil* with Luke, wrapped in what he called *blanket*, and he had an arm about me, with a strap around both our bodies so I should not fall. At other times I woke to find we had stopped for the middle-day heat or for the setting sun, and Luke was holding me as he trickled water between my lips from the hole in one of his water bowls. Once he soaked a piece of woven material in water and wiped my body to quiet the devils. The water was cool and beautiful, but I was troubled and tried to say he must save it for drinking.

Sometimes I woke to wonder if we had both died and were in a place of spirits, but I could not think for long as my mind kept spinning and changing and going down into the darkness

again. Then at last came a time of long darkness from which I
woke slowly, at first not opening my eyes, for they felt heavy,
yet knowing that the devils had been driven from my body and
that my mind had come together again.

I was lying on something soft and under a covering of something soft. I was not in the sun and could feel no breath of wind;
neither could I scent the *kamil*, or Luke, or any of the scents I
knew well. It was as if I had woken in another world, with new
scents all about me, and among them was the scent of a strange
person close by.

I stirred, turning my head but still afraid to open my eyes.
Then a hand came to rest on my brow, very gently, and from
that hand a great peace and comfort seemed to flow into me,
warming me and wiping away all fears. A soft voice said, "Mitji? Mitji . . . ?" and I opened my eyes to look up into the face
of a *walypala* woman.

Like me, she was not beautiful, for her nose was small and
straight, her mouth not thick and her jaw not wide, but her eyes
were the color of the sky and full of heart-warmth. Her hair was
not fiery, like mine, but the color of honey, and she wore it
curled up on her head in a way that showed her neck and throat.
For a moment I seemed to see her with other eyes, perhaps as
my eyes had seen in the early dreamtime before I was made,
and then it came to me that among the *walypala* tribe she might
indeed be beautiful.

Except for her head and neck her body was completely covered with a woven material in a blue color darker than her eyes,
and with pieces of another color making a pattern on it. She was
still resting her hand on my head, smiling down at me, and now
she spoke again, slowly. "I . . . woman . . . belong . . . Luke."

I nodded my head in the way I had learned from Luke, to tell
her I understood. She patted my cheek and said, "Luke . . .
say to me . . . Mitji very good." She touched my shoulder, then
laid a hand on her breast. "You . . . me . . . friends."

I felt my eyes fill with tears, but they were tears of gladness,
and after a little while I said, "Friends," which was difficult for

me then, as I had little practice in the first and last sounds of the word. Then I said, "I . . . Mitji. You . . . ?"

The woman said, "I . . . Rosemary."

This also was not an easy word for me to say, but I managed it after three attempts. Then for the first time I took my eyes from her face and looked about me. I was in a great *tent* made of wood, so big that if I had stood with my arms outstretched I would only have half-spanned it. I was lying not on the ground but on something above the ground, and the ground itself had a covering of wood and pieces of woven material. In one side of the *tent* was a big hole with straight sides, but no wind came through because the hole was covered with the see-through substance that made part of Luke's *lamp*.

Slowly I gazed around the *tent*. If Rosemary had not been holding my hand I might have been frightened again, for I could hardly believe the number of strange objects it contained, standing on the ground, hanging on the walls, and even hanging from the roof of the *tent*. I could find no words to say, no questions to ask, and at that moment a part of the *tent* wall moved and a man came through the hole. For a moment I saw beyond him and realized with new amazement that where I lay was only one part of an even bigger *tent*.

The man was a stranger, and I watched him nervously as he came toward me. Then I caught his scent, and I cried out in surprise, trying to sit up, for this was Luke, without his beard, with his hair cut short, and wearing different body-coverings. He looked younger now, and bigger than I remembered him.

"Luke," I said, "Luke . . ." and reached out my hands to him.

He took them for a moment, smiled, then made signs as he said, "Tomorrow-tomorrow . . . Mitji good . . . body strong again."

There was so much I wanted to say, but the words would not come. Somehow Luke had brought me to his *tent* where the *walypala* tribe lived, and here he must have paid a powerful sorcerer to defeat Yuma's death-magic. I remembered the red

spots that covered my body, and looked down at myself to find
I was wearing a body-covering of wonderfully soft woven material. It reached to my knees, but I felt under the *blanket* and
quickly pulled the body-covering up, wriggling a little so that I
could lift it to my neck. I had time only to glimpse that the red
spots on my chest and belly had vanished except for one or two
faint marks before Rosemary caught at the body-covering and
pulled it down, her eyes and mouth becoming round in surprised
alarm.

Luke laughed and spoke to her. She blinked, then smiled and
patted my cheek again as if to tell me that I had done nothing
to anger her. I did not understand at the time, but one of the
first things I learned in the days to come was that a *walypala*
woman did not allow a man to see her body, only her head and
part of her arms, unless she was the man's wife. In the same
way a man also kept his body hidden from everybody but his
wife, and both wore body-coverings all the time, even when
sleeping under a *blanket*.

These astonishing ways were something I had yet to discover,
for in the brief moments since my awakening I knew only that
this gentle *walypala* woman had called me her friend, and I was
so overjoyed that the tears now spilled from my eyes. Rosemary
reached out, smiling, and dabbed my cheeks with something
soft and white. "Eat now Mitji," she said. "Good soup. Then
sleep. Rest. Grow strong. You are home now."

I CANNOT HOPE TO TELL OF ALL THE SHOCKS AND STRANGENESS
and new things I met with in the days and weeks and months
following that moment when I woke with Rosemary's hand on
my brow. Everything, *everything*, was different from all I had
ever known. Even the world was different, with countless tribes
in many lands separated by great waters. Some tribes had found
ways to make fearsome weapons, like Luke's *ry-ful*, and to make
big, big things, even as big as a high hill, a thing that moved on
top of the great waters carrying many people in its belly. A *ship*.

Some of the things I saw and learned were wonderful, some were frightening, and some beyond my grasp. To discover that the world was made round, like the sun; to learn that it was so big a man would have to make a full day's march every day for four years to go around it; to know that Luke and Rosemary had come from the top of the world to the underside in a ship—all this was something I would never have believed if anyone other than Luke and Rosemary had told me.

It was mainly Rosemary who taught me the English tongue and then went on to teach me reading and writing. Fortunately I was good at imitating sounds, and since I was desperate to learn I made good progress in talking. Within a few weeks I could understand almost anything simple said to me, and could say many things without having to stop and think too hard. At first most of our conversation was about practical matters, and it was perhaps six months before I began to understand more difficult things, like the stories about God and His Son, Jesus, which Rosemary read aloud each evening from a big black book called the Bible.

It would take too long to tell of all that I felt, all that I learned, and all that I had to unlearn during this time. I can set down only a small part of it, using words long familiar to me now, but which then were unknown to me.

The "tent" in which Luke and Rosemary lived was of course a house, built of timber and with four rooms. They had given it a name as if it were a person—"Shalimar." Some three days passed before I was well enough to go out of the house, and I then imagined I would see other such "tents" of the *walypala* tribe, but to my surprise the house stood quite alone. From it a dusty track of beaten ground ran away to the west and curved around the end of a high ridge of rock.

Later I learned that the nearest place where other white people lived was a town called Lawton, a few miles to the west. Lawton had a community of over one thousand people, but it was hard for Rosemary to make me understand what such a number meant, and when I learned that only two days' march away was an even bigger community called Kalgoorlie, with *twenty thousand* souls, it seemed to me that the whole world must live there.

Luke Bowman, for that was his full name, had built the house himself three years before, helped by two men from Lawton. It stood near a small gully where an underground stream broke the surface for no more than fifty paces or so before vanishing again into gravelly ground, but the stream was said never to fail, so Luke and Rosemary Bowman had no difficulty in getting water. Beyond the gully was a big patch of ground where Luke grew plants called vines. Here the soil had been tilled and then enriched to some extent with darker soil brought in from elsewhere. A big metal tank with a pump stood near the gully, and from this ran pipes carrying water to the cultivated patch of ground.

The very idea of causing food to grow instead of seeking it wherever it could be found was astonishing to me. I discovered later that the grapes were of a kind called Black Corinth, and when ripe they were dried in the sun on wooden trays to become raisins. These were then packed in boxes and sent to a place called Perth—amazingly even bigger than Kalgoorlie—where the raisins were cleaned and stripped of their stems before being put into smaller boxes and sold to places called "shops" where people could buy them to eat. At the time it seemed a very strange and roundabout process to me.

To the north of the house were pens and sheds with two goats, a dozen chickens and a rooster, some beehives, and a stable for a pony and a cart. To the south lay a vegetable garden and a very small patch of ground where Rosemary grew some flowers. Our *kamil* was gone, for it had been hired by Luke and did not belong to him.

During my first eight months I saw only one other person apart from Luke and Rosemary. Twice each month Luke took the cart into Lawton to bring back stores, and on two occasions he returned with another man, an aborigine who came to help Luke with some heavy work in extending the stable. His name was Nomi, he wore clothes and spoke a few words of English.

I was milking a goat, another new wonder to me, when Nomi first arrived. As he jumped down from the cart I saw he was of our people and called to him. He was not of the same tribe, and his speech was strange to my ear, but many words were similar, and he showed great surprise when I asked how he came to be living among the *walypala*. He did not answer but began to ask who I was and how I came to know the tongue of his people. Then Luke came hurrying from the other side of the cart, looking troubled, and called to me, "No, Meg, no! Go into the house and don't speak to him anymore." Meg was the English name Rosemary had given me because it was easy for me to say and to write, and also it was a little like Mitji.

I hurried to obey Luke. I was troubled that I had done something wrong, but Rosemary reassured me, saying that she and Luke felt it best not to tell people I had come from a tribe in the outback, and that she would talk about this with me another day, when I had learned more of the language and could fully understand.

Next time Nomi came he called to me as I passed across the vegetable patch, but I pretended not to understand, and answered in English.

Rosemary Bowman was an angel. It was some time before I came to realize that she was a beautiful angel and that perhaps among white people I was not as ugly as I had always thought myself to be in my own tribe, who were the only other human creatures I had known. Rosemary was also beautiful inside, warm and kind and of quick understanding. It was little wonder to me that Luke loved and treasured his wife so dearly, for within days of knowing her I would have defied the fiercest of the night-walking *mamu* for her.

From the first, Rosemary set herself to bring me up afresh as if I were a child, but wisely she did not use childish words and always spoke to me in just the same way as when speaking with Luke. In the beginning I did many things wrong from ignorance, but she was never angry, never shocked, never showed disgust at those ways of my upbringing that were quite out of place among civilized people.

Instead of my girdle and tassel I wore clothes—stockings and shoes, drawers and shift, petticoat and dress. It took me longer to become used to the shoes than to anything else. When eating I sat on a chair, at a table, and used a knife and fork and spoon to eat food cooked by Rosemary on a cast-iron range or in its oven.

I went to a special small "tent" to ease myself, and I washed my face morning and evening, my hands several times during the day, my body and hair every two or three days. This body-washing took place in the kitchen. I sat in an iron bath that hung on the outhouse wall when not in use, and I was helped by Rosemary, with Luke shut in the sitting room so that he would not see me naked. I laughed about this at first, for he had seen me naked through all the days of our travel. Rosemary laughed, too, but said I had come into a different world now and must try to think as the white tribes think so that I would not make mistakes in the way I behaved.

I slept in a bed in a small room of the house, wearing a nightdress. Luke and Rosemary slept in two beds in a larger room. I was puzzled that they did not lie together as man and wife, and when I had learned enough words to talk easily with Rosemary I asked her why.

She looked suddenly sad, and bit her lip. I saw tears come to her beautiful eyes, and I wanted to gash my leg with a spear to show how sorry I was to have made her sad, but she took my hand and said, "Meg dear, you must never ask such a question, even of a friend, because this is a private matter—Oh, you won't understand what 'private' means yet. Well, it is a *secret* thing. To speak about men and women lying together is not polite. It is very *very* bad manners."

"Polite" and "manners" were words I heard many times from Rosemary while she was teaching me the ways of the white tribes.

A few months after my coming to Luke's home I was working

on the vegetable patch with him, still feeling wonder at the marvel of making food grow continually in one place instead of having to wander from place to place to find it, when a troubled thought about Rosemary came to my mind. I said, "Luke, why is Rosemary more white than you? Her face is like milk, with no blood in her cheeks. Is this so with all white women? And Rosemary's body is not strong. She can only work to grow her flowers for a small time, then she must rest. Sometimes her breathing is quick, and at night I hear her—I don't know the word, you never speak it—the sound she makes is like this." I coughed.

Luke made no answer for a moment, and I went on, "Is this so with all white women? Or . . . or is there a sickness in Rosemary?"

Luke leaned on his hoe and ran a hand through his thick yellow hair, looking at me. At first his eyes were hard and his mouth tight, but then he seemed to realize I meant no harm. His face changed, he shrugged, and said in a tired way, "Rosemary has a sickness. We don't talk about it, so please don't speak of it to her."

I was hot in my clothes under the sun, but still a shiver ran through my body. Sickness was caused by magic, so it was clear to me that some white sorcerer was pointing the bone at my beloved Rosemary. Luke himself had magic, for he had cured the sickness Yuma had put upon me, but evidently Luke's magic was not strong enough to help Rosemary against a skilled sorcerer. The only way would be to strike at the sorcerer himself and destroy him. I wondered why Luke had not taken his *ry-ful* and done this, then decided it could only be because the sorcerer was protected from all *walypala* weapons.

A blend of terror and anger made sweat break out on my body as I moved closer to Luke and said in a low voice, "Hear me, Luke. My spear, my boomerang, my throwing club, you brought them on the camel with us, and they are in the outhouse." I looked over my shoulder to make sure Rosemary had not come out to tend her little flower garden, and then I went on, "A bad

man with strong magic is pointing the bone at Rosemary. Tonight you must take me to the house where this bad man lives,
then you go back to Rosemary. I will leave my clothes here when
I go with you, and take my weapons, and hide near his house.
Tomorrow when he comes from his house I will follow him and
throw my boomerang to make him fall, and then I will run very
fast to kill him with my spear." I wiped the sweat of fear from
my eyes, thinking of what the sorcerer's spirit might do to me.
"Then I will come back to you, and Rosemary's sickness will
go."

For long moments he stood looking down at me with round
eyes. At last he said softly, "Oh, Meg . . . Meg. How old are
you? Fourteen? Fifteen perhaps? But with that red hair and fierce
green eyes and those white teeth half bared you look like a full-
grown alley cat protecting its young."

"Like what? What is an alley cat?"

"A kind of wildcat but in a town. Never mind." He rested a
hand on my shoulder, then took my arm and led me to a bench
standing in the shade cast by the house. "Come and sit down,"
he said. "I must talk to you."

Once we were seated he took off his wide-brimmed hat, wiped
his brow, and said, "Meg, first you must understand that it's
wrong to kill another person."

A killing for punishment or revenge seldom happened among
my people, but there were occasions when it was considered
quite correct. It seemed to me that Rosemary's sickness was a
proper occasion, but I no longer felt much surprise at any of the
strange ways of the white tribes.

"It is not polite?" I asked. "Bad manners?"

Luke looked up at the sky and said something to Jesus. I did
not hear an answer myself, but then Luke said to me, "More
bad than that. Very, *very* bad. Now hear me, Meg. White people
have no magic. No man can point the bone. Sickness does not
come from magic. It does not come from bad spirits. It comes
from . . ." He paused, rubbed his chin, and sighed. "It comes
from small, small animals. Take as many such animals as there

are stars in the sky, and they would be less than a grain of sand. They enter the body, enter the flesh and the blood, and bring sickness. We have no magic. We have doctors, medicine men, who can sometimes take away sickness, but not always.''

To believe such an amazing thing was to have my world turned upside down, but I knew Luke would not say anything untrue to me. "Do you say my sickness with the red spots was not sent by Yuma?" I asked.

He smiled and nodded. "That is what I say. Your sickness is a sickness of the white people and usually comes to children. It is called *measles* and is very bad for the people you lived with because their bodies have little strength against it. *Measles* can come only from another person who has the sickness. Did some new person come to your tribe a little time before you left?"

I was about to say no, but then remembered that Katapi, a woman from another tribe, had been exchanged with one of our women to become Nyiki's wife. It was she who had brought with her the small round *mapanpa* Yuma had shown me, with the face of Mitjiquin on it, Elder of Elders of all the white tribes.

When I told Luke of this and described the *mapanpa*, he nodded. "It was a piece of money, a coin called a penny, with the head of Queen Victoria on one side and Britannia on the other. It means the woman you speak of must have met with white people, or perhaps with another and another and another who had met with them. That's where the *measles* came from. The sickness does not come till many days after." He held up a hand with spread fingers three times. "Sometimes as long as fifteen days. It may be that some of your tribe have died from the sickness.''

He felt in his pocket and took out several coins. "Look, was it like this one?"

I looked at the penny but was afraid to touch it. "Yes, but these marks under the sitting-down lady were not the same. No, wait. The first two were the same."

"You have an amazing memory, Meg. These are numbers, for counting. Rosemary will soon teach you about them. Here they give a date, a particular year, 1891—but that won't mean anything to you." He sighed. "Lord, you do have so much to learn."

"I will learn everything, Luke. My heart is very warm to Rosemary, very warm to you." As I spoke he turned the coin over, and I said, "Who do you say the woman is?"

"She's Queen Victoria, a kind of chief over many tribes in many lands."

"Yuma knew that, and he said she had a magic name."

"What was it?"

"I must not speak it aloud, Luke."

He frowned, but said quietly, "I've told you, Yuma's magic *cannot* touch you."

I hesitated, then said, "The first part was like my own name, Mitji. The second part was like the first part of the woman's name as you spoke it just now."

"Queen? Mitji-queen?"

"Can I truly say it without hurt?"

"Truly, Meg."

I screwed up my courage and said, "It was Mitjiquin. Yes."

Luke sat thinking for a moment, then suddenly he laughed. "Mitji means 'white woman' to aborigine people, doesn't it? That's what you told me."

"Yes, but I think it is not a true word of our people, just as I am not a true person."

"They're not your people, Meg, and it isn't a true word. Mitji is a corruption—that means a twisted way—of saying 'Mrs.' You know how we speak of a married woman. Rosemary is Mrs. Bowman. The tribes by the sea must have picked it up when our people first came to this land, and Mrs. became Mitji because they don't use the 's' sound." He laughed again. "So Mitjiquin is their way of saying Mrs. Queen."

I could not see what he was laughing at, but before I could ask another question Rosemary came from the house carrying a tray with a big jug of lemonade and three glasses. Then I decided just to sit and listen to Luke and Rosemary talk. I would ask no more questions now, for I already had so much to think about in all that Luke had told me about the white tribes having no magic.

Much later, when I was able to look back on those early days, I could appreciate just how wise and how sympathetic Rosemary was in her teaching. Although I was always learning simple things like words and numbers and plain facts about this strange new world, she understood that there were matters in which I had to unlearn beliefs and attitudes I had been taught from babyhood, and I could discard these for new beliefs and attitudes only a little at a time. To instruct me in a whole new way of life all at once would have clogged my brain and driven me to despair.

It was an evening some weeks later when I was first told something that made me gasp, even though by then I thought nothing could surprise me. We were in the sitting room, and I was feeling a little proud because for the first time I had cooked supper all by myself from the supplies Luke brought in from Lawton every two weeks. This small pleasure was marred by my anxiety for Rosemary, who was resting on the settee. It was one of her bad days, when she barely had strength to drag herself about the house, and I was thankful that I had at least learned the rudiments of cooking and cleaning and keeping house, so that I could take the burden from her.

Something else was troubling me. I had a feeling that Luke was beginning not to like me, though I did not know why. He was never unkind to me, but often he seemed to avoid me as if my company was an annoyance to him, and I could sense that the heart-warmth he had once shown to me was cooler now. That evening I was sitting in an armchair near Rosemary, reading to her from a book with pictures and words for teaching small children. Luke sat at the table working on some things called accounts. Two lamps made the room beautifully bright, and I no longer found it uncomfortable to sit in a chair instead of on the ground.

After a while Luke sighed and gathered his papers together.

Rosemary heard him and opened her eyes. "Luke dear," she said, "I think Meg has read enough for this evening, and I think we should tell her those things we decided upon last night. She is ready for them now."

"All right, my darling." Luke put his papers away in a drawer, moved to kiss Rosemary's cheek, then sat down in the other armchair, facing me but not quite looking at me. I was reminded of the way he had avoided looking at my body when we were in the outback, but I understood that now. I could not understand why he had begun to avoid looking at me again now that I wore proper clothes.

"We want to tell you something about yourself, Meg," he said, "but I'm going to begin with a question. Why do you think your skin is white?"

I was puzzled, for I had explained this before to Rosemary. "It's because I'm not a true person," I said. "I wasn't born like real babies. A totem-spirit made me, and Manyi found me."

Luke said, "That's all quite wrong, Meg. Quite wrong. You were born in exactly the same way as all babies in the world are born."

"But . . . I am sure I did not come from Manyi's body," I said, baffled. "Her baby had just died, so I could not have come from her so soon."

"No. You came from the body of a white woman." Luke looked directly at me for a moment. "Your mother was a white woman. Your father was a white man." He gave a small shrug. "And one of them doubtless had red hair, not that it matters."

I put a hand to my head, trying to think. Then I said, "My father? You mean the chief man of the family?"

"Well, I suppose so. But really I mean the man who . . . who . . ." Luke took a big breath and looked at Rosemary. "How do I say it?" he asked.

Rosemary gave him a sympathetic smile and turned to me. "Meg, we must speak of things now that we would not speak of if other people were present, because it would be bad manners to do so. But while you and I and Luke are alone it is not bad manners, because you are like our child and we must teach you."

I said, "Is it about lying with a man?"

"Well yes, dear, partly." She stared as if struck by a new thought. "Have you done this thing yourself?"

I shook my head. "No. All the other children of ten summers and more did when they played together, but nobody wished to lie with me because I was not a true person."

Luke looked at the ceiling, and for the second time I heard him mutter something to Jesus. Rosemary sat up straight and said "Luke!" very sharply.

He said, "I'm sorry, sweetheart, but . . ." He leaned back in his chair and closed his eyes. "You carry on."

She smiled her warm smile at him and turned to me again. "Meg, you know that a baby is born by coming out of the mother's body, but do you know how the seed of that baby entered her body?"

I said, "Yes, Rosemary. The spirits are waiting everywhere to be born, and they enter a woman as she passes the places where they wait. They enter her through her foot, or hand, or her mouth as she eats, and make a baby inside her."

Luke blew out a long breath from between his lips, his eyes still closed. Rosemary said, "No, Meg. That is wrong. There are no spirits who make babies. It is when a man lies with a woman that his seed enters her and grows into a baby. That man is the father of the baby."

"Oh no, Rosemary, no," I said. "The lying together is good for making a woman ready to *receive* the spirit, but—" I broke off, putting a hand to my mouth. "That is what *all* our people believe! You mean . . . it is not true?"

"It is not true," she said, shaking her head slowly. "Oh, my poor Meg, how difficult it all is for you." She glanced at Luke. "But we will talk of that another time, just you and I. For the moment we simply want you to know what you are. People who are born wrongly, different from others, are called freaks. You are *not* a freak aborigine, Meg dear. Your mother and father, and their mothers and fathers before them, almost certainly came from England, as Luke and I did, or perhaps, with such hair and freckles as yours, from a place called Scotland, which is joined to England and where they speak the same language. Tomorrow I will show you in the atlas.''

Luke opened his eyes and said, "I favor Ireland—'' but Rosemary broke in quickly, saying, "Hush, my darling. She's trying to absorb it, and we can barely imagine how hard it must be for her.''

This was true. I sat for a long time struggling to put aside things I had known to be true all my life, but that were not true. It was as if within me I was being thrown this way and that by a great wind. Slowly the wind grew quiet, and a warm feeling began to glow in my heart. I was of the same tribe as Rosemary and Luke. I was a true person of that tribe. I was not a freak to be mocked and made an outcast.

Sometime later I came back to myself to find Luke and Rosemary watching me, though Luke looked quickly away. I said, "Where are my mother and father? Why did they give me to another tribe when I was a baby?''

Rosemary said quietly, "We don't know, Meg. It seems there is no way to find the truth of what happened now.'' She looked troubled and went on slowly, "Sometimes it happens that a mother is . . . is in difficulty and cannot keep her new baby, but even so we cannot think how you could be abandoned to an aborigine tribe living so far from civilization.''

"They lived nearer to the setting sun and farther from the middle-day sun when I was small,'' I said. "The elders said we must move on a big walkabout to keep away from places where the white man was coming.''

Luke said, "So they were once a good distance southwest from where Meg left them, and nearer to us. There were even aborigines on the outskirts of Perth only a few years ago.'' He shrugged. "Not that it helps.''

A fresh thought had come to me, and I said, "I don't think I was a new baby when I came to the tribe. I have . . . well, it is not a thing I remember, but a kind of dream I cannot quite remember. I thought it was from the dreamtime before I was made, but in it there is the sound of voices, and the feel of arms holding me, and . . . and smells and colors, but all different from anything I knew with my people in the real world. Do you think these things I remember as dreams could also be real?''

Rosemary said, "I'm sure they are, and if you recall the sound of voices this may be partly why you have been able to learn English so readily. I think these must be the memories of a child no more than two years old—and little less, either. If your mother had . . ." She hesitated, then began again. "If you had been parted from your mother earlier than that, I don't think you would remember anything, and if it had been later you would remember more. We don't know how that separation came about, but please try not to think badly of your mother, and please don't make yourself unhappy by puzzling over it.''

I smiled at her and said, "No, I won't be unhappy, Rosemary. What happened then does not matter. All that matters is that I have come back to my true tribe, and you have taken me into your home." Sudden fear struck me, and I could feel my chin trembling as I said, "Please, you won't send me back? It is such a heavy thing to live among people who look upon you as a freak, as one who is not a true person. I will always work hard for you and for Luke, and will eat only a little food—"

"Hush, hush, hush, Meg!" Rosemary broke in. "Of course we'll never send you back, and don't you ever dare to eat less than you want." She opened her arms, and I ran to where she sat, kneeling by the settee to put my arms round her, troubled by the frailty of her body, but thankful to feel her embrace me and stroke my hair. "There aren't so many years between us," she said with a soft laugh, "but to me you're the child I could never have, Meg dear. I'm so glad you're happy with us."

"There are not enough words to tell how happy, Rosemary." I heard Luke say in a hard, dry voice, "You're easily satisfied, both of you. This is not exactly a life of ease I'm providing for you."

Rosemary said, "You gave up a life of ease for me, my darling. I'm grateful, and more than content."

I lifted my head from Rosemary's shoulder to look at Luke and said, "For me it is a life of much ease, after the outback. But that is not why I am so happy, Luke. I am happy because here you and Rosemary have given me heart-warmth. That is more"—I groped for the word—"yes, more precious than all other things."

For a moment I saw pain in Luke's very blue eyes, but then he looked away and got up to put more wood in the stove. Since my coming here, summer and autumn had passed, and now winter was beginning. During my years with the aborigines I had never minded the colder seasons, for they were not severe, and now I found Shalimar rather too warm, since I had to wear clothes. But Rosemary needed the warmth to keep her from long coughing spells.

With the coming of winter there was less work to be done and more time for Rosemary's teaching. This pleased me greatly, for I hungered after learning as a starving man hungers after food, but I was careful not to make Rosemary tired. When I saw that she might soon begin to flag, I would persuade her to rest while I copied words and figures, or practiced simple reading, or pored over an atlas.

Each time Luke returned from Lawton with supplies he would bring some newspapers and magazines with him. I loved these even more than the long row of books on a shelf in the sitting room, for they had wonderful pictures in them of people and places, not only in Australia, which I now knew was the great continent where we lived, but also in other parts of the world, particularly in England, which was the mother country from which most Australians had come. The pictures helped me to understand far better than any words a world I had never seen, and when Rosemary said that soon she would have Luke take me with him to Lawton I was filled with eager anticipation.

When at last the day came I hardly knew whether I was more nervous or excited at the prospect. I spent several hours reading the night before because my thoughts were too busy for me to sleep, but I was up early and glad to be busy as I fetched water and prepared breakfast for us all. While we were at the table Rosemary said, "We had better explain, dear, that some time ago Luke told the people he deals with in Lawton that a young cousin of mine had come out from England to stay with us, so your name will be Meg Gaynor. That was my surname before I married Luke, you see?"

I nodded, pleased. "Oh yes, I'm glad to have your name, Rosemary. Is it because you don't want people to know I grew up among a tribe of aborigines?" I laughed because I could make little jokes about myself now. "And that I didn't know I was a *walypala* all the time?"

Rosemary gave a quick smile, but her eyes were serious as she said, "We don't like telling an untrue story, Meg, but we feel sure it's best for you. If people know that you're a British girl who was . . . lost or abandoned as a baby and brought up by primitive aborigines, you'll be besieged by newspaper reporters and all sorts of people who will want to question you endlessly and write about you. Luke and I feel we must protect you from such a thing until you're a little older and more used to this new world that you've barely seen anything of so far. Then you can decide for yourself whether you want the truth to be known."

I shook my head quickly. "I don't want to have people asking me lots of questions. I think they will make me frightened. I just want to live here with you and help to make the farm pay, and later I would like us all to go to England for a holiday and see the queen."

Luke drank his tea and stood up. "We'll take your boomerang with us," he said, "and you can demonstrate with it at a royal garden party. I'll wager Mitjiquin has never seen the like of that before."

"Oh dear," I said uneasily. "I must find some time to practice. I don't want to make a bad throw in front of the queen."

Rosemary laughed. "He's making a silly joke, Meg dear," she said. "Take no notice."

We left Shalimar at eight o'clock in the trap, with Luke wearing his only suit and holding the reins of the pony, Henrietta. I wore my best dress and coat, with a pretty green bonnet. The dress was one of Rosemary's that she had remade for me, the coat Luke had bought secondhand in Lawton, and the bonnet was a new one he had bought for my birthday. It was also a Christmas present, but Christmas had come very soon after my arrival at Shalimar, and I had known nothing of the occasion. We did not know when my true birthday fell, but Rosemary decided we would make it the middle day of May, halfway between her own birthday in January and Luke's in September, so the bonnet was a belated present for that day and for Christmas.

Besides not knowing my true birthday, we did not know how old I was. I could count ten summers that I remembered; I had become a woman during my last summer with the tribe, and I had been at Shalimar for eight months, so after some discussion Rosemary had decided that we would regard my first birthday here as being my fifteenth.

I felt very proud of myself sitting beside Luke as we jogged along the track to Lawton, for I was sure I looked a truly civilized person in my beautiful clothes, and I was glad to be Luke's companion, for he appeared most important in his gray suit and with his thick golden hair. But my pride and excitement were shot through with anxiety. I had clung to Rosemary when we said good-bye, half afraid to leave her, half worried about leaving her on her own. Within my memory she and Luke were the only living white people I had ever seen. Although I longed to be among others of my true people, I feared they might easily see I was not like them and would regard me as an outcast, just as I had been regarded by the tribe I had believed my own.

I confided these fears to Luke as we drove, and he shook his head. "You've nothing to worry about, Meg, I promise. You have a great gift for learning, you work very hard at your lessons, and you're an excellent mimic, so even now I don't think people would suspect anything from the way you speak.'' He flicked some flies from Henrietta's back with his whip. "I won't let anyone engage you in a long conversation today, but you can come in regularly with me from now on and gradually get more used to talking with other people. You're learning more words and getting more practice all the time, and next year I'll take you to Kalgoorlie for the day without the slightest worry. By then you'll probably be better educated than quite a few of the people you'll see there.''

I relaxed a little and said, "If so, it will be all thanks to Rosemary. She has been like a sister and mother and teacher all in one. I'm so lucky, Luke.''

He turned his head to look at me curiously for a moment. "Yes, she's wonderful,'' he said quietly. "But God knows it was high time you had a bit of luck, Meg.''

By reading and looking at pictures and asking endless questions I thought I had prepared myself for the sight of Lawton, but the reality was quite overwhelming. There were buildings twice as high as Shalimar, and people by the hundred. There were horses and carts and traps, shops and market stalls, places to eat and places to drink. I forgot my fears and sat round-eyed as we trotted along the dusty road, my head turning as I tried to take everything in.

Luke glanced at me with a smile. "You could put Lawton in a corner of Kalgoorlie,'' he said, "and Kalgoorlie in a corner of Sydney, and Sydney in a corner of London or any of the big cities of Europe. But there's a lot more space here than in Europe, and this is a country that's going to grow, Meg.''

I nodded dumbly, clutching the little handbag Rosemary had given me with a few copper coins inside. Next moment, as we turned a corner, there came from our left the most hideous and ear-splitting scream I had ever heard, shrill and terrifying. I almost sprang from the trap in my alarm, but Luke caught my arm and I clung to him, trembling.

"Gently, Red, gently,'' he said soothingly, but half laughing, "you're quite safe.'' That was the first time he ever called me

Red, and he spoke the word so kindly that afterward I was always happy on those occasions when he used this special nickname. It was strange that this should be so, seeing how much I had always hated my red hair and freckles during my days with the tribe. But at the time when I heard that fearful scream as we drove into Lawton, I hardly realized that Luke had called me by a different name, and I only remembered it later.

"That was just the engine driver sounding his whistle," he said. "Look, there's the station."

I turned my head and felt new shock at the sight of the enormous iron monster that stood there puffing steam from its upturned snout. Then my heart slowly ceased pounding, and as Luke let me go I realized that this was a locomotive such as Rosemary had described and I had studied many times in pictures. Behind the locomotive were the carriages making up a train, and there were two rails, gleaming brightly as they ran away across the land for as far as I could see.

"Will we . . . will we really have to go *inside* one of those things when you take me to Kalgoorlie?" I whispered.

"Yes." He patted my hand. "It won't hurt you, Meg. In fact, I think you'll love it when the time comes. Now let's do our shopping, and then we'll go along to St. Mark's and tell the vicar he's to have the pleasure of our company on Sundays in the future."

Apart from the vicar, I exchanged words with five other people that morning in Lawton, and to my delight not one of them gave me a puzzled look or seemed to think me strange. The vicar must have noted my darker-than-usual complexion, and asked Luke if perchance I came from some branch of Mrs. Bowman's family stationed in India. Luke said this was not so, but added with a confiding air that there was Spanish blood, possibly with royal connections, in his wife's family. I wondered what Jesus would think about that, but I said nothing.

We returned to Shalimar in time for luncheon and worked as usual throughout the afternoon, but after dinner that evening I talked until I was hoarse, telling Rosemary every detail of all I had seen and repeating every word that had been said to me or that I had said.

One evening a few days later a thought came to me as I was slowly reading aloud a piece in a magazine about Queen Victoria (I no longer called her Mitjiquin). She had gone to spend some time at a castle called Balmoral so that her family and friends could shoot some birds known as grouse and then attend some sports called Highland Games, which appeared very strange in the pictures.

I looked up from the magazine and said, "Rosemary, I remember that soon after Luke brought me here you explained that you had both come from England. Did you not like it there?"

She rested her embroidery in her lap and looked at Luke, who sat with a last held between his knees, mending a pair of boots. "May I tell Meg about us?" she asked.

He hammered a nail home, picked up a sharp knife, and began to trim a leather sole. "Yes, I don't see why not."

"You're sure?" She seemed a little puzzled. "Is there something wrong, Luke?"

He looked up, ran a hand through his tawny hair, and gave her a smile full of heart-warmth. "No, there's nothing wrong, sweetheart. By all means tell Meg the story."

It took a little while in the telling, and once or twice I had to ask for something to be explained more fully, for there was much that I found hard to comprehend even though I understood the words. The people in the story behaved in ways quite alien to anything I had known so far in my life, and I realized that all *walypala* were not like Rosemary and Luke.

As Rosemary talked I learned that Luke's full name was Luke Edwin Bowman and he came from a rich family in England. This country was divided into counties and his family had a house in the county of Surrey, a house as big as some I had seen in magazine pictures. Luke had an older brother and a married sister. She had not had to marry someone from another tribe as the aborigines did, for there were no such tribes in England. Luke's father owned a lot of land and was one of the elders of the country, called a Member of Parliament. His mother was a beautiful lady who, as far as I could understand, did nothing at all.

Luke himself was now twenty-nine years old and had been what people called the black sheep of the family. This meant he did not behave in the way he was expected to behave. He had been made to leave a place of learning called a university, and after a quarrel with his father he had packed a bag, taken work on a ship to get to America, and then for the next five years had worked his way all around the world doing every kind of job. With the atlas, Rosemary showed me the countries where Luke had worked during this time.

When he returned to England at last, he made a great effort to mend the quarrel with his father, and there was a reconciliation. Luke settled down in the family home, hoping to help with the management of the estate and perhaps to bring in new ideas he had discovered during his travels, but his help and suggestions were always waved aside. Soon he became restless and began to revert to some of his old wild ways, much to the embarrassment of his parents. But then something happened that changed his whole life. He met Rosemary Gaynor.

Rosemary was employed as a governess in a big house a few miles away in the next village. I learned that a governess was a lady of good education but poor circumstances, employed as a private teacher for the children of wealthy parents. Rosemary's father had been a grocer, and he had put every penny he could spare into giving her a good education, before dying in his early fifties. Her mother had died of a lung complaint a few years after Rosemary was born, and there were no other children.

Within a few weeks of their first meeting, Luke and Rosemary had fallen deeply in love, and Luke announced to his family that he intended to marry her. This caused a terrible upheaval, for although there were no tribes in England there were different classes of people. Luke was told that it was out of the question for him to marry a governess, a grocer's daughter. She was not of his class, and it would cause endless tittle-

tattle among the gentry of the county. Luke's father, Mr. Edwin
Bowman, declared that if the marriage took place he would
disown Luke, and Mrs. Bowman begged her son to forget such
foolishness and marry a nice young girl she would choose for
him.

Rosemary was much distressed by all this, and told Luke it
would be best if she went away and allowed him to forget her, but
he would have none of this. If she loved him, he said, then they
would marry, and Rosemary found that her love for this man was
something she could not deny. The outcome was that he called for
her one day at the house where she worked, took her to London
with her small trunk of belongings, established her in lodgings
there with a respectable woman, and married her as soon as the
banns had been read for the third time.

For a year they lived in a small house by the Thames, rented
for a few shillings a week. Luke found work with a cabinetmaker,
using one of the skills he had acquired during his travels, and
Rosemary earned a little by giving music lessons. They were far
from rich, but not quite poor by average standards, and they were
utterly and supremely happy together.

Then, after a year, Rosemary developed a cough that would
not go away. There was a sickness in her lungs, and the doctors
Luke called in said that the only cure would be for her to move
to a different climate, preferably to a sanatorium in Switzerland,
or failing that, to anywhere with a dry atmosphere.

They had no money to pay for treatment over a long period
in a Swiss sanatorium, so Luke swallowed his pride and went
to his father for help. This was refused, but Mr. Bowman said
that if Luke and his wife would emigrate to Australia, a dry and
healthy country, he would pay their fares.

When Rosemary came to this part of the story I glanced at
Luke. He was resoling the other shoe now, but his face was dark
with anger, and I saw that his knuckles were white as he gripped
the rasp. Rosemary was watching him, too, and she paused to
say gently, ''No bitterness, my darling. Please, no bitterness.''

Without looking up, he said in a taut voice, ''We'd spent

Rosemary's small savings on doctors' bills. My father paid thirty-six pounds for the two of us to travel third class on a mail steamer. Less than he'd spend on a new dress for my mother.''

Rosemary sighed and got to her feet. Moving to where Luke sat, she took his face between her hands and tilted his head so that he looked up at her. ''We made our choice, Luke,'' she said quietly, ''and they owe us nothing. So let there be no bitterness.''

The blackness fell away from him and he took her wrist, turning his head to kiss the palm of her hand. ''I'm sorry,'' he said, smiling. ''Just a flash of the old Luke, from the time before I found you.''

She laughed, bent to kiss his brow, then moved back to the settee. ''So we came to Perth,'' she said. ''That's the big town near the sea, with over thirty thousand people, yet it's still tiny compared with London. A most kindhearted doctor there, who would take no money, said I needed always to be in very dry air, and that this area beyond Kalgoorlie would be the best place. He advised us to apply for a Free Homestead Farm, and we were granted one hundred and sixty acres here for payment of only one pound.'' She looked at her husband again. ''We were so lucky, weren't we, Luke?''

He nodded, paring away a sliver of leather, and said, ''When we landed in Perth a telegram from England was waiting for me. I'd been left some money.'' He looked up and grinned, blue eyes twinkling. ''A hundred pounds, Meg, but it wasn't from anyone in my family. During the years that I was roaming the world I once did a good turn for an elderly Indian gentleman in Bombay. Chased away some footpads who were trying to rob him. He was very grateful, and asked for my name and home address. And when we arrived in Perth there was this telegram from some London solicitors to say the old chap had died and left me a hundred pounds in his will.''

''Is that a lot of money?'' I asked.

Luke laughed. ''It is when you only have eight pounds,'' he

said. His eyes rested on me as he spoke, but then abruptly the laughter went out of them and he bent quickly to his work again.

Rosemary said, "It's a condition of a Free Homestead Farm that within two years you must build a house which is not of less value than thirty pounds. We lived in a tent while Luke built this house in just six months, and we called it Shalimar from a line in some poems known as the Indian Love Lyrics—'Pale hands I loved beside the Shalimar. . . .' That was in memory of the Indian gentleman, and the house cost us not quite sixty pounds."

"Wait! Wait!" I exclaimed, and took up the pencil and pad I always kept near me. After writing on it for a few moments I looked up and said, "Then you have forty pounds left. I've just done the sum, Rosemary."

She nodded, smiling. "Clever girl. But that was almost three years ago, and I'm afraid we haven't forty pounds left now. We had a lot of expense starting our little farm here, and although I think we're making a profit now, we're only just over the hump."

"Hump?"

"Oh dear. Yes, I'll explain that." Often during conversation I had to ask the meaning of some strange word or phrase I had not heard before. Now Rosemary explained what she meant by "over the hump," reminding me of the humps on the camel I had found in the outback. In all these past months I had been so busy learning endless things about the new world I had entered that I had completely forgotten about the camel. Now I recalled the shock of seeing it that day, and my disappointment later when I found the first *walypala* I had ever set eyes on—and he was dead.

I spoke of this now to Rosemary, and went on, "I didn't know how to ask at first, and later I forgot, but who was that dead man I found in the outback when I followed the camel tracks? I think he must have been the one who hurt Luke, but I don't know why."

"Well," said Rosemary slowly, "that's quite a long story, dear, but I think you've learned enough now to understand it."

She paused as if to gather her thoughts, and suddenly I saw that her face was very pale. Then she began to cough, and it was the small, dry, wearying cough I had sometimes heard at night.

In a moment I was at her side, my arm about her. "No, don't try to tell me now, Rosemary," I said quickly. "I'm so sorry, I've made you tired. I know, I'll warm you some milk with some honey in it for you to drink. That will ease your cough."

Luke was watching us, his hands still now, his eyes troubled. "Yes, do that, Meg," he said.

As I stood by the range in the kitchen, waiting for the milk in the saucepan to grow warm, I felt a great fear for Rosemary. The thought came to me that although I knew differently now, I wished her sickness *was* caused by a sorcerer. I had become a civilized person and was no longer a savage, but I would have taken my spear and my boomerang and I would have found that sorcerer and killed him, even though Luke had told me it was wrong.

After Rosemary had sipped some of the warm milk and honey the cough abated and a little color came back to her cheeks. Luke was sitting beside her now, his arm about her, as she gave me a feeble smile and whispered her thanks.

I said, "Now that you live here where the air is always dry, will your chest be made well, Rosemary?"

Luke turned his head to look at me, and I almost flinched before the glare of fury in his eyes, realizing I must have said something very bad, but not knowing what it might be. There was a little silence; then Luke looked away and Rosemary said in her gentle voice, "Yes, I'm sure I shall be better soon. Now, why don't you sit and read to me for a little while, Meg dear?"

I was thankful to Rosemary for giving me something to do at this moment, and went quickly to the shelf beside the fireplace to pick out one of the books there. Luke got up, frowning, and went back to his boot mending as I began to read. A few minutes later, when I paused and glanced up, I was relieved to see that his anger had passed and he looked almost sorry for having shown it. But I was angry with myself now, for in asking if

Rosemary's chest would be made well I had forgotten for the moment how Luke hated any questions about her sickness. This was stupid of me, and I told myself I must never be so thoughtlessly unkind again.

FROM THIS TIME ON I ACCOMPANIED LUKE ON ALMOST EVERY occasion that he made a trip to Lawton, and each time my confidence grew. I had come to Shalimar in summer and made my first visit to Lawton the following spring. Now the seasons turned again, and each day of every season was a joy to me. I worked, I read, I listened, I learned, I gave thanks for my endless blessings and good fortune, and by the time we celebrated my second birthday at Shalimar, with sixteen candles on a cake Rosemary made, my life as Mitji the freak aborigine seemed like a distant dream. The only sadness I ever knew now arose either from Rosemary's poor health or from those occasions when Luke became grim and angry as if I had offended him in some way, though I never understood why. But the bad moments always passed eventually, and he would be friendly toward me again.

One evening in the early spring of my second year at Shalimar, when Luke was once again making repairs to our working boots, Rosemary asked me to do my nightly reading from an old *Strand* magazine we had brought home from Lawton that day among other newspapers and magazines. I was pleased because this was quite advanced reading and also because I enjoyed the stories and articles I had stumbled through in other *Strand* magazines as I lay in bed at night before going to sleep.

Taking the easy chair so that I sat facing Rosemary, I let the magazine fall open on my lap. Then sudden shock seemed to freeze my whole body, and for a moment I was swept by the old primitive fears of magic, fears that had been part of my life until only two years ago. I was looking at a photograph in the magazine, a very clear picture as big as the palm of my hand. It showed a portrait of a girl my own age—my own age indeed, for the girl was myself.

FOUR

UNTIL TWO YEARS BEFORE, I HAD NEVER REALLY SEEN MY FACE, for there were no mirrors where I had lived all my remembered life. Once or twice I had seen a hazy reflection in a bowl of still water, but that was all. On first coming to Luke's home I had studied myself in the bedroom mirror with great fascination—and not a little despair at finding I was even uglier than I had imagined.

As time went by and I came to see Rosemary as beautiful, I realized that my tribe's notion of beauty in a woman was by no means a general standard, and this cheered me considerably. After my first few days at Shalimar, when I was strong enough, Rosemary had washed my hair, and later, as it grew longer, she taught me to braid it and make what she called a bun at the back of my head. During the day, while I was working, I wore a garment called dungarees, with my hair loose but tied back at the nape of my neck with a ribbon. In the evenings I wore a dress and put up my hair in a bun. I had always hated my red hair, but Rosemary said it was beautiful.

Now, looking at the photograph in the magazine, I could not tell the color of the girl's hair, but it was worn in a bun and the face beneath it was my own. For long moments I felt very frightened without quite knowing why. Then Rosemary said, "Go on, dear. Start to read."

With an effort I focused my eyes on the words at the top of the page. " 'Portraits of cel—celebrities,' " I read slowly. "What does that mean, Rosemary?"

"A celebrity is a famous person, and you know what a portrait is. Are there pictures on the page, Meg?"

"Yes," I said. "One, two . . . six altogether, on two pages. The first three are of men, and the words say, 'These portraits represent the Marquess of Salisbury at three important' "—I hesitated—" 'epochs'? Is that right?"

Rosemary nodded, her eyes closed. "Yes. Three important times, or periods. You can look it up in the dictionary later. But you pronounce that name Sawlsbury—it's one of those difficult spellings. Go on, dear."

" 'At three important epochs in his career.' Oh, it's the same man at different times of his life, I think."

Luke sniffed loudly and said, "That's right. It's a regular feature in *The Strand*. They write about half a dozen well-known people each month, raking up old photographs of them. I remember last month they had Lillie Langtry among the celebrities, but most of them are thoroughly boring people. Can't you find something more interesting than old Salisbury?"

"Who is he?" I asked.

"Prime Minister of England. That means the chief man after the Queen."

"Yes, I remember now." I spoke automatically, gazing at the opposite page, which showed a picture of a small girl in a long dress with pantaloons peeping from below the skirt, then the picture of myself in a pale dress with a frilled neck, and lastly a picture of a lady some years older but recognizable as being the same person as the other two. I opened my mouth to speak of this astonishing matter to Luke and Rosemary but then held my tongue. When I looked again, I felt that perhaps I was mistaken.

There was a likeness, certainly, but it might have been no more than that, and I had to remember I was not very experienced in recognizing real things by looking at pictures. When I had first come to Shalimar I had been unable to discern what was portrayed in some of the pictures I looked at. Now I decided that I would read the words about the lady in the pictures later, on my own, but my eye caught two or three words under the last photograph and I said, "What is a . . . a society beauty, please?"

Luke was sweeping the scraps of leather into a dustpan. He laughed briefly and said, "A rich woman who does no work and mixes with other rich people of the same kind. She may or may not be beautiful."

That decided me to remain silent. I felt I would look very vain and foolish if I announced that I looked like a girl who had become a society beauty. Luke said, "Oh, come on, Meg, we don't want to hear about so-called celebrities. Can't you find one of those Sherlock Holmes stories you read in bed when you should be asleep and then tell us about at breakfast?"

I shook myself free of the surprise that had gripped me and began to riffle through the pages of the magazine. "Wait a minute, I'll see. Ah yes, here's one called 'The Adventure of the Yellow Face.' "

Luke came to sit with Rosemary and took her hand. "Well, go on," he said. "But leave out the first two paragraphs. They're never more than a pompous introduction by Dr. Watson."

"My darling," said Rosemary, "those stories are usually nine or ten pages long, and she can't read a whole one tonight." She opened her eyes to look at me. "Just read the first two pages, Meg dear, and we'll have two more tomorrow."

"Yes, but you'll stop me if I say a word wrong? I mean, wrongly?"

"Yes, of course. Now take it slowly, and don't worry if you stumble a little."

I drew in a deep breath, put all thought of the girl in the photograph from my mind, and began to read, though not without frequent hesitations.

"One day in early spring he had so far relaxed as to go
for a walk with me in the Park, where the first faint shoots
of green were breaking out upon the elms, and the sticky
spearheads of the chestnuts were just beginning to burst
into their five-fold leaves. For two hours we rambled about
together in silence for the most part. . . ."

I had little idea of the meaning of what I was so laboriously
reading, but knew I would read the same pages again and yet
again, on my own, word by word, with a dictionary at my elbow,
until at last I understood them.

Later that night, when Luke and Rosemary had gone to bed,
I sat at the little table in my room to read for an hour, but I did
not reread any of the story about Mr. Sherlock Holmes. The
page on which the lamp cast its pool of light was the page with
the photograph that had so startled me, and I began to read the
words accompanying the pictures with a small feeling of unease
for which I could think of no good reason.

"We are indebted to Lady Glencullen for the photograph on the right, which shows her as a child of seven.
This picture was taken at her family home in the Irish
village of Kilgarran, where her father, Mr. Thomas Mulvaney, was well known as a breeder of fine cattle. Miss
Mary Caragh Mulvaney, as she was then, received private
tuition both at her home in Kilgarran and in London,
where the family usually spent most of the Season.

"The picture below shows Lady Glencullen at fifteen,
two years before she was presented at court as a debutante
and four years before her marriage to Mr. Laurence Glencullen (later Sir Laurence Glencullen), a senior official in
the Colonial Office at that time, who in the following year
inherited the Glencullen fortune.

"In the early years of the marriage Lady Glencullen
traveled widely with her husband in the course of his duties. He was knighted and transferred to the Home Office
in 1891, since when she has devoted herself to various

works of charity in a practical and down-to-earth fashion which has attracted admiration from all quarters. She combines such work with that of being one of London's most notable hostesses.

"The photograph below (right) was taken at Sir Laurence's country home in Kent quite recently, and we do not hesitate to caption it with the words, A SOCIETY BEAUTY, for in our opinion Lady Glencullen is even more beautiful twenty years later than she was as the young lady of fifteen shown on the left."

I read the words three times, grasping a little more of their meaning each time, and when I had finished I studied the pictures again, especially the one showing the young lady. Two years ago I would have thought her ugly, and I did not think her beautiful now, but I agreed with the writer that she was truly beautiful in the recent picture. There was a warmth and gentleness in her face, in her eyes perhaps, which reminded me very much of Rosemary.

With the magazine in one hand, I picked up the lamp and moved to look from the mirror on the wall to the photograph of Lady Glencullen as a young lady. *Was* I greatly like her when she had been my age? Well . . . perhaps not greatly. There was a likeness, but I no longer felt that first startling impression of seeing myself in the photograph. Lady Glencullen came from Ireland, and Rosemary had once or twice mentioned that I might have Scottish or Irish forebears, judging by my red hair and freckles. So it was possible that Lady Glencullen and I were just similar types from the same tribe.

I returned to the table and settled down to reread the first two pages of the Sherlock Holmes story. Then I studied the next two pages, so I would be able to read them aloud more readily the following evening. In the adjoining bedroom, Rosemary coughed several times. I knew she must be awake, and I tiptoed into the passage. Her door stood slightly ajar, and when I eased it open a little I could tell from Luke's slow breathing that he was asleep. I whispered, "Can I do anything? Fetch you a warm drink?"

She whispered back, "No, dear. It's just a little cough. I'll take a spoonful of medicine."

"You're sure?"

"Yes, quite sure. Now, go to bed, Meg. You've sat up reading for quite long enough."

"All right. Sleep well, Rosemary, and God bless you."

To be honest I was still rather puzzled about what I would once have called the *walypala* god, but I knew the meaning of those last words I had spoken to Rosemary, and I meant them with all my heart.

Next day as I worked with Luke to clear the irrigation gullies into which we pumped water from the little river I said, "Please, Luke, have I done something wrong? Something to make you not like me?"

He paused, staring hard at me, then said, "Why do you ask that?"

"Well . . . it's hard to explain, but sometimes you seem to have a cold feeling for me, as if I had done wrong, but I can't think what it might be. I try very hard to do all things that you and Rosemary wish."

Luke leaned on the narrow rake he was using and stared down at the ground. "You've done nothing wrong," he said quietly. "You're a very good girl, and your being here has given Rosemary more happiness than I ever thought possible." He looked at me then with the especially friendly smile I had sometimes seen when we were in the desert together and during my early weeks at Shalimar. "I'm grateful to you," he went on, "and I should be. Rosemary and I are in your debt several times over."

When I had worked out what he meant I stared in surprise. "In my debt? But how, Luke? You give me a home, food to eat, clothes to wear, and you teach me to be a civilized and educated person. All the giving is yours."

He reached out as if to rest a hand on my shoulder, then drew it back. "No," he said. "You saved my life, you've brought real joy to Rosemary, and you made it possible for us to get through your first year here without having to borrow money."

Again I was taken aback. "Money? I brought nothing with me, Luke. I did not even know what money was."

"The yellow stones you found on the dead man," he said. "They were small gold nuggets you gave me that day in the desert." He grinned and shrugged, eyes twinkling in the way I always liked to see. "Not a fortune, but worth quite a lot to poor and needy folk like us, Red."

I felt myself to be glowing with delight as I said, "Is it true? Did I really bring such a gift with me?"

"As true as can be."

"Oh, Luke, I'm *so* happy." I took a step forward and would have hugged him impulsively to show my joy, but he moved back, his grin fading, and said almost brusquely, "Well, that's how it is, so don't go imagining I'm angry with you if I'm sometimes a little quiet. I'm probably just . . . thinking about something. Now, come on, young lady, let's get this finished. It'll be time to eat soon."

THREE WEEKS LATER LUKE SAID WE WOULD TAKE THE DAY OFF and catch the train to Kalgoorlie. I thought he meant we would all go, but that was foolish of me. Rosemary had accompanied us to church once or twice, but she found even the short trip to Lawton very tiring, and could not possibly have endured a full day of travel.

I was excited at the thought of seeing Kalgoorlie, but not apprehensive as I had been on my first visit to Lawton, for I spoke English quite naturally now and was not afraid of talking to people other than Luke and Rosemary. We set off early, wearing our best clothes. After so many visits to Lawton I was no longer in fear of the train but looked forward to riding in it. Luke had said I would enjoy this, and his words proved true. Being in a carriage was like being in a long room, and Luke found a seat for me by a window so that I could watch the land rush by as we traveled at enormous speed across the plain. I sat entranced by the wonder of it all, though once I was touched by sadness as I thought of Yuma and the copper penny he believed to hold such magic. Again I felt deep thankfulness at my good fortune in having escaped from a life of such hardship and ignorance into the world of comfort and knowledge I now enjoyed.

I was ready for Kalgoorlie and felt no fear as we left the train. It was busier and more crowded than Lawton, but it did not come as such a shock, for I could see only a part of it at a time, so it did not overwhelm me. This was a wonderful day for me, made all the better by Luke's being warm and friendly and seeming to enjoy the pleasure I was showing.

When he went to a bank, I sat on a bench just inside the door to wait while he spoke to a man in an office there, and as I waited, two ladies passing by gave me a smile and said, "Good morning." They were older ladies with graying hair, so I got quickly to my feet and made a small curtsy as I said, "Good morning to you." Much to my delight, I was not at all nervous at my first encounter in this great town, and I think I must have been beaming with pleasure, for one of the ladies inclined her head and said, "How nice to see such a happy face."

After the bank our first visit was to a man who took photographs. There I sat in a chair trying to look calm and natural while he buried his head under a black cloth and made a great flare of light with some special powder in a small T-shaped object held in his hand. Rosemary had made Luke promise to have my photograph taken, and the photographer assured us that he would have two prints ready when we called back that afternoon. I was bubbling with excitement, and tried to get Luke to have a photograph of himself taken for me. At first he would not hear of it, but I kept pleading and persuading until in the end he laughingly agreed.

Later he took me to a restaurant where we had luncheon served to us at a table by a girl called a waitress, without our having to cook or wash up or do anything for ourselves. We did not talk much, but I was listening to all sorts of conversations between other people, not to be impolite but simply to practice my understanding of English spoken by people with different accents.

After lunch we strolled about the center of the town for a while, and Luke called at one or two places where he hoped to be able to sell an increased raisin crop next season. I saw many more men than women, but not one of them looked nicer than Luke. Sometimes, watching the women dressed in skirts that reached to their ankles, as mine did, I thought with an inward smile how shocked they would be if they knew I had spent my life until two years ago running about naked.

I spoke this thought to Luke as we walked, who grinned and said, "You certainly shocked *me*, Mitji."

I laughed at this use of my old name and said, "Yes, I realize that now. I suppose I ought to feel shy and go pink in my cheeks when I remember, but somehow it still doesn't seem important to me. I expect it will take a long time for me to become a completely civilized person."

He glanced down at me with a look I found hard to understand and said, "Don't change too much. Being completely civilized isn't everything."

Later that afternoon we did a little shopping for Rosemary, then went to a small restaurant to have some eggs and bacon and tea. As we sat waiting to be served, a man with some newspapers under his arm came in. He was older than Luke, rather thin, with a long nose and sharp eyes. The suit he wore was of a brown check, and when he took off his brown bowler hat I saw that he had dark hair parted in the middle and slicked back.

He showed surprise when his eyes lighted on Luke, and at once he came toward us. "Hello, Bowman. Must have been you I saw going into Jack Waller's photographic studio this morning, but I thought I was mistaken. What are you doing in Kalgoorlie?"

Luke said coolly, "Hello, Tasker. I'm minding my own business. What about you?"

The thin man grinned, unabashed. "Just up from Perth for a few days, taking a look around to see if there's any story worth picking up."

"Well, good luck. But don't try to pick up a story about what an English girl feels like if she's married to a man who's the black sheep of a wealthy English family and who's farming a bit of land outside Lawton. My wife doesn't want to talk to reporters—but I think I've mentioned that before, haven't I?"

Tasker nodded. "You put your fist through my hat when you mentioned it," he said without rancor.

"Lucky it was only your hat."

Tasker shrugged. "All right, mate. I was just doing my job, but you've made your point." He glanced at me for the first time. "Afternoon, miss."

I inclined my head as I had seen the gray-haired ladies do, and said, "Good afternoon, Mr. Tasker. How do you do?"

He looked at me with amused surprise. "I don't do too bad, thanks. You're Miss . . . er . . . ?"

Luke said, "Meg, this is Harry Tasker, a reporter for a newspaper in Perth." He looked at the thin man. "Tasker, this is my wife's cousin, Meg Gaynor. She lost her parents a couple of years ago and came out from England to live with us."

"Glad to know you," said Harry Tasker, but with little show of interest. He looked at Luke again. "Any message for the old folks back home?"

Luke frowned. "Message?"

A grin spread across Harry Tasker's face. "I'm going home next month. Just finishing my last tour for the *Record*. Got a job on a new daily coming out in London. They want somebody with knowledge and experience of Australian affairs—"

He had glanced at me again as he spoke, and abruptly he stopped in midsentence, staring at me with great intensity and a kind of blank bewilderment. A moment before, our waitress had arrived with a tray, and Luke was occupied with her as she set our dishes of eggs and bacon down on the table, followed by the teapot and crockery. By the time Luke looked up, the man had recovered himself and stood frowning and pulling his long nose very thoughtfully as if trying to remember something.

Luke said, "Australian affairs? Well, you ought to be all right there. Bon voyage, Tasker." He gestured at the table. "We're about to eat now, if you don't mind."

Harry Tasker seemed to emerge from a reverie with a little start. "Oh. Right. I'll leave you to it." His eyes rested upon me again with a kind of wonder, and then he looked quickly away. "Ah, there's a table vacant, and I could eat a horse. Nice to meet you, Miss Gaynor. Good-bye, Bowman. Remember me to your wife."

"I'll do that," Luke said pleasantly, passing me the salt and pepper. "Take good care of your new hat."

Having heard that Luke had put his fist through the previous hat, I almost giggled at those last words, but I doubted that Harry Tasker even heard them, for it was clear to me as he turned away that his mind was fully occupied with some other matter far more important. Remembering the startled way he had looked at me, I began to feel a little uneasy as I poured tea for us.

"That man gave me such a strange look," I whispered. "You didn't see it because you were dealing with the waitress, but he seemed to have a sudden shock, and then he stared and stared. Did I do something that made him guess I'm not Rosemary's cousin, but came out of the bush?"

Luke smiled and shook his head. "Not a chance, Meg. He was more likely surprised at your very good manners, or perhaps it dawned on him that you're a very pretty girl, sitting there with your big bright eyes and your green bonnet. He has something of a reputation for liking pretty girls."

As I passed Luke his cup of tea I said, "I'm so glad you think I'm pretty. It makes me feel warm inside."

He frowned and his eyes grew cold. "Don't get big ideas about yourself," he said.

I shook my head, troubled. "Oh, I won't, Luke. I promise. It's just that . . . well, I know I'm not really pretty because my face isn't soft enough, but I grew up thinking I was an ugly freak, and it's quite nice to know I'm not as bad as that.''

"You're a great deal better than that," he said curtly, "but in fact you're not pretty. Now, let's drop the subject and eat up before this meal gets cold.''

I was puzzled by Luke's words and manner, but I remembered the time when he had told me quite definitely that he did not dislike me, so I decided not to be upset. We were only halfway through our meal when Harry Tasker left the restaurant with a nod in our direction.

I said, "I thought Mr. Tasker told us he was very hungry. He can't have had time for more than a cup of tea.''

Luke shrugged. "Newspaper reporters don't behave like normal people, Meg. Perhaps he just thought of an idea for a story.''

I shook my head wonderingly. "It seems a strange kind of work, finding out about other people and then writing about them for *other* people to read.''

Luke smiled, and I was glad to see that he was warm toward me again. "Yes, it's strange work," he said, "but the reporting of scandal and disaster seems to be an essential part of our completely civilized world.''

After a little thought I remembered the word I wanted. "You're being cynical," I said.

He laughed outright. "Good for you, Red. Come on, now. Pour us another cup of tea each. Then we'll go and buy some magazines for Rosemary.''

I poured the tea. "I didn't like Mr. Tasker much. I didn't like his scent.''

Luke stared. "Scent? He doesn't wear scent!''

"No, I mean his natural scent. Everybody has a scent. Some of the ladies we've passed today wear perfume, but I can still detect their natural scent behind it.''

Luke ran a hand through his hair and said, "After all this time you're saying you can smell *me*?''

I laughed. "Of course I can. If I covered my eyes I would know as soon as you came within a few paces of me.''

He sighed ruefully and said, "Oh my God."

"But yours is a good scent. So is Rosemary's."

"Well, let's be thankful for that." He studied me curiously for a moment. "You've come so far, Meg, I sometimes forget what you were like, but of course you could even scent water when we were in the outback."

"I could, but not nearly as well as the littlest child in the tribe I lived with. I can only do it at all because I didn't want to be a freak, so I used to concentrate very hard on what my nose told me. I think most white people only ever notice strong scents, but you can train your sense of smell to be quite good—if you have to. Among aborigines it can mean the difference between life and death, so it's very important. Do I speak quite nicely now, without much accent, and saying all my 's' and 'f' sounds properly? Oh, and my aitches? You know, when I first heard of a horse we called it *wurpa*. That was as close as we could get to such a word."

He looked puzzled at the change of subject. "Why, yes. You have no accent and you speak very much like Rosemary."

"I'm so glad. That's what I've been trying to do from the beginning."

He nodded rather soberly. "You have great powers of concentration, Meg. I remember how it was when you were bringing me out of the desert. You never missed the slightest sign that might indicate food of some kind. That ability has served you well in all you've had to learn."

I glowed inwardly at his praise, but did not tell him so in case it made him turn cold again. Half an hour later we collected the photographs, and I was fascinated to see these tiny images of Luke and of myself. It was quite different from seeing photos of people I had never known. I thought I looked rather haughty, but Luke was smiling and looked very nice.

As we strolled through the main street of the town again I said, "Luke, I've noticed that two or three of the ladies we've passed wear strong perfume and put paint on their faces, so they seem different from others. Are they special persons?"

He frowned. "You'd better ask Rosemary about that—" he broke off, looked uncertain for a moment, then gave an impatient shake of his head. "Oh, to the devil with it, you've hardly led a sheltered life and you're certainly not going to be shocked. Those women lie with men for money. They're what are called harlots in the Bible, but don't use that word in company."

I was not shocked, but I was amazed. "Money? I don't understand. In my tribe, a man could lend his wife to a friend, but if a woman lay with a man in exchange for a gift of any kind, her family menfolk would kill her. I know everything is different among aborigines, Luke, but I thought this thing was wrong among *us* also. I mean, everything I've read in books, and parts of the Bible, and in the marriage service in Rosemary's prayer book—"

"Yes, it's wrong, Meg," he broke in rather irritably, "but you'll find that the people of our tribe do quite a lot of things that are wrong. Those women are looked down upon with contempt by other women, who will have nothing to do with them."

"I see." I thought for a few moments as we walked on. "Are the men who pay them looked down upon with contempt?"

He gave a brief dry laugh. "Strangely, it doesn't seem to work out like that."

"Luke, please don't ever pay one of those women. It would hurt Rosemary so much."

He stopped short, halting me and turning me to face him, and my heart sank when I saw the anger in his eyes. Then he seemed to control himself with an effort. "You can be quite sure I will never do anything to hurt Rosemary in the slightest degree," he said in a tight voice. "And I suggest that the next thing you should concentrate upon is to avoid saying outrageous things to people."

I held back tears and said, "Forgive me, Luke. I'm still very ignorant."

He released my arm. "All right, we'll forget it, Meg."

"Oh yes. Please. You mean forget it as if it truly never happened?"

He drew in a deep breath, then seemed to relax, giving me a nod and a little smile. "How you do get to the heart of things," he murmured. "Yes, that's what I mean, Mitji. Come on, now. It's time we made for the station."

I felt much relieved as we walked on, telling myself that I still had much to learn about the ways of my true tribe, the English, and that I must think carefully before speaking. This would not be easy, for I loved to practice conversation and would go on chattering endlessly with Rosemary or even talk aloud to myself if I was working alone.

On the way to the station Luke explained that there was only a single track between Kalgoorlie and Lawton, but there were plans to build passing-places with two tracks, so that trains going to and from Lawton could run at the same time. As we came on to the platform I saw Mr. Tasker sitting on a bench. I was surprised, for he had not spoken of going to Lawton. When I pointed him out, Luke said, "Oh, he's just hanging around on the lookout for anything or anyone interesting—unless maybe there's a night train leaving for Perth."

We passed close by the bench as we made for the train. Mr. Tasker had some newspapers on his knees, and Luke gave him a nod, saying, "Found your story yet, Tasker?"

The thin man shrugged, his sharp eyes watching me. "I think I've got a big one," he said. "Might be too good for what the *Record* pays me."

"Good luck, then," Luke said vaguely, and we moved on, but not before I noticed that on top of Mr. Tasker's newspapers was a well-worn copy of a *Strand* magazine. I looked back when we reached the door of the carriage and saw that the reporter now held the magazine open and was looking from its pages toward me and back again. I realized then what must have happened, and smiled to myself. Mr. Tasker had evidently seen the same copy of the *Strand* magazine as I had, and when we met in the restaurant he had been struck by my likeness to the photo of the girl who had later become Lady Glencullen. On leaving us, he had gone to get his copy of the magazine, then waited at the station so that he could see me again and confirm his earlier impression.

Well, now he would know that there was indeed a likeness, though not as striking as perhaps he had first thought. I marveled that he had gone to any trouble in the matter, for in the new world I had entered only two years before there must surely be among its teeming population quite a number of girls who looked somewhat like me.

One thing was certain, I decided. Mr. Tasker would never find an interesting story for his paper in the dull fact that there was a lady in England who, years ago when she was fifteen, had resembled a girl of about that age he had met in Kalgoorlie today.

Dusk fell during our return journey, and I found new excitement in rushing through the gathering darkness at such speed, with the iron wheels clattering rhythmically on the rails for mile after mile, carrying us farther in an hour than I had ever before traveled in a day. When we left the train at Lawton I looked back at it and thought how ignorant I had been to feel terrified when I first saw it, as if it had been a living monster.

Henrietta had been left in the stables by the station, and as soon as she was harnessed to the trap we set off on the hour-long drive to Shalimar. This had been the most wonderful and exciting day of my life, and I felt immensely grateful and content as we jogged along the track, leaving the scattered lights of Lawton behind us. I had become a little sleepy on the train, but the night air soon revived me, and my head began buzzing with remembrance of all my new experiences and all I would have to tell Rosemary.

We drove in silence for a while. Then Luke said, "Meg, do you remember that about a year ago you asked how I came to be where you found me that day in the outback, when you followed the camel tracks back from the dead man with the gold nuggets?"

I nodded, then realized he could not see me in the darkness, and I said, "Yes, but I had a feeling you didn't want to speak of it, so I haven't asked again."

"You're more than entitled to know," he said with a little sigh in his voice, "and it's no secret, but I don't like to speak of it in front of Rosemary because I know it distresses her. I'd like to tell you now, while we're alone."

"Well . . . only if it's not a secret, Luke. I can't have secrets from Rosemary."

"It's not secret from her, I promise." He was silent for a few seconds, then went on. "We had a really good crop in the season before you came to Shalimar, and I sold at a nice profit. Then the buyer went bankrupt, and we were paid only a quarter of what we were owed. I had doctors' bills to pay, medicine to buy, and I didn't know how to get through the year. I was desperate. Then I met a man in Lawton, a prospector called Joe Catesby. You know what a prospector is?"

"Yes, Rosemary told me about the Kalgoorlie gold rush. A prospector is a man who looks for gold, isn't he?"

"Or silver, or opal—anything valuable. Catesby said he'd struck it rich a year before, in the outback a long way northeast of here. He'd found a tremendous seam of gold, but it was hidden away in a network of valleys, and he'd run out of supplies and almost died finding his way out. He had a rough map, and he was going back to find the place and stake his claim, but he wanted a partner to help him. He wanted a camel, plenty of supplies, and a couple of rifles for shooting game—I suppose he meant kangaroos—to eke out those supplies."

I heard the wryness in Luke's voice as he said, "We never saw anything to shoot, except an occasional bird on the wing, and a rifle's useless for that. Well, to cut a long story short, after Catesby approached me I talked to Dan Lomax, who owns that store in Lawton. Dan agreed to pay for the hire of a camel, to give us six weeks' supplies, and to provide two rifles on loan and a small quantity of ammunition. It was agreed that whatever came of the expedition, Dan would be entitled to one sixth of the profits, I would have one third, and Catesby one half."

I said, "But wasn't Rosemary worried about your going into the desert? And weren't you worried about leaving her?"

"I was worried to death," said Luke, and I heard his voice shake for a moment. "But by midwinter we'd have been living on slops, and Rosemary needs good nourishing food. You know that. You know how brave she is, too, and she understood that I was putting all I had into finding a means of staying on at Shalimar, where the climate suited her. There was no work in Lawton, and we both knew that if we had to move to Kalgoorlie for me to find work it would mean . . ." He stopped for a second or two, then went on. "Well, her cough would have become much worse."

Luke fell silent, and I guessed he was recalling the agony of the decision he had been driven to make in the hope, not the certainty, that the expedition would succeed and all would come right in the end. "You were delirious for the last two days of our journey home on the camel, Meg," he said at last, "but by the second day we reached that low peak you can see on a clear day from the knoll east of Shalimar. Well, that's the way we headed out, Catesby and I. Then we went on along the route by which you brought me home, and on beyond that till we came to this strange area of rocky cliffs, all seamed and split, with twisting ravines running this way and that for mile after mile."

"Our tribe passed that way once when I was young," I said, "before Manyi went away. But we didn't stay. It's a great range of rocky hills extending for many miles, an empty place, with little food to be hunted or gathered and little water. The elders called it The-place-of-too-many-ways."

"That's true, by God," he said heavily. "We roamed those ravines for day after day, trying to make sense of Catesby's ill-drawn map, with our water running out and our supplies dwindling. I suppose I was a fool ever to enter into partnership with Catesby. He was a pig of a man, and we often quarreled. There came a time when we gave up and turned for home. I thought we'd left it too late, and I was right. We were almost at the end of our tether when we stumbled into a little dry valley quite close to the edge of the maze. And that's where the gold was. That was the place Catesby had found before.''

Behind us the lights of Lawton had faded completely, and in that moonless night there was darkness all around us now. I knew Luke had let the reins go slack, for Henrietta could follow the trail by scent, as I could have done myself on foot.

"We came out with a small bag of nuggets," said Luke. "There was no time for more. I did have the wits to make a good map of our way out, so that we could find the place again, for it was only by sheer luck that Catesby had blundered into it twice. You could search for a year without finding that little valley unless you knew where to look. When we started for home we had only three bottles of water between us. We threw away the two empty tanks the camel had carried for our main supply, and after two days we reached the spot where you found me. It was then that Catesby decided he wanted all that was left of the water, plus my share of the gold.''

"I could tell from reading the sign that there had been a scuffle," I said. "Was that when he made the gash on your head?''

"Yes. I was wary of him, and he didn't quite take me by surprise, but he caught me on the head with his rifle butt, and down I went. The rifle must have gone off by accident. I heard it as I fell, and that's the last thing I remember, but I think the shot must have startled the camel and made it bolt.''

"I found the lead bullet splattered on a rock," I said, "and I know he chased the camel for several hours before he died. He must have taken the last of the water with him, for there was none where I found you.''

Luke said slowly, almost as if speaking his thoughts aloud to himself, "That was something I'll remember till I die. It's burned into my brain, that moment of coming back to consciousness to find a strange, golden-skinned, red-haired little creature with a grubby face holding me in her arms . . . a golden urchin, giving me water from her lips.''

I said, "I now know it wasn't good manners, Luke, but I couldn't risk spilling any."

He gave a brief laugh. "I wasn't greatly concerned about good manners at the time. Anyway, that's the story of how it all came about, Meg."

After we had driven on for a while a new thought struck me, and I said, "If you made a good map, then surely you could find the place again, the place where the gold is?"

"Yes. But unfortunately the map was in the pocket of a little canvas haversack, strapped on the camel with other gear. When you brought the camel back, the strap was broken and the haversack had gone. It could have happened anywhere at any time, when the camel lay down, or brushed against a rocky bluff, but however it happened, the map's lost forever."

I made a picture in my mind of the route I had taken after finding the camel, and recalled that in following its tracks I had sometimes cut across places where the creature had wandered about in a circle. "I didn't see a haversack," I said. "If I had, I would have brought it with me."

Beside me I felt Luke shrug. "Harder to find it now than to find the valley with the gold."

"But, Luke, perhaps you could find the valley in that place-of-too-many-ways if I came with you. I'm sure I could always find enough food and water just for us, even there."

He said almost brusquely, "That's out of the question. You're not an aborigine girl now, and you can't possibly go off into the outback for weeks on end with a man. God knows how long it might take. And quite apart from all that, I'm never going to leave Rosemary again."

"Oh, of course. I'm sorry, I should have thought of that."

We drove on in silence for a while, and I found myself frowning as I tried to capture an elusive thought. Something Luke had said in the last ten minutes had struck a chord within me, but I could not think what word or phrase might have done this, and I had no idea what it signified. Perhaps I was tired after my exciting day out, I decided. Perhaps after a night's sleep I would be able to uncover my hidden memory, just as Mr. Sherlock Holmes uncovered criminals in the *Strand* magazine.

I assumed that Luke had finished telling me about his near-tragic expedition into the desert with Joe Catesby, but after a while he spoke again. "When we got back to Shalimar you were still delirious. I told Rosemary what had happened, and she took charge of you. Next day I took the camel into Lawton and handed it over to Dan Lomax with the two rifles and the rest of the gear we'd borrowed. I left you out of the story I told him, Meg, and let him think the camel had come wandering back on its own, and that I'd been able to get myself home safely. But I told him the truth about all the rest of it. I offered him one third of the nuggets, but he refused them. Said he'd only take enough to cover his expenses, and that I'd more than earned the rest."

"He seems a nice man, Luke."

"Dan's a good fellow and well respected. He said he'd always been uneasy about Joe Catesby, and he came with me to the police station to report Catesby's presumed death, and how it had come about. The police weren't at all surprised. It seems Catesby had a record of violence, and they suspected he'd killed a partner of his in the outback three years ago. Anyway, they believed my story, and were quite happy at the prospect of not being troubled by Joe Catesby again."

In the distance a pinpoint of light told us that Shalimar was near. Luke said, "Then I came back home, and waited two days for you to wake up out of the deep sleep that followed your fever."

I was suddenly surprised by a great yawn that I tried in vain to stifle. Luke said politely, "Am I boring you, miss?" I could tell from his voice that he was joking, and I laughed as I said, "I haven't been bored for a single moment since I woke up from that sleep to see Rosemary's face for the first time. Thank you so much for taking me to Kalgoorlie today. It was very kind of you."

With the last words I put my hand on his arm, but he shook

it off at once and said curtly, "No need to make a fuss about it."

"I'm sorry, Luke."

"And don't keep apologizing."

"Oh, I'm s—" I stopped myself in time and said, "I'll try not to." I felt a little sad as we finished the journey, and told myself I must remember that Luke did not like to be touched. This was hard for me to understand. During my years with the tribe I had never known the warmth of touching after Manyi stopped suckling me, and I loved it now when Rosemary patted my cheek or held my hand as she explained something to me, or slipped her arm through mine as we took a little stroll together when the heat of the day had passed. I realized that man-and-woman touching was different, but I felt sure Luke knew I had no wrong thoughts in putting my hand on his arm. It was only to show heart-warmth.

When we arrived home it was to find that Rosemary had had one of her bad days, and I felt very guilty about having left her alone for so long. I quickly prepared some supper, and later, when I had washed up, I sat with her on the couch, holding her hand, and began to chatter away, pouring out an account of all I had seen and felt throughout this wonderful day. She watched me with smiling eyes, seeming very happy for me, and sometimes laughing at my excitement.

I was very tired when I went to bed, but it was some time before I slept, for I could not help wondering what it was that kept tugging at my memory of the time when I had found Luke near to death in the outback. I had the feeling that I knew something of possible importance, but could not put my finger on what it was. This frustrating feeling nagged at me for a day or two, but I could recall nothing to explain the cause, and finally I was able to put it out of my mind.

In the days that followed it was a wonder Rosemary did not become thoroughly tired of my chatter, for I must have recounted every detail of every moment of my trip to Kalgoorlie. In any event she seemed to enjoy listening to me, and was interested to find that I remembered so many tiny things that most people would never have noticed. We agreed that this must be because I had lived in the harsh outback for almost all my life, a cruel place that would quickly kill you if you failed to notice the tiny signs that led to food and water.

There were only two things I did not speak of to Rosemary. First, the story Luke had told me on the journey home from Lawton, for he had said this was upsetting for her; and second, the silly matter of Mr. Tasker seeing my likeness to the photograph in the *Strand* magazine. I would not have minded if I could have joked about it, but could not bear to suggest that I bore a resemblance to "a society beauty," for Rosemary had taught me that to be vain about oneself was very bad manners.

Christmas came, and my present from Luke was a new dress that Rosemary altered a little to make it a perfect fit. "And none too soon," she said when at last she was satisfied. "You're bursting out of your old dress, and we can't let the seams out any more." This was true, and I was delighted with such a lovely present, for it made me feel very elegant and grown-up.

On Christmas morning we took Rosemary into Lawton for the special church service, then returned home and cooked a tremendous meal of turkey and Christmas pudding. Because our crop was good this year, Rosemary and Luke had insisted, against my tearful protests, on paying me money for the work I did on the farm and in the house, so I had been able to buy presents for them, a pretty brooch for Rosemary and a pocket-knife for Luke. Rosemary's present to me was a beautiful book called *Peoples of the World*, full of photographs, which I found endlessly fascinating.

Autumn came, our crop sold at a good price, and Rosemary's cough seemed at least to be no worse. I remembered never to touch Luke, and learned not to feel sad when sometimes he was cold toward me. I worked joyously in the house, on the farm, and at my lessons, and I felt grateful for every golden moment of this wonderful life that Luke and Rosemary had given me.

Then, toward spring, four months after my trip with Luke to Kalgoorlie, a man came to Shalimar and tried to kill me.

FIVE

It began on a Sunday, a day when Rosemary always insisted that we should rest and do no work that was not essential. Luke was usually restless on a Sunday, and sometimes in a bad mood. I had the feeling that he needed to be busy in order to keep his mind away from matters he did not want to think about. I did not know what those matters were, apart from his worry over Rosemary's health.

After breakfast I went out to feed the chickens we kept in a coop near the barn and to collect any eggs. Halfway to the coop I caught a faint scent and at the same time noticed two small round indentations and a short curved line on a patch of dusty ground. I knew the sign was part of a print left by a boot with metal studs in the sole, but not by one of Luke's boots. He only used plates on the toes of his boots, and in any case the man-scent was not his.

As I finished feeding the chickens Luke came out to fetch two buckets of water from the pump by the stream, and I said, "A man was here during the night. I wonder what he was doing."

Luke stared. "A man?"

"Yes. I caught his scent just now, and there's some sign in that patch of dust."

Luke glanced to where I was pointing. "I can't see any sign," he said dourly. "You're imagining things."

"No, really I'm not. I know a man was here."

He seemed to be taken by sudden anger and snapped, "Why the hell would anyone come prowling around here? It doesn't make sense for a moment." He started to move on toward the pump, then paused to look back at me. "It's a waste of time, Rosemary, trying to make a young lady of you if you're forever going around *smelling* people."

Rosemary had appeared in the doorway as he spoke, and now she looked distressed as she said, "Luke, please don't be cross with her, my dear. Meg has done nothing wrong."

I said quickly, "It's all right. I just have this bad habit. I'm sorry I upset you, Luke."

He closed his eyes for a moment, then opened them again and smiled with an effort. "No. It's not a bad habit, and I'm the one to apologize. Sorry, Meg."

As he turned and went on toward the stream Rosemary said, puzzled, "What was that all about?"

I shook my head. In my mind there was no doubt that a strange man had prowled around our home during the night, but I did not want to worry Rosemary or to say anything that might annoy Luke again, so I just smiled and used a saying I had learned a few days before. "It was just a storm in a teacup," I said.

That afternoon, while Rosemary lay on her bed to rest, I asked Luke if I might go for a little walk as far as the knoll that rose in a hillock about a mile to the east of Shalimar. He was reading a London newspaper several weeks old, and looked up with a puzzled air when I made my request. "Walk to the knoll?" he repeated.

"Yes, if you don't mind."

He shrugged. "No, I don't mind, but I doubt that you'll find it particularly interesting." When I did not answer but just stood waiting, he said, "All right, off you go."

Throughout the morning I had been wondering where the

stranger could have come from. It seemed most unlikely that he had walked all the way from Lawton, and if he had ridden it was strange that I had found no sign of his mount, nor heard it during the night, for like the aborigines I had grown up with I had very acute hearing. It occurred to me that if a stranger was curious about Shalimar he might have ridden out from Lawton during the day, keeping out of sight behind the long curving ridge to the north until he reached the knoll. There he could have remained hidden by the scrub that clothed it and kept watch on us till dark, when he had come in on foot for the purpose of . . . what?

This was a question to which I had no answer. The man had caused no harm, done no damage to us or to Shalimar—but I did not like his scent. There had been a darkness in it that made my flesh creep.

I quickly picked up sign of him on leaving the house. His trail was so fresh it was easy to follow. I did not even have to stop and peer at the ground, for which I was thankful, since Luke might have been watching me from the window. The stranger had come from the knoll on foot and had gone back again by a slightly different path, which was natural since he had been moving in darkness.

It occurred to me that he might still be hidden on the farther side of the knoll, and when I reached the point where the gentle upward slope began I spent ten minutes moving around the foot of the knoll in a full circle, watching, listening, scenting to detect any presence, but there was none. I walked up the slope, still following the trail, and found where the man had lain hidden just beyond the crest. Lower down, by a stubby crag, I found where he had tethered his horse, not a big creature to judge by the imprint of its hooves.

During my early days at Shalimar I had been astonished by a seemingly magical object Luke had shown me, which brought distant things very close when you looked through two short tubes joined together. I had long since learned that these were called field glasses and were not in any way magical. It was simply a scientific fact that two pieces of glass, shaped in a particular way and fixed one behind the other, had this remarkable effect. As I stood on the slope where the man had hidden and looked toward Shalimar I thought how well he could have studied us through field glasses as we went about our daily work. And then after dark, when our lamps had long been put out and we were asleep, he had come to the farm to . . . to do what?

It was baffling. I wanted to talk about it with Luke, who might have found some possible explanation if only I could persuade him to believe me, but I shrank from going to him again and insisting that there had indeed been a prowler about our home, and that I was right and he was wrong. After all, the stranger had caused no trouble, and it seemed foolish for me to risk angering Luke for no good reason.

When three days had passed with no sign of the prowler's return I began to lose the feeling of uneasiness I had at first. Luke had got over his Sunday black mood, and we were working comfortably together again. It was toward the evening of a hot day, made hotter by the task at hand, but I was now a much more civilized person and hardly ever wished that I could take my clothes off to work. One of the iron tires on our trap had split, and it was necessary to fit a new one. Luke had made the tire, a flat strip of iron bent into a circle with the ends riveted and fashioned to a very exact measurement so that it was not quite large enough to slip over the wooden rim of the wheel.

Together we had dug a shallow pit a few inches deep and made a fire in it. Now the new tire lay in the glowing embers, and beside the pit lay the wooden wheel, its rim supported on four thick chocks of wood. Rosemary sat watching in the shade of an awning Luke had rigged for her near the porch. Luke and I stood on opposite sides of the pit, both in our working clothes of shirt and dungarees. In each hand we carried a length of wood with a bent nail at one end, by which we could lift out the hot tire between us. Nearby stood two buckets of water for cooling the iron.

I was greatly intrigued by this operation, for Rosemary had

explained that when metal was heated it expanded, which meant that our iron hoop would grow a little larger. Then we could slip it over the rim of the wheel and immediately cool it with water, when it would contract and grip the wheel so tightly that it could never be removed except by cutting.

Luke stood watching the metal change color. "We don't want it red hot," he said. A bead of sweat trickled down his brow, and I laughed as I wiped away sweat running into my eye at the exact moment that he did the same thing. I was happy to see him in a good mood today. Since my coming to Shalimar, over two years ago now, he had taken to calling me by different names. When he was content and at ease, he might call me Mitji, or Red. Mostly he called me Meg, sometimes amiably, sometimes in a restrained way. If he was in a black mood, he used no name at all when speaking to me.

Now, without taking his eyes from the iron tire, he said, "All right. Here we go."

I leaned forward to slip the bent nails under the tire, a little distance apart, and Luke did the same on the other side. Together we lifted the iron hoop, moved sideways, laid it on the wheel, and nudged it quickly into position so that it dropped onto the chocks. At once we let fall our hooked sticks and each turned to a bucket, using cupped hands to splash water all around the tire, so that it contracted evenly, steaming and sizzling at first, then rapidly changing color as it cooled. I heard the rim and spokes creak under the strength of its grip. Then Luke straightened up and said, "Good enough. Let's get that fire doused."

"I can see to that while you get the wheel back on the axle before it grows dark," I said.

Luke hesitated. "You'll have to make sure there are no sparks left among the embers. The wind's getting up."

"I'll be careful, Luke, really."

I carried several more buckets of water from the stream to pour on the embers and raked the ashes back and forth to make sure they were thoroughly doused. Dusk was falling as I completed the task, and then I helped Luke harness Henrietta and put her to a brisk trot to test the repaired wheel. Rosemary had gone into the house to start cooking the vegetables for dinner as we put the trap away and stabled Henrietta for the night.

Luke took the lamp he had lit from its hook in the stable. "What's for dinner?" he asked.

"Rabbit casserole and dumplings. We put the casserole on earlier, so it will be ready by the time the vegetables are done."

He nodded, lifting the lamp and looking me up and down. "Good. I'm starving, and you must be, too. We're also as dirty-looking a pair as you'd find anywhere. Come on, Red, let's get washed and changed."

All my life I had hated my red hair, but I did not mind it now because I had long since learned that I was not a freak but a true white person, and I always felt warm inside when Luke called me by a friendly name. As we walked to the house together I wanted to hold his arm for closeness, but I was careful not to.

I took a bucket of warm water into my room to wash with, brushed my hair thoroughly, changed into my dress, sat down with Rosemary and Luke to a splendid dinner, and went to bed very happy. But that happiness was to vanish during the night, together with Luke's friendliness of the day, for at three in the morning I woke to the smell of smoke.

In a second I was out of my bed and running through the kitchen in the shirt I wore as a nightdress. I wrenched open the door, rushed out, and felt my heart pound with shock as I saw that our toolshed was in flames. It was just a small shed, standing some paces from where we had made the fire yesterday, but in it were the spades and forks, axes and saws, rakes and hoes we used in our daily work.

I ran back into the kitchen shouting, "Luke! Wake up! Fire!" Then I picked up one of the two buckets of water we always left full at night and went stumbling out with it. The stony ground made no impression on my bare feet, for the soles were so hardened by my life with the tribe that they would always be as tough as the leather Luke used for mending our boots.

The shed was no bigger than the width of its door on all four sides, and I knew it could not be saved, but that was of small importance compared with the tools it held. Getting as close as possible, I hurled the water from the bucket so that it hit the top of the door and dropped down, hissing and steaming. For a moment the fire on this side of the shed was reduced to small flames flickering on charred wood. Desperately I ran in and caught at the drop-latch handle. It seared my fingers, but I was able to wrench the door open, and next moment I was snatching at the tools stacked inside, hurling them clear.

Behind me I heard Luke roar, "Come back! Back!" But the flames were getting a new grip. I knew I had only seconds left to save what I could, and I kept snatching at the tools, throwing them wide of the fire. A flaming piece of wood fell on my shirt sleeve, and a glowing red ring began to eat its way outward from the hole in the cotton. The heat was stifling now, and I was blind with smoke. Then suddenly I was drenched with water as the contents of the second bucket were hurled at me, soaking me from head to toe. Next minute strong arms snatched me up and carried me clear to windward.

Luke set me down, took me by the shoulders, and shook me, glaring as he shouted, "You—you blasted little *fool*!" I saw that he wore only trousers and unlaced boots, and my teeth began chattering with shock as I looked beyond him to see the remains of the shed collapse. Turning my head, I saw Rosemary, slippers on her feet, a coat over her nightdress, hands pressed to her cheeks as she stared at the fire. Then she came hurrying toward me, her eyes huge in the flickering light.

"Meg! Are you hurt?"

"No . . . I'm all right."

"How on earth did it happen?"

"It happened because I trusted her to douse that fire in the pit last night," said Luke in a voice that creaked with fury, "and she didn't do it properly."

"Oh, I did, Luke! I did!" I cried, struggling to hold back tears. I could feel that my hands were burned, and a patch just above one knee, but the pain of Luke's anger hurt far more deeply.

"I'll see to this one myself," he said, picking up the two buckets and turning toward the stream.

"I'll help," I said, starting after him, but Rosemary caught me by the arm.

"Leave him be, Meg," she said quietly. "You saved most of the tools, which is the important thing. Now, come into the kitchen and we'll get that wet shirt off so I can have a look at you."

I had blisters on two fingers of my right hand and on the palm of the left, also a burn on my knee and thigh. They were not bad burns, but I felt utterly miserable as I sat on a chair with a towel wrapped about me while Rosemary dabbed the burns with limewater and dusted them with flour before dressing them with gauze and plaster. If I turned my head I could see Luke pass the window time and again as he carried fresh buckets of water to quench the fire.

"Rosemary, I'm *sure* I soaked the embers properly last night," I said shakily. "I was so careful."

She looked up from dressing my knee and smiled consolingly. "Don't be upset, Meg dear. I'm sorry Luke is so cross, but he'll soon get over it. I think it might help if you don't argue too much as to how it happened."

So Rosemary, too, believed I was responsible. When I thought about it, I could not blame her, for how else could the fire have started? Unless . . . unless . . .

I waited impatiently for Rosemary to fix the patch of gauze on my thigh. As she did so she began to cough. I got up quickly and said, "You go straight back to bed, Rosemary, and take some of your cough medicine. Oh please, please do, or Luke will be all the more cross with me."

"Well . . . perhaps I will." She got to her feet, a handkerchief held to her mouth, and I helped her to her room.

As soon as she had taken her medicine and lain down I ran to my own room, threw off the towel, pulled on my working shirt and dungarees, and hurried out through the kitchen. The fire was out now, the charred wood steaming rather than smoking from the dousing Luke had given it. He came past me carrying full buckets, speaking no word as he set them down and began to rake the burnt remains of the little shed this way and that to uncover any hidden embers.

The sky was full of stars and there was a bright half moon, so I had no need of a lamp as I moved about picking up the tools I had thrown from the burning shed and carrying them to the kitchen porch. Once Luke called in a flat voice, "Leave that. I'll see to it." But I went on as if I had not heard him, taking care not to dirty the dressings on my hands.

To my relief, only a fork and a rake had been badly burnt; the rest of the tools seemed to have escaped damage. We would need a new fork, but the rake would require only a new handle. When I had gathered all the tools, I moved away from where the shed had been as if looking for any I had missed, and as I got beyond the intense smell of burnt wood blending with water and wet earth I caught the scent I had half expected.

Fifty paces from the shed, in the direction of the knoll, I scented the stranger. There was not enough light to find sign, but I knew I would see it in the morning. The man was out there now, somewhere on the knoll, or still on his way back there, or perhaps he had already picked up his horse and was riding through the night to Lawton, keeping to the far side of the ridge. One thing was certain: he had come to Shalimar once we were asleep, and he had started the fire. Whether by accident or design I did not know, but it seemed wildly unlikely to me that he had lit a pipe while prowling, and that a dropped match or knocked-out tobacco ash had caused the fire. Yet why, *why* should a stranger who wished us harm simply set fire to our little toolshed when he might have burned down the stable, the barn, or even the house?

Luke called, "What the hell are you doing out there?"

I walked back to where he now stood by the porch, wishing I could have told him that a prowler had come to Shalimar again and must have caused the fire. But I did not dare to, for I knew he would not believe me and would become even angrier with me, thinking that I was simply trying to shift the blame.

He stood with hands on hips, his body grimed and sweaty, staring at me with cold blue eyes. "How bad are your burns?" he demanded.

I struggled to keep my voice steady as I said, "Not bad, thank you. They'll soon be better. I'm sorry this happened, Luke. Very sorry. But I think most of the tools are all right. The fire only destroyed a fork and a rake handle."

"And the shed."

"Yes. I'm sorry. Shall I warm some water for you to wash?"

"No, I'll attend to that." He looked down. "Where are your boots?"

"When I smelled the fire I didn't stop to put them on. I don't need them, Luke."

"No. Well, there's half a bucket of water here, so you'd better wash your feet and go back to bed."

"I'll fill the other bucket for you first—"

"No! Just do as I say. Stop arguing and go to bed."

I took the bucket into the kitchen, washed and dried my feet, and went to my room, calling a soft "Good night" to Rosemary. I took off my working shirt and dungarees, put on a clean shirt, and slipped into bed, but it was a long time before I slept. There was pain in my hands, pain in my heart, and my mind was plagued with the puzzle of why a stranger had come to remote Shalimar to spy upon us and to burn down our toolshed. It was senseless, too absurd even to suggest to Rosemary.

When at last I slept I had found no answer to the puzzle, but my sleep was uneasy, for deep within me lay the feeling that tonight's happening was not the end of the mystery, and there was more to come. I did not dream that it would come within a matter of hours.

* * *

WE WERE ALL SUBDUED AT BREAKFAST NEXT MORNING, BUT I was thankful to find that Luke's anger had passed. His manner was a little forced, but he called me Meg and spoke amiably to me, which was more than I had hoped for.

Immediately after breakfast he announced that he would take the trap into Lawton to buy a new fork and rake handle as well as timber to rebuild the shed. I asked if he would like me to go with him to help in any way, but he declined quite pleasantly and said he would prefer me to stay with Rosemary and do some lessons, so that I could rest my hands and give them a chance to heal.

Because of what had happened, I think my own manner was forced, but I tried to be natural as I said, "I could do some work on the fence, Luke." This was a wattle fence we were putting up as a windbreak along the western side of the farm, a series of wooden posts driven into the ground with thin branches woven between them. I was deft at this weaving, and Luke had praised me several times.

"Leave the fence today," he said firmly. "Just give those hands a rest and stay with Rosemary. I'll be back before noon."

I had put on working clothes as usual, but when Luke drove off I changed into a dress for my lessons with Rosemary. Truth to tell, I was glad to have my mind occupied, for I felt shaken by the events of the night. When we settled at the table with books and pen and paper I said, "You were right. Luke isn't angry with me this morning."

"No," Rosemary said thoughtfully, and sat staring at her hands for a moment or two. They looked thin and frail, perhaps more so than they had a few months ago, and there were dark circles under her eyes. "Meg," she said slowly, "if anything should . . . happen to me, will you promise to look after Luke?"

I stared in alarm. "Happen to you? What do you mean?"

She gave a half smile. "It's a foolishly oblique way of saying if I'm taken ill, or if I have an accident, or . . . or even die."

I felt my face go pale. "You mustn't! I couldn't bear it, Rose-mary!"

"Now, don't be a silly girl. I'm just saying that *if* something happened and Luke was left alone, I'd like to feel that he would have you to look after him. You see, he's a man who *needs* somebody, Meg. He was very different before we met, and he can only be . . . well, can only be his *best* self with the right person."

I said, shaken and confused, "But not me, Rosemary. Some-times he doesn't like me at all. And anyway, you mustn't be ill or have an accident, or—or anything."

She looked at me and gave me her full gentle smile. "I'll try not to. But just to please me, promise you would do your best to look after him, Meg. Please?"

"Yes, of course, I'd always do anything for you. You know that."

"Good. Now, let's forget all about it. What shall we start with today? Some reading, I think, but we'll make it poetry to begin with. Then a few sums, followed by a history lesson. Will that do?"

"Oh yes. It sounds lovely. Can we start with Mr. Keats, please?"

For the next half hour I was very happy, even though I was often reading words I only partially understood or perhaps had never met before. Somehow the meaning came through to me, and I reveled in the rich magic of words put together in a way that struck chords deep within me.

"You're becoming drunk on poetry," said Rosemary at last with a smile. "Come along, now. Let's try some more everyday writing from a newspaper."

With a touch of reluctance I picked up one of the newspapers Luke had brought home from our last trip to Lawton and opened it at random. "I'll read you some of these small pieces of news," I said. "They're always more interesting than the long pieces about politics and important people. Now, let me see. . . ."

I read a few paragraphs about a minor accident in Coolgardie when a man on a bicycle had collided with a horse, then another piece about a play being acted at the Theatre Royal in Perth. Rosemary had explained what a play was, and it was a dream of mine that one day I might see one. The only acting I had ever known was when the older men of the tribe instructed the newly initiated boys in the ways of different birds and animals by miming their movements.

I began to read a short piece of news:

"DEATH OF PERTH REPORTER

"Our London correspondent informs us that the death has occurred of Mr. Harold Tasker at the hands of a person or persons unknown. As readers may remember, until a few months ago Mr. Tasker was a reporter employed by this newspaper—"

I broke off with a gasp. "Mr. Tasker! That's the man I met when Luke took me to Kalgoorlie!"

I looked up to see Rosemary staring in surprise. "Yes, I met him once," she said. "He tried several times to make a story out of Luke being disowned by his family and starting a new life here. Did you say 'death at the hands of persons unknown'?"

"Yes." I looked down at the newspaper again and began to read on.

". . . Mr. Tasker was a reporter employed by this newspaper, who left to take up a position in Fleet Street.

"His body was found on the morning of 15th December in an area of courtyards and narrow streets just off Fleet Street, known as the Inner Temple, one of the Inns of Court where barristers have their chambers.

"The Middle and Inner Temples occupy an area stretching from Fleet Street to the Embankment, and Mr. Tasker's body was found at the foot of some steps near

Fountain Court. He had been killed by several severe blows to the head with a blunt instrument. As yet the police have not been able to identify the perpetrator of this vicious murder. Mr. Tasker's sojourn in England had been brief, and his colleagues believe it unlikely that he had made any enemies, so the motive for this crime is a mystery.

"Mr. Tasker was unmarried, and had no close relatives so far as is known. The police will welcome any person who can give them information which may help in bringing a brutal murderer to book."

As I looked up from the newspaper, Rosemary gave a shudder. "How dreadful," she murmured.

"Yes," I said. "I didn't like him much, but I'm sorry somebody killed him. That's a horrible thing. It only happened twice while I was with the tribe, and I saw it on one of those occasions. It was much worse than somebody just dying. That happened quite a lot, especially with the children. I think about a quarter of them died before reaching five years old. Did I ever tell you that when a person died everybody had to stop saying his name, and if an ordinary word just *sounded* like his name we had to make up a new word to replace it—?"

I stopped, for Rosemary was staring past me with an uneasy frown. "There's a man coming," she said. "He's on foot."

I turned quickly to look through the window. A big man was coming toward Shalimar. He wore grubby-looking corduroy trousers with a wide leather belt, a faded checked shirt, and a broad-brimmed hat pulled so low that as he walked with bent head his face was completely hidden. Fear stabbed through me, sharp as a knife blade, fear born not of reason but of instinct, and I acted without conscious thought.

"Wait here," I said, and ran through the kitchen, realizing as I did so that I intended to get my spear and boomerang from the outhouse, where they had hung unused for so long. But I was too late. The man was only fifty paces away now and could easily cut me off if I ran for the outhouse—unless I managed to do so before he saw me, for his head was still bowed. Then he looked up, and I could see no face, only a black cloth with two slotlike openings cut roughly in it, one for the eyes, the other for the mouth. It was a strangely blood-chilling sight.

I did not realize that Rosemary had followed me to the door, but now I scented her and heard her gasp close behind me. In the same moment the faceless man reached to the back of his belt, drew a long knife, and broke into a run.

Terror possessed me. I turned, thrust Rosemary back so fiercely she stumbled and caught at the table, and then I cried, "Bar the door!" and slammed it shut behind me as I turned toward the faceless man again. He was thirty paces away, and I moved sideways along the back of the house, not quickly, watching him in case he tried to enter the house, for if he did I knew I would have to attack him from behind before he could harm Rosemary.

I could hear myself panting with fear and a kind of wild fury. I could feel my lips drawing back from my teeth like the lips of a snarling dog, and my heart was pounding fiercely. Then I was swept by a strange blend of new fear and relief as the man swung toward me. I plucked my skirt to my thighs and began to run, throwing a glance over my shoulder to make sure he did not turn back to the house, wishing I was not hampered by my dress and my shoes, trying amid a chaos of thoughts to decide what I should do.

I had nothing to use as a weapon. Our tools were now in the outhouse with my spear and boomerang, and all were out of my reach. My throwing club was—

I caught my breath as I suddenly remembered. In my task of interweaving twigs and withies for the fence we were building I had discovered that the throwing club was a most useful instrument. It was as long as from my elbow to my wrist, swollen bulbously at one end, then tapering away down the handle to a blunt point. I had found that by gripping the heavy end I could use the tapering handle very effectively for prying withies apart and poking ends through. When we had finished our work on the fence yesterday morning I had left my useful weaving instrument there with the pile of sprigs and withies we would be using to continue the task, and now I swerved to the west, glancing quickly over my shoulder again.

The man was still in pursuit. He had gained no ground, but my heart clenched with fresh alarm as far beyond him I saw the figure of Rosemary. She had come from the house carrying something in her hand—from my brief glimpse I thought it was the heavy poker we kept by the range—and she was trying to run after us, one hand pressed to her breast.

I knew what this must cost her, knew the harm it must be causing to her frail health, and fear for myself was swept suddenly away by ferocious hatred of the evil man who was doing this to my beloved Rosemary. We were near the unfinished end of the fence now, and as I raced around the pile of wattle material I dropped the hem of my skirt and bent to snatch up the short club. Then I continued around so that I faced the oncoming man.

He was twenty paces away and a frightening sight. The lower slit in the black cloth showed his mouth agape with the effort of running; the upper slit showed glaring eyes under great hairy eyebrows. I stood with my left shoulder and left foot toward him, the throwing club in my hand, vaguely aware of the bandage on my fingers but feeling no pain from the burns, for my mind was too concentrated elsewhere to feel pain. I did not hesitate, but threw hard as he came to within ten paces. The last time I had used this crude weapon was in the desert with Luke, when I had brought down a bird about to take wing. This throw was easier, and the heavy bulb of the club took the man squarely in the middle of his forehead, its impact magnified by his own forward impetus.

He stopped as if he had run into an invisible wall, staggering for a moment on rubbery legs, head thrown back, the dreadful knife falling from his hand, and then he slumped to the ground. I ran forward and snatched up the knife, just as on a day long ago I had snatched up my spear to dispatch a kangaroo so that Yuma might have his *mapanpa*.

I did not know for how long the man would be stunned. He lay facedown, his hat a yard or two away. I could see a little movement as he tried to lift his head, and one hand groped slowly across the ground as if seeking purchase. I stood over him with the knife, but could not bring myself to kill him as I had killed the kangaroo, though I shall never know what I might have done if there had been no lesser alternative. As it was, I picked up the throwing club from where it had fallen and hit the man hard on the back of the neck.

He gave a gasping grunt and lay still. I called to Rosemary, "Keep back, keep back!" and was thankful to see her sink to her knees, a hand still pressed to her chest. At once I bent and slit the man's shirt sleeve with his knife, then ripped the sleeve away and tore it in two strips. Twisting the strips into crude ropes, I tied one tightly to each of his wrists, then heaved him over onto his side and doubled his knees up until I could lash his wrists firmly to his ankles. This was the way we tied a dead kangaroo for carrying on a pole. I had no plans for carrying the faceless man, but felt satisfied that this was a good way to secure him.

I looked toward Rosemary and called, "It's all right, he can't hurt us now." She got slowly to her feet and walked to us, the poker hanging limply from her hand. "Oh dear God, Meg," she said in a choking voice, "he was going to *kill* you, wasn't he? But why? Why?"

"I don't know." My heart had slowed to a normal pace now, but I felt very strange and wobbly. I bent to untie the knot at the back of the man's head and pulled the mask away. The face revealed was that of a stranger, a man in his forties with a narrow brow and bony ridges above his eyes, an unshaven face, coarse and brutal, with a crooked scar down one cheek.

Rosemary said, "You were . . . you were wonderful, Meg. I don't know how . . ." She shook her head helplessly. "Perhaps he wanted a woman. I mean, to lie with her by force. God knows what would have happened if you hadn't been here." She stared down at the man with horror still in her eyes. "I've never seen him before."

I said, "Neither have I, but I've scented him before. Twice."

"Scented him?" She looked at me in bewilderment, then suddenly began to cough and put a handkerchief to her mouth. I moved to support her, dropping knife and club to hold her in my arms. When the spasm passed I was shocked to see blood on the handkerchief. It seemed that everything was happening at once, and I hardly knew what to do.

"Rosemary dear," I said urgently, "you *must* go and lie down, but I daren't leave him for long in case he manages to escape." I glanced at the man, and from his breathing I judged that he might begin to come to his senses soon. "I'm going to run and get my spear," I said. "It will only take a minute, and he won't be ready to start struggling yet. You go back to the house, Rosemary, but don't hurry. Go very slowly, and rest as soon as you get there. Please don't worry about me, I'll be quite safe."

She said uneasily, "You—you won't kill him?"

"No, I couldn't. I'm really quite a civilized person now. I'll just stand guard till Luke gets back, to make sure he can't get away and hurt us."

"But Luke might not be back for ages yet."

"It doesn't matter how long. Now, please start back while I run and fetch my spear."

I was gone for no more than a minute, and I passed Rosemary with a smile and a word of reassurance as she walked slowly to the house. Five minutes went by before the man recovered sufficiently to take in his situation, and then he began to curse and swear most savagely, glaring at me and tugging fiercely at the rough ties I had made from his shirt sleeve. After two or three seconds I gave him a sharp jab in the thigh with my spear, and as he yelped with pain I said, "Lie still and be quiet."

At once he began cursing and wrenching at his bonds again, so I gave him another jab and repeated my words. After the third jab, and with the spear poised for a fourth, he lay still and began to speak in a whining voice, saying that he had drunk too much in Lawton the night before and had no idea how he had come here or what he had been doing.

I ignored him, offering no answer, and after a while he fell silent. Later he started whining again, then lost his temper and received another quick jab to quiet him. It was hot in the sun, and later he asked for water. Again I ignored him. We would both wait until my task was done before either of us could drink.

I did not grow weary as I stood guard over the man through-out that morning, for during my years with the tribe I had learned the way of closing my mind when long periods of waiting came. Often I had lain hidden for hours in the hope of seeing game, with just a small part of my mind alert. So it was now, for I already knew all that I was ever likely to know about this man who had tried to kill me, and there was nothing more to think about for the time being.

At last, when the sun was high, I heard a sound and looked across to the house. The trap was moving along the trail, laden with timber and with Luke at the reins. I saw it halt, saw him go into the house. A minute passed, then he came out, breaking into a run. As he came near I saw that his face was drawn with anxiety and I called, "Is Rosemary all right?"

"She's not very good." His voice was jerky as he slowed to a halt. "But I think she'll be all right after some rest. What in God's name has been happening, Meg? Is it true this man tried to kill you?"

"He came at me with that knife." I nodded to where it lay. "Rosemary said perhaps he wanted to make me lie with him, but it didn't seem like that."

The man started his whining story again. Luke picked up the knife, bent over him, and said in a terrible voice, "Shut your mouth or I'll kill you!"

The man groaned, then was silent, slumped hopelessly where he lay. Luke said, "We have to get him into police custody, but

I can't leave Rosemary now. Meg, could you drive into Lawton on your own and fetch somebody from the police station?''

"Yes, I can do that, but you'll have to keep guard on this man."

Luke said grimly, "I will. Just watch him for a minute while I unload the trap and bring it here. We'll dump him on it, drive him up to the house, and tie him to a chair in the kitchen."

Ten minutes later, in my dungarees now, I climbed to the driving seat of the trap and gathered the reins. I had often driven Henrietta about the farm on various jobs and was not worried about driving her to Lawton.

Luke put a bottle of water at my feet and reached up to rest his hand on mine. "Thank you, Meg," he said in a strangely harsh voice. "If Rosemary had been on her own when that swine came . . ." He closed his eyes for a moment, then shook his head wordlessly and stepped back.

I said, "Tell her I'm quite all right, and make sure she rests." Then I touched the whip to Henrietta's back and began the hourlong journey to Lawton. I had not gone more than a few hundred yards when my body began to shake, my chest to heave, and I was racked by dry sobs as all the fears I had been holding down since my first sight of the faceless man that morning broke from my control. Tears came, and I drove blindly for a while, but then the trembling and weeping passed. I whispered an apology to Henrietta as I dried my eyes and blew my nose, feeling greatly ashamed of myself.

I felt tired and was half asleep when we reached the outskirts of Lawton. Here I was lucky, for I was hailed by Sergeant Kelly as he came from his house to go on duty at the police station. I had met him once or twice when I came to Lawton with Luke. He was a big cheerful man, who called me his "colleen" and joked about my red hair and freckles, though in a kindly way.

When I started to tell him why I had come in alone, the smile vanished from his eyes and I saw a very different man. "Wore a black mask and came after you with a *knife*?" he said, the muscles of his jaw knotting with anger. "Is Mrs. Bowman all right?"

"Well, her health isn't very good, and she was badly shaken when she ran to try to help me, but the man didn't hurt her. I was the one he chased."

"Is he some murderous lunatic or d'you think he meant to force you—" The sergeant broke off abruptly. "Well, never mind that. How did you get away?"

"I ran to where Luke and I were putting up a fence. We'd left a kind of mallet there, and I threw it at the man. It hit his head, and he fell down. Then we were able to tie him up."

Sergeant Kelly whistled softly. "Dear Lord, that was a lucky throw, Meg."

"Yes. Then we watched him till Luke returned, to make sure he didn't get away."

"Can you tell me what this fellow looks like?"

"Yes, we took his mask off." I described the man as well as I could, and ended, "He had a crooked scar on his left cheek, just here." I touched my own cheek.

Sergeant Kelly nodded. "Sid Buller, and as nasty a piece of work as you'd find anywhere, though what the devil he was up to out at Shalimar I can't imagine just now. He's wanted in Kalgoorlie for robbery with violence, and perhaps murder, too, if the poor fellow he injured so badly should die. We have Sid Buller's ugly face on a poster at the station."

The sergeant thought for a moment, then gave me a smile. "We'll have to be recruiting you to the police force, my little colleen, for it's a fine job you've done today." He held out his hand. "Now, if you'll be so kind as to step down and come into the house, Mrs. Kelly will give you a nice big glass of lemonade while I go to the station and pick up a cart and a colleague. Then we'll drive back with you and take this fellow off your hands."

Henrietta was tired and not a little indignant at making the double journey with so short a rest between, and it was almost three in the afternoon when we reached Shalimar. Luke was waiting by the porch, and after saying quietly, "Thanks, Meg,"

he took the two policemen into the kitchen while I drove Henrietta around to the stable, unharnessed her, and spent half an
hour grooming her and giving her a good feed of hay and bran
mash. I was reluctant to go into the house, for I had no wish to
see once again the hatred in the face of the man I had made
prisoner, and I was thankful when, from the stable, I watched
him being marched to the police cart in handcuffs by Constable
Nash, who remained there with him.

Luke called me to the house, and I found Rosemary at the
table in the sitting room with Sergeant Kelly beside her, reading
from some sheets of paper. She looked very pale, and I went to
her quickly, putting an arm about her shoulders.

"Are you all right, dear?" she whispered.

"Yes, quite all right, but why aren't you lying down? Have
you eaten? Can I make tea for you?"

"In a moment." She gestured to Sergeant Kelly. "We must
just finish this business."

Luke, standing with thumbs hooked in his belt, his face somber, said, "Rosemary has written out a statement for the police,
and in a moment the sergeant would like you to read it through
and sign it if you think it is correct."

I nodded and held Rosemary's hand in silence until Sergeant
Kelly finished reading. He looked up, then pushed the papers
across the table toward me. "There you are, my little colleen,"
he said gently. "Just say if there's anything you don't agree with,
or anything that's left out."

I was well used to Rosemary's handwriting, which was very
clear even though here her hand had shaken from time to time.
There was silence as I read. When I had finished I looked up
and said, "Yes, everything here is just as it happened."

Sergeant Kelly said, "Did Buller say anything to you at any
time? Did he call on you to stop when you were running away?
Did he make any threats? Did he say he would hurt you if you
didn't . . . give in and do as he told you?"

I shook my head. "No, he didn't utter a word the whole time.

I mean, not until after he came around to find himself tied up. Then he said lots of words, some I've never heard before.''

"That doesn't surprise me," the sergeant said dryly. "Look now, Meg, the fellow says he came to Lawton by train last evening, stole a bottle of whisky from a bar, and got drunk as a lord. He says he must have wandered out of the town and lost himself, wandering on, still drinking from his bottle till he fell asleep. He swears he remembers nothing of what he was doing until he woke to find himself trussed like a turkey and you prodding him with a spear.'' The sergeant frowned. "A spear? Where did that come from?''

Luke said, "It's a souvenir I picked up a long time ago from an aborigine.''

"I see.'' The sergeant tapped the sheets of paper neatly together. "Do you think it's possible, Meg, that Buller was drunk and didn't know what he was doing?''

"No, it isn't,'' I said. "If that was true he wouldn't wear a mask to hide his face.''

Sergeant Kelly grinned and gave a nod of acknowledgment. "It's a neat brain you have under that carroty hair of yours, young lady.'' The grin vanished and he pursed his lips. "Now, I have to ask you: what do you think was the man's intention? Was he attempting to kill you, or attempting to . . . harm you in some way?''

I thought for a while, then said, "I don't know, Sergeant. He came at me with the knife, he chased me with the knife. His face was hidden, and he didn't speak. I don't know what was in his mind.''

"Well . . .'' The sergeant pondered. "Since he didn't lay a hand on you, it's going to be hard to prove his intention. He could claim he intended to do no more than frighten you, but fortunately we have at least one other very serious charge against him we *can* prove, and that will put him in prison for a long time.''

Luke said slowly, "Have you asked if anybody sent him, Sergeant? I mean, sent him to harm my wife?''

The sergeant frowned. "Who'd do that, Mr. Bowman? What makes you ask?"

"I'm not sure." Luke rubbed his brow. "It just seems so deliberate for the man to come all this way from Lawton. Perhaps I'm thinking about Joe Catesby, the man I went prospecting with, remember?"

Sergeant Kelly nodded. "What about him?"

"He didn't come back. Perhaps he has friends who think that was my fault, and they hired Buller to harm my wife, as revenge."

"After two years and more?" The sergeant shook his head. "Out of the question. And anyway, Joe Catesby had no friends."

Rosemary said, "When Meg pushed me into the kitchen and slammed the door he didn't try to get in. He tried to get at Meg."

The sergeant looked at me. "I can't believe you've made any enemies here since you came out from England, my little colleen," he said. "No, I think it's just that Buller is a violent man. Maybe he had robbery in mind when he came out here, or maybe it was something worse. Assault on a female. He's pretty much an animal, and he may not even remember what was in his mind. We can only be thankful you were lucky enough to stop him." He stood up, folding the papers carefully. "I'll let you know what happens, Mr. Bowman, but I doubt if these ladies will be called as witnesses. This statement will do, unless he denies the whole thing, and he can hardly hope to do that."

When the policemen had gone, taking their prisoner with them, Rosemary broke down in tears. I made her undress, put her to bed, and sat with her while she ate a dish of bread and milk with honey and raisins. When she had finished and I bent to kiss her cheek, she clung to me, just whispering my name. Luke sat in the corner all this time, anxious and troubled but not knowing what to do.

I gave her a small dose of the laudanum she sometimes used to help her sleep at night and told her she would feel much better after a few hours of rest. Then I moved to where Luke sat and whispered, "Will you stay with her until she sleeps? There's something I have to do."

He gave me a distracted look, seemed about to ask a question, then shrugged and nodded. In the kitchen was a saucepan of stew we had prepared the night before. I set it on the range to begin cooking, then went out and began to walk toward the knoll. Twenty minutes later I came upon what I had expected, a horse tethered in a little hollow on the far slope of the knoll, where I had found sign of it before.

She was a rather poor mare, ill-fed, ill-cared-for, and with a saddle in need of repair, but she seemed pleased to see me and munched gladly at some handfuls of yellow grass I brought her from a patch nearby. In the worn saddlebag was a dirty blanket, a bottle of water, some stale food wrapped in a greasy cloth, half a bottle of whisky, and a pair of battered binoculars.

I had sometimes ridden Henrietta about the farm with just a blanket on her back, but this was the first time I had used stirrups or sat in a saddle. I called the mare Tankai because she reminded me of a skinny old woman I had known in the tribe, and I coaxed her to an easy walk around the knoll and across the flat ground toward Shalimar. When we were a few hundred yards from the house Luke came out. He looked about him, saw us, and stood quite still, staring. I was not surprised to see the astonishment on his face as we came close. "Is Rosemary asleep?" I asked as I slipped down from the saddle.

"Eh? Yes," he said blankly, "but where the devil did this come from?"

"She was tethered on the far slope of the knoll," I said. "That man Buller couldn't say anything about it without admitting he was here deliberately, so I didn't say anything either. She's not much of a horse, Luke, but if we sell her the money will help pay for the new fork and toolshed. I'm afraid there's nothing of value in the saddlebag except these old binoculars." I held them out for him to see.

Luke looked at them, looked at me, looked up at the sky, then at me again. One moment I thought he would laugh, the next that he would be angry, for all kinds of different expressions passed across his face. At last he turned away, sat down on the bench by the wall, rested his elbows on his knees, and held his head in his hands. I moved to stand before him, careful not to touch him as I said anxiously, "What is it, Luke?"

He shook his straw-colored head without lifting it, and after a moment or two he said, "That was the man you scented a few days ago, wasn't it?"

"Well . . . yes, it was."

"And I almost bit your head off when you told me."

I forced a little laugh and said, "You're not used to a girl who scents people, that's all."

"It's not all. He set fire to the toolshed last night, and you scented him again then, when you went wandering off a little way toward the knoll."

"Yes. I'm sorry I didn't tell you. I knew he'd watched us from the knoll because I walked out there after that first time and found where he'd lain hidden and where he'd tethered the horse."

Luke looked up. "And you didn't dare tell me then, or last night after the fire, because you knew I'd fly into a raging temper and say a lot of harsh words."

I stood silent for a moment, not knowing what to say and feeling deep pity for him because I could see the real pain in his eyes. Then I managed to smile, and said, "It's only because you're worried about Rosemary, and anyway it's all past and done with now. Shall I tell you what I think about that man, Luke?"

He sighed, stood up, and briefly touched the knuckles of one hand to my cheek. "Am I forgiven?"

"Yes, yes of course. Oh, I mean, there isn't anything to forgive."

"We'll agree to differ on that. Now, listen, Red. In future don't put up with it if I'm bad-tempered. I've seen you get angry with yourself often enough when a piece of work wasn't going quite right. It's the way you looked in the outback before you collapsed. Your jaw starts jutting, and your eyes go narrow and glare, and your freckles stand out, and you look like an Irish alley cat about to spit and claw. Well, it'll serve me right if you get angry like that with me if I ever again treat you as unfairly as I have over this business of the man you scented.'' He was silent for a moment, then went on, ''Now, tell me what you think about him, because I don't know what to think. My brain seems to have gone to sleep.''

I said, ''When I was with the tribe, sometimes a man was taken with a very strong passion for a particular woman. It was like a fever, taking away his senses so he would try to lie with her even though he knew her family would kill him if they found out. Well, that man Buller had no reason to want to kill me, so it can only be that he wanted to take me away and make me lie with him. I think perhaps he must have seen me in Lawton and was seized with a passion for me—a woman need not be beautiful for this to happen,'' I added hastily. ''She can be quite plain. It's just something that happens.''

Luke said quietly, ''Don't fear that I'll think you vain, Meg. Go on.''

''Well . . . then he could have found out that I lived here with you and Rosemary, and he could have ridden out to spy on us from the knoll. He wouldn't try to take me while you were here, so perhaps that's why he set fire to the toolshed last night. If some tools were destroyed, then you would have to go into Lawton for new ones, so Rosemary and I would be left alone.''

Luke gazed past me with distant eyes for some seconds, and then he sighed again and lifted his shoulders in a small shrug. ''I can't think of anything else that makes sense,'' he said.

We stood for a moment, both thinking. Then I said, ''Well, I'd better see to Tankai.''

''Mmm? Who?''

I laughed. ''Tankai. Our new mare. That's what I call her. I'll feed and water her and give her a good rubdown. Oh, I'd better get you something to eat first. You must be so hungry.''

Luke put out a hand to stop me as I turned away. ''No,'' he said. ''You've had a cruelly hard day. You're tired, you've got a dirty face, and we've neither of us eaten since breakfast, so you must be hungry yourself. I'll see to the mare. You go and have a wash and comb your hair. Then we'll make do with bread and cheese and fruit for luncheon; there's plenty of that.'' He smiled suddenly, a true heartwarming smile. ''No arguments. Go on, Mitji, do as I say.''

ROSEMARY GOT UP TO HAVE DINNER WITH US THAT EVENING and seemed much recovered. As if by unspoken agreement we did not talk of what had happened but spent an hour or so after dinner playing a card game called cribbage, which Rosemary had taught me some months before.

When I went to bed that night I lay awake for a while, but strangely I did not think about the dreadful minutes when that faceless man had appeared or recall the long knife in his hand or the sound of his booted feet as he pursued me. Instead I found myself with two thoughts running through my mind, though they had no bearing upon each other. One was of the reporter, Mr. Tasker, murdered by an unknown hand in faraway London. The other was of Rosemary, speaking words that chilled my blood when she made me promise to take care of Luke . . . if anything happened to her.

SIX

To my relief we had nothing more to do concerning Sid Buller but read about him some weeks later when a report appeared in the Perth *Record*. It said that he had been sentenced to twelve years' hard labor for robbery with violence, and there were four other offenses to be taken into account, for which he was awarded a further three years of imprisonment, to run concurrently.

We guessed that his actions at Shalimar made one of the four offenses, and I gasped when Luke explained what was meant by "concurrently." In the tribe we would have thought this a ridiculous idea, since it meant that the man was no worse off for the extra crimes. Luke grinned when I told him this. "You're reading *Oliver Twist* at the moment, aren't you?" he said. "That's the book where Mr. Bumble says, 'The law is a ass—a idiot.' He was right, wasn't he?"

The summer passed, and it was on a day in autumn that I drove into Lawton with Luke for our weekly visit to the Methodist Church, only to find we had missed the service because it had been brought forward by an hour. Mr. Grindle, the vicar, was pottering about in the porch as we arrived. He was a plump, kindly man with thin, graying hair, and he gave us a doleful smile when Luke asked why the change had been made.

"I have a rival, my dear sir," he replied with a sigh. "Indeed, there are three churches of different denominations in this town, and we all have a rival now. The Reverend Simon Fordyce and Mrs. Fordyce arrived two weeks ago, and hold open-air services every Tuesday, Friday, and Sunday.''

Luke showed surprise. "A traveling preacher?"

"Just so. And a most effective one, I fear. If my clerical colleagues and I wish to have anything like a reasonable Sunday congregation we have to hold our morning services *before* Mr. Fordyce holds his." Mr. Grindle wagged his head ruefully. "Even so, my morning flock has dwindled, since many are not prepared to suffer *two* sermons in succession."

"Well, we'd better go and take a look at him," said Luke. "Mrs. Bowman won't be at all pleased if I have to tell her Meg has missed her ration of preaching this Sunday. Oh, no offense, Vicar."

"None taken, my son," said Mr. Grindle amiably. "I'll come along with you, if you can find room for me. It's never too late to learn."

Luke said, "Welcome aboard, then." We edged together on the seat, and I exchanged greetings with Mr. Grindle as he clambered up to sit beside me.

"How is Mrs. Bowman?" he asked. "It's a long time since I saw her. Oh dear, I really must make an effort to drive out to Shalimar."

"She's much the same," Luke said briefly, and shook the reins to set Henrietta walking.

Five minutes later we came down a gentle slope to where a crowd of some sixty people, men and women, were gathered about a small cart. On the cart stood a man in a clerical collar, speaking in a richly vibrant voice. Beside the cart stood a harmonium with a woman seated at it. She was quite tall for a woman, and well fleshed without being plump. Her hair was golden, just a little darker than Luke's. She wore a pale gray dress with a matching toque hat tilted back to show an oval face with large blue eyes and a strong chin. Sitting with hands in her lap, she had turned a little on her stool to watch the preacher, and I judged her to be a few years older than Rosemary.

Mr. Simon Fordyce was dark, bare-headed, with bright cheerful eyes set in a rather square face. About the same age as Luke and of similar lean build, he wore fine checked gray trousers and had taken off his jacket to reveal a black shirt with a clerical collar attached to it.

As we drew near I began to hear his words. They were like those Luke called the hellfire words we had once heard from a Presbyterian minister when he preached at our church, but there was a curious difference. Minister McTaggart had thundered menacingly against sin. Mr. Simon Fordyce also spoke with passion against it, but his eye was so merry, his manner so engaging, and his words so picturesque that the effect was not at all the same as Minister McTaggart's.

". . . and let us dwell for a few moments upon Adam and Eve," he was saying with warm enthusiasm. "Use your imagination. See them in your mind's eye as they roam the Garden of Eden. They were naked, dear friends. Naked! But unashamed! Unashamed of the exquisite warm flesh of the beautiful bodies God had made!"

A faint quiver, a soundless sigh, seemed to pass through his crowd of listeners, and the preacher lifted a hand with upraised finger, his eyes widening. "But the devil was at hand," he went on in a penetrating whisper. "The Lord of Sin was hidden in that garden, murmuring softly in Eve's innocent ear, describing the rich joys that her sublime body could offer to Adam, and of the wondrous pleasures that his could give to her . . ."

He paused to drink from a glass of water on the little wooden lectern where the Bible rested, and the congregation seemed to hold its breath waiting for him to resume. Quietly Luke helped me down from the cart, and with Mr. Grindle we moved around the edge of the little crowd till we stood near the lady at the harmonium.

"The Lord of Sin is with us still!" the preacher thundered so suddenly that we all jumped. "And shall I tell you his most

potent servant, who dwells in the hearts of man and woman
alike? Shall I name that demon who drives our weak flesh toward
the goal of ecstasy? It is *lust*, my friends! LUST! Aye, there is
lust in *your* heart, sir!'' He pointed at random. ''And in yours,
madam! And yours, and yours!'' His finger moved accusingly,
then turned toward his chest. ''Also in mine! And, my good
friends, I confess to you there is *lust* in the heart of my dear wife
there.'' He gestured toward the woman at the harmonium, and
for a moment all heads turned to regard Mrs. Fordyce with
interest, the men with a measure of speculation. Mrs. Fordyce
lowered her eyelids in bashful acknowledgment.

Luke glanced at me, made a grimace of amused bewilderment, lifted his shoulders in a baffled shrug, then turned his
attention to Mr. Simon Fordyce again, who smiled conspirato-
rially upon his congregation. ''Lust is the prime enemy against
whom we must do battle,'' he said in a quiet voice, ''and it is
vital that we should *know* our enemy. Let us therefore reflect
together on that which passed between Adam and Eve on that
fateful day at the beginning of Time, and upon other tales of
lechery with which the Good Book admonishes us to virtue.''

For the next ten minutes Mr. Simon Fordyce proceeded to do
this, picturesquely and with great animation. I saw that Luke
was half listening but taking more interest in a study of the
congregation, and I found myself doing the same. Nobody had
brought children to listen to Mr. Fordyce, I noticed. The women
ranged from young to middle-aged, and some kept nodding
shocked agreement as the preacher condemned the wicked ways
he described in such rich and lively fashion. The men ranged
from young to old, and listened with open-mouthed fascination.

Mr. Fordyce ended his sermon with a vivid description of
Samson's lechery with Delilah, pointing out that it had caused
his downfall, then read some verses from the Song of Solomon
and announced that the closing hymn would be ''Onward Christian Soldiers.'' He had distributed, he said, a few printed sheets
with the words of the hymn, and would be grateful for help in

collecting these after the service. "Perhaps the young lady here would be kind enough . . . ?"

He was pointing at me, smiling, and I felt myself blushing foolishly as I dipped my head and muttered a word of assent. While the lady was playing some preliminary bars of the hymn I heard Mr. Grindle whisper to Luke, "Have you ever heard a more moral sermon preached in more immoral fashion? And half the good Christians in Lawton come flocking to hear him!"

Luke grinned. "Not just the Christians, I fancy. He's a clerical equivalent of *La Vie Parisienne*." I did not understand this until Luke explained to me later that it was a French magazine with a reputation for impropriety.

A number of people must have come solely to hear Mr. Fordyce preach, for during the hymn, which was led by Mrs. Fordyce with a fine contralto voice, quite a few of the congregation began to drift away, the men in particular.

When we had sung "Amen," Mr. Fordyce said, "Before the final blessing, dear friends, I must announce that this is our last service in Lawton for the time being. We have been sent to these colonies in Australia by the Christian Research Association, an amalgamation of several religious bodies, to study the particular problems of expanding Christian service in this vast continent."

He gazed around at the dwindling congregation, hands on hips, his face alive with good humor, and I thought he looked more like a hero from one of the adventure stories in the *Strand* magazine than a preacher as he went on: "So my dear wife and I will be traveling to many towns and villages, also to homesteads in outlying areas, to learn what we may. It is our hope that when we return to England we shall be able to render a report that will bring you fellowship and practical assistance from the churches of the Mother Country. And now, shall we bow our heads for the blessing?" He lifted an outstretched hand.

When the blessing had been said I found myself collecting the small hymn-sheets that people handed me while Mrs. Fordyce played a soft voluntary on the harmonium as the congregation dispersed. Behind me I heard Mr. Grindle say to Luke,

"Well, thank heaven they're going, Mr. Bowman. Perhaps we duller clerics may get some of our congregation back now, and certainly there should be less, ah . . . untoward excitement among our flocks."

Mr. Simon Fordyce came toward us, a hand outstretched. "Grindle, my dear fellow, how kind of you to join us."

"I don't know about kind," said Mr. Grindle with a resigned smile. "You're a shocking chap, Fordyce, and I can't make you out at all, but I confess I'm glad you're moving on. Now, here's Mr. Bowman and his wife's cousin, Miss Gaynor. They have a farm a full hour's drive from Lawton, and they haven't had the pleasure of attending a service of yours before."

"I should certainly like to repay their visit," said Mr. Fordyce with easy friendliness as he shook hands, first with me, then with Luke. "My wife and I will call on you, if you permit, Mr. Bowman." Amusement sparkled in his eyes. "I'm not really a shocking chap, as Grindle says."

Luke seemed a little taken aback, and I thought he was seeking an excuse to put Mr. Fordyce off, so I said rather hesitantly, "I'm sure Rosemary would like that, Luke. It's so long since she saw anybody but us."

He rubbed his chin, then nodded. "Yes, that's true. All right, Mr. Fordyce, perhaps we can agree on a date so that you can take a bite with us. Shalimar isn't the Ritz, but we'll do our best. How long have you been out here? And how was England when you left?"

I moved away, leaving the men talking, and collected the last of the hymn-sheets. Mrs. Fordyce was still playing softly, watching me. She smiled and called, "Bring them here, my dear, if you would be so kind."

As I walked across to the harmonium I saw a man moving toward Mrs. Fordyce from the other side, a thickset man with a stubble of beard and a grubby face, swaying a little on unsteady legs, a corked bottle sticking out of his jacket pocket. I had seen him two or three times before in Lawton and had been puzzled the first time until Luke explained curtly that the man was drunk—and then had to explain to me what this meant. His name was Marcus, and I later found that the police often had to arrest him for being drunk and causing a disturbance. Now I felt troubled and uncertain what to do as he came up to Mrs. Fordyce from behind and laid a hand on her shoulder.

"You're the—*hic*—lady wi' good ol' lust inna heart, mmm?" he muttered in a thick voice.

The three men a little way off had seen nothing, and I kept my own voice low as I said fiercely, "Go away at once! At once, do you hear?"

Mrs. Fordyce was quite unperturbed. "Don't worry, dear," she said, and stood up, turning to face the man, who leered at her and said something more, though I did not catch it. What happened next I could not quite make out, but I saw Mrs. Fordyce's skirt flounce out as if she had moved her leg suddenly, and next moment the man staggered back, falling to his knees, hunched forward with head almost touching the ground, and groaning.

Mrs. Fordyce adjusted her hat, looked down at the man, and murmured, "Don't give me any trouble, sonny-boy. I've handled more drunks than you've had haircuts."

I must have been open-mouthed with surprise as she turned to me again with a cheerful smile and took the hymn-sheets I had collected. "Thank you so much, my dear. We'll pop them in this bag. Then I must get my husband to help me lift the harmonium onto the cart."

Mr. Fordyce called out, and I saw that the three men were looking in our direction now. "Is everything all right, Eliza?" he inquired.

"Quite all right, Simon," his wife replied serenely. "The gentleman is just offering up a private prayer." Then she winked at me as she turned away, and I felt myself suddenly drawn to her. With her strapping body, rude health, and bold eyes she was quite different from my beloved Rosemary, and in my limited experience quite unlike a vicar's wife. But I could sense great warmth and kindness in her, I admired her cheerful confidence, and I was glad that we might be seeing her again.

Driving home with Luke, I spoke of the incident with Mrs. Fordyce and the drunken man and asked if I was right in thinking that she and her husband were an unusual pair for such a vocation. "Perhaps a lot of clergymen and their wives in England are like that," I reflected, "but I only know the ones in Lawton."

"I doubt if you'll find another pair like the Fordyces anywhere," said Luke, shaking his head and half smiling. "I've met his type in various parts of the world, and they've never been clergymen before. Adventurers, yes. Rogues, yes. Traders, explorers, gamblers, men of business, yes." He gave a laugh. "Never a vicar, though. And Mrs. Fordyce is a handsome young woman who wouldn't look out of place on the stage."

I was driving the trap home, and Luke sat with an empty pipe in his mouth, as he sometimes did, for he never smoked, even out of doors, for fear of aggravating Rosemary's cough. He glanced at me now and said, "If they tried to tap people for money I'd wonder if they were a pair of tricksters, posing as cleric and spouse, but Grindle told me they seem to be very comfortably fixed for money, and in fact have been very generous in giving to various church charities in Lawton." He took his pipe from his mouth and put it in his pocket. "What did you think of them yourself, Red?"

"Well, I hardly spoke with the man, but I liked Mrs. Fordyce very much."

He nodded. "I took to the man, and I expect I'll share your view of the lady when I've seen a little more of her."

"Yes. I'm glad they're coming on Thursday, and I'm sure Rosemary will be pleased. I'll help her make a nice luncheon for them."

During the next few days I became hugely excited. These would be the first guests ever to visit our home since I had come to Shalimar. Some of my excitement rubbed off on Rosemary, for we were very happy as we made plans for the occasion, deciding how to organize the day's work, what to serve for luncheon, and how to arrange matters so that we could make our scanty cutlery and crockery provide for five instead of three.

Because Rosemary was happy, Luke was in good humor, too. When we sat pondering what meat we could afford, he announced that he would send Mitji out with her spear to bring back some juicy kangaroo steaks, together with some fat witchetty grubs for dessert. Although he was joking, I did consider the idea of kangaroo meat, but for no longer than a moment, because I knew from experience that it might take weeks for me to make a successful hunt. In the tribe, kangaroo meat had been only an occasional treat.

When the day came, the visit of Mr. and Mrs. Fordyce was a great success. They were at once on easy terms with Rosemary, and she with them. I knew from my study of magazines and photographs that ours was a poor home by many standards, but our ways and manners were of the best, and I was proud of Shalimar, proud of our little farm, and proud of Luke and Rosemary, who had given me a new and wonderful life.

Our guests came at noon, stayed for luncheon and for the afternoon tea we had prepared, and did not leave until an hour before dusk. During that time we showed them around the farm, answered many questions, displayed the scrapbooks Rosemary and I had kept, and asked about their experiences in visiting Australia for the Christian Research Association. Rosemary always said grace for us before meals, but on this occasion she asked Mr. Fordyce to do so. He assented cheerfully, but apart from this and the fact that he wore a clerical collar there was nothing about him to suggest that he was a man of the church.

During the day there were times when the two men strolled together, talking. It came to me then how glad Luke must be to have a man to talk with, for he had so few opportunities to do so, and I imagined how I would feel if I had to spend almost every waking hour in the company of men, without Rosemary or any other woman to talk to. When I went to tell the men that tea would be ready in ten minutes I strolled with them for a while and heard Luke asking about the London Season, the English weather, and cricket. Rosemary and Mrs. Fordyce had talked of other things to do with England, and I had said very little, for it would have been easy for me to make a foolish mistake and reveal that I had never been there in my life.

When Mr. and Mrs. Fordyce left, it was with the promise that they would visit us again whenever they were passing through Lawton, and to our pleasure we saw them several times at Shalimar during the next few weeks.

My seventeenth birthday came, and only two days later a most terrible blow fell upon us, the worst I could imagine. Rosemary suddenly collapsed, and it became agonizingly clear to me that she was dying. I was shaken by horror and filled with shame at my stupid blindness, for only now did I realize that even when I first set eyes on Rosemary she had been dying slowly. She had known it, and Luke had known it.

Now she was dying quickly. At last I knew it, and I was torn by pain and fear.

IT WAS OVER IN FOUR DAYS, AND DURING THAT TIME I FELT I was living through a bad dream. On the first day Luke brought Dr. Vernon from Lawton. He examined Rosemary, told her heartily that she would soon be better, then signaled to me to remain with her while Luke went out to the sitting room with him.

Rosemary gave me a tired smile and whispered, "He'll leave some cough mixture. Perhaps something strong to make me sleep. But I won't be here for long, Meg dear."

I took her thin hand in my own and shook my head wordlessly, unable to speak, knowing that she spoke truly. I had seen a number of old folk die during my years with the tribe. I knew the look that comes into the eyes when death is near, and I could see that look in Rosemary's eyes now.

Her fingers tightened feebly on my hand for a moment, and she said, "Look after my Luke for me. . . . He'll need you so badly—'' A fit of coughing seized her, and I quickly lifted her frail body to a sitting position, supporting her to ease the strain. When the fit had passed I wiped her face and continued to hold her while she recovered her breath. With her head resting on my shoulder she murmured weakly yet urgently, ''Promise, Meg. . . . He gave up everything for me . . . and I've been a poor wife for such a man. Take him away, Meg dear . . . and in a little while marry him. He'll be lost without you. Please . . .''

''Yes, yes, I promise,'' I said quickly, stroking her brow. Even her astonishing plea for me to marry Luke made little impression on me at that moment, for my only concern was to prevent her talking because I knew it would bring on another fit of coughing. I would have promised anything to avoid that.

''Thank you . . . thank you,'' she whispered, and sagged against me, her eyes closing as if content to let go now that she had my promise. I laid her down gently and sat holding her hand, a small part of my mind beginning to register amazement at what she had asked. Later, when Dr. Vernon had gone and Rosemary was sleeping after a dose of some new medicine he had left, Luke called me into the sitting room and told me in a flat, lifeless voice that the doctor could do nothing to save Rosemary and did not expect her to live for more than three or four days. His face was haggard and he stared past me as he spoke. I wanted to take his hand, to put my arms around him for comfort, or to have him put his arms around me, but I knew he would not want me to touch him.

I could find no words to tell how my heart ached for him—and for myself. To say that I was sorry meant nothing in comparison with the grief that racked me, but I thought of the nursing Rosemary would need in whatever time was left to her, and I knew she would wish Luke to be spared all that this would involve, so I rubbed the tears from my eyes and told a lie. ''Rosemary wants me to nurse her, so you must move into my room, Luke, and I'll take your bed.''

He drew in a long breath and let it out again slowly, still not looking at me. "All right," he said. "If that's what Rosemary wants."

In the time that followed we lived in a waking nightmare, taking turns to sit with Rosemary by day, sometimes reading to her, seldom talking because when she tried to respond it would bring on a fit of coughing. I made meals for us all, but Rosemary would take no more than a little broth, and Luke and I had no appetite. For much of the time the doctor's medicine kept Rosemary asleep, and for this I was thankful. I was thankful also that she made my lie into truth by begging me in her frail whispering voice to attend to her needs because she did not want Luke to have the task of nursing her through the indignities of her last days.

I slept lightly at night, alert for any sound from Rosemary, sometimes lying awake and listening to her troubled breathing, dreading that it might stop at the next breath yet at the same time wishing for the misery of her suffering to end. Twice I had strange dreams. In one I was living with the tribe again, Mitji the freak, and Rosemary came, smiling and healthy, to tell the elders that I was not a freak and that I belonged to the great and powerful tribe ruled by the magical Mitjiquin. But they would not believe her, and stabbed her with their spears. I tried to stop them, but the sorcerer had put a spell upon me so that I could not move, and I stood rooted to the ground, weeping as they killed her. Then the spell was lifted and I was about to mourn her in the way of my tribe, by gashing my arms and legs and scalp, but her spirit spoke to me, telling me that this was not the way of my true people, and I woke to the sound of her coughing. I was trembling, my body wet with sweat as I quickly climbed out of bed to give her a dose of the cough medicine.

The other dream was less horrible but more bewildering. I was in the outback with Rosemary. She was dressed as usual, but I was naked except for my girdle and tassel of emu feathers, and I carried my boomerang, spear, and throwing club, just as I had when I left the tribe. We were walking toward an object lying on flat sandy ground, and as we drew near I saw that it was a skeleton, with one bony hand clutching a small pouch. I knew that this skeleton was the remains of the dead man I had found in the outback with the little pouch of glittering yellow stones that I later discovered were gold nuggets.

We walked around the skeleton, Rosemary holding my arm and saying in her gentle voice, "Oh, the poor man, the poor man . . ." Then she turned to me and said, "You will take care of my Luke for me, won't you, Meg dear? He'll need a little time, of course, but I know he'll want to marry you."

In my dream I did not answer but stood leaning on my spear, looking down at the skeleton and trying to remember something I knew was important, though I had no idea what it could be. After a while I said, "We'd better go this way, then," and I began to follow the tracks the camel had made, just as I had done on the day I found Luke. I think the dream ended by simply fading away, but when next I woke I remembered this much of it clearly.

At three in the morning of the fourth night I was roused by the sudden quietness of Rosemary's breathing. When I lit the lamp and went to her she was awake but barely conscious, her face waxen, her pulse flickering feebly. Her lips moved, and though she made no sound I knew she had tried to utter a single word: "Luke."

I hurried to tap on his door and tell him to come quickly. In seconds he emerged, fastening the belt of hastily donned trousers, bare to the waist. My throat had closed, and it was a struggle to speak as I said, "Oh, Luke . . . I think it's very close now. She asked for you."

He closed his eyes tightly for a moment, face twisting with pain, then moved past me into the bedroom and stood gazing down at his wife in despair, hands moving and twitching as if seeking something to do. Rosemary lay on her back, eyes half open, her breathing almost stilled. Her lips moved again. This time I did not know what she was trying to say, but I knew she was at the point of death, and I murmured, "Take her in your arms, Luke. Hold her close."

He gave me a strange, wondering look, then sat on the edge of the bed and very gently lifted Rosemary so that she was half lying, half sitting, cradled in his arms, her head against his chest. I heard her give a sigh, and I whispered, "Call me when you need me." Then I gathered up my clothes from the chair where they lay and carried them through to the sitting room so that I could dress there. I had not wanted to leave Rosemary. I did not think even Luke could grieve more deeply for her than I, but I was trying to act as I had learned from Rosemary that our own people acted, and I felt it would be wrong to intrude upon Luke's last moments with the wife he loved so dearly.

I had dressed, washed my face, combed my hair, and made some tea when Luke came through to the kitchen. He wore a shirt now and sat down heavily at the table with his back to me. Resting his head in his hands, he said, "It's over. Oh, dear God . . ." His voice broke.

I whispered, "Oh, Luke, my heart aches for you." Forgetting myself for a moment, I put a hand on his shoulder. "I'm so very sorry."

He turned his head to look at me, dazed, yet with an expression that chilled my blood, for mingled with the grief I seemed to see shame and anger, though I could not fathom their cause. Then he spoke in a low, husky voice, and his words cut me to the bone. *"Get out of my sight,"* he said.

I snatched my hand away and took a pace back, telling myself not to be hurt or angry. Rosemary had been the light of Luke's life, and only minutes ago she had died, cruelly young. At such a moment a man who worshipped her as Luke had done might be forgiven any wild words. I said, "There's tea in the pot there, Luke. I'll go and see to Rosemary."

Her poor wasted body seemed light as a child's when I washed her, put a clean nightdress on her, and did the best I could to brush her hair and make two neat braids. When I had finished I found Luke sitting on the bench in the garden as the first light of dawn touched the sky. He had shaved now and was dressed in the one suit he owned. His head of golden hair rested back against the timbers of the house and his eyes were closed.

As he heard me cross the threshold he said without opening his eyes, "I'll drive into Lawton now. Back by early afternoon with the undertaker. You'll stay with Rosemary?"

"Yes, of course. Would you like to see her now? She looks very . . . peaceful."

He nodded, stood up, and went into the house. I did not follow, but stood looking at Rosemary's flower bed, trying not to cry. In a little while Luke came out again and stood beside me. After a moment or two I heard him say in a low voice, "I'm sorry, Red."

I shook my head. "It was nothing."

"You're a good girl. Thanks for all you've done."

"I loved her, too."

"Yes."

He turned away, and I watched him go to the stable. A few minutes later he drove the trap out and set off along the track to Lawton without looking back. For long hours after his going I busied myself about the house and farm, cleaning, tidying, hoeing, weeding, anything to keep me occupied so that my mind would remain benumbed and I would not have to think of a future without Rosemary.

At noon I went to her room and read aloud one of her favorite pieces from the Bible.

> "Two are better than one; because they have a good re-
> ward for their labor.
> For if they fall, the one will lift up his fellow; but woe to
> him that is alone when he falleth; for he hath not an-
> other to help him up.
> Again, if two lie together, then they have heat; but how
> can one be warm alone?
> And if one prevail against him, two shall withstand him;
> and a threefold cord is not quickly broken.

Better is a poor and a wise child than an old and foolish
    king, who will no more be admonished.''

When I had read the verses I made myself eat a little soup
with bread, then went on with the job we had begun recently of
cutting a new irrigation channel to extend the vineyard. At two
o'clock Luke returned, followed by two men with a long cart
on which rested a newly made coffin. They wore tall black hats,
and I had seen the older man several times at church. He was
Mr. Nugent, the undertaker. I joined Luke as Mr. Nugent and
his assistant carried the coffin into the house.

"Can I get you anything to eat or drink?" I asked.

Luke shook his head. "I'm all right. Put a few things in a
bag, Meg. You'll be going back to Lawton with them."

I stared. "Going back?"

"Yes." He made an irritable gesture. "I've arranged for you
to stay with Sergeant Kelly and his wife until things are sorted
out. You can't stay at Shalimar alone with me. The funeral is
tomorrow. I'll see you then."

I was startled and felt a quick wave of irritation myself, but
held it down as I said, "I can't do that, Luke. I promised Rosemary I'd take care of you."

"Thank you," he said with cold politeness, "but that won't
be necessary. Just do as I ask."

As he began to turn away I pushed a wisp of hair from my
eyes and said, "Nobody in Lawton is going to think bad things
of you if I stay. Even if they did it wouldn't matter. I'm not going
to leave you alone here—" I broke off, flinching, for he had
spun around upon me with such fury that for a moment I thought
he would strike me. His face was ashen, his eyes glaring, and
he spoke in a terrible whisper. "Don't argue, damn you! Not
another word! Go and get ready! Now!"

After the first instant of shock I was so angry I could have hit
him for treating me with such harshness. I felt my jaw beginning
to jut, my eyes narrowing and returning his glare. I knew my
face would be ugly now, with my freckles and red hair and snub

nose making me look, as he had once said, like an Irish alley cat about to spit and claw, but I did not care. For long moments there was such tension that it was as if lightning might strike the ground between us. Then suddenly I recalled that Rosemary lay dead and I was facing a man with a broken heart.

All anger drained out of me, and I closed my eyes for a moment. Then I said in a small voice, "All right, Luke," and turned away to go into the house.

I sat in the kitchen until the men carried Rosemary out in her coffin. Then I put a few clothes and belongings in a canvas bag and went out to where the undertaker's cart was waiting. Mr. Nugent said, "You ride up front with me, young lady. Jim'll ride with the coffin."

I thanked him, handed up my bag, and walked to where Luke stood a little way off. "What time is the funeral?" I asked.

"Ten o'clock at the Methodist church. Mr. Grindle will take the service," said Luke, gazing past me.

"I'll see you there, then." I paused, lowering my voice so that the men by the cart should not hear, and said carefully, "Rosemary asked me to take care of you. I gave my promise. Don't make me fail her."

His mouth tightened. "Those were Rosemary's last moments, and she couldn't have known what she was saying. You're released from such a promise."

I was about to tell him that Rosemary had sought the same promise from me long before, but this was not the moment to argue. I put out a hand and almost touched his arm in the friendliest gesture I dared to make. "We'll talk about it tomorrow," I said. Then, after a little hesitation, I spoke the thought that had come to my mind. "Please, Luke . . . don't hate me because I'm alive and your Rosemary isn't."

His whole body jerked as if with shock, eyes widening above the dark patches of worry and grief beneath them. For long moments he simply stared at me dazedly. Then he turned away and went into the house.

SEVEN

SERGEANT KELLY AND HIS WIFE RECEIVED ME VERY KINDLY. They were wise enough to say little about the tragedy of Rosemary's death and to let me help with household tasks. Lying in bed in their small spare room that night, I did not expect to sleep well, but I must have been unusually tired after all the sorrow and tribulations of a very long day, for I slept almost as soon as I laid my head on the pillow.

At some time in the early hours I found myself suddenly awake. There was no sense of having awakened from a dream, but running vividly through my mind was a recollection of my recent dream about being in the outback with Rosemary and seeing the skeleton with the pouch of gold nuggets clutched in its hand. I recalled Rosemary's words in the dream, speaking of Luke: *He'll need a little time, of course, but I know he'll want to marry you.*

This was an echo of similar words she had spoken to me in reality after Dr. Vernon had visited her shortly before she died. She had begged me to take care of Luke, saying he had given up everything for her and that she had been a poor wife for such a man. I had not quite taken in the meaning of those last few words at the time, being too deeply concerned with easing her distressful coughing, but now as I lay in the darkness I thought she could only have meant that for at least as long as I had been at Shalimar, and perhaps much longer, she had not been able to share Luke's bed. Then she had said, *Take him away, Meg dear . . . and in a little while marry him. He'll be lost without you. Please . . .*

Looking back, I knew I could not have withheld the promise she wanted, but I felt there must be little hope of my keeping it, for it was not in my power to order Luke's life. I could not go to him and say it had been Rosemary's wish that he should marry me. He would never believe it; I could hardly believe it myself now. And he had even rejected the notion that I should take care of him by her wish.

For a moment or two I wondered what my own feelings were about being married to Luke, for until now I had thought of it only as what Rosemary wished. Marriage in the tribe had been quite different from marriage between white people. I tried to imagine what it would be like if I were married to Luke, then hastily put the thought aside, for Rosemary was not yet dead twenty-four hours and it seemed a betrayal of her to think in such a way.

I turned over in the bed, hoping to go to sleep again, and as I did so I had a final recollection of my earlier dream. I recalled leaning on my spear, looking down at the skeleton holding the pouch, and trying to remember something I knew that was very important. I was still trying to pin down that elusive piece of knowledge when sleep overtook me again.

I HAD NO SUITABLE CLOTHES FOR A FUNERAL, BUT MRS. KELLY lent me a black scarf to tie around my head and a black armband to wear. Luke called for me at half past nine. His eyes were sunken and his face drawn, but he spoke to me gently and managed to smile as he greeted me. At the church, when Mr. Grindle conducted the service, the only people present apart from Luke and myself were Sergeant Kelly and his wife, one of the churchwardens, the harmonium player, the undertaker and his men, and a wrinkled old couple who seemed to know the service by heart and appeared to enjoy taking part. Mrs. Kelly later told me they were among the oldest inhabitants of Lawton and made a practice of attending every funeral.

I wept when the coffin was lowered into the grave and the first handfuls of earth were thrown upon it. I would have given anything simply to have Luke hold my hand, but he stood with a pale, stony face until the graveside part of the service ended, then turned away with the rest of us, leaving the gravedigger to complete his task.

Mrs. Kelly invited Luke back to the house for a cup of tea, and as we sat there Luke spoke words to Sergeant Kelly that shook me to the very core of my being.

"I made arrangements about Meg when I was in Lawton yesterday," he said absently, stirring his tea. "She'll be going back to England with Simon Fordyce and his wife. They have connections with a number of missions and Christian associations there, and they're quite sure they can find her a suitable position with one of them."

Sergeant Kelly glanced at me, then looked back at Luke and said slowly, "Well . . . that's all right then, I suppose."

By this time I had gathered my wits, and I said in astonishment, "Back to England? What do you mean, Luke? I don't want to go away anywhere! How can you have made arrangements with Mr. and Mrs. Fordyce? It's almost three weeks since they were last here. I don't understand—"

"It's for the best," Luke broke in sharply. "It was no secret to them that Rosemary was"—his voice wavered—"that she had only a little time left. I told them that without Rosemary I wouldn't be staying on here, and they offered to take charge of you."

"But nobody told me!" I cried.

He looked down at his cup. "We couldn't. Rosemary didn't want you to know she was dying . . . not until the very end, when it couldn't be hidden." He grimaced without humor. "Shalimar is the last place on earth I want to be now. I only went there because it gave Rosemary another two or three years of life. When I've sold the whole place—house, furniture, crop, everything—for as much as it'll fetch, which is precious little, I'll be moving on.''

I put down my cup and saucer with an unsteady hand, fighting back tears as I said, ''But who will look after you, Luke? I promised Rosemary.''

He looked about him with an air of controlled exasperation, and Mrs. Kelly said gently, ''That's impossible, Meg. Whether Mr. Bowman goes or stays, it's out of the question. You must see that.''

I sat looking down at my hands, clenched in my lap, and after a little silence I said, ''What did you mean just now when you said you had made arrangements about me while you were in Lawton yesterday, Luke?''

''I sent a wire to the Chester Hotel in Kalgoorlie. That's where Simon Fordyce and his wife stay in between their trips to outlying parts. They may get the wire tomorrow, or it may wait a couple of weeks for them, but when they do they'll come up here to collect you and take charge until they sail for England.'' Luke's voice held no expression, and he did not look at me as he spoke.

I shook my head in despair. There was nothing more I could say, and beyond my grief at failing Rosemary I began to feel fear of the unknown future that would soon be opening before me. I had spent my childhood among people as primitive as their forebears had been ten thousand years before. Rosemary and Luke had educated me and brought me into the civilized world of my own kind—but only to the fringes of it, this I well knew from my reading and studies. Compared with London and other great capitals, Kalgoorlie was no more than a village, yet to me it had seemed unbelievably huge and densely populated.

How would I get on with the strange people of England? I had lived most of my life as an aborigine, and although Rosemary had taught me so much, it was mostly hearsay, from books and pictures and her own knowledge. In all my seventeen years I had spoken with only a handful of English people, and I had no experience of civilized life beyond what I had known at Shali-

mar. I could chop wood, fetch water, cook and sew well enough
according to Rosemary; I could hoe, weed, pick grapes, build
a fence, groom a pony, drive a trap; and I had at least been well
schooled in correct behavior. Perhaps, I thought, some of this
would be of help to me in the new and frightening life awaiting
me on the other side of the world. I hoped so, but I did not
know.

All I did know, sadly, was that nothing I had learned in childhood would help me. In England, if ever the truth about me
were known, they would surely find it comical that I could use
a boomerang, bring down a bird with a throwing club, or find
food and water in a barren desert. They would be unlikely to
admire a girl who could identify people by their scent, who
could recognize dozens of small animals by the faintest of tracks,
who could follow human tracks a week old—

Something fell abruptly into place in my mind, and I had to
suppress a gasp at the realization that a mystery was solved. I
now knew what the important thing was that I had not been able
to recall, either in my dream or when I lay awake struggling to
pin down the tantalizing memory.

Luke and Sergeant Kelly were talking now, but I was only
vaguely aware of their presence, for I suddenly knew there was
something I could do that might at least go part of the way
toward keeping the promise I had made Rosemary. My mind
was in turmoil as I tried to decide the best way to go about it.

Twenty minutes later Luke said good-bye to us and left for
Shalimar. Before going, he thanked Mrs. Kelly for allowing me
to stay and told her he would provide money so that Mr. and
Mrs. Fordyce could buy some decent clothes and other necess-
ities for me in Perth before I began the voyage to England.
Selling Shalimar would yield a hundred pounds or so, he said,
and he could borrow from the bank against that if need be.

He spoke as if I were not in the room, and it was hard to
prevent the hurt from showing in my face. I longed for him to
feel toward me what I had always called heart-warmth in the
tongue of my childhood, for we had lived and worked together

for close on three years now, but it was almost as if he could not bear to look at me. Then I reminded myself that it was Luke who had saved my life when the sickness had come upon me in the desert and almost killed me. He had brought me safely to his house and to my beloved Rosemary, who had given so much of herself to educate me in the ways of my own people. Luke had provided me with a home, had fed me and clothed me and been kind to me. Now, with Rosemary's death, the light had gone out of his life, and it was selfish of me to feel hurt by his manner at such a time.

Next morning when I got up I braced myself to tell Mrs. Kelly that regardless of what anyone thought I intended to return to Shalimar until Mr. and Mrs. Fordyce arrived to take me to England. I expected strong opposition, but in fact my task was made easy by two facts. First, a wire had arrived from the Kellys' daughter in Kalgoorlie saying that she had broken her arm in a fall and asking her mother to come and look after her two young children.

"I don't know what to do about you, Meg," Mrs. Kelly said worriedly as she stood at the range making breakfast. "It's not fitting for you to stay here with Bob." She turned to her husband. "We can't ask Millie Turner; her baby's due any day now. Is there anyone else you can think of?"

I said quickly, "Don't worry, Mrs. Kelly. I've made up my mind to go back to Shalimar. I know it's not considered fitting, but I'll be quite all right with Luke, and the fact is, Mrs. Bowman herself asked me to take care of him."

Mrs. Kelly's first look of shock faded to one of unease and then to hesitant relief. "Well, I don't know, dear," she said doubtfully. "I mean, I'm sure it would be quite all right, but . . . what do you think, Bob?"

Sergeant Kelly stood by the window rereading the wire. At his wife's question he looked up and gave a brief nod. "Might be best all around," he said bluntly. "George Farmer at the store told me Luke Bowman bought himself three bottles of whisky before he left for home yesterday."

Mrs. Kelly bit her lip. "That's very worrying. It's a bad time for him to be on his own out there. I suppose if Mrs. Bowman herself felt it was all right for Meg to stay, then . . . ?"

The upshot was that Sergeant Kelly, who was off duty that morning, drove his wife to the station at nine o'clock, then returned to take me to Shalimar. I was so occupied with my plans that I made the foolish mistake of saying I did not want to trouble him and could easily walk to the farm. He stared at me in astonishment. "Walk? It's five miles under a baking sun, Meg. You'd be ill before you got there."

I managed to prevent myself saying that I had spent much of my life walking many more miles than that under a baking sun, and instead I smiled and shook my head as if at my own foolishness. "Oh dear. I wasn't thinking. I feel so muddled after all that's happened."

We reached the farm an hour before noon, and I asked Sergeant Kelly to stop a quarter of a mile away. "Luke might tell you to take me back," I explained. "It's better if I arrive alone. That's why I had that silly notion about walking. I won't argue with him, Mr. Kelly, I'll just get on with whatever needs doing about the house and farm until he accepts that I'm going to stay. You needn't have a moment's worry about me."

He nodded. "Best way to handle him, most likely. You're a good girl, Meg. Luke Bowman isn't the easiest of customers." When he had handed me my bag and driven away I began to walk along the dusty track toward the farm. The sky was very blue, the sun beat down strongly, and I was glad now that I had not walked from Lawton. It was true that I was well used to sun and desert, but only as a near-naked aborigine, not wrapped in a shift and a long dress, wearing drawers and stockings and shoes.

There was no sign of Luke about the farm. The door of the house stood open. I went in, put down my bag, and found him sprawled on his bed in shirt and trousers, one foot still booted. A whisky bottle in the kitchen, three-quarters empty, told the tale. He had been too drunk to undress, and was still in a stupor.

I took his other boot off and put a blanket over him but made
no attempt to rouse him. The next hour I spent cleaning quickly
through the house, feeding the chickens and ensuring that Henrietta had fodder and water. I emptied the bottle of whisky into
the stream, found two full bottles and emptied them also. Then
I sat down and wrote a short letter in my best handwriting.

> Dear Luke,
>   Mrs. Kelly was called away, so Sergeant Kelly brought
> me back. He believes I am staying here, but there is some-
> thing I have to do, and I shall be away for about ten days.
>   I have thrown away all the whisky. That is what Rose-
> mary would wish.
>   Please, Luke, be as you were when she was here.
>   Your friend,

I hesitated, then wrote "Red" as my signature. That was what
he always called me when he felt warm toward me. After a
moment or two I added,

> P.S. I have borrowed your pocketknife.

I went into his room and put the letter on the chair beside his
bed, standing one of his boots on part of the paper so that he
could not miss finding it. I shook him gently to see if he was
near to waking, but he remained slumped, breathing heavily.
Satisfied, I took Luke's pocketknife from the dressing table,
went to my bedroom, and with scissors from Rosemary's sewing
box I cut a spare cotton underskirt down to about fifteen inches
in length. I unpinned my hair, made it into a single braid, then
took off my shoes and all my clothes and fastened the tiny skirt
at my waist.

Barefoot, as I had lived most of my life, I padded into the
kitchen, filled Luke's big water bottle from the pitcher by the
sink, and drank four large mugs of water. A drawstring bag
holding pegs for the clothesline hung on a hook by the door. I

took it down, emptied out the pegs, and put in a loaf of bread and a big jar of our own raisins. I broke ten eggs into an empty jar, screwed the lid on firmly, and put it with the rest of my food.

I stood thinking for a moment, then went to fetch the remains of my underskirt and added this to the bag. Slinging the water bottle and food bag on my shoulder, I went out by the kitchen door to the outhouse to collect my spear and throwing club, boomerang and digging stick. Again I paused to consider my preparations, but could think of nothing more I needed.

A white man who tried to do what I was about to do would surely die, but I was no longer Meg Gaynor, supposedly from England. Already I was Mitji the aborigine, my nose twitching with the scent of the stream, the chickens, the pony, the goats, the house, the very ground where I stood. I could scent Luke's recent presence here strongly, and I knew that even after a week or more I would still be able to pick up the lingering scent of Rosemary. My eyes were again the eyes of an aborigine, busily noting every detail of my surroundings, aware of the tracks of a crow leading to the stream, of a beetle scuttling into the shadow of the wheelbarrow, of some ants moving in a ragged file to a nest somewhere beyond the stable. To me, all these were food, were life itself, but for the moment I had no need of them, for I was far better provisioned for the journey before me than I had been on the day I ran away from the tribe.

I glanced at the sun, then turned and looked northeast toward the point where the mountains on the distant skyline broke in a broad gap through which Luke had brought me unconscious to Shalimar. Beyond those mountains I would be on terrain I knew, terrain I had walked with Luke riding the camel beside me, until the sickness felled me and took away my senses. That was long ago, but because I had been what I had been, I could bring to my mind a clear picture of every stage of that journey, which to any but an aborigine would have been almost featureless.

I stood still for a moment, sharpening my senses, renewing instincts I had not used for some time. Then I said, ''Please,

God, help me." It was not much of a prayer, but ever since I had started going to church I had felt uneasy about the way people seemed to keep pestering God at length for what they wanted, and I thought He might be better disposed to somebody who did not take up too much of His time.

After the prayer I said aloud but quietly, "It's the best I can do, Rosemary. I really have tried, but it's all I can do."

Then, without looking back, I set off at an easy pace toward the distant hills.

WHEN PLANNING MY JOURNEY I HAD WONDERED IF MY LIFE OF ease at Shalimar might make the task ahead of me very difficult, but within a few hours I was reassured. By the time I reached the first line of hills I no longer felt it strange to be walking almost naked through the outback. My feet were still like leather and would probably always be so now. I could never hope to have dainty lady's feet.

I had brought the remains of my underskirt to drape over my shoulders if the sun began to make them sore, but my skin did not burn. Although my body had been covered for almost three years it was still brown compared with Rosemary's, even though it had seemed white to me during my years with the tribe. No doubt those years had tempered my skin against the sun for all time.

During the greatest heat of the afternoon I rested for two hours in a patch of shade thrown by a rock, and when I moved on I began to practice the use of my spear and boomerang and throwing club, selecting a target, throwing, then picking up the weapon as I moved on. In this way I wasted no time, and after a little practice I was glad to find that I had not lost my old skill.

Because I had been so well provisioned when I set out, I was able to journey for the first two days without having to seek food or water, and on the third and fourth days I needed only to go a little out of my way to find some tubers and water frogs, which provided both food and moisture to supplement the remains of what I had started with. As a result I made very good time, and on the evening of my fourth day of travel I reached the place where I had first found Luke. Many seasons of wind and weather had scoured away all sign, except for the misshapen bullet still lying by the rock.

I camped there that night and rose at first light to hunt food and find water, heading east toward the hillside a mile or two away, where I had found plentiful food and water before. I returned two hours later with a goanna lizard, which in the tribe we had called *kurkati*, a small possum, and two big handfuls of kalpari seeds. Using Luke's pocketknife, I quickly skinned and cut up the meat, then made a fire and cooked the pieces in hot ashes. While at the hillside I had dug for water in the same place as before, drunk as much as my belly would hold, then filled the water bottle and also the two empty screwtop jars in which I had carried the eggs and the raisins.

When the meat had cooled I ate a few pieces for my breakfast, together with some kalpari seeds, and put the rest in my drawstring bag, reflecting that I now had ample food and water to last three or four days. In one respect at least I had changed since my years with the tribe, for then I had never thought of providing beyond the needs of the day. But in other respects I seemed to have changed little. For three years I had been eating wonderful civilized food, yet this morning I had enjoyed the lizard and possum meat, and I did not feel at all strange squatting naked in the desert as I carefully packed my drawstring bag for the day's march.

"Luke was almost right, Rosemary," I said to the great emptiness about me. "I'm an aboriginal alley cat. But don't be ashamed of me, dear. I'll be civilized again when I go back."

Two hours later I reached my journey's end at a ridge of red rock. I had come through this broken ridge from the other direction, leading the camel, on the day that I found the dead man and later found Luke. There were many gaps in the ridge, but today I had retraced my path exactly, with a clear memory-picture of it in my mind, and I did not have to search longer

than a few moments for the crevice in the rock face where I had
thrust the dead man's shiny leather pouch.

On that long-ago day I had believed that the white-leaf thing
with black lines on it contained in the pouch was a thing of
magic, a dangerous *mapanpa*. Later I had forgotten all about it
until a dream had jogged my memory and told me that I knew
something important. Even then I could not identify the elusive
thought, and it was only on the day of Rosemary's funeral that
the recollection had taken sudden shape clearly in my mind.

The mysterious object in the pouch, the white-leaf thing with
black lines, had been as strange and mystical to me as the copper
penny Yuma had shown me many days before. But now I knew
that it was a piece of paper with a map drawn on it, the map
Luke had made showing the exact location of the gold-bearing
ground he had found with Joe Catesby. Luke believed that the
map had been lost somewhere in the desert. He could not know
that I had found it in the pouch on Joe Catesby's body, and that
after studying it and finding it beyond my understanding I had
not thrown it aside where the dead man lay because I feared this
might displease his spirit. I had carried it with me for a good
distance before hiding it in a crevice of rock as I passed through
the ridge.

I stood holding the pouch in my hand now, looking down at
it, sad and ashamed of myself. From the day Luke told me the
story of his search for gold I had possessed a key that would
open the door to riches for him, and I had stupidly failed to
recognize it. He could have made Shalimar into a magnificent
farm; he could have built a fine house there; he could have taken
Rosemary to the best doctors in the world, and perhaps saved
her life. If only . . .

I thrust the pouch into my bag, knelt down, covered my face
with my hands, and wept. After a while I stood up, gathered
my weapons, and turned for home. I could not keep the promise
I had made Rosemary to take care of Luke, because he would
not allow it. Now I was trying to do the next best thing, to give
him riches so that he could be free from worry and have servants

to look after him. I hoped this might prove even better than if I looked after him myself, for he would be able to have servants with far more skills than I possessed. I was not very sure about this, I could only hope, but it was the best I could do.

My journey home was uneventful. I knew that soon I would be going to the far side of the world, and I did not want to think about the new and strange life awaiting me there, for it frightened me. So I walked in a kind of waking sleep, keeping my mind closed, alert only for what was second nature to me, the noting and sensing of every detail of my surroundings as I made my way for mile upon mile over scrub and desert, salt marsh and sandhill, ridge and valley of the silent and sunbaked outback.

At dusk five days later I camped in a shallow gully at the foot of the last line of hills before the plain where Shalimar stood six or seven miles away. I could easily have reached the house that evening, but I knew Luke would be angry if I arrived just as I was. He would probably be angry with me anyway, but I planned to rise at dawn and dig for the water I could smell beneath a patch of blue-gray grass I knew as *jiwara*. I would wash my face and hands and body, make myself as clean and tidy as possible, then drape the cut-off piece of my underskirt over my upper body before going on to Shalimar. I had nothing to cover my legs, but with luck I hoped to enter the house unseen by Luke so that I could quickly put on a dress.

I ate the remainder of my food that night and slept on a patch of sand the wind had piled up at one end of the gully. At dawn I woke, picked up my digging stick, and moved to the patch of *jiwara* some fifty paces away at the foot of a little slope, taking the water bottle but leaving my drawstring bag and weapons where I had slept. The ground proved hard, and it took me almost half an hour before I reached water an arm's length down. Even then it seeped only slowly into the hole, and I guessed this was because most of the underground water here was being drawn off by the stream that broke surface for a short distance close to where Luke had built Shalimar.

I was kneeling by the hole, bottle in hand, watching the water in the bottom of the hole slowly rise, when a small sound brought my head round with a jerk. Next moment Luke appeared around a spur of sandy rock, mounted on Henrietta. I dropped the bottle and came to my feet as if on springs, startled, horrified, and curiously annoyed with him for coming upon me unawares in this way. Luke was equally taken aback, and for a frozen moment we simply stared at each other. Then I cried indignantly, "Oh, *Luke!*" and turned to run for the shallow gully where I had left my belongings.

Snatching the piece of cotton underskirt from the bag, I slipped my head and arms through the upper hole and gripped the material at the top to hold it in position so that it covered me from armpits to waist. When I turned, Luke had dismounted and was marching toward me, his face dark with anger.

"Where the *hell* have you been?" he demanded in a voice that was almost a shout. "I've been worried sick about you, you *stupid* girl!"

I had been about to say I was sorry he had found me not properly dressed, but his shouting revived my annoyance, and I glared back at him. "I left a note. I *said* I'd be back in about ten days. Didn't you read it?"

"Don't give me that alley-cat look! Of course I read it! But—"

"There's no 'of course' about it! When I left Shalimar you were drunk as a duke!"

"A *lord!*"

"What?"

"Drunk as a lord, not a duke—Oh, never mind! What the devil did you think you were doing, acting like an aborigine going walkabout? My God, you could have died out there!"

I swung an arm to point to the wastes behind me and almost lost control of the underskirt. "Died? Now who's being stupid? I *lived* out there for most of my life, didn't I? And stop shouting at me! What do you think *you're* doing, sneaking up and taking me by surprise? I was going to get washed and—and covered up before coming on to Shalimar.''

"Sneaking up?" His voice rose indignantly. "I've been riding out this way before first light for the past three *days* hoping I might sight you from the top of the hill. Simon Fordyce and his wife are coming for you today, and what was I supposed to tell them?''

"You could have told them anything you like!" I flared. "You could have told them Rosemary *begged* me to look after you, but you won't let me, so I went to fetch something I remembered leaving in the desert, something that should at least make sure you won't have to worry about money anymore.''

I reached into my bag, plucked out the pouch, and threw it at his feet. "There's your map, Luke, the map you made of the place where you found gold. Joe Catesby had it. I found it that day on his body and thought it was a magic thing, so I took it away because—Oh, the reason doesn't matter.''

He bent slowly to pick up the pouch, staring at it wonderingly, and I went on, "I hid it somewhere before I found you later that day, but it was only last week I remembered and realized it was a map. *Your* map! I'd have *told* you where I was going if you hadn't been in a drunken stupor, and shame on you for that—"

I broke off sharply, all my hurt and anger and distress draining suddenly away as I saw how weary and drawn he looked. I recalled that I was shouting at a man who only days ago had lost the wife who was everything to him. "Oh, Luke, forgive me," I said, moving forward slowly till I stood in front of him. "I'm sorry I shouted at you. I was upset because I wanted to be clean and decent before you saw me . . . and it wasn't true when I said I would have told you what I was going to do. I wouldn't, because I know you would have stopped me, but it's done now, and I'm back, and please let us not be cross with each other.''

He had taken the map from the pouch, unfolded and looked at it, and was now slowly putting it back again. As I finished speaking he gave me a small, tired smile. "We're both sorry,

Mitji. But I do wish I'd said it first.'' He looked down at the pouch and shook his head. ''Now this.''

I said, ''It's nothing compared with—with losing Rosemary. But it was all I could do.''

He studied me curiously for a few moments, and then a hint of sad humor came into his gaze. ''We'd better get back to Shalimar. You may feel you're pretty well muffled up in that whatever it is you're wearing, but there's a lot of you still showing, and it's not exactly formal wear for receiving the Reverend Simon Fordyce and his wife.'' He gestured toward the pony. ''Will you walk or ride?''

I smiled and said, ''I'll walk, please.''

''All right.'' He looked down at the pouch, then slipped it into his pocket. ''And thanks, Red. Many, many thanks.''

I tore a short rip in the top of my makeshift bodice so I could knot it firmly above my bosom, then gathered up my drawstring bag, water bottle, and weapons. Two minutes later I was walking across the plain with Luke riding beside me on Henrietta. We did not speak much, for there seemed little to say on either side. Later that morning I would be leaving, and Luke would be on his own to do whatever he might decide. I was reluctant to think about either of those things, and perhaps he felt the same, but at least we moved in friendly silence together.

After about half an hour Luke said, ''You went back to beyond where you found me?''

''Yes. A few miles beyond.''

''It's a long time since you were in the bush. Was it hard for you, Red?''

''No, it was just . . . ordinary. After the first half day it was as if I'd never been away.''

''Still happy with a diet of lizard and witchetty grubs?''

I laughed. ''You're so spoiled, that's the trouble with you *walypala*.''

There was a heavy haze over the land, and even when we came to within a mile of Shalimar the house was still hidden from us. Five minutes later, as often happened in the early morning, the sun sucked up the mist and a light breeze dispersed it, so that the house came suddenly into view, and Luke said, "Oh my God, they're already here."

A large trap stood by the house, a woman on the seat, a man standing beside it. Although they were too far away for us to distinguish their features I knew they were Mr. Fordyce and his wife, and I could see they were both looking toward us.

I stopped in alarm, and Luke reined in the pony. Then he said slowly, "It's no use, Meg. They've seen us, and the best liar in the world couldn't invent a reasonable story to account for your appearance now. Only the truth will do that."

"I suppose so. But then perhaps they won't take me to England?" I added with sudden hope.

Luke slanted a downward glance at me. "We'll see about that," he said grimly.

Together we moved on, and as we came at last to within speaking distance I saw that Mr. Fordyce was leaning against the trap with folded arms, watching us from under the brim of his hat with surprise that contained a hint of amusement rather than shock, or so it seemed to me; and his wife's expression was much the same. I had not felt embarrassed with Luke, for we had traveled for days together when I was Mitji the aborigine, but now I was acutely aware of my legs being bare to well above the knees, and I felt the color rising in my cheeks.

Then Mrs. Fordyce said coolly, "It seems to me, Simon, that as a minister of the Lord you might well avert your gaze."

Unhurriedly he turned his back on me and looked up at her. "My dear," he said cheerfully, "what a very proper notion, and how remiss of me not to have thought of it myself."

Luke slipped from the pony and moved in front of me. "Go to the kitchen, Meg," he said. "We'll give you an hour to bathe and change while I explain to Mr. and Mrs. Fordyce."

Dropping my weapons, I went quickly to my bedroom, gathered up the clothes I intended to wear, picked up my brush and comb, and ran back to the kitchen, closing the door after me. We had always kept one iron bucket of water warming on the range and another of cold water at hand. Now I set the bath on the floor and poured both buckets into it. Sitting in the tepid water, I soaped and scrubbed myself, then wrapped a towel about me and sat on a chair to brush my hair. There was no time to wash it, but I brushed steadily for five minutes to get rid of all sand and grease, then braided and coiled it in a bun.

All this time I could hear the murmur of voices from the sitting room, and I wondered how Mr. and Mrs. Fordyce were receiving the truth about me. I cut my toenails, put on my underwear, then dragged the bath out of the back door and tipped the water down the soak-away. I wiped it out, hung it on the wall, then put on my stockings, shoes, and dress and looked at myself in the mirror beside the sink. I could see only my head and shoulders, but it seemed to me that I looked quite a respectable person again.

I did not pause long, for I knew that within an hour or so I would be taken away from Shalimar, and I wanted to keep my mind too busy to think about that. For a few seconds I stood reminding myself of all that Rosemary had taught me about good manners and polite behavior. Then I opened the door, went into the sitting room, dropped a little curtsy, and said in my best voice, "Good morning, Mr. and Mrs. Fordyce. I do apologize for this delay in presenting myself. May I offer you a cup of tea? Or perhaps you have not yet taken breakfast?"

Three pairs of eyes gazed at me curiously, for even Luke seemed taken aback by the abrupt change. Then Mrs. Fordyce smiled and patted the seat beside her on the small settee. "Thank you, my dear," she said, "but we'll have a late breakfast in Lawton together. Come and sit down for a moment."

I obeyed, making sure to keep my knees together and my hands folded in my lap. Simon Fordyce said, "We came to collect you very early so that we could catch the nine o'clock train. I'm sorry our arrival caught you—er, unprepared."

I said, "Oh, please don't mention it." Then, as I could think of no other polite phrase to say, I looked to Luke for help.

"I've told Mr. and Mrs. Fordyce how you were lost or stolen

or abandoned as a baby, Meg," he said, "and how you grew up among the aborigines. I've also told them where you've been this past week or so." He shot a slightly puzzled glance at each in turn. "I must say that for such a surprising story they've taken it very calmly."

Simon Fordyce wagged his head solemnly. "Extraordinary events are not infrequent in my calling, Mr. Bowman. Since I preach the miraculous it is not difficult for me to accept the surprising. Isn't that so, Eliza?"

"Very well put, Simon," she said without looking away from me, then went on, "We agree with Mr. Bowman that at least for the time being it is best to say nothing to others about your background, Meg. It can serve no purpose and may well cause embarrassment."

"Yes, Mrs. Fordyce."

There was a little silence. The lady and her husband sat looking at me with a kind of baffled fascination. It was as if despite Mr. Fordyce's claim to be accustomed to extraordinary events, they both found it hard to credit that the girl sitting demurely before them had just traveled alone and barefoot and almost naked through the Australian outback for well over a hundred and fifty miles. No doubt it did seem amazing to those I had once called *walypala*, but to me it had not been a very demanding journey.

Mr. Fordyce broke the silence by dropping his hands on his knees and saying, "Well, we must be getting along. Have you packed your things, Meg?"

I said, "No, sir, but it won't take long. I have only a few things to put in a bag."

"Yes. Well, Mr. Bowman has provided some money, as promised, and we shall be able to set you up in clothes and other items in Perth."

I stood up and said, "Thank you, Luke. You're very kind."

He frowned. "It's little enough, and doesn't compare with what I owe for all you did for Rosemary. Now, go and put out any of her books you'd like to take with you on the kitchen table and I'll make a parcel of them for you. Then hurry and pack your things."

I was close to tears as I went to Rosemary's bookshelves and made a random choice of some favorite books: *Nicholas Nickleby* and *The Pickwick Papers* of Mr. Charles Dickens; *Plain Tales from the Hills* by Mr. Rudyard Kipling; *Tess of the D'Urbervilles* by Mr. Thomas Hardy; *The Adventures of Tom Sawyer* by Mr. Mark Twain, an American gentleman; Miss Jane Austen's *Pride and Prejudice*; and finally a collection of works by all the great poets, called *The Golden Treasury*.

Later I was glad that with the books I had chosen I could travel in imagination to England and India and America and could go back in time to the days Jane Austen and Charles Dickens had written about. I carried the books into the kitchen, added my scrapbook and *Peoples of the World* to the pile, then went to my bedroom and put some underclothes in a canvas bag together with my brush and comb and other toilet accessories, reflecting in a remote kind of way that I would have to give my fingernails some attention, for they were rough and chipped from my journey.

I wished I had a photograph of Rosemary, but at least I had the one of Luke that had been taken during my trip to Kalgoorlie, and this I put in my handbag between two pieces of stiff cardboard to prevent its bending. I put on my green bonnet, hung my coat over my arm, picked up my bag, and went back into the sitting room, clenching my teeth and trying to hold back tears that would betray the sadness and fear in my heart.

Luke was alone. He said, "They've taken your parcel of books and have gone to wait for you in the trap. I just wanted to say thank you again for what you did." He seemed to avoid looking directly at me, but I could see pain in his eyes now, and something else I could not understand, a haunted look of guilt.

I said, "It wasn't much after all you and Rosemary have done for me. Please take good care of yourself, Luke. I'll write to you from England."

"No," he said quickly. "No, don't write. I don't know where I'll be, and anyway"—he shrugged—"there's no point."

I swallowed hard but did not speak, for I could not trust my voice. He felt in his shirt pocket and said, "Like you to have this. . . . Well, I know Rosemary would have wished it." He held out his hand. On the palm was a small, heart-shaped silver pendant on a chain. I had seen it many times, for Rosemary had always put it on in the evening when all work was over.

Now I could not stop the tears running down my cheeks, but somehow I managed not to let my voice break as I said, "Oh, Luke, thank you. May I wear it now?"

"Yes. Of course."

"Will you put it on for me, please? My—my hands are not very steady."

He frowned. "All right. Turn round."

I obeyed, and when he had fastened the small clasp I slipped the pendant down inside my dress and turned back to him. "It's the most treasured gift I shall ever have."

"Glad you like it." He stood with hands resting on his hips, looking down at the floor between us. "Well . . . they'll be waiting. Good-bye, Meg."

"Good-bye, Luke." I stood looking at him, hoping he would take my hand, perhaps even kiss my cheek, but afraid to make any such move myself. After a few seconds in which he did not stir or lift his head my hope died. I picked up my coat and my bag and went out to where Mr. and Mrs. Fordyce waited with the trap.

EIGHT

TEN DAYS LATER AND AN HOUR AFTER DUSK I STOOD BY THE rail of a ship called *Callisto*, hundreds of miles from land, watching the green luminosity of the water foaming along the ship's side and wondering vaguely if I was dreaming a long, long dream from which I would wake to find myself curled up on the ground under a brushwood shelter with a dingo at my back for warmth.

If I had been plucked from the tribe and brought straight to this ship I think I would have been hysterical with shock and fear. The tiny community of Lawton had surprised me, the small township of Kalgoorlie had astonished me, and Perth had amazed me by its immensity both in size and in numbers of people. I thought my reading and studies had prepared me for whatever I might find as I began my journey with Mr. and Mrs. Fordyce, but the reality outran my imagination so greatly that it took my breath away.

More was to come when we reached the adjoining port of Fremantle. My first sight of the sea, that unbelievable amount of water stretching to the far horizon, was difficult enough for a desert-bred primitive to comprehend, but the ship itself, *Callisto*, was a miracle so gigantic that it left my mind benumbed. How was it that a great iron structure as big as a hundred houses could float on the water and move faster than a man might run, carrying hundreds of people living in unbelievable luxury?

I was never to see what must surely have been a huge kitchen to provide meal after meal for all those passengers, but I was constantly aware of the waiters bustling to and fro and of the many servants attending to our needs. There were bathrooms, lavatories, lamps everywhere that lit by electricity at the touch of a switch, and I had a cabin entirely to myself, with a bed and wardrobe, chair and small table, and even hot and cold water from taps over a basin.

There were different classes of passenger on the ship, but we were traveling first class, which surprised me a little because I had not thought of Mr. and Mrs. Fordyce as being rich people. It was some time before I learned about these different classes, because for the first two days at sea I suffered badly from seasickness. Between bouts I lay on my bed hating the sea and wishing I was back in the tribe even as an outcast freak, for I was convinced I was dying. However, by the third day I seemed to have got what Mr. Fordyce called my sea legs, and by the fourth I was eating heartily, thoroughly enjoying the sea and the sea air, and lost in dreamlike wonder at all the marvels of the great ship carrying us across the planet Earth.

In many ways I was excited by my entry into this astonishing new world, but underlying all such feelings there was an ache in my heart. I mourned Rosemary and missed her bitterly. I missed Luke also. There had been times when he had hurt me by his words and attitude, but there had been other times when we worked or talked together as comfortable friends with a flow of warmth between us.

Mr. and Mrs. Fordyce were very kind. In the early days of the voyage I dreaded being spoken to by any of the other passengers, either at meals in the dining room or when strolling or sitting on the deck, for it was all so new to me that I felt as great a freak among my fellow passengers as I had ever felt among the aborigines. During this time Mr. and Mrs. Fordyce were particularly careful to keep an eye on me and protect me from being drawn into a conversation where my ignorance might prove embarrassing, but by the end of the second week I began to lose my fears and feel quite at home.

Mr. Fordyce and his wife puzzled me. They were good company and got on well with our fellow passengers, but sometimes I almost felt they were acting a part, for when we were alone they seemed to relax and become quite mischievous, making whispered comments about various of our shipboard companions that were so apt I found it hard not to giggle.

Eliza Fordyce had a gift for finding a likeness between certain people and various creatures. "Here comes Miss Mole," she would whisper, "and I haven't a worm to offer her." Then, aloud: "Oh, good afternoon, Miss Tenby. What a delightful hat. How I envy you your milliner." And when the woman had walked on, flattered: "The one fruit missing from that confection is a banana."

I had seen only pictures of moles, bulldogs, walruses, and other creatures to whom she likened some of our fellow passengers, but I found her comparisons very accurate, and one day when we were sitting on deck with her husband playing a game of dominoes I said, "Do I look like an alley cat, Mrs. Fordyce?"

She stared, looked at Mr. Fordyce, then at me again. "Whoever told you that, Meg?"

"It was Luke. Mr. Bowman. An Irish alley cat, he said, but it was mainly when I was angry about something."

She laughed. "Well, I'm sure he wasn't talking of your morals, dear, but he was right about looks. With that red hair and green eyes and turned-up nose, I think you might well be compared with a rather dangerous-looking stray, especially if you were angry."

"A stray?"

Simon Fordyce said, "An undomesticated cat, Meg. A stray creature surviving without human help." He studied me thoughtfully. "Yes. That fits. Were you upset to be called an alley cat?"

"Oh no. I was only ever upset if Luke was annoyed with me. It wasn't often," I went on quickly. "He was really so kind to me, but of course he was desperately worried about Rosemary, and I didn't know that."

"Of course," said Eliza Fordyce gently. She picked up a domino, then glanced to one side. "Here comes Mr. Rabbit," she said, lowering her voice, "accompanied by his spouse, Mrs. Bloodhound." Next moment a small nervous man holding the arm of a large lady with heavy jowls came by.

Mr. Fordyce said benevolently, "Good morning, good morning." polite greetings were exchanged, and when the couple had passed on he muttered severely, "Behave yourself, Eliza. Remember my calling."

"That is my constant endeavor, Simon dear," she replied piously, then closed one eye at me as she played her domino. I suppressed a smile, but was at once reminded of the occasion when she had winked at me after dealing so surprisingly with the drunken man at the prayer meeting. Again I felt puzzled at how different Mr. and Mrs. Fordyce were from any of the other clerics and their wives I had seen in Lawton. Perhaps, I reflected, it was because they came from England. Perhaps vicars and their wives were different there. It was not until we had been at sea for almost four weeks that I by chance made a discovery about Simon and Eliza Fordyce that was astonishing, and another about myself that was alarming.

THE FIRST STAGE OF OUR JOURNEY WAS FROM FREMANTLE TO A place called Colombo, which was the capital of the island of Ceylon. This took thirteen days, and once I had got my sea legs I loved to stand and study the big map of the world on a wall near the purser's office, watching the line of our progress marked on it each day, and memorizing the names of countries and big cities and ports.

We were able to go ashore in Colombo for a few hours, and here I found myself in a world quite different from the three I

had so far known—the tribe, Shalimar, and the floating world
of *Callisto*. Once the carriage we hired had taken us beyond the
port area of Colombo I was fascinated by the teeming numbers
of people, the jabber of voices, the clothes so bright and color-
ful, the street stalls and the bazaars.

There came a moment when I made Simon Fordyce laugh as
he stood waiting with me on a corner while Eliza Fordyce bar-
gained firmly but amiably for some silk material that had caught
her eye. I had my own eyes closed when he said anxiously, "Are
you all right, Meg?"

I said, "Yes, thank you, Mr. Fordyce. I'm really enjoying
myself."

"But you have your eyes closed."

I opened them and said apologetically. "Oh dear. I'm sorry."
I looked about me to make sure none of our fellow passengers
was near, then went on, "There are so many wonderful new
smells, and I was just trying to—to make a note of them in my
mind."

He stared. "Smells?"

"Yes. Where I grew up it was very important."

"Lord, yes, I remember now. Luke Bowman told us you can
scent water and animal trails and even people." He sniffed ap-
praisingly, then grinned. "Some of the smells here don't seem
particularly attractive."

I smiled and shrugged. "Aborigines don't think of smells as
being good or bad in the way that white people do."

I knew from my reading that there were many elephants in
Ceylon, and I had hoped to see one, but Simon Fordyce pointed
out that any tame elephants would be mainly used for work
outside the cities and towns, so I would almost certainly be
disappointed. In this, to my great good fortune, he proved
wrong, for later we saw an elephant that had been brought to
the docks for some special purpose. We were able to study this
huge and astonishing creature that I had seen only in photographs and drawings till now, and I had the opportunity to take
note of its very distinctive and quite pleasant scent.

From Colombo we sailed for nine days to reach Aden, which
was hot and dry and dusty, more like the land I had grown up
in and therefore less strange and interesting to me than Colombo. When *Callisto* sailed on from Aden we entered the humid
and oily heat of the Red Sea, and it was here, two nights later,
that I discovered the truth about the Reverend Simon Fordyce
and his wife, Eliza.

At two o'clock one morning, I lay in my bed unable to sleep.
The cabin seemed airless, and even though I had taken off my
nightdress and lay with only a towel across my stomach I was
moist with sweat. At last I climbed out of bed, put on the nightdress and my dressing gown, and peered cautiously out into the
corridor. All was quiet, and I had only to go a few paces before
reaching the swinging doors that opened onto the promenade
deck. Here, by a big locker containing deck chairs, I found a
deep patch of shadow and stood there breathing deeply.

The air was still hot and moist, but there seemed more life in
it than the air in my cabin had offered. After a while I moved
along a little way to a corner of the superstructure and sat down,
hoping that if I spent an hour here on deck I might be able to
sleep when I returned to my cabin. I had barely seated myself
comfortably when I heard a voice so close above my head that
it made me jump. A moment later I realized it was Simon Fordyce's voice, and that I was sitting under the window of the
cabin he occupied with his wife, next to my own. The louvered
shutter was closed, but the window itself was open, a faint light
penetrating the drawn curtain.

"I don't believe it!" were the words I had heard, spoken with
a note of indignation. Then there was silence but for faint sounds
I could not identify, a muttering from Simon Fordyce, a laugh
from his wife. I was about to move, for I did not want to eaves-
drop, when Simon Fordyce said, "Ah, damn it, woman! Forty
points for a capot! How the hell do you do it if you're not false-
dealing the cards?"

Eliza Fordyce said, "I don't need to false-deal when you
choose to sink a couple of stiff brandies in this humidity, sonny-

boy. All I need is a clear head, and that's another five guineas you owe me."

A chuckle. Then: "Cut you double or quits, my beauty."

"Not when I've just seen you put a crimp in that ace, you crafty twister."

I sank back with my mouth open, stunned. I had understood only part of what had been said, but of one thing I was certain. English vicars and their wives might be different from others I had known, but they could not possibly be *this* different! Surely they did not gamble at cards, and cheat, and use the strange words I had just heard.

There was a little silence broken only by a yawn from the man and the rippling sound of cards being shuffled, as I had seen the whist players shuffle them in the ship's card room. Then Mrs. Fordyce exhaled a long sigh and said, "God, it's sticky."

"Try taking your nightdress off."

"Don't start that, it's too damn hot. And while we're about it, don't get any ideas about young Meg."

"Ideas?" Mr. Fordyce sounded surprised, and I was startled myself.

Mrs. Fordyce said quite amiably, "I've spotted you looking at her in a particular way sometimes, Simon. One eyebrow raised, the other eye half screwed up, very speculative. I've known you long enough to recognize that look. You're interested."

There was a hint of laughter in his voice as he said, "Well, I don't think I'd realized that. But now you mention it, Eliza, my dear . . . why not? I'm a free man, am I not?"

"You're trying to provoke me so I'll hit you, and then we'll get into a struggle, and we both know how that will end up, but it's still too damn hot. However, as a matter of interest I'll tell you why you're not to get any ideas about Meg. For one thing, she's part of a job we're being paid for—in fact, she *is* the job, and it's foolish to indulge in any distraction. Secondly, the man in the dark room wouldn't like it, and if you make an enemy of him you're a bigger fool than I take you for. Thirdly, I've come to have a great respect for that girl and I'm very fond of her, so anyone who takes advantage of her innocence in our civilized world will have *me* for an enemy. And finally, sonny-boy, *I'm* your woman, so look no further."

Part of a job? Man in the dark room? Great respect? I'm your woman?

There was so much to baffle me in so few words that my benumbed mind could barely take it all in. Clearly Simon Fordyce was no vicar, and Eliza was not his wife, but beyond this I could not fathom what her words had meant. Then Simon Fordyce spoke again.

"To be honest," he said thoughtfully, "I hadn't yet realized that I was attracted. I thought I was merely intrigued by a quite astonishing girl. However, I take your point as regards the job, as regards the unwisdom of annoying our enigmatic employer, and as regards your liking for young Meg, which I share. But on your last point, my little treasure, let us remember that although we have long been professional partners and our frequent pretense of the married state offers us splendid opportunity for mutual pleasure, there is no commitment between us and never has been. So for you to claim that you are my woman is no more valid than for me to claim that I am your man."

"Brandy always makes you pompous," said the woman I had thought was Eliza Fordyce, "and it's too hot to argue. Do you want another hand of piquet?"

I did not hear the answer, for I had risen and was moving toward the swinging doors, my thoughts in turmoil. One thing was clear to me: I could not let the situation continue, could not go on day after day pretending ignorance. Besides, I wanted to know what "the job" was, and who was the man in the dark room, and what was to happen to me when we reached England.

A few seconds later I was tapping on the door of the cabin. After a moment or two it was opened by Simon Fordyce, wearing a silk dressing gown over pajamas. Beyond him I could see his companion, also in a dressing gown, her hair down and tied back loosely at the nape of her neck, sitting at the small table

by the window, her hands casually folded over what I knew to
be a pack of cards.

"Meg?" Simon Fordyce stared in surprise. "Are you unwell?"

"No." My hands were clasped tightly in front of me, and
my whispering voice was jerky. "I'm sorry. I couldn't sleep,
and I went out on deck and sat down, but I didn't realize it was
under your cabin window, and then I heard you talking. I didn't
set out to listen, but then I heard about . . . about me being *the
job*, and about *the man in the dark room*, and—" I looked past
him. "And about you and Mrs.—oh dear, I don't know what to
call her now."

He pursed his lips in a soundless whistle and stepped back.
"You'd better come in, Meg," he said quietly.

I moved forward, and as he closed the door after me the
woman at the table gave me a rueful smile and said, "Keep to
Mrs. Fordyce in public, Meg dear. In private you can make it
Eliza and Simon." She reached out her arms. "Come here."

As I went to her I could not help thinking how I envied her
that smooth oval face, that golden hair, and those large blue
eyes. It struck me that in her pose as a vicar's wife she had
somehow contrived to disguise how beautiful she was. Now she
took my hands and made me bend to receive a kiss on the cheek.

"I'm glad you heard," she said. "Now we've no choice but
to tell you as much as we can, though I'm afraid that's not much.
Take Simon's chair. He can sit on the bed."

I obeyed, feeling greatly relieved by her manner, for I had
feared there might be anger at my discovery. Simon Fordyce
was closing the window. "We'll just have to swelter for a while,"
he said, moving to the bed, "in case anyone else decides to sit
under our window." He sat down and rubbed his chin thoughtfully. "Hard to know where to begin. I suppose the simplest
way to start is by saying that Eliza and I work for a man who
sent us out from England to make sure you were protected."

I stared. "Protected? From what?"

He gave an apologetic shrug. "That's one of several things

we don't know, Meg. But isn't it true that a few months ago a man came to Shalimar and tried to kill you?''

"You mean Sid Buller?'' I shook my head in perplexity. "Well, I'm not sure he intended to kill me. Later everyone thought it was . . . something else.''

"Rape?'' said Eliza bluntly. "Rosemary didn't think so. She saw the swine chasing you with a knife, and she told me she was sure he meant to kill you.''

I said, "But even so, what you tell me seems impossible. How can anybody in England know I exist, let alone send you out to protect me? And anyway, Sid Buller was safely in prison before you arrived, so he was no longer a danger.''

Simon Fordyce sighed. "I don't know how our employer became aware of your existence,'' he said, "but as for protecting you, I assume Sid Buller didn't try to kill you for any reason of his own. He was hired by somebody, and that somebody might well take steps to try again.''

I looked from Simon Fordyce to Eliza, still completely baffled. "It doesn't make sense,'' I said. "There's nobody in the world with any reason to have me killed.''

Eliza had been idly shuffling the cards, dealing some out in rows, and gathering them up again. Now she glanced at me and said, "Meg, did you ever know a man named Tasker?''

I stared in new surprise. "Well, when Luke took me to Kalgoorlie one day we met a man called Harry Tasker, a newspaper reporter, but it was just a matter of him and Luke exchanging a few words. I didn't really know him.''

Simon said, "Did you know that Tasker returned to England and was murdered there, in London?''

I nodded. "Yes, I happened to see it in a newspaper one day when I was reading for Rosemary.'' I frowned at the recollection. "That was just moments before Sid Buller appeared, and I don't think we ever talked about it later. I was too busy with fetching the police and looking after Rosemary because she'd made herself ill trying to help me.'' I looked at Simon. "But what has Mr. Tasker being murdered in London got to do with me?''

He shook his head. ''I don't know, Meg. I only know it *has* something to do with this whole business, because our employer engaged us to investigate Tasker shortly before sending us out to Australia, but we didn't get very far because the man was murdered.''

By this time I was so confused that I found it difficult to frame a coherent question, and in the silence Eliza said, ''When we found you living at Shalimar under Luke Bowman's wing we were satisfied that you were well protected. He didn't intend to leave you or Rosemary exposed to another Sid Buller.'' She hesitated, and her hands toying with the cards grew still as she said gently, ''But we were concerned about what would happen when Rosemary died. We knew from the doctor that it couldn't be long delayed. Luke knew it, too, and he asked if we would take you home and find you a position in England. He wanted to be sure you were in good hands, and that's what our employer wanted also. He telegraphed us to take charge of you when the time came.''

I looked down at the cards on the table and said, ''I think I was the only one who didn't know Rosemary was dying. She knew well enough. Did anybody ask her what she wanted done about me when it happened?''

Simon and Eliza exchanged a look. Then she said, ''We couldn't ask that, Meg. We pretended to be a preacher and his wife, as we have done on other occasions, because it allowed us to do things and ask questions that would seem out of order otherwise. It allowed Simon to announce that we would come out and visit you at Shalimar—without being invited. It allowed him to question Dr. Vernon about Rosemary's health and to discuss it with Luke Bowman. But even as a man of the cloth he could hardly talk to Rosemary herself about what was to happen with you when she passed on.''

I said with an ache in my heart, ''No, I suppose not. But she wanted me to take care of Luke, and I gave my promise. She even wanted me to marry him.''

There was a silence in the cabin but for the distant throbbing of the ship's engines. Then Eliza said quietly, ''A deathbed promise can't always be kept, Meg. Rosemary would know you could only keep it if Luke assented.''

''Yes. I didn't think of that at the time, but anyway I would have promised her anything.'' I sat trying to collect my thoughts for a while, and then I said, ''So this is as much as you can tell me? A man in London sent you all the way to Australia to see that I was protected and to take me under your care because he believes somebody wants to kill me?''

Simon nodded and mopped his face with a handkerchief. ''That's about it, Meg.''

''It doesn't seem very likely.''

Eliza reached across the table and touched my hand. ''No, it doesn't. But what we've told you is true.''

The atmosphere in the cabin was very close, and I longed to be outside, even in the heavy air of the Red Sea, but there were still questions in my mind. I said, ''Please, may I ask . . . who are you? You're not Mr. and Mrs. Fordyce, and you're not a vicar and his wife, but you've spoken about someone you call your employer, and I'd really like to know . . . well, what you are.''

Eliza put the pack in front of me and said, ''Cut them.'' Wonderingly I obeyed. She picked up the pack and began to deal a row of cards faceup. ''Our names are real,'' she said. ''That fellow on the bed is Simon Fordyce. I'm Eliza Fordyce because I changed my surname a good few years ago now. It's convenient for when we're supposed to be man and wife, or sometimes brother and sister. The name I was born with doesn't matter.''

She studied the cards, frowning a little. ''Simon is a doctor's son, but he was orphaned when he was six, and brought up by a maiden aunt who spent a number of years beating a decent education into him, for which he ought to be grateful but isn't.''

I turned my head to look at Simon and found he had lain back on the bed with eyes closed and was dozing. Eliza went on, "At sixteen he left his maiden aunt when she announced her intention of having him articled to a solicitor, a notion that horrified him. This was only one cause of his going, the other being that he was discovered to have seduced the young wife of an elderly professor at the university near the town where he lived. Do you understand what I mean by seduced, Meg?"

"Yes. Rosemary explained words like that to me."

"A woman of good sense. Of course, the sleeping beauty there vows that it was the other way round and *he* was the victim of seduction, but I've never believed that." Eliza looked up from the cards with a wry smile. "He ran away to sea, and I met him eight years later, when he was twenty-four and I was eighteen. He'd left the sea and was working for our employer by then, so I joined him, and we've been partners for the past ten years."

I watched her lay out another row of cards, vaguely aware that she was not playing patience, as I had first imagined. When I realized she had finished speaking I said, "Aren't you going to tell me about yourself, Eliza?"

She glanced up, and I caught a wickedly mischievous sparkle in her blue eyes. "Me? I'm a vicar's daughter, dear. How else would I have learned to play the harmonium?"

I gasped, and despite my confusion at all I had just learned I had to stifle a little burst of laughter. "I'm sorry. I expect you're joking," I said.

"Not at all." She gave me a look of mock dignity. "My father intended me to be a boy called Elijah, but had to put up with a girl he christened Eliza. Oh, it's true enough, Meg. He was one of those big hearty vicars, and he never forgave me for not being a boy, though I tried hard to be like one when I was young, just as you told us you did when you were with the aborigine children. My poor mother was a mouse who simply fawned on my father. I don't think there can be much of her in me."

She frowned at the cards again, as if annoyed with them, and moved some of them about. "By the time I was sixteen I decided I was a girl and that it was a waste of time trying to be anything else. Then I read something in a magazine one day and became completely stage-struck, convinced I was a combination of Sarah Bernhardt, Eleanora Duse, and Sarah Siddons, but somewhat better. So I ran away to become an actress."

She made a mild grimace. "We seem to have a lot in common, Meg, except that you had a sensible reason for running away, and mine was stupid. Well, in the next year or two I learned a great deal that I would never have known if I'd stayed at the vicarage. There was much of it that I doubt my father knew. I also discovered very early on that I wasn't much of an actress, but I did have a pretty figure and a fair voice for singing sentimental ballads, so I managed to get a few engagements at the bottom of the bill in the cheaper music halls."

Eliza stared indignantly at the cards, then at me, then back at the cards again. "Damned fortune-telling nonsense," she said. "That's quite impossible. What was I saying?"

"About singing in music halls."

"Ah yes. Well, that's where Simon found me, and he had a job to do for his employer that called for him to have a young wife, or at least a girl to pass as his wife, so we just . . . came together then, and we've remained together ever since." She laughed and swept the cards together. "What my father would call 'living in sin.' "

I said, "But you don't mind?"

Eliza looked at the man on the bed, then at me, and I glimpsed a shadow deep in her eyes. "Oh, I mind all right," she said softly. "But in ten years he's never asked me to marry him, and I'll be damned if I'll ask *him*."

We sat in silence for a few moments. Then I said, "Thank you for telling me all this. I'm still confused, and I don't understand why you were sent from England, but I'm glad to know about you and Mr. Fordyce—I mean Simon. When I was on deck and heard you speaking, you mentioned 'the man in the dark room.' Is that the one who is your employer?"

Eliza nodded. "That's right."

"Well . . . who *is* he?"

"I've often wondered myself." She reached out with a foot, the dressing gown falling back from one long bare leg as she kicked Simon gently on the hip. "Hey, wake up, Your Reverence. It's bad manners to fall asleep with two beautiful women in your bedroom."

Simon Fordyce blinked, propped himself on an elbow, gazed at me in puzzlement for a moment, then sat up and yawned. "My apologies, ladies," he said. "It's the result of a clear conscience and pure living. I sleep the sleep of a little child."

"It's the result of not having any conscience at all, more likely," said Eliza.

"A cruel thrust, my beauty. What have you two been talking about?"

"I've told Meg about you and about me. Now she's just asked who the man in the dark room is."

"Ah, now there's a question." Simon stood up and paced across the little cabin. "I can't give you an answer because I don't know, Meg. He first engaged my services through a solicitor in the Middle Temple, in London. Later I met him but never saw him. When he has work for me, I'm summoned by the solicitor and I'm ushered into a small room, or office perhaps, which is in darkness. All I can make out is the shape of a man sitting in an armchair there. He gives me instructions in a voice I can only describe as beautiful. If I have any questions, I ask them. Some he may answer, some he may decline to answer. Then I return to Eliza in our London flat and we set out on whatever new venture has been set before us."

I said, "And that's all you know of him? You've never tried to find out his name or have sight of him?"

Simon shook his head. "Never. Eliza is beset by curiosity. I prefer the mystery. To judge by the work we do for him and the money he pays, it's safe to assume he's very rich."

"What sort of things do you do for him?" I half smiled. "I

mean, apart from going to Australia to protect a girl nobody has ever heard of?''

Simon paused by the table, felt the pack of cards there with a delicate touch, and cut an ace. "We do whatever Mr. Josiah Smith wants," he said with a nod of satisfaction as he replaced the cards. "That isn't his real name, of course; it's an assumed name that we've been told to use when dealing with him or with his solicitor. Sometimes a job might take a week, sometimes many months. What have our last three jobs been, Eliza?"

She sat with chin on hand, watching him quietly with an expression I could not interpret, and said, "Well, not counting our investigation of Harry Tasker, there was the diamond mine those people had salted in South Africa, and before that we were given the job of ruining a particularly unpleasant gambler in the South of France, and before that there was the business in Rome when you almost got caught stealing that icon from Bonello."

I was startled, and said, "Stealing?"

"Recovering." Eliza smiled as she spoke. "It had already been stolen from a church."

I did not understand this, but thought it would be impolite to pursue the question, so I said, "Why did some people put salt in a diamond mine?"

Simon laughed. "No. In simple terms they took a lot of diamond-bearing ore and put it in a hole in the ground to make it appear to be a rich diamond mine, which they then tried to sell."

"To Mr. Smith?" I asked.

"I've no idea, Meg. He didn't say."

I thought about a stolen icon and a ruined gambler, and I said, "He seems a kind person, sending you to look after me, but are all the things you do for him good things?"

Simon lifted an eyebrow. "We rarely know what his purpose is, so again I've no idea. We perform the tasks he sets us, and he pays us for doing so. Beggars can't be choosers."

"But . . . well, you're not a beggar, are you?"

Eliza laughed. Simon said, "No. But I'm not a vicar either.

I'm a laborer in the vineyard, and I do whatever I'm called upon to do."

I said, "Please excuse me. I didn't mean to criticize."

He studied me curiously for a moment, then said, "In a devious world I find you remarkably direct. When you heard us talking and realized we're not what we pretend to be, you might well have kept quiet hoping to find out more. You might even have been afraid. But you came straight here and told us what you heard. You're an uncommon girl, Meg."

"Am I? I suppose that's because I've had an uncommon life. Then I was taught by Rosemary, and I'm sure she was a very uncommon teacher. Do you think I shall see the man in the dark room when we arrive in England?"

Simon shook his head. "You're not going to England. We're taking you to Switzerland, to a place called a finishing school. It's where wealthy people send their daughters after they've left school in England, to make them into proper young ladies."

I looked at him in astonishment. "Switzerland? A special kind of school? But why is he sending me there?"

Simon smiled. "He hasn't said. When we found you with Luke and Rosemary Bowman we reported by telegraph that you were in good hands. After visiting Shalimar we realized that Rosemary was very ill, and we later made arrangements with Luke to take charge of you when the worst happened. He sent for us when she died, and we telegraphed our employer for instructions. He replied that we were to take you to Clairmont Finishing School in Neuchâtel, where all arrangements would be made to receive you."

I said rather dazedly, "You spoke of wealthy parents. Won't this cost your employer a lot of money?"

"Certainly it will."

"But you don't know why he is doing it?"

"We really don't, Meg."

A trickle of sweat rolled down my brow and stung my eye, but I was mentally in such a muddle I barely noticed it. "What will you do after you've taken me to this finishing school?'' I asked.

''Eliza and I? Oh, we shall go back to England and amuse ourselves until Josiah Smith's solicitor tells us that the man in the dark room has a new task for us.''

I rubbed my eye, feeling my heart sink as I tried to see into the future. I had lost Luke and Rosemary, I would soon lose Simon and Eliza. Alone and without friends, I was about to enter yet another world that would be completely strange to me, and perhaps I would have to learn yet another language. It was only three years since I had been Mitji the freak aborigine, and sometimes I was still swept by a primitive fear of the endless and complicated demands of civilization. Added to this there was now an unknown man in a dark room who appeared to have taken charge of me because my life was threatened. It was all very frightening, and I had to make a great effort not to let fear show in my face.

''How long shall I be at this school?'' I asked.

Simon rolled his eyes in comic despair, and it was Eliza who answered. ''We don't know that either, Meg. We only know that we are to give you the solicitor's address and you may write to Mr. Josiah Smith, care of that address, whenever you please, to let him know how you are getting on, and if there is anything you need.''

She hesitated, then went on, ''Simon doesn't like me to guess at our employer's motives, but I've taken no vows of obedience to Simon or any man, so I guess as much as I please, and I think he's sending you to the school in Switzerland because it's a good place for you to hide.''

''Hide?'' I echoed blankly.

''Yes, dear. Don't look so bewildered. You have a good brain, so make use of it. If somebody hired Sid Buller to make away with you, that same somebody might want to keep track of you with a view to another attempt. As a matter of fact, a man embarked with us at Fremantle who very much aroused our suspicions. We're sure he was engaged to keep track of you;

that's why we've been careful to let everyone know that you're coming to England with us. But in fact we shall unexpectedly leave the ship at Marseilles, and go to Neuchâtel by train.''

I said slowly, "Was it that thin man with big ears and a small black moustache, who dined at the next table to us? Mr. Cranwell?''

Simon sat up straight, looking surprised. "That's right. But how did you know?''

"He was in my cabin only a few days after we left Fremantle. It was during the day, and I'd locked the door, but he must have got in somehow, and I think he looked through my belongings.''

Simon said, "How the devil do you know that?''

"I picked up his scent when I came back to the cabin. I know the scent of the cabin steward and the cleaner, but this was different, like the scent of Mr. Cranwell at the next table. It seemed impossible, so I thought I must have made a mistake, but perhaps I didn't.''

"I keep forgetting about your peculiar abilities," Simon said thoughtfully. "No, I'm pretty certain you didn't make a mistake, Meg. Be sure to tell me if anything like that happens again.''

"Very well. But I don't see how he can have been hired to follow me," I said. "He left the ship at Colombo.''

"Not of his own free will, dear," said Eliza. "On our last evening ashore there he was waylaid by footpads in one of the alleys behind the bazaar, and so the poor man missed the boat. Ships never wait when it's time to sail, you know.''

For a moment I could not quite make out what was puzzling me about Eliza's words. Then light dawned, and I said, "But if he missed the boat, how can you know that he was waylaid by footpads?''

"Simon saw it in a vision," said Eliza solemnly, and winked.

I sat feeling suddenly drained of energy. It was three o'clock in the morning, I had hardly slept, and in the past hour I had undergone a whole series of shocks and surprises. My brain seemed to have stopped working, and I could think of no more questions to ask about the mysterious Mr. Josiah Smith, or about my unknown enemy if one really existed, or about my own future.

I said, "Thank you for telling me all this. If you will excuse me, I think I'll go to bed now."

Eliza nodded, and I saw sympathy in her eyes. "Try to sleep, Meg," she said. "Leave thinking about it all until later. Good night, dear."

I wished them both good night and went to the door. With the window shut, the cabin had become very hot, and I vaguely planned to spend ten minutes cooling down on deck before going to my own cabin. I was just about to open the door when a random thought struck me. It had little to do with all that we had just been speaking about, but it concerned my first sight of Simon Fordyce and his wife, when he had preached that remarkable sermon about the sins of the flesh.

"If you want people to think you're a vicar," I said, "why do you preach the kind of sermon I heard in Lawton? Luke could hardly believe his ears. The way you spoke was much more likely to excite people into doing the things you were supposed to be preaching against."

Simon Fordyce fingered his chin. "I suppose it just comes out that way," he said solemnly.

Eliza gave a sniff of contempt. "It comes out that way because he's a wicked devil with the gift of the gab who can't resist getting respectable people thoroughly stirred up, that's the truth of it."

"They enjoy it, my sweet," said Simon blandly. "You should see the women's faces when I announce that I have lust in my heart, and the men's faces when I tell them you have lust in yours."

"I see them, all right. One of these days you'll go too far, sonny-boy, and then there'll be trouble. I should think your disgraceful sense of humor has already piled up enough trouble for you in the next world without inviting any more in this."

He wagged his head with mock gravity. "There speaks the

vicar's daughter. Fear not, dear Eliza. I intend to repent in due course, but not just yet.''

She stood up and said sharply, ''Don't be cynical and irreverent in front of Meg. I won't have Rosemary's teachings undermined.''

His face changed. ''Ah. Yes. I'm sorry, Eliza.''

She came to me by the door. ''Go to bed, dear. I know you won't speak of this to anybody, but do try to behave with us as you have done all along, and in particular don't mention a word about our leaving the ship at Marseilles. We managed to leave Mr. Cranwell behind in Colombo, but he may not be the only one keeping an eye on you.''

I said almost desperately, ''I'm a girl who grew up among aborigines and only came out of the bush three years ago. How can I possibly *matter* so much to people I've never seen or heard of before?''

Eliza sighed and took my hands. ''We don't know,'' she said. ''All we can be sure of is that you *do* matter very much indeed.''

Half an hour later, still awake, I lay on my bed with a dozen different tentacles of thought turning in my mind. The man in the dark room . . . Mr. Tasker murdered in London . . . all that I had just learned about Simon and Eliza Fordyce. Who was my unknown enemy? Did one really exist? And had Sid Buller truly intended to kill me that day? Rosemary had been very sure of it. If she was right, had he been sent to do so? If she was wrong, there was not a shred of evidence to indicate that I had an enemy, or to support the story Simon and Eliza Fordyce had just told me. In which case, did the mysterious Josiah Smith really exist? And if so, what did he want of me?

After a while I got up, put on the light, and went to the little cabin wardrobe. On one of the shelves was a brown paper parcel, still unopened, containing seven of Rosemary's books together with *Peoples of the World* and the scrapbook I had begun to keep as soon as I was able to read a little. So far on the voyage I had borrowed books from the ship's library for my reading, but now I felt I wanted something familiar and well loved to stop my mind churning restlessly away on questions I could not hope to answer.

I untied the parcel, then stared in dismay. My scrapbook was missing. In it had been all kinds of pictures and pieces of interest I had cut from the old newspapers and magazines Luke brought in from Lawton, and tucked at the back was the page I had cut from the *Strand* magazine, showing three photographs of the lady who as a girl of my own age had looked very much like me. I had felt embarrassed at the idea of pasting it in my scrapbook, but at the same time unwilling to throw it away.

Now both the page of photographs and the scrapbook were lost. I sat on my heels, trying to remember the morning when I had hastily packed my belongings. I was sure I had included my scrapbook with the books of Rosemary's I had chosen, but it was Luke who had parceled them up for me while I folded and packed my clothes. He must have left the scrapbook out by mistake.

I felt close to tears at the loss, for this was a precious souvenir. Rosemary had helped me in the beginning, and the scrapbook was very much bound up with my memories of her, but Luke would no doubt throw it away when he sold Shalimar and cleared everything from the house. Sadly I set aside *Nicholas Nickleby* to browse in, packed the other books away, sat myself on the bed propped up with pillows, and opened the chosen book at random. The miraculous light from the glass bulb above the bed lit up the page, and I began to read.

> Into these bowls Mrs. Squeers, assisted by the hungry servant, poured a brown composition which looked like diluted pincushions without the covers, and was called porridge. A minute wedge of brown bread was inserted in each bowl, and when they had eaten their porridge by means of the bread, the boys ate the bread itself, and had finished their breakfast; whereupon Mr. Squeers said, in a solemn voice, ''For what we have received may the Lord make us truly thankful!''—and went away to his own.

Dotheboys Hall. A dreadful place. Very different from the school for daughters of wealthy parents I was soon to join in Switzerland, I reflected, my mind wandering from the page. I had never seen snow except in pictures, and could not easily imagine a place like Switzerland. With my limited experience of the civilized world I found it very difficult to visualize myself arriving at Clairmont Finishing School there.

I would have found even more difficulty in visualizing the startling circumstances under which I would one day depart from it.

NINE

I BECAME A PUPIL AT CLAIRMONT FINISHING SCHOOL IN JULY and remained there for ten months and eight days. July was a winter month in Australia, but I had long ago learned from Rosemary that it was a summer month in Europe. During the first few days I was quite terrified, for I found myself among girls as strange to me as if they had come from another planet, and I was evidently just as strange to them.

Rosemary had taught me good manners, but my companions here seemed to have countless small ways of behavior that it was necessary to adopt if you were not to be treated as something of an outcast. To me, some of their ways seemed unkind or ill-mannered, and I found myself completely at a loss. I was not helped by the fact that although almost half the girls were English they all spoke French to each other for much of the time.

Simon and Eliza Fordyce brought me to the study of Mam'selle Herault, principal of the school, on the Sunday afternoon of our arrival in Neuchâtel. They had already told me that I had been registered at the school as Meg Smith, ward and niece of Mr. Josiah Smith, care of Messrs. Molton, Hardacre, and Lane, solicitors of the Middle Temple. As far as Mam'selle Herault knew, I had been born and brought up in Western Australia by my parents, who had recently died in a boating accident.

A porter took my case and small trunk, and a maid was sent with him to unpack for me in my bedroom while Mam'selle received us in her study. Mam'selle Herault was a thin lady of about forty with a very severe manner and a way of tilting her head back to gaze down her nose as she spoke. She informed us that Clairmont was a finishing school only for young ladies from the very *best* of families, and she trusted that I would feel at home in joining them.

I would have been frightened of Mam'selle Herault if it had not been for Eliza, who had changed her own manner to become a quite different kind of vicar's wife, not in the least overawed and ready to match comment for comment and question for question. Simon had also changed his manner to become dull and pompous, leaving everything to his "wife" and simply nodding ponderous approval now and again. I might have laughed if I had not been so nervous.

Mam'selle spoke good English with a quaint accent that I found pleasing to my ear. When the preliminary skirmishes made clear that the wife of the Reverend Simon Fordyce was not to be subdued or made to feel inferior, Mam'selle seemed to become less formidable. She asked me some questions about the voyage, which I tried to answer sensibly, then went on to tell us that there were at present twenty-two young ladies at Clairmont, with a teaching staff of five and a very adequate staff of servants. This being Sunday afternoon and a fine day, the young ladies had been taken to Lake Neuchâtel, only a few hundred meters away, where those who wished could bathe while others went boating.

"Both activities are of course closely supervised," said Mam'selle. "Tents are provided for bathers, and the boats have awnings to afford protection from the sun. Do you swim, Meg?"

"Er . . . no, Mam'selle."

"Then perhaps you may learn. We have two or three young ladies who are swimmers and might give you instruction. Our doctor highly recommends it for health reasons, and it has become a most acceptable diversion for the better class of person these days. You do not have a bathing dress?''

"No, Mam'selle." I felt stupidly guilty at having to admit it.

Eliza said, "My husband and I will be staying at the Hotel du Lac for a few days until Meg is properly settled, Mam'selle Herault, and in that time I will take her shopping for whatever she may require. The clothes she brought from Australia do not provide an adequate wardrobe, and although I know that Mr. Josiah Smith has provided you with ample funds for whatever Meg may need during her attendance here, I wish to see her fully provided for myself before we relinquish our responsibility for her."

"Quite so, Mrs. Fordyce. Now perhaps you would care to see Meg's room and to make a tour of the school, so that you may reassure Mr. Josiah Smith as to its excellence. I understand he will not be coming to view it himself?"

"That is our understanding also," Eliza said with a gracious smile, "is it not, Simon dear?"

Her "husband" appeared to rouse himself from something of a doze and grunted, "Eh? Er . . . yes. Absolutely."

Mam'selle rose from behind her desk, giving me a slightly worried look. "I do recommend the purchase of a parasol," she said. "A pale complexion is desirable in a young lady, and Meg seems to have allowed her face to receive too much sun."

If ever I went swimming, I thought, my body would be seen to have received too much sun also. Eliza must have had the same thought, for she said without hesitation and with great authority, "Meg's coloring is a matter of pigmentation, Mam'selle, not of sun. According to the specialist her parents consulted on this matter she has a slight but quite harmless excess of a corpuscular secretion which produces the effect of tanning by the sun. To my mind it is desirable in her case, since it makes the freckles on her nose and cheeks less obvious than they would be if her skin were pale."

Simon Fordyce nodded. "Corpuscular secretion," he echoed vaguely.

Mam'selle looked wise and said, "Quite so."

I was to share a large bedroom with the Honorable Emily Fortescue, a plump girl with brown hair and a sulky manner, daughter of an English nobleman. I first met her that evening at supper when I was formally introduced to the rest of the pupils, and she made it plain from the beginning that I was unwelcome as her room companion. In the common lounge before we went to bed, a few of the girls spoke pleasantly to me, a few had the scent of hostility about them, and the rest busied themselves with their particular friends and paid no attention to me. I smiled and tried to be friendly whenever opportunity offered, but I felt utterly out of place among these beautifully dressed girls from rich homes with many servants, where they had lived in unbelievable comfort and ease.

Going to bed that night, when I spoke to Emily she would answer only in French, saying, *"En français, jeune fille! Parlez en français!"*

I did not even know what that meant till later. It was a great relief when Eliza came next day to take me shopping. I did not tell her how frightened I was to find myself alone in such company, but she must have guessed, for once we were in the carriage she took my hand and said, "Poor Meg. I do feel for you, dear. Is it quite awful with all those rich young misses?"

"Yes, it is," I acknowledged, "but I expect I'll get used to it. You know, there was a time after I first came to Shalimar when I thought all *walypala* women were like Rosemary, but they're not."

Eliza said, "All *what* women?"

"Oh, I'm sorry. White women. Rosemary was the first I ever saw."

Eliza sighed. "You're quite right, dear. They're not all like her, and if Mr. Josiah Smith had any sense he would have lodged you with a nice farming family somewhere, not delivered you to the mercies of a clutch of hoity-toity, spoiled females. You would have been just as well hidden on a farm. But men are so stupid in many ways, as you may have observed, Meg."

I thought about Luke, then about Simon, the only two white men I knew at all well. "They're sometimes puzzling," I said. "I don't know about their being stupid."

Eliza laughed. "Dear, honest Meg. I hope they don't change you too much. There are quite enough of us devious people about." She patted my hand. "I don't doubt you'll have a few early troubles, but you'll find your feet all right in the end, for you're an adaptable girl and you know a great deal more about survival than the rest of us."

Three days later Simon and Eliza Fordyce left Neuchâtel. It was not easy to hide my sorrow and anxiety when I was left alone with them to say good-bye in the drawing room adjoining Mam'selle Herault's study.

"Are you beginning to settle down, Meg?" asked Simon.

I managed to smile. "Not really, but I'm trying. You said I may write to Mr. Josiah Smith, and I will. May I have your address so that I can write to you also? And if just sometimes you could find time to write back a few lines . . ."

My voice trailed to silence, for Simon was slowly shaking his head and Eliza was biting her lip with a troubled air. "I'm sorry," said Simon. "This is the end of our task, and we're not permitted to keep in touch with you. Perhaps Josiah Smith thinks you might be traced through us if we exchange letters." He gave a rather forced smile. "Besides, I've no doubt he'll have other work for us soon, and then we shall be off again."

"Oh. Yes. I see." There was an aching emptiness within me. I swallowed hard, returned his smile, and said, "Well, I can only thank you both for taking care of me, and wish you well in your work together. I shall think of you often and remember you in my prayers."

Simon turned away and looked out of the window. Eliza glanced at him and said bleakly, "Yes, I'm ashamed, too, Simon." Then she came forward, kissed my cheek, and embraced me, holding me for a moment as she whispered, "I doubt if I'm in very good standing with the Almighty, but I'll say a prayer for you, too, Meg dear."

Stepping back, she dabbed her nose with a small handker-chief and said brusquely, "All right, Simon, surely you can spare the girl a kiss to say good-bye? I won't begrudge you that."

She turned away to the window. Simon seemed to hesitate, but after a moment he came toward me, reaching out his hands to take mine. He looked at me carefully, then leaned forward very slowly. I could have turned my head aside, for he was allowing me ample time to do so, but I remained still and closed my eyes, waiting for his lips to touch mine. It was a very gentle kiss, lasting no more than a second, but I was to recall it many times in the months to come, for it was the first kiss I had ever known from a man, and even the memory of it brought me a bewildering sensation of strange happiness and longing.

He released my hands and stepped back as I opened my eyes. "It's been a privilege to know you, Meg," he said, beginning to turn away. "And as for you, Mrs. Fordyce, you're a rare and generous woman. Now, let's be going, and no looking back."

Seconds later the door closed, and I was alone.

AFTER BEING TERRIFIED DURING MY FIRST FEW DAYS AT CLAIR-mont I was merely miserable for the next several weeks, but then gradually life seemed to get a little pleasanter for me. There were several reasons for this. First I found that not all the girls were self-confident and haughty. There were three or four who, like me, were shy and unsure of themselves, and in time I found I had a cautious friendship with a French girl and two English girls. I was also helped by having a quick ear and a gift for mimicry, so I was very quickly able to make progress in French. This was our common language, though often in private the two English girls and I would use our more familiar tongue.

I was never to feel at home as I had done at Shalimar, but as I became familiar with the routine of the school and the different personalities of my fellow pupils I began to feel less lonely and miserable. The French girl, Nicole, was a good swimmer, and during those early weeks she taught me to swim, which I much enjoyed and for which I was most grateful to her. It was soon after this, and while I was still trying to find my feet at Clairmont, that something happened to make the whole school regard me with new eyes.

From the beginning it was clear that certain girls dominated others in varying degrees, but one girl stood out in this respect. She was English, a little taller than most of us, with glossy dark hair and pale brown eyes that contained strange little flecks of darker brown in them, a handsome girl with a strong face, penetrating voice, and waspish tongue. Her name was Clarissa Fitzwilliam, and she was the uncrowned queen among the girls of Clairmont, though not a popular queen.

Clarissa reminded me of a dingo I had known when I was with the tribe. He had dominated the other dogs by his aggressive ways, giving sharp nips to the flank or taking out a tuft of hair from the neck, not for any real cause but simply to keep the other dingoes constantly aware that he was their master.

Clarissa was of similar nature. She had three or four followers who fawned on her; the remainder seemed to dislike her and to be afraid of her. She was a strong girl and went in for a great deal of casual pinching and hair pulling that was supposed to be a joke. I was not a victim of her spiteful ways, perhaps because of an encounter on only my second evening at Clairmont. We were in the common lounge after supper when she came up with her cronies demanding in English to know my name, where I came from, and who my parents were.

I had stood up to answer politely when she addressed me, but as she continued in a hectoring manner I felt the hair at the back of my neck begin to bristle and my nostrils begin to flare. I said, "My name is Meg Smith, I come from Australia, and my parents are dead."

Her eyes narrowed, and she looked me up and down. "Don't be pert with me, miss!" she said sharply.

I did not answer, for I could not think what to say, but simply stood meeting her gaze with growing anger. The room was very quiet, and later I realized that the other girls expected her to give my hair a tug or my arm a hard pinch. Her hand moved slightly, then stopped. Perhaps Clarissa was deterred by what Luke Bowman had called my alley-cat glare, but whatever the reason she stepped back after a moment or two with an angry shrug.

"It seems Mam'selle is taking Gypsies as pupils now," she announced. "I really don't know what Clairmont is coming to." Then, as I learned later from my roommate, Emily, she said the same thing again in French for the benefit of the girls who spoke no English.

In the days that followed I often saw Clarissa bullying one girl or another, but they seemed too afraid of her to complain to Mam'selle, and I felt it was nothing to do with me—until one night, after we had gone to bed, I heard Emily crying softly. I sat up, lit my bedside candle, and went across to her. I knew that Emily had no liking for me, and to be honest I cared little for her, but I was troubled to hear her weeping.

"Emily, what is it?" I whispered. "What's wrong?"

She began to mumble falteringly in French, but I said impatiently, "Oh for heaven's sake, say it in English so I can understand easily."

She propped herself on an elbow, rubbing tears from her cheeks. "It's that Clarissa," she whimpered. "You know how she picks on a girl and keeps on at her, pinching and pushing. Well, all this week it's been *m-me*! My arms and legs are all bruises, and my head is so sore from her tugging my hair."

"All this week?" I said, vaguely surprised. "I hadn't noticed. I suppose I've been so busy studying my French books."

"You'd notice if she picked on *you*," Emily moaned resentfully. "Why doesn't she? Why doesn't she pick on you? It's not *fair*!"

"Well, I can't help that," I said, patting her hand, "but stop crying and try to go to sleep now, Emily. If Clarissa picks on you again tomorrow I'll tell her to stop."

"You will?" A gleam of hope touched Emily's eyes, then

faded quickly. "But then she'll only turn on *you*." The gleam returned. "But you will speak to her, won't you, Meg? You promise?"

"I promise. Now, go to sleep."

I got back into bed, feeling annoyed with myself for becoming involved with Emily's troubles and not quite sure how it had happened. If I did interfere I would certainly become the target of Clarissa's anger, which was what Emily hoped for, but as I lay there I found I was not greatly troubled by this prospect, so it was not hard for me to put the matter out of my mind and go to sleep.

It was customary for all the young ladies of Clairmont to gather in the large common lounge of an evening, to read, talk, do needlework, or play such games as drafts or dominoes. We also had Mam'selle's permission to use playing cards, provided we played only patience or piquet or bezique. On the day after my nighttime talk with Emily I was pleased to hear that we would all be taken for a nice long walk by the lake that afternoon. This had not happened before, and I looked forward to the exercise, but I could hardly believe it when after walking sedately for less than a mile we rested for half an hour and then made our way back to the school.

"I thought Mam'selle said a long walk," I whispered in halting French to Nicole, who was walking beside me.

She looked surprised. "Certainly it was a long walk, Meg. What do you mean?"

I shook my head, bewildered. "It doesn't matter." I could not very well tell her that I had often walked ten times as far without feeling I had traveled a long way. Perhaps because of my disappointment I was in an unfriendly mood that evening. I had forgotten about Emily and Clarissa, and settled myself in a corner to read a few more pages of *Les Misérables*, with a French/English dictionary at my elbow. After a little while I became so immersed in my reading that I was hardly aware of anything going on around me until I heard a sudden loud squeal.

I looked up to see Clarissa with a rolled parasol in her hand,

standing over Emily, who was huddled in an easy chair clutching
a piece of embroidery, whimpering and darting appealing looks
in my direction. Clarissa had two of her cronies with her and
was prodding Emily with the parasol as she spoke.

"Why are you so fat, Emily? Do you not realize how offen-
sive it is to the rest of us? See how fat you are there"—she gave
a prod with the parasol—"and there, and there."

A few of the girls watched with sycophantic smiles. The rest
were pretending to take no notice but watching furtively, each
one glad that she was not the current victim. Anger began to
kindle within me. I laid my book aside and lifted my voice as I
said, "Leave Emily alone, Clarissa."

Clarissa spun around, glaring, and the whole room was suddenly hushed. It seemed for a moment that she was unsure who
had spoken; then her gaze fastened upon me. "*What* was that?"
she demanded incredulously.

"Leave her alone, please. Stop tormenting Emily."

Clarissa's eyes glinted. "And what has that to do with you,
Miss Gypsy? You don't even like her!"

I stood up and moved forward until I faced Clarissa. To my
surprise I was suddenly enjoying the moment, and I had a vague
notion that perhaps this was because I had held such a mixture
of feelings pent up within me since my arrival at Clairmont that
I was eager for an opportunity to release them. "Emily and I
share a room," I said. "I won't have her tormented."

Clarissa stared at me, fury in her eyes, her mouth working
strangely, but beyond that fury I could see dawning apprehension. She knew, as every girl in the room knew, that if she failed
to outface me now, if she yielded to my demand, her dominance
would be destroyed. "Have a care, miss," she said in a tight
voice. "You would do well to go and sit down."

"And you would do well to leave Emily alone."

"Your advice is declined."

"Clarissa," I said, "if you continue to behave like a spoiled
child, I shall treat you as such."

"Pooh!" she said contemptuously, and gave Emily another

prod with the parasol. Next instant I had her nose pinched hard between the knuckles of my first and second fingers. Clarissa was half a head taller than I and probably physically stronger than the other girls, but I had lived most of my life with a primitive tribe in barren wastes where simply to survive called for endless labor. As a freak female, I had been treated as a boy, played boys' games, and become hardy as a boy; then I had spent three years doing hard manual work at Shalimar. I was stronger and quicker by far than Clarissa.

It was no effort for me to twitch the parasol from her grasp with my free hand. Then, as she squealed nasally, I pulled her forward by the nose so that she fell across Emily's lap. Her long braid touched the floor. I put my foot on it to hold her down, rested a hand on her back, and delivered three hearty whacks to her rump with the parasol before tossing it aside and giving her a push so that she rolled off Emily's lap and sprawled on the floor, panting shrilly, sobbing, dazed with shock and almost hysterical.

The room was like a tableau, with every girl frozen in the pose of whatever she had been doing moments before. Round eyes stared at me. Gasps and whispers filled the air. Clarissa got to her knees, tears running down her cheeks, her nose glowing red, mouth hanging open. ''I—I—I'll *tell*!'' she cried in a strangely muted shriek. ''I'll tell Mam'selle! She'll *expel* you!''

My heart lifted. If I were expelled, perhaps Mr. Josiah Smith would have to bring me to England, where I knew the language. Anywhere there must surely be better than Clairmont. I took Clarissa by one ear and drew her to her feet. ''Excellent!'' I said. ''We'll go to Mam'selle at once. Come along, Clarissa.'' I started toward the door with her, then glanced back. ''You too, Emily. You can show your bruises and tell where they came from.''

''Oh yes!'' Emily came eagerly to her feet, and I was at the door when Clarissa sank to her knees, clutching at my wrist to ease the strain on her ear.

''No! Please, Meg! No!'' There were fresh tears, different

tears now, and I knew Clarissa was suddenly very much afraid, for I could scent the fear that gripped her.

"You wanted to tell Mam'selle," I said.

"No . . . no, I don't. I'm sorry. She'll write to my father and he—he'll fly into a rage." She was babbling now, scarcely coherent. "He'll have me brought home, and—Oh, you don't know what he's like. Even when I was small he'd have me locked in a dark room for hours as a punishment. I was so frightened, and I never knew what I'd done wrong. Oh *please*, Meg!"

I let go of her ear and helped her to her feet, feeling sudden pity for Clarissa and shame for myself.

"Please . . ." she sobbed.

"It's all right," I said hastily. "Don't be afraid."

At my elbow Emily said indignantly, "You're surely not going to take any notice of *her*? Come along, Meg! Let's take her to Mam'selle, and I'll show my bruises. Then we might get *her* expelled!" Emily, now that she felt safe, was eager for revenge.

I looked at her and said, "You be quiet." There must have been something threatening in my look, for she flinched in alarm and said placatingly, "All right. It was only a suggestion."

I remembered how cruel the children of the tribe had been to any weakling, any freak, any bully deposed by a stronger bully, and I felt suddenly tired. Taking Clarissa by the arm, I led her from the room and closed the door. "You'd better go and wash your face," I said. "Then come back and sit talking with me as if we were now friends. Help me with my French if you like. That ought to stop the other girls taunting you or picking on you. After half an hour I shall go to my room, and I think you might go to yours. They're bound to talk about what's happened, so we might as well let them get it over with."

She stared at me in bewilderment from red-rimmed eyes. "Why—why are you helping me when you d-don't like me?"

I scowled at her, thinking of Luke. "A friend once set me a good example. Now, do please go and wash your face."

She gave me another startled glance, then hurried away. I watched her go, still thinking of Luke Bowman. He had never

liked me, I knew that now. There had been times when he tried
hard, but he could never hide his feelings for long. Yet despite
those feelings he had taken me into his home, given me food
and shelter, comfort and kindness, and, above all, the golden
privilege of having Rosemary to teach me and to guide my first
steps into a frightening new world. But I had no intention of
explaining all that to Clarissa.

Dear Luke,
    This evening I did the most shocking thing. Do you
remember that girl Clarissa I told you about? Well, recently she chose Emily as a victim. I don't much like
Emily, but she was weeping in bed last night, and I promised to help her.
    About half an hour ago, in the common lounge, I took
Emily's part when Clarissa was tormenting her, and it
came to a positive challenge (as sometimes used to happen between women in that place where I grew up). The
outcome was that I gave Clarissa some whacks with her
own parasol. I expect I also gave her what you used to
call my alley-cat glare, too! I can't imagine what Rosemary would think of me, and I really am ashamed, but
somehow I was just drawn into a situation in which I
seemed to have no choice as to what I might do.
    At first Clarissa was beside herself and threatened to
tell Mam'selle, so . . .

I sat writing in the diary I had begun to keep when we left
Fremantle, not a proper diary but a large account book I had
bought for the purpose. As always, I wrote as if penning a letter
to Luke, because in this way I found that my thoughts flowed
more freely. Luke was the first living white man I had ever
knowingly seen, and the only person left in the world toward
whom I could feel a sense of belonging. By writing to him in
my diary I was able to feel less lonely, though I had to put out

of my mind the realization that I did not know where in the wide world he was now, and that I would never see him again.

When I had completed my latest entry I put the diary away in my drawer and took out some writing paper for my weekly letter to Mr. Josiah Smith. I had never told him that I was unhappy at Clairmont, and the letters were always quite short, for I did not imagine he would be interested in our trivial daily events. Certainly I had no intention of telling him what I had done to Clarissa earlier this evening.

Dear Mr. Smith,

I am glad to be able to tell you that I am making quite good progress with my French now, and was commended for this by Mam'selle yesterday. The weather here remains fine, and my friend Nicole is delighted that as a result of her tuition I am now able to swim.

The other day I spoke to Mam'selle about three books I would like to read, and she said that she would send for them at once. I was troubled that this would be taking advantage of your generosity, which I had no intention of doing, but Mam'selle assures me that you have provided ample funds for any such expenditure.

Please accept my most grateful thanks for your kindness, sir. I hope it is in order for me to ask that you pass my good wishes to Mr. and Mrs. Fordyce whenever the opportunity may arise.

Yours sincerely and respectfully,
Meg Smith

My life at Clairmont, which had already begun to improve, changed very swiftly after my confrontation with Clarissa. Overnight I became much respected, with all the girls anxious to be friendly and several eager to transfer their loyalties from Clarissa and become my cronies. I did not respond to this, but kept thankfully to the three who had first been pleasant toward me, Nicole and the two English girls, Ruth and Fiona.

After a few days of being very subdued, Clarissa recovered some of her old arrogance, but to me she was always polite, and since many of the girls were now more ready to stand up to her there was none of the baiting and badgering that Emily and others had suffered.

By midautumn I had become used to this new world of Clairmont and no longer felt miserable, but there were times when I was bored, as I had never been at Shalimar, and there were times when I felt I was spending my days in trivial activities. I liked my friends very much, but because they did not know the truth about me I was never able to feel as close to them as I had been to Rosemary and to Luke. I often longed to have a friend who was truly close to me, and there were times when I felt imprisoned, suffocated by constant supervision, and longed to be out amid the valleys and lakes and mountains, studying creatures and plants new to me, going somewhere, doing something, fending for myself again.

Then I would feel ashamed and tell myself angrily that I was no longer a savage running naked in the outback. By a kind of miracle I had come into Rosemary's care, and by her example and her teaching and her unselfish giving of herself she had made it possible for me to learn the ways of my own people, so that I could live among them as a civilized person. I was now a quite capable and well-educated young lady who would one day . . . do what?

There my thoughts stuck, for I had no idea what my future might hold, and no communication from anybody outside Clairmont. I did not know how long Mr. Josiah Smith would keep me here, or what he planned for me when I left. Simon and Eliza Fordyce had told me that somewhere an unknown enemy was seeking me, intending me harm, but this seemed fanciful now.

Winter came. I wrote my weekly letters to Mr. Josiah Smith and talked to Luke in my diary. Sometimes as I lay in bed at night I tried to find Luke with my mind, to know if he was safe and well. This ability was something taken for granted as natural in the tribe. A woman who had married into another clan and gone away would have a baby. Her parents would know at once, as if a message had come into their minds from afar. I had no such power. I had tried to find Manyi, the woman I looked on as my mother, when she went away, but without success. I had thought the power was missing in me because I was a freak and not a true person. In a sense that was right, for I was indeed of a different race, and it was foolish of me even to try to find Luke with my mind. But I had never forgotten my promise to Rosemary, and though I had not been able to keep it I wanted so much to be reassured that Luke was safe and well. So I tried, and failed.

As Christmas drew near, Mam'selle told me that I would not be going to England for the holiday period and that she would make arrangements for me to remain at the school. At once I had invitations from each of my three friends to spend Christmas at their homes. Mam'selle sent a telegram to Mr. Josiah Smith's solicitors and received a prompt reply to the effect that I was not to come to England but could accept a friend's invitation to spend Christmas with her on the Continent, providing Mam'selle Herault was satisfied that I would be in the care of a good family.

As a result I was a guest for three weeks at Nicole's beautiful house near Grenoble. Her parents and older brothers were rather formal, so I was thankful for all I had learned of etiquette from Rosemary and from living at Clairmont. When asked questions about my life in Australia I had to use my imagination to some extent, but in this I had already been helped by Eliza Fordyce, who in the last days of our voyage had concocted a quite simple but plausible background for me. The first few days of the Christmas holiday were something of a strain, but after that I began to feel at ease and to be glad of the experience I was gaining.

I sent Christmas greetings to Mr. Josiah Smith, together with a fine lawn handkerchief on which I had embroidered his initials in silk thread. My needlework was not very skilled, but at least I had bought the handkerchief not from my allowance but with my own money, by selling my kangaroo claw to Gerda, an Austrian girl, for a few francs. This was the claw Yuma had given me for helping him secure his magic bone.

On Christmas morning I wrote in my diary to Luke.

Dear Luke,

I am thinking especially of you today, for this is Christmas Day and I know how deeply you will be missing Rosemary. I miss her so much myself, but somehow I find peace in remembering her, and wherever you are I hope that you will also find peace and comfort.

I am wearing her pendant, which you so kindly gave me. I don't wear it all the time, for fear the chain may break and I may lose it, but I wear it every Sunday when going to church, and I wore it when I went last night with Nicole and her family to Midnight Mass. In Neuchâtel I go to the Protestant church, but a lot of the girls are Catholics and quite often I attend a service with them in the little school chapel, though I'm not allowed to take Communion. I don't think Rosemary would mind which church I go to and I don't suppose God minds.

Tomorrow I will tell you all that happens today, Christmas Day. I have plenty of time in the mornings, because I still wake early while the house hardly begins to stir before half past eight o'clock, except for the servants, of course.

Now I am going to ring for them to fetch hot water for my bath. Oh, Luke, how different it all is from when you first brought me home. I still remember how alarmed I was when Rosemary first tried to get me into that bath. . . .

Nicole and I returned to school. Switzerland lay under a blanket of snow, and I shivered through days colder than any I had imagined when seeing pictures of snow-clad lands in the magazines I had pored over in Shalimar. For a week or two I was utterly miserable, but then I saw that the other girls and the local people were untroubled by the cold, even seeming to enjoy the snow, and I decided I must pretend to do the same.

To my surprise, pretense soon became reality, and I found myself greatly invigorated, looking forward to walks and games in the snow and envying the local skaters gliding so smoothly on any small frozen patch of water.

The weeks passed, and with spring came the day Rosemary had decided was to be my birthday. If she had guessed my age correctly, this would be my eighteenth birthday. My friends gave me little gifts, Mam'selle arranged a small birthday party for me in the evening, and I went to bed that night feeling very grateful for such a happy day, never dreaming that this would be my last night at Clairmont.

No pupil was allowed to leave the school alone, but we were permitted to walk down into the village in pairs of an afternoon, to buy from the shops there or to sit by the lake for a while. On the day after my birthday I accompanied Fiona, who wanted to buy some embroidery thread from the haberdasher's shop.

Fiona was a good-natured girl, but she always took a long time to make up her mind. After she had dithered for a while I went to stand in the doorway, hoping she might grasp that I was growing a little impatient, for it had been agreed that we would walk by the lake for a while when she had made her purchase.

Coming down the hill from the school I had been vaguely aware of an old man with a donkey cart of fruit a little way behind us. This was Armand, a familiar figure in Neuchâtel. Now I saw him again, a few paces from the doorway of the shop, standing by his cart and fidgeting as if waiting for somebody. As soon as he saw me he took hold of the bridle and began to lead his donkey along the cobbled road, only to halt in front of me. *"Vous voulez des beaux fruits, mam'selle?"* he asked, gesturing toward the baskets of different fruit on the cart.

I was a little surprised, but smiled and shook my head. *"Merci, Armand."*

He looked anxious, then nodded toward my hand and said, *"Votre gant, mam'selle."*

My glove? I wondered what he was talking about, and raised my gloved hand to look at it. At once he thrust a scrap of paper into my palm, then turned away and began to lead his donkey and cart on down the road. I gazed after him in astonishment before looking down at the piece of paper I held. It was quite small and had been folded twice.

I half turned, about to tell Fiona what had happened, but held my tongue at the last moment, not quite knowing why. Slowly I unfolded the paper, and my heart jumped as I found myself staring down at a few words in writing I knew well.

The summerhouse. As soon as you can manage it. Tell nobody. Urgent.

                                                            Luke.

TEN

I TUCKED THE SCRAP OF PAPER INSIDE MY GLOVE AND STOOD gazing across the street with unseeing eyes as I groped for comprehension.

Luke? Here? Even in a dream I would have found it unbelievable, but this was no dream, for here was Fiona calling me to help her decide between two shades of blue. I recommended one at random, thankful that she was too preoccupied with decisions to notice how distracted I was.

How on earth had Luke found me here? And why? To my sorrow he had seemed to want no further contact when we said good-bye in Shalimar on the morning of my return from the outback with his lost map, but now he had sought me out. There was so much I could not understand. Why had he chosen to send me a message so secretly? There was nothing to stop him calling at the school and announcing himself as an old friend from Australia—except that my name was now Meg Smith, not Meg Gaynor. But Luke knew nothing of Josiah Smith, or that the Reverend Simon Fordyce and his wife had been impostors, unless he had found out in some way. But even then . . .

My thoughts became so tangled that I had to stop even trying to guess what Luke was about. By this time Fiona and I were walking by the lake and she was chattering away about a rumor that Mam'selle Jaffe, the youngest of the Clairmont staff, had a beau in Neuchâtel. I spoke a few words automatically now and again, but my thoughts were elsewhere.

The summerhouse was close to a high wall at the bottom of the long garden at the back of Clairmont, and was screened by a thick shrubbery. It was rarely used, mainly because it was a favorite haunt of spiders, beetles, and other crawling insects, whom the young ladies of Clairmont regarded with great fear, much to my secret amusement. I wondered what they would think if they knew how often I had eaten various relatives of these creepy-crawlies.

As soon as you can manage it, the note had said. I knew that Fiona would be glad rather than disappointed when I cut short our walk, and only twenty minutes later we reached Clairmont. Looking at the clock in the hall, I saw there was an hour to go before we assembled for tea—cups of tea and tiny sandwiches in the English fashion, a proud feature of Clairmont's curriculum.

Fiona settled down with her embroidery on the long veranda among some of the other girls, and I went to my room to fetch a book. It was my habit to spend an occasional hour in the summerhouse for the very reason that it was usually shunned by other girls and so made a haven for me when I wanted to be quite alone for a little while, to think, or dream, or simply to empty my mind and give it rest in the way I had learned among the aborigines.

A narrow path wound through the shrubbery, and I felt my heart beat more quickly as I emerged into the clearing where the summerhouse stood. The door and walls were half glazed, and the glass was a little grimy, but I could see nobody inside.

I opened the door. There were some folding chairs stacked against one wall, a few spiderwebs here and there, and the usual community of beetles and woodlice scuttling about the timber floor or tucked away in crevices. I brought a chair out into the spring sunshine, unfolded it, and sat with my book on my lap. All was quiet, and if it had not been for the evidence of the note tucked in my pocket I might have wondered if I had dreamed that Armand had thrust it into my hand.

I sat there without thought or speculation, watching some ants carrying burdens bigger than themselves as they scuttled across the grass-grown joints of the flags surrounding the summer-house, but my senses were alert, and five minutes later I heard a faint sound beyond the wall. As I stood up and turned, I saw through the glass of the summerhouse two hands appear on top of the wall, then Luke's head and shoulders. He hauled himself up, swung his legs over the wall, and dropped to the ground.

He wore a tweed jacket with a belt, breeches strapped below the knee, long woolen socks and boots, and a cap tilted back on his thick mop of yellow hair, a style of dress I had seen in pictures of English sporting gentlemen. He did not see me at once because the summerhouse was between us, and he was brushing dust from his jacket when I stepped into plain view and whispered, "Luke."

He froze, staring at me as if not quite recognizing me for a moment, and I realized that he had never before seen me so elegantly dressed, my hair so fashionably groomed, my hands smooth and my nails carefully manicured. Then he relaxed and almost smiled. Before I could prevent it I found myself running toward him, tears coming to my eyes, arms reaching out to embrace him. "Oh, Luke, how lovely to see you! How wonderful!"

His face changed, and he caught me by the shoulders, holding me at arm's length. "No time to waste," he said in a low voice. "You're in danger. I have to get you away from here tonight."

I was stupefied. "Tonight?" I echoed incredulously. "But that's impossible. What do you mean? I've been here almost a year now as Meg Smith, and nobody knows except Mr. and Mrs. Fordyce and a gentleman called Mr. Josiah Smith, who pays for me to be here. Why should I suddenly be in danger?"

"For God's sake, don't argue!" he said urgently, glancing about him. "Is anyone likely to come here?"

I shook my head. "No. But if they do I'll hear them in plenty of time."

A little of the tension went out of him, and he nodded slowly. "Yes, of course you would. I'd forgotten." He drew in a deep breath. "But there's no time to explain everything. I've been hunting for you for weeks to get you out of harm's way, but the school principal is hardly likely to believe my reason. She'll call the police if I try to take you away openly, so it has to be tonight, Meg."

I said, "Simon and Eliza Fordyce said I had an unknown enemy, and now you seem to be saying the same thing, but I think you must all be mistaken. Why should anyone wish me harm?"

His hands tightened on my shoulders. "Because you are *who* you are," he said fiercely. "That's why."

I was utterly confused. "Luke, please . . . I don't understand you. I'm just Meg. Just Mitji. You know where I came from."

His voice was suddenly soft, but his hands held me as strongly as ever. "Oh yes, I know where you came from. *But you don't!*" He gave me a little shake, as if in exasperation. "It's too long a story to tell now, so it comes down to this. Do you trust me? *Do you, Red?*"

There could be only one answer to that question. No matter how startling his words and manner, no matter if he were mistaken, deceived, or deranged, this was Luke Bowman, and I could give him only one answer. "Yes," I said. "Of course I trust you."

"Thank God for that," he said fervently, and let me go. "Is all the school asleep by midnight?"

"Yes, even the staff. When I was first here I sometimes wandered out into the garden at night because I felt imprisoned in my room. Emily sleeps like a log—she's the girl I share with—so nobody ever knew I'd been out."

"All right. Can you pack a bag for an overnight journey without Emily knowing?"

"Yes, I'll only need a few minutes. How long a journey?"

"Up to thirty-six hours by train and boat, depending on connections. I'm taking you to London, where you'll be safe."

I had passed beyond surprise or the urge to question now, but was still in a daze of mixed emotions. I longed to go with Luke, no matter where he took me, and I was eager to go to London, but troubled about causing my friends and Mam'selle Herault anxiety. I said, "May I leave a note for my friend Nicole? Just to say . . ." I put a hand to my head. "Well, could I just ask her to tell Mam'selle not to worry about me, and say I'm quite safe because I've gone away with my oldest and dearest friend?"

Luke stared at me with what seemed a blend of pain and anger. "All right," he said, "you can say that. Now, listen, I want you here, with your bag and ready for the journey, by one hour after midnight. There's an early train that comes through from Zurich. I don't want to pick it up at Neuchâtel because somebody is bound to see us there. I want to pick it up farther on, at Travers, where it stops soon after seven A.M., but that means we'll have to walk about fifteen miles along the valley during the night. Can you manage that?"

"Fifteen miles? Oh really, Luke. Don't you remember a girl called Mitji?"

He half smiled. "I remember."

"But you mustn't be cross with me when I take my shoes and stockings off—" I stopped short, listening. "Somebody's coming."

"Damn!"

"Don't swear in front of me. Rosemary wouldn't like it. Quick—off you go."

He gave me a look of bewildered exasperation, then ran for the wall, drew himself up, and rolled over the top to drop down on the far side. Twenty seconds later, as I sat with my open book on my lap, Fiona emerged from the path through the shrubbery, grimacing with distaste.

"Oooh, how *can* you sit here among all these horrid creepy things, Meg? Look! There's a beetle as big as a *plum*!"

I laughed, and said with a calm that surprised myself, "Well, think how big you are to him. What is it, Fiona?"

She came forward warily, holding out her embroidery. "It's this blue silk," she said worriedly. "Do you think it *really* goes well with the other colors, or should I have bought that more greeny sort of shade?"

THE MOON WAS ALMOST FULL AND THE SKY WAS CLEAR THAT night. I had packed a small case, but it was heavy because it contained the books I had brought from Shalimar. Despite my protests, Luke insisted on carrying it, so for me the journey was easy. I had packed a toque hat for later, and wore a scarf on my head, tied under my chin. My skirt was doubled up, with the hem pinned at my waist, leaving my legs free and unhampered from just above the knee. My shoes and stockings I carried in the bag formed by my folded skirt.

Not another soul was on the road that night, but still we walked in silence, exchanging only a whispered word or two now and again. By dawn we were sitting on the ground in a little grove of trees only half a mile from the station at Travers, sharing some chocolate Luke had brought with him and quenching our thirst at a rivulet that bubbled from a rocky cleft and wound its way down into the village.

An hour later, curled up at the foot of a tree amid long grass, I roused from a light sleep at the sound of a cart passing on the road below. It was after six o'clock now, and people were stirring. Luke was asleep beside me, and I thought how strange it was that here in the civilized world we two should be traveling again in much the same way that we had once journeyed through the barren outback.

I shook him to wakefulness and said, "We have to move soon, Luke."

He blinked, took out his watch, stared at it, then grunted, "Didn't mean to fall asleep. Might have missed the train, damn it."

"Luke, stop swearing."

"Sorry. Sorry, Red."

"To tell you the truth, the men in the tribe used to swear a great deal, using most dreadfully obscene words. It was quite complicated, and regarded as something of an art, so I'm really not shocked when you say damn. It's just that—" I hesitated.

"I know," he said. "Rosemary wouldn't like it." He sighed and rubbed his eyes. "You never told me about the way aborigines swear before."

"No, and I'm not going to tell you now. I don't even know the words in English."

He laughed. "I should hope not."

I was happy to hear him laugh, happy that for the present at least there was warmth between us, and happy when he stood up and reached down a hand to help me to my feet. I put on my stockings and shoes, then unpinned the hem of my skirt from the waist and let it fall to my ankles. "Stand still," I said, and began to brush away the fragments of grass that clung to his clothes. When I had finished he performed the same service for me. After waiting to be sure that nothing was moving on the road we emerged from the trees and began to walk toward the station as if we had come from one of the houses on the outskirts of the village.

I said, "Haven't you any luggage of your own, Luke?"

He nodded. "I have a case at the station. Left it there three days ago after I first discovered you at Neuchâtel."

All the unanswered questions came sweeping back into my mind then, but I knew that this was not the time to voice them. Instead I said, "Who am I supposed to be for the moment? I mean, I didn't have to go to Clairmont to learn that a lady and gentleman don't travel alone together unless they're properly related."

He nodded, frowning. "Yes. You'll have to be my sister or my wife."

"I haven't a wedding ring to wear, so I'd better be your sister."

"All right."

"Well, don't look so bad-tempered about it."

"Ah! You're starting to wear your alley-cat face."

I bit my lip and stared ahead. After a few seconds I said, "Was I? Then I'm sorry. I'm Meg Bowman, your sister, and I won't make alley-cat faces at you. Let's be friends, Luke."

He touched my shoulder lightly. "We're friends."

AT EIGHT O'CLOCK THAT MORNING WE CROSSED THE FRONTIER into France and came to Pontarlier, where we took a different train for the two-hundred-mile journey to Paris. On this train Luke paid for a sleeping compartment, and we both slept for four hours until luncheon was served during the last part of the run to Paris. Luke had only a smattering of French, so I was able to show off by talking fluently to the waiter when we ordered.

There was much I wished to know, much Luke had to tell me, but I felt no urgency now. We would have to be alone before we talked of important matters. In any event I had spent the past year with no idea as to what the future held for me, and now that would surely be changed dramatically; but after being left in ignorance for so long I could easily wait a few more hours without impatience.

During luncheon Luke asked me to tell him how I had fared at the Clairmont Finishing School. It did not take long to give quite a full account of my time there. I described the staff and some of the girls, gave a general idea of our daily routine, told of my Christmas visit to Grenoble, and announced proudly that I had learned to swim; but since there had been little variety in our daily life at Clairmont there was not a great deal more to say.

As I spoke, Luke watched me so attentively that I felt embarrassed and said awkwardly, "Oh dear, are you counting my freckles or have I got a smudge on my face from the engine?"

"Eh? Oh no." He made a gesture of apology. "Sorry if I

was staring. It's just that you seem to have grown up . . . yet you're exactly the same." He fingered his glass of wine and glanced about him. "We'll be taking a cab across Paris to the Gare du Nord, and from there I'll reserve a first-class compartment for us to Calais. Then I can tell you about . . . everything."

I said, "A whole compartment must be very expensive, and I only have a few Swiss francs with me, my pocket money allowance. Are you sure you can afford all the expense I'm causing you?"

He looked at me with his head on one side, as if puzzled. "Meg, hasn't it occurred to you that I might be quite rich now?"

"Rich? Oh! You mean—" I hesitated, then lowered my voice. "The mine? The gold you found?"

"Yes."

I was swept by a glow of joy. "Oh, Luke, how wonderful! I'm so glad for you. Do please tell me about it."

"Well, as soon as you left, I sold Shalimar, hired two camels and ample equipment, and went prospecting again. It was easy to find the place this time, because I had the map." He glanced at me. "I'd also learned a little about surviving in the bush from a funny kind of freak aborigine girl I used to know."

I smiled and he continued, "I brought back some ore samples, went to Kalgoorlie, registered my claim, then took samples to the Perth Fidelity Mining Company. They organized a small expedition to go out there with me, including a geologist and a mining expert. Their report was very favorable, and the result was that I sold my claim on the mining rights to the Perth Fidelity for eighty thousand pounds plus ten percent of the claim's future yield."

I gasped, then began to laugh. "Oh, Luke! When you think how we had to watch the pennies—" I broke off, put down my knife and fork, and pressed my hands to my eyes to stop the sudden tears.

"Meg?" he said anxiously. "Are you all right?"

"I'm sorry." My voice was a shaky whisper. "If only I'd

remembered earlier . . . if only I'd gone to get the map sooner, long before Rosemary died . . .''

"Stop that!" His voice was low but peremptory, and I looked up, startled, to meet his angry gaze. "Don't you dare to hold yourself guilty for that. It would have made not a scrap of difference." He took a handkerchief from his pocket and passed it across the table. "Now, dry your tears, wipe your nose, and eat your meal." He watched me narrow-eyed, and I obeyed him meekly. The last thing I wanted was to have any bad feeling between us that touched upon Rosemary.

As I handed back the handkerchief he relaxed again and said, "You don't feel you're entitled to a share?"

I wondered what he meant, and repeated, "A share? What share?"

"A share in the proceeds of the Bowman Mine, of course. I'd never have found it again without the map."

Now I glared. "Oh, don't be ridiculous! I promised Rosemary I would take care of you, but you wouldn't let me, so fetching the map was the next best thing I could do, that's all."

His bright blue eyes, the first blue eyes I had ever seen, sparkled with sudden laughter. "It's just as I said. You haven't changed a bit. I needn't have worried about what that school might do to you. Could you try not to glare as if you're about to point the bone at me?"

The last words took me by surprise, and I had to laugh myself. "Only men can point the bone, so you can't say I'm a witch."

His eyes sobered, and he looked out of the window. "I'm never too sure."

I drank some water and said, "You've only told me about yourself up to the time when you sold the claim to that mining company. Go on from there."

"Well . . . then I misbehaved myself rather badly for quite a long time. Not in Lawton, not even in Australia. I traveled here and there around the Far East, then around Europe, and drank a lot too much, and quarreled with various people." He frowned. "I can't think why I'm confessing my sins to a young miss from finishing school."

"It's better than telling lies," I said, "though I suppose you could have told me to mind my own business."

"Ah. That didn't occur to me."

"When did you stop misbehaving?"

A waiter came to take away our plates, and Luke waited till he had gone. Then he said quietly, "When I looked at your scrapbook."

I sat up straight in astonishment. "You kept my scrapbook? Wherever did you find it? I thought I'd put it with the other books you packed for me, but it wasn't in the parcel."

Luke continued looking out of the window. "I must have missed it," he said vaguely. "Anyway, I came across it in the kitchen later, and when it was my turn to leave Shalimar I put it in my trunk."

"Oh. Whyever did you do that?"

He leaned back in his seat and looked at me sourly. "I've no idea why. I just did. And what came of it is something we'll leave until we're on the train for Calais."

"All right, but there's no need to snap at me. May I have some more coffee, please?"

My first sight of civilization had been Shalimar. Then came Lawton, Kalgoorlie, and, much later, Perth. On the voyage to Europe I had seen Colombo, Port Said, and Marseilles, and in going by train to Neuchâtel I had seen other cities, but Paris took my breath away with its majestic beauty, and for most of the cab journey from the Gare de L'Est I had my head out of the carriage window, calling excited questions to Luke, which he had no time to answer before I called the next.

We were fortunate with our connection, and an hour later we sat alone in a first-class compartment, facing each other as the train began to rumble out through the northern suburbs. I was still thinking about the wonders I had seen in Paris when Luke rose, lifted his suitcase down from the rack, laid it on the seat, opened it, and took out a long envelope. Inside the envelope was a piece of printed paper, folded once. He drew this out and passed it to me.

"I found this tucked in the back of your scrapbook," he said as I unfolded the paper.

In my hands I held the page I had cut from a copy of the *Strand* magazine, almost five years old now, showing three photographs taken of the same lady at different times of her life. Luke said, "Your name is Moira Glencullen. You are the daughter of Sir Laurence and Lady Glencullen. She is the person in those photographs. Your father was Scottish, your mother Irish. I'm sorry to have to tell you they both died only a few years ago, shortly after that article appeared in the *Strand* magazine."

Strangely, I felt very little sense of shock as I looked again at the photograph showing the lady as she had been at the age of fifteen. It simply struck me that I had been right in thinking how great was the likeness between us when I first saw the picture. I looked up and said, "But you won't call me Moira, will you? I hope you'll go on calling me Meg." I hesitated. "Or Red, sometimes."

Luke glared at me and banged his hand on his knee in exasperation. "Don't you understand what I've just told you, damn it? That lady and her husband were your parents, and you were their only child! But you're an orphan now—you're also an heiress! Yet all you can do is sit there and tell me you'd rather not be called Moira! Doesn't what I've said *mean* anything to you, Meg?"

I said apologetically, "Not very much. I'm sorry, but please try to understand. Of course I'm interested, but you and Rosemary told me long ago that I wasn't an aborigine and that I must have had white parents. Now you tell me their names and show me this photograph of my mother. But they don't seem real to me. It's all so . . . so *remote*. Your whole world was completely unknown to me until I was—well, somewhere between fourteen and fifteen. To me, Manyi was my mother. She suckled me and brought me up. To me, you and Rosemary are my family. You brought me up in this new world." I touched the photograph.

"I can't feel for these people as you expect me to, and I'd be a hypocrite if I pretended. But I really am intrigued, because there must be a quite fascinating story behind all this. I'm just finding it hard to think of myself as part of it."

He sat gazing at me in the half-bewildered, half-despairing way I had seen so often before, but at least his anger had vanished, and I was glad of that. Eventually he gave a little laugh and said, "All right, Red. Perhaps it's best that you feel detached, for I rather dreaded telling you that your parents were dead."

I said, "My mother can't have been very old. How did it happen?"

"As the article in the magazine says, she gave a lot of her time to charitable work, and apparently she didn't dispense her bounty from a distance, but genuinely involved herself in helping very poor people in the East End. That's the area of London where the poorest people live, and that's where she was infected with typhoid fever, from which she never recovered. It seems she must have carried the infection to your father, for he died within four days of her own death."

I found that my eyes were moist, and said, "That poor lady, and her husband, too. I can only think of them as strangers, but it was still a dreadful tragedy. She seems to have been a very nice lady, doesn't she?"

"Yes. By all accounts they were both admirable people."

I sat watching the fields of green corn flash by, thinking about my mother and father, trying to make them less remote. After a while I said, "They must have been living in Australia when I was born. Or perhaps soon after?"

"You were born in England," said Luke, "on the fifth of May, and you were eighteen years old on your recent birthday, so Rosemary was only a few days out in her choice. You were taken to Western Australia when you were one year old, and your father, then Mr. Laurence Glencullen, was commissioned lieutenant-governor of the colony there. He was knighted a year later."

I was puzzled. "Surely such people could never abandon their own child? It simply isn't possible."

"That was only a guess we made, Meg. It seemed the only explanation. But you weren't abandoned. You were kidnapped by two criminals of very low intelligence from the garden of your home in Perth and taken by them some miles into the outback, to a cluster of tumbledown huts, long abandoned, where a gold strike had been falsely reported years before. You were then almost two years old."

I felt my stomach contract at the thought, and whispered, "Oh, my poor mother."

"Yes, indeed," Luke said bleakly. "But it can't have been very pleasant for you either, Meg."

I shook my head. "I don't remember anything."

"Even so . . ." He shrugged and left the sentence unfinished. "It wasn't a carefully planned crime. Your nurse turned her back for a few minutes, and perhaps you wandered out of the garden. In any event, you were seized and carried off in a small cart, to be driven to this cluster of shacks several miles out of Perth. Next day a crudely written note was delivered to your distraught parents, saying you would be returned unharmed on payment of five hundred pounds."

I said, "Oh, Luke, how awful for them. But how do you know all this?"

"It was reported in the English and Australian newspapers at the time, though I don't recall it myself. Sixteen years ago I was probably too young to be bothered with newspapers, but I've now read the whole story in the *Times* files. Your father called in the police, and when the note from the kidnappers arrived he followed the instructions given as to where he was to leave the money—under a sack in an open cart which would be standing on the corner of Albert Street at midnight. But a trap was set, and the man who came to collect the money was caught. His name was Brockbank, a known criminal, and as I've said, both he and his accomplice were of poor intelligence."

I sat listening to the story of my kidnapping as if it were something that had happened to a stranger, for either I had been too young to remember even the most formless detail, or shock had wiped all memory of it from my mind.

"At first the man blustered and protested his innocence," said Luke, "but after twenty-four hours he changed his tune and tried to blame it all on his companion in the hope of getting a lighter punishment for himself. So at dawn next day the police, with your father and Brockbank, rode out to the abandoned shanties, and there they found . . . nothing except a few signs of recent occupation in one of the huts. Brockbank was almost mad with rage and fear, cursing his partner in crime most vilely. That man's name was Vane, and he was picked up two days later trying to stow away on a boat sailing from Fremantle. You remember that's the port for Perth?"

"Yes, of course I do. We sailed from there."

"Well, it transpired that Vane had been left with you in a tumbledown shack, but when his partner didn't arrive by dawn he thought either Brockbank had been caught or that he had run off with the money and didn't intend to share it. Vane was a weak character, and he panicked. He left you asleep on a blanket, or so he said later, and set out for Perth, but making a wide half-circle to get there in case the police were seeking him. He managed to make his way through Perth to the port, but there he was caught when trying to stow away. The rest you either know or can guess, Meg."

"Yes," I said slowly. "I suppose my tribe must have passed that way after Vane had gone and I was alone. Manyi had just lost her baby, and she had milk to give me. I expect I was hungry and crying by then. They didn't realize I was somebody's child, Luke; they had never seen a white person before. They believed I had been put there by an ancestor-spirit for Manyi to find." I thought for a moment. "They must have been much farther south and west than we ever traveled again. Or perhaps Manyi was with another clan then, and later came to ours in marriage. I vaguely remember her having a husband who died when I was small."

Luke gave a little shrug. "Whatever the details, Manyi must have taken you, and then you were brought up as an aborigine." He shook his head slowly, with a touch of sober wonderment. "Lord, but destiny weaves strange webs. We were at opposite ends of the earth the day your tribe passed through that huddle of deserted shanties, Meg, but if Manyi hadn't found you I would have died in the outback on a day twelve years later."

I said, "So would I, if you hadn't taken me home for Rosemary to nurse."

We sat in silence for a minute or two. I was trying to absorb all Luke had told me, and I think perhaps he was allowing me time to do so. At last I said, "I'm glad to know who I am, but to be truthful it doesn't seem very important. I'm just the same person I was before I knew, so it doesn't change anything."

"It changes a great deal," Luke said sharply. "Your father owned large estates in Scotland and the Home Counties, and you therefore stand to inherit a great fortune."

I felt a stab of anxiety, and said, "Oh, Luke, I'm such a fool, but that makes me feel quite frightened. Surely if nobody knew I was alive all these years, then somebody else must have inherited by now?"

"No. Now, listen, Meg. When the police couldn't find the stolen baby, they decided that either Vane or Brockbank or both of them were lying and that in fact you had been done away with and buried somewhere in the bush, so the two men were tried for murder and eventually hanged. No doubt they thought this most unfair, but to my mind hanging is too good for kidnappers, so let's waste no sympathy on them. It seems, however, that your mother always retained a tiny flicker of hope that you might have been deposited with a woman confederate who became attached to you and who feared being caught if she tried to return you to your family."

I said, "That was a very slender hope, wasn't it?"

"I suppose when you love somebody you clutch at the smallest straws." He looked out of the window. "I know I did with Rosemary."

"Yes. I'm sorry, Luke. Please go on."

"Well, your mother always hoped that one day, by some miracle, you might be found and restored to her. That was a slender hope, too, but the fact is you *have* been found. I don't know if your father shared that hope, but in deference to his wife he had a will drawn up that allowed for such a remote possibility. The terms stated that in the event of his death and his wife's death, after certain small bequests the whole of his estate was to be held in trust by their lawyer, Adrian Webb, for your benefit until such time as you would have reached the age of twenty-one. If by that date no proof of your survival had emerged, your death was to be assumed and the fortune was to pass to an old friend and business colleague of your father's, John Lafayette, to be used exclusively for charitable works at Lafayette's entire discretion."

I felt a stinging pain behind my eyes as I said, "I expect the idea of charitable works was at my mother's request, too. I'm so proud of her, and I do wish I remembered her. It seems my father must have loved her very deeply, and that's something else to warm my heart. But, Luke, however did you find out about the will and . . . well, all about me and about my parents?"

He gave a wry smile. "You're always curious about what other people might consider the least important things. Do you want me to tell you *how* I found out before I finish telling *what* I found out?"

"Well, yes, if you don't mind." To me it was Luke's activities that were of interest, not remote lawyers and wills.

"Well, it began one day when I was in Paris and I discovered that page with the photographs in your scrapbook. I found it impossible to believe there could be such a likeness to Lady Glencullen unless you were related, so I went to London and looked up the obituaries of your mother and father in the newspaper files. There was mention of their only child, Moira Glencullen, being kidnapped in Perth and murdered, so I looked up details of that story, and then it was easy to see what had happened—easy for me, because I knew Mitji, a girl of the right age who had been brought up among aborigines.''

I said, ''Did you go to the lawyer, the one mentioned in my father's will? You said his name just now, but I've forgotten it.''

''Adrian Webb, a very well-known and very successful solicitor with chambers in Grays Inn. Yes, he was named in the obituaries, so I went to him with my story and told him how Moira Glencullen had survived and was alive today. He's no old fogy but a man in his middle forties, and although he has a most benevolent manner it hides a very shrewd brain. At first he simply didn't believe me, and though he was too polite to say so in plain terms I fancy he thought I was a trickster of some sort. But I had a very detailed story to tell, Meg, about how you found me that day and how I later brought you home to Shalimar. It wasn't the kind of story anyone could easily make up, and I had nothing to gain by doing so. But what convinced him in the end was when I produced a photograph of you, the one taken when we went to Kalgoorlie, and set it beside the photograph in the magazine. He had no doubts after that.''

''My photograph!'' I exclaimed. ''I didn't dream you might have kept it, Luke. You were so grumpy when I left, but you must have felt at least a little bit friendly to keep my photograph.''

He struck his knee with his fist in a gesture of exasperation. ''There you go again! What really matters is that I convinced Adrian Webb of the truth, but you're more concerned that I happened to keep a photograph of you, which has no importance whatsoever.''

''Well, it's important to *me*,'' I declared. ''I can't help it if you and I think different things are important, but there's no need to go on at me about it. What happened after you convinced Mr. Webb?''

Luke leaned back and shrugged. ''He suddenly began to see how everything fitted together. You were the right age for Moira Glencullen, you were in the right place for a child taken by aborigines years ago near Perth, and you were the image of your mother, especially when I was able to tell him that you had green eyes and red hair. It was then he revealed the terms of the will and went on to say that steps must be taken at once to protect you, because in his opinion if John Lafayette discovered that you were alive you would be in grave danger. Then I told him your life had already been in danger some eighteen months ago at Shalimar.''

I said, startled, "But I thought Mr. Lafayette was a friend and colleague of my father's. Are you saying that *he* was responsible for what Sid Buller did?''

Luke said quietly, "People can be mistaken about their friends, and there's a large fortune at stake. Buller would have been hired through intermediaries, of course, for men like Lafayette know how to go about these matters. At all events, when I told Adrian Webb of Buller's attack on you he became greatly alarmed, because he was certain that John Lafayette was behind the whole affair, and this showed that somehow or other Lafayette had come to learn of your existence *well over eighteen months before*! But Webb kept asking how this could be, and who could have known—other than somebody in Western Australia who had seen Meg Gaynor and by some strange freak had recognized her as Mary Glencullen's daughter.''

I said, "I know who it was, Luke. Do you remember that day you took me to Kalgoorlie and we met Mr. Tasker, the newspaper reporter? Well, he looked at me very intently in the restaurant, and later he followed us to the station, but by then he had a copy of that two-year-old *Strand* magazine with him, so I think he must have guessed who I was even then.''

Luke nodded agreement. "Yes, he was the one. I realized that, too. He evidently thought there was money to be made out of it, for as soon as he reached England he must have obtained a copy of your father's will from Somerset House, which gave him the name of John Lafayette, a gentleman with large diamond- and gold-mining interests in southern Africa. I don't know why Tasker went to him instead of approaching your trustee, Adrian Webb. It's true Tasker was a bit of a knave, but he wasn't a wicked man. He couldn't have known that going to John Lafayette would almost cost you your life, and he certainly didn't know it would cost his own. He must simply have thought that the old friend and business colleague of your father's might produce a large reward.''

I said, "When the solicitor decided that somebody must have recognized me in Australia, what made you think of Mr. Tasker?"

"He was the only one to fit the bill. A reporter, old enough to have been working on a newspaper at the time of the kidnapping, so he would remember the story; a man who had seen you in Kalgoorlie nicely dressed and with your hair groomed, when you would look most like your mother's photograph; a man who might well keep old copies of the *Strand* magazine for reference; and a man who was leaving for England shortly. It all added up to Harry Tasker, so I suggested the name to Adrian Webb, who said he would make inquiries of a friend at the *Times*. Only a day later he told me of Tasker's murder the previous year, and said it was clear now that the man must have approached John Lafayette with the information that Moira Glencullen was alive— with the results for him and for you that we now know. One murder, one attempted murder.''

I said, "Do you really believe John Lafayette was responsible for Mr. Tasker's death? It seems so . . . so cold-blooded.''

"We're sure of it, Meg. As Adrian Webb says, the same person who hired Buller to get rid of you must have hired somebody to get rid of Tasker, so he could never tell anybody else that Moira Glencullen had reappeared after all these years. Tasker may even have guessed that you had been taken by aborigines. As a reporter he could easily have found out that Nomi, that aborigine from Lawton, worked at Shalimar for me occasionally, so he would question Nomi about you and learn that once in the early days you spoke to Nomi in his own tongue.''

The train rattled on. From time to time we passed through a small village, and occasionally I saw people working in the fields, but I was only vaguely aware of this, for I was struggling to understand the bewildering story Luke was telling me. After a while I said, "It was only by showing my photograph that you convinced Mr. Adrian Webb who I was. How could Mr. Tasker have convinced John Lafayette when he didn't have a photograph to show?"

"That puzzled us," said Luke. "But Adrian Webb insisted that Tasker *must* have had a photograph of you, and then I remembered Tasker had seen us going into Jack Waller's photographic studio that day in Kalgoorlie. He said as much when he spoke to us in the restaurant. So all Harry Tasker had to do was go to the studio, ask a question or two, tell a plausible story, and order a print of the photograph taken of the young lady who had come in that morning with a fair-haired man, Miss Gaynor and Mr. Bowman."

I nodded. "Yes. I suppose it wasn't very difficult. Oh, Luke, it's horrible to think that by what he did that day the poor man brought about his own death." We sat in silence for a while; then a shiver passed through me, and I said, "I've only half believed it till now, but Simon and Eliza Fordyce said I had a dangerous enemy. They didn't know who it was, but now I realize it must be John Lafayette. It's so strange, though. How could my father have had a trusted friend who is a truly wicked man, ready to kill for greed? And why would a man who owns diamond and gold mines do such things to get even richer?"

"You mentioned the Fordyce pair," Luke said bleakly, "and we'll come to them in a moment. Let's take your last question first. You've achieved wonders in less than four years, coming from a Stone Age community and fitting into the modern world so well that nobody would ever think you'd had anything other than a normal European upbringing. But like most young ladies, you have no experience of the world of men, the world of commerce, industry, and politics, so I have to tell you that although most men are decent-enough fellows with average faults and virtues, there are some who even if they owned half the world would strive endlessly to acquire the other half, and this evidently describes Mr. John Lafayette. Now, for your first question . . .''

He fell silent for a few moments, as if gathering his thoughts, then he went on, "I never knew your father or mother, though I wish I had. It seems strange to me, as it does to you, that they could have been so easily deceived as to trust a man who had such an evil heart as John Lafayette must have. I said as much to Adrian Webb, but he told me that as a lawyer he has seen the same kind of thing time and again, men reposing their trust in scoundrels and villains with plausible tongues and convincing ways. It happens to shrewd, hardheaded men as well as to innocents. No doubt this was the case with your father."

I said, "Yes, I suppose it must have been. Anyway, it happened, and the reason doesn't really matter. May we have the window open a little, Luke? It's getting rather stuffy in here."

He leaned forward to lower the window halfway, murmuring, "Ah yes. So much more important than the Fordyce pair."

"Oh, I forgot. You said we would come to them in a moment, didn't you?"

"I did. Suppose you tell me what you know about them first."

"Well, now I'm going to surprise you, Luke. Mr. Fordyce *isn't* a vicar at all!"

Luke winced. "God save us all. Sometimes you're so bright, and sometimes you're . . . just the opposite. Do you think I don't *know* the Fordyces were impostors? Do you imagine I didn't try to find you in London once I knew you were in danger? Do you think I didn't try to seek out the Christian Research Association, the organization Simon Fordyce was supposed to be working for? It doesn't exist! The Fordyce pair are hired adventurers!"

I said, "Luke, I've never noticed this before, but when you're angry, and talk quickly like that, your ears move up and down. Are mine the same when I talk while I'm wearing my alley-cat face?"

He gazed at me with mouth slightly open, eyes growing steadily rounder, then suddenly he collapsed back in the corner and began to laugh helplessly. "Dear God," he gasped. "What am I going to do with her? Oh, Red . . . you're priceless."

As the laughter faded he took out a handkerchief and wiped tears from his eyes. I was glad he had called me Red, but I pretended to be severe as I said, "It's very rude to laugh at a person."

"True," he agreed a little breathlessly, "but it's also rude to comment upon a person's ears moving."

"Oh dear. Yes, it is. I do apologize."

"And I apologize for laughing."

"Luke, when you were saying all those things about Simon and Eliza Fordyce I wasn't ignoring what you said. It's just that I already know they're adventurers. They told me on the ship."

Luke sobered and looked at me quietly. "What else did they tell you?"

"Well, it's all rather mysterious, but they work for a very rich man called Josiah Smith. He sent them to Australia to protect me, because somehow he discovered that I have an enemy, and we know now that it's John Lafayette, because Adrian Webb told you. I don't know why Mr. Josiah Smith decided to be my guardian angel, and neither did Simon and Eliza Fordyce know. In fact—and this is really strange, Luke—they have never actually seen him. He deals with them through a solicitor, and they call him 'the man in the dark room,' because when he has work for them they go to the solicitor's office and Mr. Josiah Smith sits in a completely dark room to give them instructions."

"A curious habit," Luke said dryly. "Do you know what instructions he gave regarding you?"

"Oh yes. They were to make sure I was in safe hands, and when they found that you and Rosemary were looking after me they were well satisfied. But they realized"—I hesitated—"but they realized how ill Rosemary was, so they arranged with you that they would take charge of me when the time came. I didn't want that, Luke. I wanted to stay and look after you."

He looked out of the window, stony-faced. "Never mind about that. Just go on."

I suppressed a sigh and said, "That's all, really. On the ship I learned that they're not married, though I think Eliza would like to be, but they have been together for a long time. Eliza is a vicar's daughter who ran away to be an actress but turned out to be not very good at it. They work for this mysterious gentleman, Mr. Josiah Smith, but they don't seem to know a great deal about him. They didn't know who my enemy was, and they didn't know who I really am either. I think Mr. Josiah Smith *must* have known who I am and have known about the will and the danger from Mr. Lafayette, but I can't imagine how *he* could have learned the truth about me."

"I can tell you that," Luke said brusquely, still gazing out of the window. "Our old friend Tasker told him."

"Tasker? But you just said Mr. Tasker told John Lafayette—who then hired some criminal to silence him."

"That's right." Luke turned his head to look at me again. "Puzzling, isn't it? Unless you happen to know that Josiah Smith and John Lafayette are one and the same man."

ELEVEN

I STOPPED THINKING AND WATCHED A DONKEY CART PILED WITH hay moving along a track between two fields. A peasant woman sat sideways on the donkey; a boy plodded beside her wearing a wide-brimmed hat of straw on the back of his head. After a while, when my befuddled brain had rested for a minute or two, I said, "How can the same man be my protector yet want me dead? How can the same man have had Sid Buller hired to kill me, and then have sent Simon and Eliza Fordyce all the way from England to protect me? For this past year Mr. Josiah Smith has paid for me to attend a very expensive finishing school in Switzerland so that I would be safely hidden away from my enemy there. It simply doesn't make sense."

"I used much the same words to Adrian Webb," said Luke, "and as he pointed out, it may not make simple sense, but it does make devious sense, and Lafayette is a very devious man. The Sid Buller attempt was his first and immediate response to learning from Tasker that you were alive and that his future control of the Glencullen fortune was therefore threatened. Oh, and as Adrian Webb didn't need to point out to me, you can ignore the condition set out in the will that Lafayette must use the fortune exclusively for charitable purposes. Since he is given sole discretion, there would never be anybody to check or to challenge what he did."

I shook my head, still finding it hard to believe what Luke had said. "Why wasn't there another attempt after Sid Buller failed?"

"Because it would have been too obvious. Nobody was sure about Buller's intentions, and the police favored the notion that it was a matter of taking a woman by force, either you or Rosemary. Buller wisely kept his mouth shut, because if he admitted being hired to kill you he would have been even worse off. But if later you had died from foul play, then it would have been plain that this was a second attempt, with Buller being the first, and a lot of very serious inquiries would have begun. Lafayette didn't want that, so now he changed his tack. He became your protector and benefactor, but under his assumed name of Josiah Smith, which he no doubt uses for any activities in which he doesn't want his true identity known. We can't be sure exactly what he plans for you, but he has plenty of time. You won't be twenty-one for three years yet, will you? So if you had an accident of some kind and died in a year's time, or maybe two, nobody would suspect him. After all, he can easily show that he, John Lafayette, has been your kindly benefactor all this time as Josiah Smith."

Luke made a sudden gesture of fury and tugged at his collar as if he felt it choking him. "It was a thousand to one that anybody else would ever know Moira Glencullen had lived beyond two years old. Tasker knew, and he was silenced by killing, which left only Lafayette himself—until I found that page of photographs in your scrapbook, Meg. It doesn't mean the danger is past, not with a man like Lafayette, but at least I've got you out from under his hand, and I'm thankful for that."

I felt suddenly tired, and found it difficult to think clearly. "I'm thankful, too, Luke," I said. "But mainly I'm just so glad to see you and to be with you. I can't imagine how you managed to find me."

"It took weeks," he said, staring into space as if remembering. "Adrian Webb set inquiry agents to watch Lafayette's house in the country. I tackled the shipping line that owns the *Callisto*, the ship you sailed on. After a lot of persuasion they looked up their past records and were able to tell me that Mr. and Mrs. Fordyce, with Miss Meg Gaynor, had disembarked at Marseilles, so that's where I went. I didn't think you would have remained there, so you could have been anywhere on the Continent. But when I tried to find if anyone resembling Simon Fordyce had bought tickets at the railway station there, people looked at me as if I was mad.''

Luke half laughed, rubbing his eyes with finger and thumb. ''It's hardly surprising I had no luck, seeing that I was asking about casual passengers who might have caught a train to anywhere some nine or ten months before. I telegraphed my failure to Adrian Webb, and he wired back reminding me that we had been told the *Callisto* had docked at Marseilles at about six P.M. and had sailed again at midnight. It was unlikely that you had traveled on by train that same evening, so possibly you had stayed at a hotel overnight.''

I said, ''Yes, we did. At the Hotel du Vieux Port.''

''So I discovered, after several days of scouring the hotels,'' said Luke. ''And then at last I had a stroke of luck. A porter at the Vieux Port remembered the three of you. He was just a boy, newly arrived from deep in the country, and you were the first person he had ever seen with red hair and green eyes. He was amazed, because he thought all English people had blond hair and blue eyes. The important thing was that he had heard you talking with Eliza Fordyce as you were leaving next morning, and he remembered the word 'Neuchâtel.' It stuck in his mind because it seemed the only word that wasn't English, and he saw it on your luggage labels as well.''

''His name was Maurice,'' I said. ''He was a pale, skinny boy.''

Luke nodded. ''He may have got less pale and skinny with the money I gave him for remembering. From Marseilles I came to Neuchâtel and took a room on the outskirts. Then I went for daily walks in the country, watching for birds with a pair of binoculars, like any other eccentric English gentleman. After a day or two I felt sure you must be at the finishing school, but it was a week before I saw you, and another three days before I was able to arrange for that fellow with the fruit cart to give you my message."

I did not say anything for a few moments, for I was afraid my voice would falter. When I was sure I could speak steadily I said, "It was wonderfully kind of you to take so much trouble over me."

He folded his arms, frowning slightly. "You must sometimes wish you were back with the tribe," he said, "where everything was very simple. No mysterious enemies, no complicated plots against you, no false friends and treachery."

I shook my head, half smiling. "I never wish that. Living with the tribe wasn't really simple. I expect it's the same everywhere, civilized or uncivilized. I never saw the kind of affection you and Rosemary gave me, but I saw plenty of enmity, fear, plots, and treachery. I saw men wither away and die because a sorcerer pointed the bone at them. Oh, it makes me feel miserable to learn that somebody wants me dead, but for different reasons it could as easily have happened in the tribe. My best friend, Yuma, threatened me just before I ran away."

A new thought occurred to me. "Luke, I don't think Simon and Eliza Fordyce are bad people. I don't think they can have known that the man in the dark room means to harm me. They treated me very kindly, you know."

Luke grimaced. "So has Lafayette, alias Josiah Smith, apparently."

"Yes, but Simon and Eliza don't"—I hesitated—"well, they don't have a bad scent. Oh, I know I'm not supposed to talk about people having scents, but it's true."

"I don't mind your talking to *me* about it," Luke said reasonably. "Can you really tell whether people are good or bad by scent?"

I shook my head. "Only sometimes. It's hard to explain, because it's not something I can distinguish in the same way I can distinguish between, say, you and another person. It's more of an instinct. Occasionally a scent makes the back of my neck prickle, and then I know the person is dangerous. But sometimes that danger doesn't affect the scent.''

"So the Fordyces could be bad and you wouldn't scent it?"

"They could," I said slowly, "but I doubt it with them, Luke. They both have something of a—a good scent. At least, I think so.''

He shrugged. "Well, it's of no importance. You're out of Lafayette's clutches now, which is all that matters. Unfortunately we can't produce any proof that he was responsible for Sid Buller trying to kill you, or any proof of his intentions in the future, so it will be necessary to see that you're well safeguarded until you're twenty-one and the inheritance has passed to you.''

I said, "I've been wondering what you have in mind for us when we reach London. Do you have somewhere for us to live? I haven't kept house since leaving Shalimar, and I'm sure London will be very different, but I learn quite quickly, so I'll soon pick it up.''

He gave an impatient shake of his head. "There's no question of *us* living anywhere, Meg. Fortunately Adrian Webb was a friend of your father and mother, as well as being their lawyer, and he has agreed to take you into his home as one of the family until all this is settled. As for me, once I've seen you safely installed I shall be moving on again.''

"Oh," I said emptily. "Oh. I see.''

IT WAS FIVE O'CLOCK WHEN WE REACHED CALAIS, AND THERE we had two hours to kill before the next ferry left for Dover. While waiting to embark we strolled around the town to stretch our legs, then sat outside a café, lingering over cups of coffee but exchanging few words. I felt strangely desolate. Somehow I could not find it in me to care much about lawyers and wills and a man who wanted me dead. Even knowing who my mother and father were failed to touch me deeply. I thought how wonderful it would have been throughout my childhood to have had such parents to love and to be loved by, but that was in the realm of what might have been. I had no memory of them, and to me they were no closer than characters I had read of in a book.

I had adjusted to the strangeness of life at Clairmont, and now I was to be plunged into yet another new world, equally strange, living in a house in London with the family of a successful lawyer. I had no doubt that I would grow used to it in time, for I was well practiced by now in the way of adjusting to great changes, so it was not this that made me feel desolate. As we sat at the little table, idly watching the passersby, both busy with our own thoughts, I realized the true cause of my dejection. For many hours now Luke had been with me, and I had assumed that in some way we would remain together. Perhaps I would keep house for him, or . . . or . . .

I jumped and almost upset my coffee, then felt my cheeks grow suddenly hot as a startling truth was revealed to me. I wanted to be with Luke. Always. For all my life. I loved Luke Bowman, and if I flushed now it was not from maidenly modesty, for my aborigine upbringing had instilled nothing of that in me; I flushed from shock and shame at the realization that I was in love with Rosemary's husband.

For long seconds I was racked by a sense of betrayal, but then the feeling passed as I recalled how Rosemary herself had begged me to take care of Luke, had even wished me to marry him. I sighed inwardly with relief. There was no betrayal. I had tried to keep my promise to Rosemary for her sake, as a service I owed her and longed to repay. It was not a service I had thought of as a burden, for I was always glad to be with Luke, but it had never occurred to me that I might be in love with him. Perhaps, though, it had occurred to Rosemary; perhaps in her wisdom she had detected the seeds of it in me.

This, then, was why I felt so dispirited now. The man I loved would be going out of my life, and there was nothing I could do to keep him. Rosemary was his only love. It was surely for her sake only, because he knew how Rosemary had cared for me, that Luke had gone to such trouble for so many weeks past in order to protect me.

I sat with aching heart, gazing out over the harbor but hardly seeing anything, afraid to look at Luke in case he read my feelings in my eyes. I was sure he would be angry if he suspected the truth, and I could not bear the thought of his parting from me in anger. Some time later I roused from a kind of waking sleep to hear him say, "The boat's in, Meg. We can go aboard now."

The sea was calm and the evening warm. I was glad to sit on deck, for with the sea to watch there seemed little need for conversation between us, and we could remain silent without any feeling of unease. Soon after eight o'clock we reached Dover and I set foot on the land of my birth, the land of which I had no memory.

"We've both traveled enough for one day," said Luke as we came out of the customs shed with a porter wheeling our luggage on a trolley. "We'll stay at a hotel tonight and take the morning train. Is that all right?"

"Yes. Yes, of course. Thank you, Luke."

He peered at me. "Is anything wrong? You're very quiet."

"No, I expect I'm just tired."

"You?" His eyebrows lifted, and he smiled. "That must be a record. I've never known you tired before. Come along, we'll just tidy up, then have dinner." He took my arm, never dreaming that his smile and the touch of his hand made my heart turn over within me.

I slept poorly that night in a pleasant room of the Queensbury Hotel, but by breakfast time next morning I felt able to keep my feelings hidden from Luke, and even contrived one of our brief squabbles, glaring at him with my alley-cat face so that he would feel all was normal. At ten o'clock we reached the huge, sprawling metropolis of London, and I was thankful I had at least glimpsed something of Paris to prepare me for the size and bustle of a great city thronged with people, horses, cabs, carts, and carriages of every kind.

We left Victoria Station with its great locomotives, its medley of noises, and, above all for me, its mingled scents of steam and hot metal, food and flowers from the stalls, horses and countless humans. Luke caught my arm as we made for the cab rank, pointing with his cane, and there in the road I saw the incredible sight of a carriage moving noisily on four wheels without a horse to draw it. I had once seen a picture of a motor car in a magazine, but to see the reality left me breathless.

Ten minutes later we were in an enormous shop with several floors one above the other, each filled with vast quantities of goods in such inconceivable variety that I had to make a huge effort to hide my astonishment, clenching my jaws to stop my mouth hanging open. Luke led me to the ladies' department, summoned the senior assistant, a plump middle-aged lady with a pleasing scent, and told her to take his sister away and provide her with a complete wardrobe for all occasions, as would be required for a young lady who had lost everything in a shipwreck. He would return, he said, in two hours' time.

I was clearly something of a puzzle to the shoplady, but she took up her task with enthusiasm, regretting that the emergency necessitated my taking ready-made clothes, but comforting me with the assurance that my brother would undoubtedly arrange for a dressmaker to visit me at the earliest opportunity. By the time Luke returned, two well-filled trunks stood ready and I felt more exhausted from trying on clothes than I had ever felt after a day's journey in the outback. Luke arrived with a cab, having collected his case and my own from the left-luggage office at Victoria, and when he had paid the bill, which I was sure must be enormous, we set off again.

A few minutes later we stopped outside a huge building with sentries standing guard by the iron gates in scarlet coats and great fur hats that I knew were called bearskins, for I had seen soldiers like this in magazine pictures.

"Buckingham Palace," said Luke. "That's where Mitjiquin lives, the lady with her head engraved on that magic penny you told me about, remember?"

"Oh . . . Yuma's *mapanpa*. Yes." I should have been deeply
interested to see the London palace of Queen Victoria, and to
think of the enormous gap I had spanned since the day I had
cast my spear to secure the kangaroo bone that Yuma wanted;
but I was distracted and filled with mingled sadness and apprehension as I realized we must be nearing our journey's end.
"Where are we going now?" I asked.

Luke took out his watch and looked at it. "Almost time for
luncheon," he said, "so it wouldn't be courteous to go straight
to Adrian Webb's house. It's only half a mile away in Belgrave
Square." He pushed up the trap in the roof with his cane and
called to the driver, "Café Royal now."

"Right, sir."

As the cabbie whipped up his horse Luke said, "I'll take you
to luncheon there first and send the cabbie on to Belgrave Square
to deliver the luggage with a note to say we'll arrive sometime
after two o'clock." He glanced down at me with that curiously
ironic smile I had seen before. "With luck you'll set eyes on
some famous people at feeding time, Meg. The Café Royal is
quite a haunt of London's literary and artistic luminaries—chaps
like Swinburne, Beardsley, Whistler, Oscar Wilde—Oh no, you
won't see Wilde; he's just gone to prison."

In fact I saw no well-known person that I was aware of during
luncheon, but the Café Royal itself was another new experience
for me, an enormous place of mirrors and red plush, with ornate
cornices to lofty ceilings, thickly carpeted floors, and splendid
table linen, plate, and cutlery. I had no trouble with the menu,
for I had been well taught at Clairmont, but I ordered only one
course, for I had little appetite.

Luke said, "Are you all right? Not feeling unwell?"

"No, no, I'm perfectly well, thank you. It's partly because
I'm nervous about going to Mr. Webb's house, but I never have
been able to eat as much as"—I lowered my voice and tried to
make a little joke—"as you *walypala*. I don't think I ever shall.
Remember how Rosemary used to worry about me at first? Then

at Clairmont I was just the same, breakfast and dinner but not much between.''

Luke nodded. ''I'll mention it to Adrian Webb to save you having to explain.'' He picked up his soup spoon. ''You'll make some fellow a very economical wife one day, Meg.''

Those idle words were like salt on a wound to me. I was only able to pick at my meal, and for the next hour I drove myself to make cheerful conversation so that Luke would not suspect my sorrow and its cause, telling him more about my time at Clairmont, of my friends and daily life there, and of particular incidents such as my confrontation with Clarissa, which caused him to laugh aloud.

At half past two we took a cab along Piccadilly to Hyde Park Corner and then on into a square of splendid houses, with beautiful lawns and gardens occupying the center of the square. Here the cab drew up at Number 24. Luke paid it off, then almost brought tears of pleasure to my eyes by offering me his arm to escort me up the steps to the deep porch.

I had learned about different grades of servant from Ruth and Fiona at Clairmont simply by listening to their conversation, and I had gained experience of a big house with servants when spending Christmas with Nicole, so I knew that the man who opened the door to us, wearing a dark suit and black tie, was the butler. He was portly, with a pink face, thin gray hair, and a dignified manner, inclining his head politely at sight of Luke and saying at once, ''Good afternoon, sir. You will be Mr. Bowman?''

''And Miss Gaynor,'' said Luke.

''Quite so, sir.'' The butler gave me a deferential smile and stood back. ''Please come in. I am Henson, the butler, and you are of course expected. The master received your note, and I have sent Miss Gaynor's luggage to her room for the maid to unpack. Your own case is in the hall awaiting you, sir. If you will come this way, please?''

Clutching Luke's arm, I walked with him across a large paneled hall with a broad staircase running up to a gallery.

Henson opened a door and said, "If you will be so kind as to wait in the morning room, I will advise the master of your arrival."

When the door had closed Luke murmured, "Sit down, Meg," and reluctantly I stopped clutching his arm, took an upright chair near the window, and clutched my handbag instead. Luke stood with hat and cane in hand, gazing out of the window.

After half a minute of silence I whispered, "Where will you be living, Luke? Shall I see you sometimes? And may I write to you now? Well, I have been writing to you all this time— that's how I keep my diary—but I'd be very happy if I could send you letters."

He continued to look out of the window, and I saw his jaw tighten. "No point, Meg, no point," he said shortly. "I'll be going abroad and traveling again very soon."

"Oh, I see." I sat trying to empty my mind of thought. Parting with Luke before, parting with my first true friend, had been cruelly painful. Now he had come into my life again for little more than twenty-four hours, just long enough for me to discover that I loved him and to make me feel that this second parting would break my heart. I was suddenly shocked to find my mind saying *mitjiquin, mitjiquin, mitjiquin*, as if in some primitive attempt to numb the pain.

Next moment the door opened, and as I came to my feet I made a huge effort to pull myself together. The man who entered wore a gray suit with a paler gray silk tie. My first impression was that he seemed to be two parts of different men. For while he was tall, lean, and broad-shouldered, his head was round, his face cherubic under short, dark, curly hair, and his brown eyes held a merry twinkle, so that from above the shoulders he reminded me irresistibly of a young Mr. Pickwick. He came quickly toward me, moving lightly and reaching out his hands so that I automatically put out my own to be grasped.

"My dear, my dear," he said warmly, "thank heaven Luke has brought you safely home." He turned his head, still holding my hands. "Well done, my dear fellow. Nobody but you could have succeeded, for you alone had Moira's trust."

I winced inwardly, but Luke said, "She would prefer to remain Meg Gaynor, and it would probably be wiser for her to do so for the present."

"Of course. And I shall certainly follow her wishes on that point." Mr. Webb looked at me again, smiling and giving my hands a little press as if of greeting. "Welcome to your new home, Meg. Your mother and father were among my dearest friends, and I was greatly moved when they made me their lost child's trustee, though I never dreamed I should have the joy of taking up that very welcome duty."

He released my hands, and I made a little curtsy as I said, "You're very kind, sir. Please forgive me if I don't say the right words, but I'm still greatly confused. I've traveled a long way and have had so much to take in during the last forty-eight hours." Though I was not quite telling a lie I was certainly giving a false impression, for if I seemed dull and slow-witted it was not from traveling or from anything Luke had told me. It was simply because I was numb with heartache.

"My dear child, I marvel that you can keep your eyes open after such an exhausting time," said Adrian Webb, "and although I'm most eager to have a long chat with you I shall insist that you rest for an hour or two, indeed for as long as you wish, and we shall talk this evening after dinner."

"Thank you, sir. I would be glad of a little time to collect myself."

"Of course, of course." He clasped his hands behind his back, beaming at me and bouncing slightly on his toes in a mannerism that would well have suited Mr. Pickwick. I could read nothing from his scent, but to the extent that I was able to feel anything at all with the sorrow of Luke's parting upon me, I felt I was fortunate indeed to be taken into the home of a man so kindly. ". . . But let us settle upon a mode of address less formal than 'sir,' " he was saying now with a glance at Luke.

"As a close friend of the family might I claim the adoptive title of Uncle Adrian, do you think?"

Before I could answer, the door opened and a lady entered. She had a thin face and moved her angular body in a strangely awkward way. Sandy hair was swept up in pompadour style around her head, her eyes were deep-set and intense, and I judged her to be in her late thirties. Adrian Webb said, "Ah, there you are, Becky. This gentleman is Mr. Luke Bowman, of whom I have told you, and here we have his cousin by marriage, Meg Gaynor, who is to be our guest." He turned to us. "Mr. Bowman, Meg, I present my dear wife, Rebecca."

Luke bowed over the lady's hand, and I dropped her a curtsy. She gave us a quick, nervous smile and said, "Good afternoon, Mr. Bowman. How nice to see you, Meg. I do hope you will be happy here."

I murmured a suitable response, still taking in the fact that I had been introduced to Mrs. Webb as a relative of Luke's, which seemed to indicate that she had not been told my true identity. Her husband said with a smile, "I was just suggesting that since Meg is to become one of the family she might address us quite informally as Uncle Adrian and Aunt Becky, if you agree, my dear."

She gave him a startled glance, as if surprised at what he had said, or perhaps surprised at having her opinion sought, but answered quickly, "Of course, Adrian, what a splendid notion. We must certainly do all we can to ensure that she is comfortable with us."

"Yes, indeed," said Adrian Webb, "and let us make a good start by allowing the child to rest. Will you take her to her room, Becky? I think you might tell Henson to have a cup of tea sent up to her, and then she can take a nap if she wishes. Maggie will be looking after her, will she not? Excellent. Then have Maggie wake her at half past six, and you can show her the house and garden before dinner, hmm?"

"Very well, Adrian." Her hands fluttered, and again came that quick, nervous smile, but there seemed to be nothing unfriendly in it. I felt that Mrs. Webb was simply a highly strung lady with the mannerisms that went with such a temperament. There had been a girl at school rather like her, whose jumpy movements had reminded me of a darting lizard. Now Mrs. Webb glanced at Luke and said, ''Shall we be having the pleasure of Mr. Bowman's company for dinner also?''

''No, ma'am, no, though it's most kind of you to ask,'' Luke said briskly. ''I'll take my leave of you now, if you'll excuse me.''

He turned to me, and I made myself look through him, for I did not dare to let my eyes focus on his face lest I should lose my composure and weep. This was my farewell to Luke, and it would have to be made under the gaze of two strangers. I had hoped to be private for this moment, had hoped for some small gesture that I might treasure, and I stupidly recalled how Simon Fordyce had even kissed my lips in saying good-bye. That would have been something for me to remember, but I knew it would not happen. I heard Luke's voice saying, ''Well, good-bye, Meg. I'm sure you'll be very happy here.''

I heard my own voice, as if it were that of another person, saying, ''Good-bye, Luke. Thank you for all your kindness. God bless you.''

Then there came a murmur of voices as he took his leave of Mr. and Mrs. Webb—Uncle Adrian and Aunt Becky, as I would now have to remember to call them. I kept gazing in front of me with unfocused eyes, so my vision became blurred and I was unaware of the moment when Henson the butler arrived and Luke was shown out; but after a while I felt a touch on my arm, and Aunt Becky said, ''Come along, dear. I'll show you your room.''

IT WAS A MAGNIFICENT BEDROOM, AND MY NEW CLOTHES, HATS, and shoes had all been put away in two great wardrobes. I was introduced to a maid called Maggie, a girl with an accent I later discovered was Cockney, who was about my own age and also had freckles, though fewer than mine. Another maid brought me a cup of tea on a silver tray, and a few moments later I was alone.

I drank my tea, took off my shoes and dress, lay on the bed and wept a little, then became angry with myself for being so ungrateful. I explored the room, looked out of the window onto a well kept garden, and put my personal belongings away in drawers—my diary, my birthday presents from Clairmont, my books, Luke's photograph, and Rosemary's pendant. When this was done I emptied my mind and slept, hoping to be refreshed for the evening. Uncle Adrian and Aunt Becky had been remarkably kind and thoughtful, but even so I felt that this first evening and my first few days in Belgrave Square would surely be something of an ordeal.

I woke at six, washed my face and hands, made my hair tidy, and put on one of the new dresses Luke had bought for me. At half past six it was not Maggie but Aunt Becky herself who tapped on the door, announcing that we would make a tour of the house and she would introduce the rest of the servants to me.

Number 24, Belgrave Square was no less splendid than Nicole's house in Grenoble. Even to me it was obvious that the furnishings, chandeliers, curtains, carpets, paneling, and every item of ornament or decoration was of the most expensive quality. From my studies at Clairmont I was able to recognize the work of Landseer and Millais in two of the many paintings that hung on the walls of rooms, halls, and passages. It was not a very long tour, for Aunt Becky did not linger anywhere as she darted from room to room with her nervous, scuttling walk, pointing out whatever seemed to me quite obvious.

"Now, here is the drawing room, dear. There is the piano in the corner, you see? Do you play?"

"Not really, Aunt Becky. I had some lessons—" I was about to say "at Clairmont" but stopped short, wondering if Aunt Becky was supposed to know precisely where I had come from. "But I only got as far as playing scales rather badly," I went on, deciding I had better be prudent until I had talked with Uncle Adrian.

Aunt Becky smoothed her hand over the gleaming surface of the magnificent grand piano. "Such a pity." She sighed. "I was never put to the piano when young, so this beautiful instrument is wasted. The boys may take it up one day, of course."

"Which boys, Aunt Becky?"

She gave me a startled look. "Oh, did Mr. Bowman not tell you that Adrian and I have two sons? There is Albert, who is thirteen years old, and Edward, who is eleven. Of course, they are at boarding school, but will be coming home for the summer holidays in a few weeks. Let us go out by the French windows and look at the garden, dear. Then we can return by way of the dining room."

As we stepped onto the terrace she blushed slightly and lowered her voice. "The boys are called after our dear Queen's late husband and her eldest son, Albert and Edward, you see? It was my own idea. I feared Her Majesty might regard it as disrespectful had she known, which of course was most unlikely, but Adrian assured me that it was a very respectful compliment. See how the tulips are coming along. I think they are my favorite flower after roses and perhaps peonies."

I was puzzled by Aunt Becky, for I felt that a wealthy and successful man like Uncle Adrian would have had a rather different wife, a self-possessed lady who spoke calmly, moved with dignity, and was never flustered. I thought no less of Aunt Becky because she was not like this; in fact, I felt there might be a bond of sympathy between us, for I well knew what it was like to be filled with anxiety, though perhaps I was able to conceal it better.

The tour ended with a brief visit to the kitchen, where Mrs. Cartwright, the cook, was busy preparing dinner. Here the servants I had not yet encountered during my tour were introduced to me, and then Aunt Becky led the way back to her sewing room, which we had visited earlier. I had been making a great effort to throw off my sorrow and try to appreciate how lucky I was to be received so kindly into this household, and as Aunt Becky closed the door I said, "Thank you very much for showing me the house, Aunt Becky. I'm anxious not to be a nuisance to you in any way, so I shall always be glad of your guidance as to whatever you would like me to do."

She came toward me with a rather secretive air, glancing over her shoulder as if to make sure the door was properly shut, and said with one of her quick smiles, "I'm delighted to have you here, Meg, and I feel sure we shall get along famously. Sit down, dear, sit down."

I took a chair on one side of a small round table, and Aunt Becky seated herself facing me, talking as she did so. "I find it a great strain to have Albert and Edward home for the school holidays. We shall be going down to Eastbourne for part of the time, as usual. We have a very nice manor house there, and I do hope you will be able to—to help keep the boys entertained. I find them rather demanding, and it is extremely difficult to get a temporary nanny just for the holidays." Aunt Becky leaned across the table, grasped my wrist, fixed me with a penetrating look, lowered her voice, and went on without pause, "You are a sensitive, Meg. I am sure of it."

"Oh. Am I?" I said, rather bewildered. "A what?"

"A sensitive, dear. Will you help me?"

"Er . . . yes, if I can, Aunt Becky."

Her voice became a whisper, her gaze urgent. "I am trying to get in touch with my dear father, Meg."

I was utterly baffled, and began to wonder if I had missed being instructed in some important fact or custom of the civilized world. Aunt Becky went on, "I *know* dear Papa has something to tell me, and I am sure you can help me get in touch with him."

I said hesitantly, "Perhaps . . . perhaps I could write a letter to him for you, Aunt Becky?"

She blinked in astonishment. "A letter? No, no! Papa passed on to the Other Side ten years ago now."

I gasped as a hazy light dawned on me. "Oh, I do beg your

pardon! I didn't understand—or perhaps I still don't understand. Do you mean that your father died ten years ago, Aunt Becky?''

She winced, then said reproachfully, ''He passed away, dear.''

I knew that expression, and it confirmed what I suspected she meant. I said, ''Please accept my condolences, Aunt Becky. I'm so sorry. But how can I help you to get in touch with him?''

''With his *spirit*, Meg,'' she said eagerly. ''Oh, please don't mention this to Adrian, for he would never approve, but I have been attending séances with a few like-minded ladies for several years now, and many spirits have spoken to us through our medium, Mrs. Cruikshank, but my dear papa has never yet found the way of communication from the Other Side, and I know he must be trying so hard.''

Her eyes filled with tears, and I found myself patting her hand and murmuring rather muddled words of comfort as I tried to collect my wits and grasp what she was telling me. In the tribe, I had been taught that the world was made during a dreamtime before man began, made by ancestral spirits that were enormous animals and birds of various kinds. These spirits could die, and then they became stars in the sky, or rocks, mountains, caves, water holes, but their essence remained, and in this form they were responsible for all births by putting the seeds of babies into women's bodies.

I was not considered a true person, but the aborigines believed that all men and women had existed in a spirit state before being born into profane life. On initiation they entered sacred time, and on death they returned to their original spirit state, ready to begin the cycle again. But I had never heard of anyone attempting to talk with those spirits.

Rosemary had taught me very different beliefs, and I had accepted them because she was Rosemary, though I was sometimes puzzled by certain things I read in the Bible or heard in church. While at Shalimar I had read in a magazine that Sir Arthur Conan Doyle, who wrote the Sherlock Holmes stories, was investigating something called Spiritualism, and the article explained what this was. Later, at Clairmont, a few of the girls had tried to hold a séance one evening, sitting round a table with the lights out and hands joined, but nothing happened except that some became frightened, others began to giggle, and the séance broke up.

I had been very slow-witted in failing to grasp Aunt Becky's meaning much sooner, but now I realized that she was a Spiritualist, perhaps a secret one, and that she had a passionate desire to communicate with the spirit of her dead father. I also realized that she felt I was gifted in some obscure way and might be able to help her.

Even as this thought came to me she said, "I have been wondering if the *venue* is wrong, Meg. Perhaps that is why dear Papa cannot reach me through Mrs. Cruikshank. I could not dream of inviting her to this house, of course, for she is a quite common person in spite of her powers as a medium. But you and I together, holding a little private séance here in my sewing room, which is completely private . . . who knows what might happen? You do *believe*, don't you, dear?"

I said uneasily, "I don't know, Aunt Becky. I don't feel it's very likely that anybody can talk to a person who has—er, passed away."

"Oh, but it's true, Meg!" she said urgently. "I've heard Mrs. Cruikshank talk to spirits many times."

I did not want to argue, so I said meekly, "I just thought perhaps it's more likely that two living people can talk without speaking, even at a distance. I once knew somebody who could do that." I had once known many who could do it, for in the tribe it was regarded as a perfectly natural ability, but I could not tell Aunt Becky that.

"Well, at least we can *try*, can we not?" she said pleadingly.

I could think of no way to refuse, and tried to sound warmly willing as I said, "Yes, of course we can. I just don't want you to be disappointed if we fail. But why do you think this house would be better as a—a venue for getting in touch with your father?"

"Oh, because it was *his*, dear!" she said eagerly. "This was

Papa's house until he passed away, and so was the house at Eastbourne.'' She hesitated, then looked down at the table with a touch of heightened color coming to her cheeks. ''Papa was a very well-to-do man, but I'm afraid he made his money in *trade*. A chain of jewelers' shops.''

I said, ''Is there something wrong about jewelers' shops?''

''Well, it's *trade,* Meg, which is not at all the thing for people out of the top drawer. It's not like being a landowner or in one of the professions.''

I felt out of my depth, and said, ''Still, it's very nice for you that your father owned this house and a manor house at Eastbourne.''

''Oh yes, he acquired a lot of property, which I inherited when he passed on, since I was an only child, and then of course it became Adrian's property since he is my husband.'' She darted a glance at the clock. ''Oh my goodness, just look at the time. We shall have Henson calling us for dinner at any moment.''

She got to her feet, and I rose with her as she went on, ''We'll let you settle down for a few days, and then we'll have a little séance while Adrian is at his office, but not a word to anyone, Meg dear. This is our little secret.''

I said, ''Yes, Aunt Becky,'' and followed her from the room, feeling bemused by all that she had poured out to me in the last twenty minutes, and not a little apprehensive about the prospect of our private séance.

At dinner we had two servants to wait on the three of us, and I thought with a pang of how Rosemary must have struggled to keep house, taking care of Luke and a primitive creature from the outback until I had learned enough to help with the work. Aunt Becky chatted in sudden bursts, fluttering nervously from time to time, but I realized that this was her usual manner. Uncle Adrian was an easy conversationalist, always relaxed and never at a loss for something to say. For my part I felt I managed quite well in conversation, for this was something much practiced at Clairmont, but I had to be a little careful since I was not sure how much Aunt Becky was supposed to know about me.

After dinner she settled down at the bureau in the drawing room to write letters to Albert and Edward at boarding school, while Uncle Adrian took me off to his study for the chat he had promised when I first arrived. He made sure I was comfortable in an easy chair, then sat behind a large desk set diagonally before the window and looked at me with a twinkle in his eye.

"I hope you're not feeling too nervous about your first séance with Aunt Becky," he said.

TWELVE

I WAS AT A COMPLETE LOSS, NOT KNOWING WHAT TO SAY AND feeling sure my face wore a blankly stupid look. Uncle Adrian made a reassuring gesture and said, "Oh, don't worry, my dear. I've no doubt Aunt Becky said it was to be a secret, but I'm very well aware that the dear soul has been trying for years to make contact through a medium with her late father."

I said cautiously, "Oh, I see."

Uncle Adrian sighed. "Every now and again she becomes convinced that some new acquaintance is a sensitive, as she calls it, and then she tries to persuade them to join her in a séance, though she doesn't always succeed. She seems to regard young girls as the most promising prospects, and managed to scare away two or three maids we've had until I put my foot down and forbade her to involve any servants." He smiled ruefully. "But as soon as I saw you I felt sure Becky would lose no time in raising the subject."

I said, "What do you want me to do, Uncle Adrian?"

"Well . . . Luke Bowman told me all about how you found him in the outback and brought him to safety. A remarkable story, and one that shows your upbringing to have made you a very level-headed girl, not easily frightened, so I would be grateful to have you humor Aunt Becky in this matter, Meg." He gave me an apologetic look. "If you don't mind."

I said, "You mean you would like me to join in a séance with her and perhaps accompany her when she goes to join other ladies in a séance?"

"Would you find it in any way disturbing?"

I reflected for a few moments, then said, "No, I don't think so, Uncle Adrian, but I feel I shall be of very little help. I'm not a sensitive, I don't think it's likely that we can talk to dead people, and I won't be able to pretend, because I'm rather hopeless at that."

He threw back his head and chuckled. "I wouldn't ask you to pretend, Meg. The sooner Aunt Becky realizes you can't help her get in touch with her late father, the sooner she'll stop pestering you to try. Obviously nothing will happen when you have a private séance with her in the sewing room, and I doubt that anything significant will occur if you go with her to this medium she thinks so well of—Mrs. Cruikshank, isn't it?"

"Yes, I think that was the name she mentioned, Uncle Adrian."

He nodded thoughtfully. "You might find it somewhat creepy, hearing messages for other people, but to be fair to this woman she has never yet claimed to have—er, got in touch with Becky's father, which she would certainly have done if she was a fraud. However, it probably won't be long before she announces that your presence is unhelpful, Meg. I suspect that your down-to-earth mentality would be considered obstructive at a séance, not conducive to good communication with spirits in the next world, so I'm sure you won't have to put up with it for long."

I hoped that would be so, for although I had never given thought to such a matter before, I now realized that I was in no way attracted to the notion of communicating with the dead, even if that were possible. I did not want messages from my mother or father, or even from my beloved Rosemary, for this would have smacked too much of the sorcery I had been brought up to fear. But despite my reluctance I felt unable to refuse what had been asked, and I said, "I'll do as you wish, Uncle Adrian, but I won't be able to tell you anything about it because Aunt

Becky has asked for it to be kept secret. It's rather difficult for me, really."

"My dear child, I see that only too well, so let me assure you that I have no wish to hear anything further on the subject, and we need never refer to it again."

I felt relieved, and said, "Thank you, Uncle Adrian. I've been wanting to ask you if anybody else knows who I am and where I came from. I've been careful not to say anything in front of Aunt Becky until I had the opportunity to ask you about it."

"Sensible girl," he said approvingly. "Not that we need to worry about my dear Becky, for apart from her obsession concerning her father she is almost entirely lacking in curiosity. She assumes that Luke Bowman is a client of mine, and she has been told that since the death of his wife he has been responsible for her cousin, Meg Gaynor. Since Luke Bowman travels on business worldwide and has no permanent residence, he has transferred that responsibility to me under a proper legal arrangement, making me your guardian and trustee."

Uncle Adrian paused to smile. "To a very great extent this is all true," he went on. "Becky knows nothing of that scoundrel Lafayette, or of the way he kept you hidden from the world at a school in Switzerland until he could safely strike you down. Your Aunt Becky simply believes that you have completed your education at a finishing school where Luke Bowman placed you, and that I have now brought you home to live with us. This is what everybody else—our family, our friends and acquaintances—will be given to understand, and as I have said, it is virtually true."

"You mean Luke has really made you my guardian, Uncle Adrian?"

He shook his head. "Ah no. He has no legal authority to do so, since you are in no way related to him. But I am of course your trustee, since I was appointed as such in your father's will."

I knew this, of course, but had forgotten it at the moment, for it was not easy to keep track of all I had discovered in the last two days. I said, "Forgive me if I shouldn't speak of this, but won't it be a great expense for you to keep me until I'm twenty-one?"

He toyed with a pencil on his desk, half smiling. "I don't think you need worry about that, Meg. For one thing, Luke Bowman is a rich man and insisted on placing ample funds at my disposal. For another, as your trustee I am allowed to draw upon your inheritance and apply such funds for your benefit at my entire discretion. However, I don't expect to use either source of monies, for I'm . . . well, a man of substance myself, and it will be no hardship to provide for the needs of one extra member of the family."

I was touched by what he had said, but it was the thought of what Luke had done that made me so happy I could not trust my voice for a few moments. At last I said, "You're very kind, Uncle Adrian, and I hardly know how to thank you."

"There's no need," he said quietly. "Your father and mother were my friends." He leaned back in his chair, thoughtful of expression, and there was a little silence. Then he sat up briskly, reached across the desk to open a box, and took out a cigar. "I now propose to smoke," he said cheerfully, "which your Aunt Becky detests, so I shall do it here in my study. I'm sure you'll soon be ready for bed after the past two hectic days, and I don't think we need to talk about anything else tonight, do we, my dear?"

I shook my head. "No, Uncle Adrian. Well, unless you have any instructions for me about what to do each day."

He looked surprised. "Good heavens no. The servants attend to all the work, of course, and Becky pays and receives a few morning calls. Apart from that, there's"—he paused, frowning at his cigar, then went on vaguely—"sewing and reading and— ah, various things that ladies do. Of course, Albert and Edward will be home from boarding school in a few weeks, and I'm sure Becky will be glad of some help in keeping them occupied. Do you play the piano? Or ride? Hmmm, a pity. But perhaps you would like to learn?"

I said, "I'd like to learn proper riding, Uncle Adrian. All I know at the moment is how to harness a horse and drive a trap or cart."

"Well, in London we find it more convenient to use cabs, but we have our own carriages down at Eastbourne, and among them there's a gig you can drive." He looked at me with his head to one side, amused. "But you won't be required to do any harnessing, Meg. We have grooms for that."

"Yes, I should have realized. Well, thank you very much, Uncle Adrian." I stood up to leave, and as I turned my eye was caught by a shelf on the wall bearing several silver cups, a row of framed photographs above them. Uncle Adrian followed my gaze as he came round the desk.

"From my younger days," he said. "I had some small prowess in athletics."

Together we moved to look at the photographs. One showed a group of young men, all with oars, another showed a different group in shirts and short trousers. It was easy to pick out the young Adrian Webb from each of these. A third photograph showed a big, wild-looking man with a shock of hair, dressed in rags. The remaining picture was again of Uncle Adrian, a few years older than in the first two, wearing a wide-brimmed hat and with a rifle resting over his shoulder. At his feet lay a dead lion.

"A record of my salad days," he said, indicating the first two pictures. "I was a double blue at Cambridge."

"I'm afraid I don't know what that means, Uncle Adrian."

"Oh, it means I represented Cambridge against other universities in two sports, rowing and rugby football." He chuckled and tapped the next photograph. "I doubt if you can recognize me here. I was in the Amateur Dramatic Society, and played Caliban in Shakespeare's *Tempest*. Do you know it?"

"Yes. I've only read six of his plays so far, but that was one of them, and I remember Caliban, the poor wild man. Did you shoot the lion that's in this last photograph, Uncle Adrian?"

"Yes, my dear, I did. And however calm and pleased with

myself I may look, I can assure you I found it a terrifying moment. That was in Kenya, soon after I came down from Cambridge and before I took my final examinations in law. The active life is behind me now, I fear.''

His words brought a thought to my mind, and I said, ''May I ask one thing, Uncle Adrian? I really would like the opportunity to explore London—I mean the central parts—for I've never lived in a big city. May I be allowed to go out walking, please? I would never get lost, I promise.''

He gave me a quizzical look. ''Luke Bowman speaks with awe of your abilities in that respect, but a city is very different from the outback, you know.''

''Oh, that only makes it easier, Uncle Adrian. There are so many more things to mark the way.''

''Well, I'm sure you know best on that score, but we mustn't forget that you have a dangerous enemy, my dear.''

I had forgotten, for despite all that Luke had told me I had a mental picture of Mr. Josiah Smith as a benign person, and found it hard to adjust to the notion that he was in fact the monstrous John Lafayette who sought my life. Now I said, ''Surely he couldn't try to have me harmed in public and in daylight, could he?''

Uncle Adrian got up and paced the room, hands in pockets, frowning. ''Most unlikely,'' he said at last, ''but it means you must walk only by daylight and always keep to public places. If at any time you feel you are being watched or followed, then you must let me know at once, you understand?''

''Yes, Uncle Adrian.''

He halted in front of me, and the touch of sternness faded from his round, cheerful face. ''You lived much of your life under the sky,'' he said gently, ''and I realize how hard it would be if you were confined to the house. Just be alert and careful, Meg, particularly if anybody speaks to you. Don't be deceived by some plausible tale designed to lure you into danger.''

''I'll be very careful, Uncle Adrian, and thank you again.''

''I'm sure you will bring pleasure to our family, Meg. Good

night, my dear." He bent to kiss my cheek, then took my arm and escorted me to the door, holding it open for me. I spent the next hour in the drawing room talking with Aunt Becky and looking at her family album. There were several pictures of her father, a big man with a severe expression, and her eyes filled with tears as she told me how he had died in his own stables at the manor house in Eastbourne after being kicked in the head by his favorite horse as he knelt to examine a hoof. It was believed that the horse must have been stung by a bee at that moment, causing it to kick out wildly.

I murmured my sympathy and turned the pages. Albert Webb, the older son, was like his mother. Eleven-year-old Edward was almost comically like his father, with the same round head that seemed mismatched on the well-built body. At ten o'clock I excused myself and went to bed. There I was able to let go of the tight rein I had kept on my thoughts and feelings, allowing myself to think of Luke and to weep a little from the heartache of losing him. After a while I said my prayers and slept.

The following afternoon, while Uncle Adrian was at his office in Grays Inn, I experienced my first séance. Before it began I was afraid I might disgrace myself by giggling out of nervousness, but in fact my only feeling was one of pity for Aunt Becky. We sat on either side of the small table in the sewing room with the curtains drawn, our hands resting on the table with fingers touching to complete a circle.

Nothing happened. I could hear Aunt Becky's breathing and my own, and I was aware of a confusion of emotions within me. I wanted something to happen for Aunt Becky's sake, but I had no wish to hear any spirit voices talking to me. Every few minutes Aunt Becky would say, "Is anybody there?" No response came, and after a while she whispered, "Are you awake, Meg?"

"Yes, Aunt Becky."

"Oh." She sounded disappointed. "I thought you might be going into a trance so that the spirits could speak through you."

"I don't know how to go into a trance," I whispered apologetically.

"I think it just happens, dear. At least it seems to with Mrs. Cruikshank. Sometimes the table moves quite violently. You haven't felt this one moving?"

"No, I'm afraid not. I don't think I'm much use at this, Aunt Becky."

"Oh dear. I felt sure you were a sensitive, even though you were unaware of it. Let us try a little longer, dear."

We tried twice more during the next two days, with the same lack of result. Then, as Uncle Adrian had predicted, Aunt Becky accepted that I had no powers as a medium and we abandoned the experiments, much to my relief. There still remained the weekly séance at Mrs. Cruikshank's home in Kensington, and this I attended four times. The other ladies present were extremely pleasant, and Mrs. Cruikshank herself seemed a very down-to-earth person. When we formed a circle around the table and the séance began she appeared to go quickly into a trance and then spoke in a deep voice. This, I learned, was the voice of her control, a Cornish fisherman who had died over a hundred years ago.

There was never a moment when I felt that Mrs. Cruikshank was pretending, but no message came from Aunt Becky's father, and the messages and advice for other ladies from various departed relatives seemed very ordinary. I could not help feeling it strange that spirits in the next world seemed to know no more than living people in this world. Perhaps these thoughts had a bad effect, for the spirit responses became fewer and briefer with each visit I made, and once again Uncle Adrian's prediction was fulfilled when Aunt Becky told me with some embarrassment that Mrs. Cruikshank thought it best that I should refrain from attending in the future.

Before this happened, and during my first week in Belgrave Square, when I was out walking for only the third time, I stopped to look in a shop window as I was making my way along Piccadilly, and on glancing back I noticed a man I was sure I had seen earlier, when I set out from the house. He wore a brown suit and bowler hat, and he also had stopped to look in a shop window. I did not know the man, but was certain I had caught sight of him the day before, in Hyde Park, and I recalled that Uncle Adrian had said I must tell him at once if I felt I was being watched or followed.

At once I hailed a cab and drove to the offices of Adrian Webb & Co., solicitors of Grays Inn, for although I had never been there before, I knew the address. They were very fine offices, and I gave my name to a clerk, who showed me to a waiting room. Only half a minute later Uncle Adrian appeared, looking surprised and anxious. "Meg? What is it, my dear?"

"I think I'm being followed, Uncle Adrian. There was a man near me in Piccadilly whom I saw when I left the house, and I also saw him strolling behind me in Hyde Park yesterday. The same man. And with all the thousands of people in London, I don't think it can be a coincidence."

Uncle Adrian ran a hand back over his short curly hair and made a wry grimace. "No, it isn't, Meg. I thought there was no need to tell you, but I should have remembered you've had to acquire the habit of noticing all that goes on about you."

I stared. "What do you mean, Uncle Adrian?"

"Is it a man in a brown suit and bowler hat?"

"Why, yes!"

"That will be Mr. Finn, and I suspect that he is now outside in a cab, if he was able to secure one quickly enough to follow you. Regard him as a guardian angel, my dear. Either he or his colleague, Mr. Mawson, is on duty from nine o'clock till dusk for that purpose."

It was not until Uncle Adrian had almost finished speaking that I understood what had happened, "You mean the man is employed to guard me?" I said in astonishment.

"Yes, Meg. Not obtrusively, of course. His instructions are to be on hand in case of need."

"But—but surely that must cost a great deal of money! Oh dear, it seems such a waste."

His eyes twinkled. "Then you must complain to Luke Bowman. This is by his arrangement."

"Luke? Do you know where he is?"

"I'm afraid not. He left no address with me."

I stood trying to collect my wits, and after a moment or two I said, "It's better that I know about Mr. Finn and Mr. Mawson, because now I won't make their task difficult by suddenly taking a cab or doing anything that might cause them to lose track of me."

"I'm sure they will appreciate that."

I did not much relish the idea of having a shadow wherever I went, but I was deeply moved to know that Luke had arranged this. Uncle Adrian accompanied me out into the street, and there we found Mr. Finn waiting in a cab. He emerged and looked embarrassed, fidgeting with his bowler as he was introduced to me, but he seemed relieved that in the future I would take care not to lose him and that I would advise him whenever I returned to the house with no intention of going out alone again that day.

Uncle Adrian said, "You'll pass this on to your colleague, won't you, Finn? Oh, and see that Mawson is on view outside the house tomorrow for Miss Gaynor to have sight of him. Understood?"

"Very good, sir."

I said, "I shall be walking back to Belgrave Square now, Mr. Finn."

"Thank you, miss. You know the way?"

"I took note of the route followed by the cab, and I shall go by way of Holborn, Shaftesbury Avenue, Piccadilly, Green Park, and Hyde Park Corner, stopping at a stationer's shop on the way. Will that be all right?"

"Most 'elpful, miss. I'm much obliged." He made a stiff little bow. "I'll wish you good day, miss."

I said good-bye to Uncle Adrian, and two minutes later I turned into Holborn, feeling slightly foolish, with Mr. Finn trailing twenty paces behind me. At a stationer's shop in Shaftesbury Avenue I bought a large book of lined paper in stiff marbled covers. This was to be my new diary, for the account book I had used at Clairmont was full now.

When I emerged from the shop Mr. Finn was lighting his pipe a little way off, watching the doorway over his cupped hands, and as I walked on he took up his position behind me.

Dear Luke,

After eight weeks, Mr. Finn and Mr. Mawson remain my shadows, and it does worry me that you should have such expense. If I knew where to write to you I would send you one of my alley-cat glares and tell you to stop, for I'm sure I have nothing to fear. I sometimes feel that what Sid Buller did at Shalimar had nothing to do with who I really am, and that "the man in the dark room" is all imagination, but I expect you would think me silly to say this.

I haven't written in my diary for almost two weeks because the boys came home on the Saturday before last and we are now down at Eastbourne in this wonderful manor house, as I told you we would be. (I wish I could really tell you, but pretending is better than nothing.) My shadows are here also, staying in a nearby cottage.

Aunt Becky and Uncle Adrian are very kind, but I must confess I was becoming bored from having so little to do. I walked a great deal in London (full of new scents!) and joined a library so that I always have plenty of books to read. I also took up painting, just watercolors, but oh, Luke! They really are quite awful. I fear I have no talent as an artist.

As I told you, I no longer sit at séances, but poor Aunt Becky never seems to lose hope of getting a message from her father, and she continued trotting off to Mrs. Cruikshank every week until we left. I don't yet know if she is in touch with a medium here. Uncle Adrian comes down only at weekends, and I know Aunt Becky is thankful to have me with her to help with the boys.

I think she must have been very lonely in London before I came, because Uncle Adrian is often out until late of an evening. I believe he spends a lot of time at his club.

She doesn't seem to mind, but I think I would feel very hurt in her place. I suppose that's because I have the example of how you loved Rosemary and were always glad to be with her.

Now, about the boys. Albert is a nice boy, like his mother in looks and with her rather nervous manner. Edward is a miniature of his father in looks but is not at all a nice boy. On the contrary, he is a little fiend who cheats at games, tells lies, and is ruthlessly selfish. However, looking after them certainly prevents me becoming bored! I have taken them to the beach three times, and for picnics in the country twice. I have also taken Albert in the sea and started to teach him to swim. He's a brave little chap, and tries hard. Edward won't go in the water, and I'm almost sure he stole Albert's pocket money from the bathing machine while we were in the sea, but I can't accuse him.

I have arranged riding lessons for the three of us at nearby stables, and we have our first lesson tomorrow. Today I put on my new riding jacket and breeches, and when I looked in the pier glass I hoped I would see a very handsome lady, but I just looked like me.

Apart from everything else, I've been playing cricket on the lawn with the boys. They don't expect a girl to be any good at all, and you should have seen their faces when I ran Edward out by throwing the ball to hit his wicket from about thirty paces! I had to pretend it was just luck, of course, and after that I was careful to be clumsy and to throw wide.

It's past eleven o'clock now, and the whole house is asleep, so I had better finish and climb into bed myself. With my love, Luke, wherever you are. God bless you.

I did not write all my thoughts in my diary. Some were too precious. I did not say to Luke that sometimes I lay awake at night, taking myself back in time, recalling those moments in the desert when I had held him in my arms and pressed my lips between his to give him water; recalling how he had clung to me and sucked at my lips for the life-giving fluid.

There had been nothing of man-and-woman in what happened then; I had been no more than the grubby golden urchin he spoke of later. But now I tried to pretend that it had been a kiss. I knew this was a deception, but the memory of my lips on his was all I would ever have of Luke, and it was only myself I was deceiving.

WE RETURNED TO LONDON TOWARD THE END OF AUGUST, AND I hardly knew whether to be glad or sorry that the boys would soon be going back to their boarding school. I had an ever-growing dislike of Edward, for he was so false. On the surface he played the part of an innocent and was always glibly flattering to me, but underneath he was just as I had described him in my diary. Albert, on the other hand, was a boy whose company I truly enjoyed. Once he had overcome his initial shyness he seemed to develop a great affection for me and treated me as an elder sister. I returned his affection, for such heart-warmth, as I had called it in the tongue of my childhood, meant everything to me.

It became a habit that once the boys were in bed I would go to their room and sit talking with them for ten minutes or so before saying good night, sometimes telling them little stories of my daily life at Shalimar, for they knew I had come from Australia, and sometimes listening to Albert recounting stories of boarding-school life that I only half understood. Edward always listened intently but rarely spoke, except to admire something I had done or to say how pretty I looked in whatever dress I happened to be wearing. This embarrassed Albert, who on one occasion announced gruffly that in his view I had an unusual sort of face but he liked it very much.

On the night before the boys were to go back to school I tapped on their bedroom door as usual and entered at Albert's call. He was sitting up in bed with a book on his lap, but there was no sign of his brother.

"Where's Edward?" I asked as Albert put his book aside.

"Oh, I don't know. He sometimes prowls about, Meg."

"Prowls about?" I sat on the edge of the bed, facing Albert. "Whatever do you mean?"

"Well . . . nothing, really."

I was about to persist when I remembered hearing tales about the schoolboy code. For one boy to "sneak" on another was the unforgivable sin. "Well, I expect he'll come prowling back soon," I said casually. "Do you think you can find time to write to me, Albert? I'd like to hear how you get on, especially if you win your colors for the school rugby team."

"Oh yes, I'll write," he said quickly. "It's funny, Meg. I used to look forward to going back to school, but I hate it now you're here."

I ruffled his hair and said, "Oh, once you're back you won't feel like that. I'm going to miss *you*, though."

"Will you really, Meg?"

"Honestly. Cross my heart." I had picked up something of the way boys talked. "I'll be sad."

He beamed. "Oh, my hat! Will you really? I'm so glad."

"Glad?" I punched him gently on the shoulder. "Don't be a rotter."

"Well, I didn't exactly mean . . . I mean, you know . . ." He frowned in thought, and after a pause went on, "You're eighteen and I'm thirteen and almost three quarters, Meg. I've been thinking, it won't be *very* long before I'm grown up, will it? And then I was thinking, well, if you didn't mind waiting, it would be nice if we got married."

By the time he completed his last sentence I had guessed what was coming, so I showed no surprise, but I was touched to my heart. "Why, Albert," I said, "that's my very first proposal, and I'm greatly honored."

"You mean you will wait, Meg?"

I said, "Albert, never ask people to make a promise they may not be able to keep, and never make one yourself. Whatever you think now, it's possible that you'll change in various ways as you grow older, and I won't let you commit yourself to a promise now. I can only say that when you *are* grown-up you can ask me again, if you still wish to.''

"But some man might come along and marry you before then, Meg."

"And you might find yourself wanting to marry a different lady before then, Albert. We'll just have to wait and see."

"Well, I won't want to marry anyone else, but all right. You won't tell Edward or anybody, will you?"

"Not a word. That's a promise I can keep. Now, tell me about Old Bony, your new form master."

Ten minutes later, when I kissed Albert good night, his brother had still not appeared. At the door I said, "I'll leave you to turn out the gas as soon as Edward's in bed. Say good night to him for me."

"Yes, all right, Meg." He picked up his book again. "This *Treasure Island* is jolly good; you ought to read it."

"I will, Albert." I went out, smiling to myself and glad that he was not too heartbroken at having failed to obtain immediate acceptance of his marriage proposal.

Then my thoughts turned to Edward, and I wondered what he was up to. Prowling, Albert had said, but for what purpose? Aunt Becky was in the drawing room, working on an enormous jigsaw puzzle. This was a favorite pastime of hers. She declared that it was a sovereign cure for her frequent headaches, and had been working on the present puzzle for weeks. Uncle Adrian was not yet home, and the servants had retired. I had gradually taken on increasing responsibility for the boys, and felt I ought to find Edward now.

As I moved along the passage I pulled back a curtain to look out on the garden with the vague notion that he might have gone out in his nightshirt and dressing gown to pick an apple from one of the three trees at the end. There was no sign of him, but I saw a band of light thrown from between curtains not fully

drawn in a room on the ground floor. From where the light fell
I knew it came from Uncle Adrian's study.

I hurried downstairs, across the hall, and along a short passage, hesitated for a moment at the door, for I had never entered
unbidden before, then opened it quickly and went into the room.
The gas had been turned on, and Edward sat in Uncle Adrian's
chair at the desk, a miniature of his father, but with only his
head and shoulders showing over the desk top. Some papers lay
in front of him, and he looked up as I entered, showing mo-
mentary surprise before giving me one of his innocent smiles
and saying, "Hello, Meg. Is it time for bed?"

I closed the door behind me and kept my voice low as I said,
"Edward! What on earth are you doing here? Are those your
father's papers you're reading?"

"I was just looking," he said as I moved up to the desk. "I
like knowing things about people."

"Edward, you're *prying* into your father's affairs! It's a shocking thing to do, and you can't possibly understand such matters
anyway! Stop it at once!"

"I can understand some things," he said, quite unruffled. "I
think he gambles a lot, Meg. Look at this notebook here—"

"No I will *not* look!" I whispered furiously. "Put it away.
Put everything away just as it was, and I'll say nothing to your
father. Oh, you should be *ashamed* of yourself!"

He began to gather up the papers carefully. "No need to make
a fuss," he said politely. "I just like to know things. It helps to
make people do what you want. I often make boys at school do
what I want by knowing things about them."

I was about to tell him that he was a little monster, but I bit
my lip. Calling him names would serve no purpose. I took a
deep breath and said, "Edward, it is *wrong* to pry into other
people's affairs. You must *never* do it again. Do you understand?"

He put the papers and notebook away in a drawer, taking care
to arrange them just so, then closed the drawer, stood up, and

gave me a contrite smile. "Yes. I'm sorry, Meg. I won't do it again."

I knew his words were false, but I could do no more. "Come along," I said firmly. "Bed."

Half a minute later we were mounting the stairs together. As we reached the top he said, "What's a mortgage, Meg?" He pronounced it as it was spelled, mort-gage.

I said, "It's something to do with people lending money, but I'm not very clear about it. Anyway, you pronounce it mortgage."

"I'll try to find out about it," said Edward. "Papa has got two."

"Never mind about that," I snapped. We were on the landing now. "Go and get yourself to bed. Albert will put the light out."

"All right, Meg. Good night." He went running off along the passage, and I turned to go downstairs again, feeling quite shaken by this young boy's apparent inability to know right from wrong and trying to put out of my mind any speculation about what he had said regarding Uncle Adrian.

The memory of his curiously adult and almost sinister interest in "knowing things about people" haunted me for several days, but then was driven from my mind by an encounter I had sometimes vaguely thought about but never really expected. I was exploring a part of London new to me, the area near the ancient Tower of London, when a hansom cab drew up beside me and Eliza Fordyce emerged.

I stood still, gazing at her, not knowing what to say. She was more fashionably dressed than she had been as a vicar's wife and as beautiful as I remembered her, but her face held none of its usual placid good humor. "Meg," she said, "I must talk to you. Please, dear, join me in the cab. Oh please."

I felt very flustered, and was aware of Mr. Mawson, who was my shadow that day, coming quickly forward as I said, "I can't, Eliza. I'm sorry, but I know the truth about Josiah Smith now. Oh, I'm sure you and Simon wished me no harm. You were just deceived—"

Burly Mr. Mawson was at my elbow lifting his hat and saying, "Any trouble, miss?"

"Er—no, no," I said in confusion. "I won't be a moment."

"Very good, miss." He stepped back a few paces but remained alert and watchful.

Eliza said, "Meg, you're in danger with Adrian Webb. I beg you to come with me now."

Greatly troubled, I said, "Oh, Eliza, I'm sure you believe what you're saying, but it isn't true. Luke discovered the truth about Josiah Smith really being someone else, John Lafayette, and—oh, it's too long to explain, but Luke found me at Clairmont and took me away to live with Adrian Webb, and I *know* Luke would never do anything to endanger me."

Eliza closed her eyes for a moment and whispered, "Dear God." Then she looked at me and said, "Where is he now? Luke, I mean?"

"I—I don't know. Abroad, I think. Eliza, please, I beg you not to continue working for your dreadful 'man in the dark room'. You don't know the truth about him."

She shook her head slowly, despairingly. "Oh, but we do," she said softly. "We do now." She looked beyond me to Mr. Mawson and gave a small hopeless shrug. "Simon sends his regards, Meg." The cab door was still open, and she turned to climb in.

As she closed the door I called through the open window, "Please give him mine, and *please* tell him what I've said."

She nodded, and said somberly, "I'll tell him." Then she rapped on the trap with her umbrella, and the cabbie sent his horse away at a sharp trot over the cobbles.

Mr. Mawson said, "Everything all right, miss?"

"Yes," I said, though I felt strangely heavy-hearted. "Everything is quite all right, Mr. Mawson." But as I walked on I half wished that Mr. Mawson had not been there, and half wondered what I would have done if that had been so. I thought it likely that I would have entered the cab to hear what Eliza had to say. Which, I told myself, would have been very foolish. All the same, when I saw Uncle Adrian at breakfast in the morning I said nothing about my encounter with Eliza Fordyce.

Next day, when I continued my exploration of that eastern part of the city from London Bridge to Tower Bridge, I half hoped and half feared that I might see Eliza again, though I did not know why I should either hope or fear another encounter, unless her words had sowed a seed of doubt in me.

I never minded how far I walked myself, but I had noticed both my shadows limping on tender feet when I went far afield, and felt I should take pity on them. From Belgrave Square to the Tower of London was a full four miles, and I usually spent an hour or so exploring the area before returning home, but to save Mr. Finn's or Mr. Mawson's feet I had now taken to returning home by cab, no doubt to their relief. Whoever was on duty would follow in another cab.

Three days after my encounter with Eliza I was in a hansom traveling west along the Victoria Embankment toward Waterloo Bridge, having spent the morning visiting the Royal Mint, Billingsgate Fish Market, and The Monument, a huge pillar of stone near Pudding Lane, commemorating the Great Fire of London. It was half past one o'clock, and I had left Belgrave Square soon after breakfast, saying I would want only a little bread and cheese with a glass of milk for luncheon. As usual, this prompted a remonstrance from Aunt Becky. I still ate lightly compared with the way most well-to-do people seemed to eat, and she was convinced I would one day fade away, despite the fact that I was always in glowing health.

The river was on my left, and as we passed the Temple Gardens on the other side of the road I remembered with a shiver that it was somewhere in the courtyards beyond that Mr. Tasker had been brutally murdered. I looked away, and next moment I felt the cab lurch, heard the cabbie shout. Then we were at a halt, one wheel up on the pavement, with my cabbie bawling wrathfully at a man with a cartload of hay who appeared to have lost control of his horse so that the cart had swerved across the road.

Looking out of the right-hand window I saw the carter shouting back as he climbed down from his seat. He was cursing, and I heard something about a bee, which reminded me of what Aunt Becky had said about the way her father had died. Next moment the left-hand door opened, and even as I turned, a long arm reached in, a powerful hand gripped my arm, and I was hauled unceremoniously out onto the pavement.

I would have fallen if Simon Fordyce had not steadied me. Then he said, "Meg dear, for the love of God, don't make this difficult." Still gripping my arm he rushed me toward the parapet at the point where Temple Steps led down to the waters of the Thames.

THIRTEEN

I WAS ASTOUNDED, BUT I FELT NO SENSE OF FEAR. IT WAS IM-
possible for me to feel fear of Simon Fordyce or of Eliza, whom
I now saw standing a few paces away with her back to us, facing
Mr. Mawson's cab, which had drawn up a little distance behind
mine.

"Simon! No! Wait!" I was resisting, trying to pull away, but
I did not kick or claw, for I could not think of him as an enemy,
and I shrank from the embarrassment of a full-scale struggle in
public. Mr. Mawson was coming toward us now, calling out. I
saw Eliza step into his path, heard her say, "Pray excuse me,
sir," saw her skirt flounce a little as her leg moved; then she
turned and walked toward us. Mr. Mawson sank slowly to his
knees, eyes rolling and mouth a round O of shock, a repetition
of what had happened to the drunkard at the service in Lawton
when I had first set eyes on Eliza Fordyce.

She caught my other arm, saying, "Do trust us, Meg dear."
Then I was being hustled down the steps from the pavement to
the water, almost lifted off my feet, seeing for the first time a
little sailing dinghy with a man in a dark blue jersey standing in
it, holding it alongside the steps. I exclaimed, "No! Listen, you
don't understand!"

"Indeed we do, Meg," said Simon briskly, and dropped me
into the boat. The man in the blue jersey steadied me as I stum-

bled, and he said with a Cockney accent, "Take a seat please, miss," pushing me down on a thwart as he spoke. Next moment Simon and Eliza were in the boat with me, the man in the blue jersey pushed off, the sail flapped and caught the wind, and in seconds the dinghy was scudding downriver at a great rate on an ebbing tide and with a good following wind.

I sat clutching my hat with one hand, my handbag in the other, trying to feel angry, or indignant, or at least afraid, but all I could feel was a kind of hilarious astonishment at the audacity of it all, and a pang of concern for Mr. Mawson. I shook my head at Eliza and said, lifting my voice above the breeze, "Oh, that poor man! You ought to be *ashamed* of yourself, Eliza."

"I'm permanently ashamed of myself, dear," she said with a smile, "and I did push a five-pound note into his top pocket."

Looking back to the Temple Steps a hundred yards away now, I saw the figure of Mr. Mawson appear at the parapet, staring after us, and on impulse I lifted a hand and waved to him, though what he made of that I could not imagine.

Simon leaned forward and took my hand. "Listen, Meg," he said, and I had never seen him more serious, "we want you to come with us to meet the man in the dark room. At the moment we're heading downriver to disembark on the south bank near London Bridge Station, and from there we want to take you by train to Sevenoaks, to the home of Mr. Josiah Smith."

I said, "Who is also Mr. John Lafayette?"

Simon dipped his head in agreement. "Yes. We, too, know that now. But let me finish, Meg. If you believe that Eliza and I would bring you to harm, if you can't trust us, when we leave this boat I'll put you in a cab back to Belgrave Square. If you come with us to talk with the man in the dark room, and if you then believe he intends harm to you, you have my word that I will bring you back to London and to Belgrave Square."

"My word also, dear," said Eliza.

We had crossed the river and were passing under Blackfriars

Bridge now. I tried to imagine that Simon and Eliza Fordyce were wicked and devious people who were leading me into a trap, but found this impossible. I said, "Can I send Aunt Becky a telegram from London Bridge to say I'm quite safe?"

"Anybody could send a telegram," said Simon. "Better if you write a note in your own hand. Charlie here will see that it's delivered within the hour." He nodded at the man in the blue jersey, who sat at the tiller now.

I said, "Yes, I'll do that." I heard Eliza sigh, saw relief flood both their faces, and realized that I had agreed to do as they asked without quite being aware of having made up my mind. "Did you arrange for that cart to swerve and stop my cab?" I asked.

Eliza's blue eyes smiled affectionately upon me. "We thought the river was a nice idea, Meg," she said gently. "You wouldn't have wanted a hue and cry through the streets of London, would you?"

THE HOUSE STOOD ON A HILL IN HUGE WALLED GROUNDS ABOVE the village of Telhurst, some two miles from Sevenoaks Station. A fine carriage with a driver and groom had awaited our arrival at the station, and as we drove through Sevenoaks I learned from Simon that he no longer dealt with Mr. Josiah Smith in a solicitor's office in the Middle Temple, but now dealt with Mr. John Lafayette in the magnificent house called Caragh. When Simon spoke that word I had a vague feeling I had heard it before, but could not remember where or in what connection.

I said, "Do you know why you always used to meet him in a dark room?"

"We still do meet him in a dark room," said Simon, "and so will you, Meg." He hesitated. "Nobody sees him except a few of his trusted servants. When he goes out by day it's in a closed carriage or a reserved train compartment with the blinds drawn. I gather he isn't a cripple, for he takes exercise by night, riding or walking the byways of the Weald of Kent after dark.

That's all we know of him, Meg, except that we're quite certain he intends you no harm."

"Have you never tried to find out *why* he behaves so strangely?" I asked. "Now that you know who he is."

Simon shook his head. "To do that, we would have to pry, ask questions, perhaps bribe. We can't do that to the man who is our employer." He smiled. "Besides, as I've said before, I savor a touch of mystery."

The carriage drew to a halt on a wide apron of flags fronting an elegant portico, and the great door swung open even as we mounted the steps together. A gray-haired butler said, "Good afternoon, Mrs. Fordyce, Miss Gaynor, Mr. Fordyce. Please come in."

We crossed a large paneled hall hung with pictures and ancient weapons, and the butler opened the door of a pleasant room with French windows looking out onto lawns and flower beds. Addressing me, he said, "Do you wish Mr. Lafayette to attend upon you now, miss, or would you prefer to take tea first?"

"Oh . . . well, I think I would like to talk to Mr. Lafayette as soon as possible, if that is convenient," I said, wondering quite seriously if I could be dreaming and might wake up at any moment. I was reassured when I pressed a hand against my chest and felt Rosemary's little heart-shaped pendant under my dress.

"As you wish, miss," said the butler. "If Mr. and Mrs. Fordyce will be so kind as to wait here, I will have tea sent in for them." He bowed slightly in their direction. "You will find copies of *Punch, The Lady,* and other interesting magazines on the table should you wish to peruse them."

"Thank you, Blake," said Simon. Then he looked at me. "Don't worry, Meg. Remember my promise."

The butler said, "If you will be so kind, miss . . . ?"

I followed him past the foot of a beautiful staircase, along a broad passage, past the open door of a handsome library with tall mullioned windows, and on to a closed door, where he halted. Grasping the handle, he said, "You will find the room in darkness except for a small lamp by an easy chair, miss. Mr. Lafayette would be grateful if you would seat yourself there."

I said, "Very well," and felt my nerves grow taut as he opened the door. I could tell the room was lofty as soon as I entered, and could dimly make out some of the furniture, rugs, pictures, and ornaments in the light of a small lamp turned very low on a table ahead of me and to my left. This was near a large fireplace, but at once I looked beyond the fireplace to where I could make out the shape of an armchair with a high back. I could see nothing of the occupant, even dimly, for the chair was facing away from me, but I had caught the human scent at once and knew that the man in the dark room was sitting there.

The door closed behind me. The scent told me nothing of good or ill. I waited for a few moments for my eyes to grow more used to the dark, but once I had moved forward to sit in the easy chair I found that the lamp was directly in front of me, so that it dimmed my vision again. A man's voice, deep, mellow, even beautiful, spoke from beyond it.

"Are you afraid, child?"

I thought for a second or two, then answered, "No, sir. I'm very puzzled, but at the moment I don't feel afraid."

"You have been told that I seek to harm you? Destroy you?"

I hesitated, but could see no way to speak tactfully, and so I said, "Yes, sir. My oldest and dearest friend told me that, and took me away from Clairmont for my safety."

"That would be Mr. Luke Bowman. Yet you are here now. Do you no longer believe him?"

I said slowly, "I no longer know what to believe. I trust Luke completely and forever. I know he believed all that he told me. But I find I cannot mistrust Simon and Eliza Fordyce. So I feel that . . . somewhere there has been a mistake, a deception. I am greatly confused."

"Poor child, you deserve better than to be enmeshed in such treachery and wickedness. What is your opinion of Adrian Webb?"

"I see little of him, sir, so I don't know him well, but he has shown me every kindness."

"Of course." There was sorrow in the mellow voice, but a thread of anger, too. "You are the daughter and sole heir of my dear friends Laurence and Mary Glencullen. I think Mr. Bowman told you that I am named in your father's will and that if you fail to reach the age of twenty-one, then the fortune passes to me, to be used for charitable purposes at my entire discretion."

I said, "Yes, that is what Luke told me."

"You realize that his information came from Adrian Webb, who is your trustee?"

"Well, I suppose so, but I'm sure Luke would have required to see a copy of the will."

"Yes. But it is quite certain that he did not go to Somerset House, where for the payment of a small sum he could have seen the *official* copy of your father's will. Please do not think I blame him. Adrian Webb is a solicitor of high reputation and great plausibility. If he could gain your father's confidence and faith sufficiently to be made trustee, it is hardly surprising that Luke Bowman failed to suspect anything amiss."

It was as if an icy finger had suddenly touched my spine, and I said uneasily, "Uncle Adrian? I'm not sure what you mean, sir."

The mellow voice said, "My dear, the true will of your father is very much as Adrian Webb described it, and not very different from whatever so-called copy he showed to Luke Bowman, but there is one vital difference. There is no mention of myself, John Lafayette, in the will. Your parents knew my reclusive habits too well to involve me in widespread charity operations. No, the person who is to receive the Glencullen fortune for that purpose if you fail to reach the age of twenty-one is your trustee, Adrian Webb."

Perhaps for as long as a minute my mind seemed to stop working completely, and then gradually a confusion of thoughts began to stir. Uncle Adrian? Was *he* my secret enemy? Was it he who had in some way contrived to have Sid Buller sent to kill me? But how had he known of my existence if it was to Mr. Lafayette that the newspaper reporter, Harry Tasker, had come with his story?

My mind jumped with a new realization. Harry Tasker had examined the official copy of the will at Somerset House. If this did not mention John Lafayette, then surely it was to Adrian Webb, my trustee, that Harry Tasker had taken his story . . . and so brought about his own death.

I covered my face with my hands, filled with horror, trying to think clearly. Uncle Adrian? With his twinkling eyes, kind manner, and Pickwickian countenance? Then in my mind's eye I saw a picture of eleven-year-old Edward, cherubic and innocent in appearance, yet capable of lying, cheating, or stealing to gain his ends. Like father, like son, except that Edward had not yet acquired his father's skill in concealment.

Mr. Lafayette said from the darkness, "If you doubt me, I pray that you will suspend judgment for twenty-four hours, so that tomorrow Simon and Eliza Fordyce may escort you to Somerset House. There you may see a true copy of the will with your own eyes. And even if you do not doubt me I shall insist upon this. You have had enough of lies, but from your father's will and testament you will learn the truth."

I lowered my hands, pulled myself together, and said, "You would hardly insist on that if what you have told me were untrue, sir. I cannot help but believe you, but what is Uncle—" The word stuck in my throat. "What is Adrian Webb's purpose?"

"I have studied the man in some depth, my dear," said the mellow voice from the armchair, "for unlike your father I had grave suspicions as to his probity, and I was concerned to discover if possible whether he would observe the charity requirements of the will, once the fortune passed into his charge. He is a man who has lived far beyond his means for many years now, and he has become a heavy gambler. I know that his houses in London and Eastbourne have been mortgaged. I believe, though I have no proof, that he has already converted large sums

from your inheritance to his own use. If you had never been
found alive, or if you were to die before reaching twenty-one,
his embezzlement would never be discovered, and he would
continue to convert your father's estate to his own use in devious
ways, perhaps by setting up false charities.''

The man in darkness stirred in his chair, and a hint of bitterness tinged his voice. ''If you will remember all the wickedness
and villainy that Adrian Webb must surely have imputed to me,
my dear, then you have only to substitute his name for mine in
order to understand what he has done, and why. When your
friend Luke Bowman arrived on the scene after discovering your
true identity it must have been a great shock to Adrian Webb,
who believed the secret was safe once he had disposed of Mr.
Tasker. But he is a clever, resourceful scoundrel, and to put *me*
into the role that he himself had played was a brilliant deception.
I am not surprised that it convinced Mr. Bowman.''

''Poor Luke,'' I whispered. ''Oh, poor Luke. He thought he
was bringing me to safety, Mr. Lafayette. He'll be so angry with
himself when he finds out.'' The last words brought a new
thought to my mind, and I went on, ''If Mr. Tasker didn't come
to you with his story, sir, how did you find out about me?''

''Not by chance, Meg. That is the name you prefer? Meg?''

''If you please, sir.''

''Well, it was not by chance that I learned you were alive. As
I said, I have been at some pains to keep a close eye on Adrian
Webb, and when he dismissed an elderly clerk of his for some
minor offense I arranged for the man to be given a clerical job
in one of my London companies. Later, in a dark room, I ques-
tioned him closely about his former master. It emerged, among
other things, that the clerk had overheard part of an exchange
between Adrian Webb and a Mr. Harry Tasker from Australia
and had later found brief notes about it that Webb had discarded.
The matter held no particular significance for the clerk, and he
simply noted that a child for whom Adrian Webb had been appointed executor and trustee was not in fact dead, as had long
been presumed. She was to be found on a farm near the small

town of Lawton, in Western Australia, living with a couple by the name of Bowman and presumably unaware of her identity. The clerk could not put a name to this child, but to me it was clear that she could only be you, Meg.''

There was a long silence. Other questions kept coming to my mind, but they were not important. For the moment I was dominated not by thought but by feeling, for within me was growing a great need to know and to understand the man who sat in darkness. He had spent a small fortune in sending Simon and Eliza Fordyce to Australia to protect me, then in bringing me to Clairmont, where he had kept me in luxury for almost a year.

It was clear from this great house, Caragh, and the huge estate that John Lafayette could well afford a small fortune, and I knew now that he had indeed been a friend of my parents. But I did not know why he had gone to such lengths for me, and I did not know why he sat in darkness.

His voice broke the silence at last. ''Will you put the lamp out, please, Meg? I am about to light another one.''

I reached forward and obeyed. As the flame vanished I heard the scrape of a match; then came a brighter light from beyond the armchair. The man stood up, turning toward me, but with the light behind him I could see only a dark silhouette. I heard him catch his breath, and then he spoke in a wavering voice as if to himself, murmuring, ''Dear Lord . . . Mary lives again.''

I said, ''You find me much like my mother, sir?''

''You—you are the image of her as she was at your age, my dear.''

I stood up, and it was as if another person took charge within me then, for I was startled at my own words as I said, ''Are you my friend, Mr. Lafayette?''

The silhouette stirred, as if making a gesture. ''I am indeed your friend, Moira Glencullen . . . or Meg. And I pray you will be mine.''

I smiled to soften my words and said, ''Then why do you take unfair advantage of me, sir? Why do you look at me when I cannot look at you? Surely that is unkind?''

I heard him sigh. "My appearance is not . . . pleasing, child. That is why I sit in darkness."

"Does appearance matter between friends?" The words still came from my lips as if my own mind had taken no part in forming them.

In a voice I could barely hear he said, "There was once a time, perhaps, when it did not matter. . . ."

I drew in a deep breath, then said quietly, "Please draw back the curtains, sir. Please allow light into this room. Please allow me to see who claims to be my friend."

There was silence for almost a minute, and in it I heard the slow ticking of a grandfather clock. Then the dark figure moved away from the armchair and across the room to the tall curtained windows opposite the fireplace. I moved myself then, so that as he drew upon the curtain cords I was standing only two or three paces away, facing him with the window on my right. The curtains rolled back, bright sunlight burst through the French windows, dazzling me at first, and then my eyes focused and I gazed at Mr. John Lafayette as he stood before me.

He was a tall man in a dark gray suit of perfect cut, lean of face, slim of body, in his late forties, standing very upright, mouth twisted a little as if in pain at some ordeal, hands twitching as he clenched and unclenched his fingers. Because I had grown up with notions that were different from those of my own kind, I was a poor judge of looks, but to me it seemed that John Lafayette's features—the brow, the mouth, the line of jaw—would have been quite handsome, except that his hair and his skin were white as milk, the irises of his eyes were pink, and the pupils red.

I was taken aback, for I had not known what to expect, and his appearance was of a kind I had never yet seen or heard of, but as I stared I heard myself say, "Is that all, sir?"

"All?" The pink eyes blinked. "Do you know what I am, Meg?" I shook my head. "I see you are different, but I don't know a name for it."

He almost smiled, and his nervously twitching hands grew

still. "Yes, they told me how direct you are." The smile faded.
"I am an albino, my dear. A freak. A spectacle. My body is
deficient in a pigment that gives most humans their coloring.
My aspect is more than unpleasing, it is frightening, and so I
hide myself away from all but a few of my trusted servants.
Have you seen enough of my repellent appearance, Meg? May
I draw the curtains now?"

Again I shook my head. "Oh no. No, Mr. Lafayette. Do you
think I don't know what it is to be different from others? To be
a freak and a spectacle? I know far better than you, for I grew
up among people who had never seen white skin, green eyes,
red hair, and freckles. I was ten times the spectacle you claim
to be, and I was only a child. I cannot say I was brave and didn't
care, for I cared deeply. But you are so *little* different, sir, and
you are a grown man. What does it matter if mannerless people
stare? You are blessed with great riches, Mr. Lafayette, and even
more important than that, you are educated and you seem to
have good health. You tell me you are an albino. If the choice
was yours, would you choose to be a cripple instead? Or an
invalid?"

I stopped speaking, feeling quite dazed, wondering where all
those words had come from. To my astonishment I saw two tears
break from the corners of those pink eyes and run down the
paper-white cheeks.

"You spoke with your mother's voice," he whispered. "That
was the voice of Mary Caragh Mulvaney."

"Mulvaney?"

"Her maiden name."

"Oh, I remember now. It said so in the *Strand* magazine."
I caught my breath. "Caragh! Yes, that was her middle name—
and you have called this house after her?"

He smiled, and a little more of the tension drained from his
taut body. "It is an Irish name that means 'love.' Yes, I called
this house after her, Meg."

We stood looking at each other for a few moments, taking
each other in, and there was hardly a trace of embarrassment in

him now, only a kind of bewilderment tinged with gladness. One thing I knew beyond all shadow of doubt—that Mr. John Lafayette was my friend.

I said, "I would like to hear about my mother, but could we walk in your gardens in this beautiful sunshine while we talk?"

For a moment he looked nervous again, then gave a shrug and smiled as he said, "If you permit me to put on dark glasses. Bright sunshine is a little distressing for me."

"If you would rather not . . . ?"

"No, no. I would very much like to. By my own fault I see too little of daylight." He took a spectacle case from his pocket and put on some dark glasses.

I studied him carefully and felt pleased as I said, "There. You now look rather mysterious, and very distinguished and . . . well, quite handsome, Mr. Lafayette."

He laughed, then stopped suddenly, as if surprised by the sound of his own laughter. "Oh, Meg," he said, "you must surely be a witch, as your mother was." He unfastened the catch of the French windows and pushed them open, gestured for me to step onto the flagged terrace, and followed me out. Hesitantly he crooked his elbow. "Would you care to take my arm, Meg?"

"I shall be pleased to."

He gave a sigh of pleasure. "This will cause such a stir. Most servants in Caragh have never set eyes on me, so we shall see curtains twitching at windows and perhaps even hear the buzz of excitement throughout the house."

"I think Simon and Eliza Fordyce will be surprised, too."

"I'm sure they will."

Together we descended three shallow steps to the lawn, and for the next ten minutes or more we simply strolled together without speaking, down past flower beds and shrubbery to a small lake fed by a stream, then across a bridge, circling back by way of a meadow and a coppice to the lawns. Twice we came upon gardeners who looked thunderstruck at the sight of us, perhaps half guessing that the white-haired man with the mellow voice who wished them good day must be their mysterious employer.

For me the respite of silence was welcome. I felt content but somewhat drained of energy, and although there was much I still wished to be told I felt no sense of urgency as I strolled with the strange man whose arm I held, my mind almost asleep except for the automatic noting of bird and insect, water and plant, animal track and any indication of food. This was a habit I had never been able to lose.

Twice as we strolled Mr. Lafayette suddenly laughed, quite softly to himself, but with a touch of exuberance, and twice he reached across to pat my hand as it rested on his arm. At last, and with something of an effort, I broke from the dreamlike mood and said, "What is to happen to me now, Mr. Lafayette?"

"I very much hope you will consent to stay at Caragh for the time being, my dear," he said soberly. "Simon and Eliza Fordyce have taken up residence here in the hope that you will do so, and my housekeeper, Mrs. Armitage, has prepared a room for you." He glanced away toward the great house. "We have no lack of rooms here, more a lack of people, which I hope you will help to correct."

I said, "What do you think Adrian Webb will do when he discovers I have gone and sees the note I sent Aunt Becky? Might he go to the police and make trouble for you?"

"He won't dare to, Meg. He will know that his trickery has been exposed and that you have come to me by consent. Adrian Webb cannot afford to bring about a situation that would involve investigation into his actions as your trustee, for he has so much to hide. Truth to tell, I have a suspicion that Harry Tasker's death was not the first that might be laid at his door. Webb married for money and laid hands on a useful fortune when his wife's father died. You know about that?"

I remembered Aunt Becky telling me in a shamefaced manner that her father had been well-to-do but "in trade." It had not occurred to me then that Adrian Webb might have married her for money, but when I recalled how ill-matched they were it seemed very likely now. I said, "Aunt Becky said her father owned quite a lot of property, and that he died after a horse kicked him on the head when he was in the stables at East-bourne."

Mr. Lafayette nodded. "His somewhat outlandish death came at a very convenient time for Adrian Webb, and there were apparently no witnesses to what occurred in the stables. The body was found some little time after death, and medical evidence suggested a fatal kick from a horse, so that is what the coroner's jury assumed."

I shivered and said, "Do you really think Adrian Webb could have . . . ?"

Mr. Lafayette pressed my hand gently. "My dear, in all cities there is an underworld, and in London it would not be difficult to procure a man's death cheaply—or a woman's, for that matter. There are brutes without souls who will do anything for money. But I am quite certain that Adrian Webb is himself capable of such an act if driven to it. Capable and competent, for he is very strong—he rowed for Cambridge in his youth—he is daring and hardy, he is infinitely resourceful, as witness his brilliant deception of Luke Bowman, and he is an excellent actor, as you have reason to know for yourself."

We were approaching the house again now from the west, and as Mr. Lafayette had predicted I glimpsed curtains moving and faces showing briefly at windows as news of their unseen master's appearance in plain view ran from servant to servant; and beyond some French windows I could see plainly the figures of Simon and Eliza Fordyce gazing across the lawns and flower beds toward us.

I said, "I'm troubled about Aunt Becky, for I'm quite sure she doesn't know the truth about her husband, and she's been very kind to me. I sent her that little note, but I know she'll worry about me."

Mr. Lafayette said, "You have some personal things at Belgrave Square, I imagine. Things you would be sad to leave?"

"Yes. I'm wearing Rosemary's pendant, but there are some

books and a photograph of Luke and—Oh dear, there's a kind of diary I keep. I hope nobody reads it.''

He laughed and patted my hand on his arm. "Don't worry, Meg. Write a note today for Aunt Becky, just saying that you have had to leave suddenly and that Uncle Adrian will explain. That way you won't have to say anything bad about him, and it will be up to him to invent a plausible story for her. Then add that you would like her to give the bearer of the note your books and personal items, which you can list for her."

I said with great relief, "Oh yes, I'll do that, sir. The photograph is on my dressing table, and the books and diary are all together on the same shelf in my wardrobe."

We had reached the path that ran past the morning room, and the French windows opened as we drew near. Simon and Eliza Fordyce stood there, and I felt Mr. Lafayette go suddenly tense, his pace slowing. I knew what he was feeling, and I tightened my hold on his arm as I whispered, "Come along, now. You look *very* nice."

I heard him give a little laugh, then felt him relax. As we came to the open windows Simon said uncertainly, "Mr. Lafayette?"

"That is correct, Mr. Fordyce." I felt the arm go tense again as if my companion was bracing himself for a great effort. Then with his free hand he took off the dark glasses and used them to gesture with forced casualness. "Young Meg has persuaded me to abandon my practice of concealment, and we are in some dispute as to which of us two is the greater phenomenon."

I fell in with his jocular manner and said, "I had my first bath at fourteen, and I eat snakes and lizards and grubs. Mr. Lafayette can't compare with me."

Both Simon and Eliza looked completely nonplussed. Then she dropped a small curtsy and said, "It's a pleasure for us to meet you at last, sir."

Simon said in a baffled way, "Yes. Oh yes indeed." He glanced at me. "And Meg is staying?"

"Meg is staying," said Mr. Lafayette, a note of thankfulness in his voice. "We have a little more to talk about, so perhaps you will excuse us for the moment. You might care to change and refresh yourselves now that you know Meg is to remain with us. Ring for anything you require, of course. Meg will be in her room shortly, Mrs. Fordyce, and perhaps you would visit her there to make sure she has everything she needs. I suggest we all meet before dinner in the drawing room. Let us say at seven-thirty, if that is satisfactory to you." He smiled. "I believe you play the piano, Mrs. Fordyce. Perhaps we can persuade you to give us the pleasure of your playing for a little while this evening. Come, Meg, my dear."

We strolled on, leaving Simon and Eliza gazing with round eyes. Two minutes later we reentered the room where I had first met John Lafayette. As we did so, my gaze was drawn to something I had not seen before and I stopped short, catching my breath. Hanging over the fireplace was a portrait, a very fine portrait of my mother in what I judged to be her middle thirties. I moved forward to study it, and John Lafayette said, "What stupidity to call her a society beauty, as that magazine did. Mary had little time for the ways of society, and she was never beautiful. Striking, yes. Captivating, certainly. But that freckled face and wide mouth were never made to enrapture poets."

With my eyes on the portrait I said slowly, "You speak as one who knew her well."

"Oh my dear . . ." The mellow voice shook for a moment. "We were children together. I loved her then, and I shall love her till I die."

I felt pain in my heart for him as I said, "Will you tell me about it?"

"There isn't a long story to be told, Meg. My grandfather was French, my grandmother Irish. My parents lived in London, where my father made a fortune in the City, and I was born there. My early years were miserable. I was, I am, a freak. An albino. The family still owned property in Ireland, adjoining Thomas Mulvaney's land near Kilgarran, and when I was twelve, and my mother died, my father sent me to live with his sister there. He thought I would be happier if I were hidden away from the world, and in a way he was right, for there I met Mary Caragh Mulvaney.''

I turned from the portrait and said, ''She can only have been a small child then, surely?''

''She was six.'' John Lafayette moved to a settee and sat down, taking off his glasses to rub his eyes. ''Mary didn't see me as a freak. In all the years of friendship she simply saw me as different in the way that we are all different, one from another. Your words, when you first saw me—'Is that all?'—they could have been her words, Meg. She had a private tutor. So did I, because I feared going to boarding school to become a freak again. The years passed and we grew up together, with Mary being my friend and champion, for heaven help anyone who made a cruel remark about my appearance. It was she who made me go to university, but without her beside me I lost my courage and became a recluse there.''

He smiled wryly, and the sad pink eyes looked at me without embarrassment. ''I feared that she would have changed when I came home on vacation, but Mary never changed. The day she became a young lady by putting her hair up she came running, running to our house, all breathless and sparkling, to show me and to ask what I thought—and I thought my heart would burst for love of her. Perhaps there came a time when she guessed, but I don't believe so. I never told her, for I knew I would never ask her to marry me. I could not bear for her to have such a—a spectacle as a husband, even if she had wanted me.''

His voice faded, and he sat gazing into space, remembering. I moved to sit beside him on the settee and waited. After a little while he said, ''I went into the City, and I was still a young man when I inherited a fortune. I increased that fortune many times over, not from greed but because I had no other outlet for my energies, and perhaps because I did not care whether I succeeded or failed. Always I worked through others, Meg. A network of people brought me information and carried out my instructions, while I sat alone to think and plan.''

He paused and shook his head. "But I am running ahead of my tale now. When Mary was nineteen she married Laurence Glencullen, your father, and though I envied him I was truly glad, for when Mary first wrote to tell me of the engagement I put inquiries in hand and learned that Laurence was a young man of fine character. When I returned to Ireland for that summer, Mary brought him to me and I was even more glad. We became good friends, Laurence and I, and we remained friends through the years that followed."

John Lafayette rested his white head against the high back of the settee and closed his eyes. "They were my only friends," he said in a low voice. "To them I was never a man in a dark room, unseen. With them it did not matter that I was a freak. Sometimes Mary became angry with me, fixing me with those fierce green eyes and reprimanding me for being oversensitive, even for being vain, holding up others with crueler disabilities as examples to me. Oh, she was right, Meg, she was right."

He shook his head, and I saw his mouth tighten. "I was too sensitive in other ways also. I shrank from interfering in the affairs of these two dear friends, and so I said nothing to them of what I suspected concerning Adrian Webb, who secured their confidence and became their lawyer. I should have told them, made them listen, offered myself as your trustee. . . ."

He gave a great sigh and sat up, clasping his hands together and staring down at them. "My heart broke for them when their tiny child was taken from them in Australia and believed dead. It broke for myself when they were both taken from me four years ago now, at much the same time that you were saving Luke Bowman from death in the Australian outback." He fell silent, then stood up with sudden energy, bracing himself as if shrugging off a burden. "Here you sit in your pretty dress and hat and gloves and I have offered you no refreshment yet. I'm so sorry, my dear. Let me show you to your room now and introduce your maid to you, and while you rest I will have some tea sent up."

I shook my head. Almost from the first moment of seeing

John Lafayette I had felt a strange affinity for him, a warmth and understanding that seemed to override the difference in our ages, to put thoughts into my mind and words into my mouth that seemed hardly to be my own. So it was now, when I said, "Yes, I would like to see my room, to wash my hands and face, and to write the note for your messenger to take to Aunt Becky, but I don't need to rest. I would like to see your village, sir, the village of Telhurst."

He blinked and put a hand to his brow with a baffled air. "Why . . . of course, if you wish. Perhaps Simon would care to drive you there, or I can have one of the grooms take you."

"No, Mr. Lafayette. I would like you to take me there, to show me the church, the smithy, the shops, the market, if you please."

The reddish pupils seemed to widen with alarm at my words, and I went on quickly, "You will have me beside you, on your arm, and we shall wish people good afternoon, and I think we may find amusement by watching them from the corners of our eyes as they stare and whisper together at sight of the mysterious Mr. Lafayette. But it will be no more than a nine days' wonder, and then they will find something else to whisper about."

He passed a tongue across pallid lips and said, "Meg . . . I can't. I haven't the courage."

"My mother would have made you. If we are to be friends you can no longer remain the man in the dark room, sir."

He drew in a long, deep breath. "You'll stay beside me, Meg? Holding my arm? You promise?"

"I promise."

"Then . . . so be it."

AT DINNER THAT EVENING I ALMOST FELL ASLEEP SITTING AT the table, for I felt more exhausted than if I had walked from dawn till dusk. I learned that the splendid dining room of Caragh had not been used since my mother and father had last been there as guests, and there was an atmosphere of excitement among the servants as they went about their duties under the watchful eye of Blake, the butler. Mr. Lafayette was at the head of the table, I sat on his right with Simon beside me, and Eliza sat on his left.

Before dinner I had been able to spend a quarter of an hour with Eliza and to give her the essentials of John Lafayette's story, which she had passed on to Simon. They were clearly intrigued to be sitting at table with the man who had been a mystery to them for so many years and who had engaged them to perform so many strange tasks, but I was thankful to them for their wit and sensitivity in that they did not studiously avoid all reference to his appearance but responded casually when he spoke of it so that it dwindled in importance.

"I shall not pretend that the village walk with Meg was a pleasure," he was saying as coffee was served and I strove to keep my eyes open. "In fact it was an ordeal, but I found it a bearable ordeal, and I know that next time it will be still easier to bear."

Eliza said, "I can't think why you have hidden yourself away from us all these years, Mr. Lafayette, and I'm quite jealous of Meg's success with you. I hope you'll invite me to accompany you to Sevenoaks one day soon." She glanced at Simon, and her eyes sparkled. "Or better still, when Meg and I go to Somerset House tomorrow morning to see the will, let us leave Simon here and have you as our escort instead. Simon is sometimes very boring, and he doesn't fully appreciate us, does he, Meg?"

I was too sleepy to invent any polite words, and I said, "I don't know what he thinks about me, but he doesn't appreciate you, Eliza."

"Eh?" Simon said in surprise. "Oh, rubbish. I hope you'll ignore that remark from the aborigine girl, Mr. Lafayette, and I also hope you'll take up Eliza's suggestion."

"London . . ." said Mr. Lafayette slowly. "So many people. I only visit my lawyers there, traveling in a closed carriage, wearing a wide-brimmed hat to hide my face as I dart from the carriage to a room in darkness."

"A waste of time," Eliza said politely. "Nothing and nobody is strange in London. If you walked the streets in a Viking helmet and snowshoes, hardly a head would turn. And tomorrow you will have a lady on each arm to support you, Mr. Lafayette."

I forced my eyelids open, for they had closed without my being aware of it. "Luke," I said vaguely, "however can I let Luke know what has happened?"

John Lafayette put his hand on mine as it rested on the table. "That has already been arranged," he said. "Luke Bowman has bought an estate in Somerset and is farming there. Adrian Webb won't tell him you have run away, because Webb knows he can't play the same trick on him again, now that you're with me. But tomorrow Luke Bowman will receive a telegram advising him that you are in the care of John Lafayette at Caragh. Since he believes me to be the blackest of villains I have no doubt he will make an early and dramatic appearance here."

My heart lifted at the thought of seeing Luke again. "Oh, I'm so glad," I said. "I didn't even know he was in England, and it will be lovely to see him. Luke was my first real friend, and I do miss him." On the last word a huge and overwhelming yawn took me by surprise. I smothered it with a hand and gulped an apology. "I beg your pardon. Please forgive me."

Mr. Lafayette leaned back in his chair, and those sad red eyes smiled at me. "You can barely keep awake, and little wonder," he said, "for you've been giving of yourself all day. Off to bed with you now, Meg, and sleep well, my dear."

"Oh thank you, and please do excuse me." Both men stood up as I rose, Eliza gave me a smiling, "Good night, dear," and I was turning toward the door when a thought struck me and I paused. "Mr. Lafayette," I said sleepily, "you said Adrian Webb would not speak to the police and would not tell Luke, but what do you think he *will* do?"

The smile faded from the paper-white face, and the strange

eyes grew somber. "I have too much respect for you to conceal the truth behind foolish reassurance, Meg," he said. "I know that in one way or another Adrian Webb will still seek to achieve his aim by bringing about your death. What I do not know is *how* he will seek to achieve it."

FOURTEEN

I WOKE AT SEVEN THE NEXT MORNING, AND WHEN I HAD taken my bath I went out to walk in the grounds before breakfast. Simon was strolling by the lake and waited for me to draw near.

"Good morning, Meg."

"Good morning, Simon."

He smiled. "And how is Miss Glencullen today?"

"You're not supposed to call me that. We don't want reporters putting stories in the newspapers about—what was it you called me last night?—that aborigine girl."

"So I did. Am I forgiven?"

"Oh, I don't mind anyway."

He nodded toward the distant house. "What an extraordinary man."

"Yes. So rich, yet so sad. I think I had more happiness in Shalimar than he has ever known."

"How can such a clever man suffer so greatly from being an albino?" Simon wondered. "I've seen normal people a great deal less pleasing in appearance."

"I expect he became turned in upon himself when he was a small boy at school. Children aren't angels. They can be the cruelest of human beings."

"And you speak from experience?"

290

"Yes." I looked at the sun. "We'd better go to breakfast. It's been arranged early, so we can get to Somerset House by ten. Are you glad to know the man in the dark room at last?"

"Very glad, and so is Eliza. He wants us to continue working for him as before, but there's a great change in him. He speaks to us now as if we were old friends."

"Well, that's not surprising. He'd like you to be, because he hasn't got any, has he? Will you be going away to do a job for him soon?"

Simon looked down sideways at me. "We're already doing a job for him, Meg, the same job we were doing in Australia, playing the part of your guardian angels."

"Oh. Yes, I see. I do hope there won't be any trouble."

"That's up to Adrian Webb."

Eliza and Mr. Lafayette were at the table and talking easily together when we arrived for breakfast. He rose as I entered, and again I found myself thinking of my mother and of their lifelong friendship and affection for each other, so it felt quite natural for me to go to him and offer my cheek to be kissed in greeting.

He did not speak for a few minutes after that, but when Simon and I had served ourselves at the sideboard and taken our seats he picked up an envelope that lay beside his plate and passed it to me. "I hope this won't make you sad, Meg, but I thought you might like to see it so you may know that your mother was truly my friend."

I smiled and said, "I hadn't thought of disbelieving you, Mr. Lafayette." The letter was addressed in large and rather untidy handwriting to John Lafayette, Esq., Caragh, Telhurst, Nr. Sevenoaks, Kent. Inside was a single sheet of writing paper bearing the same hand.

Dearest Markie,

Thank you for writing but I forbid you to come and see me at present. This wretched fever may be catching, and I have even banished Laurence to the tower in

the west wing. I will let you know when I am well
again.

> With fondest love,
> Mary Caragh

P.S. I have instructed nurse to bake this in the oven
before giving it to Moxon to post!

As I looked up, Mr. Lafayette said, "She always signed
herself Mary Caragh to me . . . and as you know, she was
never to recover."

I did feel sadness, but the tone of the letter warmed me. I
looked at it again and said, "May Eliza and Simon read it?"

"I should like them to, since they are so closely involved
in your affairs."

I waited until they had both read the letter, then said, "Why
does she call you Markie?"

"Oh, that." He gave a little sigh. "It began as a childhood joke when she was no more than twelve. She read in a
history book about a French general who commanded an
American force against the British during the War of Inde-
pendence. He was the Marquis de Lafayette, so Mary chose
to pretend I was a French nobleman incognito, and she began
calling me Le Marquis. After a while it was just Marquis,
and then at some time or other, while I was at university, she
anglicized the spelling. From then on I was always Markie to
her."

The more I learned of my mother, the less remote from her
I felt, and now I was aware of a profound grief at the thought
that if only she had lived a few more years she would have been
able to see her lost daughter again and to hold me in her arms.
I passed the letter back to Mr. Lafayette and said, "Thank you
for letting me see it, sir."

He took it, and with a touch of embarrassment said, "It troubles me that you address me as 'sir,' though I respect the cour-
tesy, and even 'Mr. Lafayette' seems too formal for Mary Caragh

Glencullen's daughter. I will not suggest you adopt me as Uncle John, for I fear Adrian Webb has poisoned that relationship for us both, but it would give me great pleasure if you used your mother's name for me.''

I thought for a moment, then said, ''I don't think that will be difficult for me. Where I grew up, all people just had single names, like Yuma or Manyi or Katapi, and young or old were simply addressed by that single name, like Markie.''

A white hand reached out to touch mine. ''Bless you, my dear. I wonder where you learned to think like that before speaking? It was not a habit of your mother's.''

I said, ''Oh dear, I don't always think first. Sometimes if I'm angry I speak without thinking at all, and I glare, Luke says, so I look like an Irish alley cat.''

For the first time I heard John Lafayette really laugh without restraint. ''Now, that's inherited,'' he said. ''I know exactly what Luke means.'' He looked at Eliza and Simon. ''I have no family, and I have been a very lonely man. Perhaps it would not be too difficult for you also to adopt Mary Caragh Glencullen's name for me. I have grown very weary of having no friends.''

AT HALF PAST TEN THAT MORNING WE LEFT SOMERSET HOUSE, Markie Lafayette, Eliza, and I, and walked to the solicitor's office in the Middle Temple, where in the past Eliza and Simon had received instructions from the man in the dark room. Mr. Hardacre, the senior partner, was of course aware that his client was an albino but was greatly surprised to discover that his days of concealment were past. Our visit was simply to introduce me to Mr. Hardacre, and when we left I was able to show off the knowledge I had acquired during my London explorations by guiding us through the maze of alleys and courtyards of the Temple to the Embankment and Blackfriars Station, where we caught a train back to Sevenoaks. All the time that we were walking, Markie Lafayette wore dark glasses, and hardly anybody gave a second glance to the man with the white face and curly white hair showing below the brim of his top hat.

We arrived home to find that the messenger sent by Markie to Belgrave Square had returned with my personal belongings. There was also a hasty note from Aunt Becky to say that Uncle Adrian had explained the need for my sudden departure, and though I would be greatly missed they were glad for me to have this unexpected opportunity of returning to Clairmont as a teacher.

When I showed it to the others Simon laughed. "Ingenious but hardly plausible," he said. "She won't believe it, will she, Meg?"

I nodded. "Oh yes. She's a very trusting person, and she would never dream of questioning anything he tells her. To Aunt Becky her husband is what he seems to be. I really feel very sorry for her."

"Poor lady," said Markie somberly. "She may one day have a terrible awakening."

At three o'clock that afternoon Luke arrived at Caragh. We had been expecting him. My maid, Lucy, was on watch at an upper window and came running down to tell us that a cab was coming up the drive. I went quickly to the hall and was peeping from behind curtains when the cab drew up and Luke fairly sprang from within, thrusting money at the cabbie and rushing up the steps of the great porch. The doorbell clanged furiously, and I felt my heart pounding as I ran to the morning room, leaving the door open by half an inch and putting my eye to the crack.

Blake had been given instructions and was crossing the hall to the front door. Nobody else was in sight. Blake opened the door, standing to one side, and this was as well, for he might have been knocked over by the way Luke burst into the hall. "Good afternoon, sir," Blake said politely. "You will be Mr. Bowman, I believe? May I take your hat and cane, sir?"

"Eh?" Luke was taken aback for a moment. Then he glared

round the hall. "Where is she?" he demanded. "Where's Meg Gaynor?"

"Miss Gaynor is awaiting you in the morning room, Mr. Bowman," said Blake. "I do suggest you remove your hat, sir."

"Awaiting me?" Luke shook his head in bewilderment, then snatched off his hat and thrust it at Blake. "Where?"

"If you will kindly follow me, sir."

I hurried across the room and sat down in an armchair with my hands folded in my lap. Seconds later the door swung open and Luke strode in. He stopped short at the sight of me, as if dumbfounded, and then relief swept his face and he came forward. "Meg! Thank God you're safe! What in heaven's name are you doing here, you stupid girl? Come along—this is no place to linger!"

I said, "Please close the door and sit down, Luke. I have something to tell you."

He stood with hands on hips, looking down at me with angry eyes. "Don't *argue,* Meg! I've no idea what Lafayette is up to, sending me that wire. All I'm concerned with is getting you safely away."

I said, "I'm safe here, Luke."

"No, you're not!"

I felt full of love for Luke and deeply sorry for the humiliation I knew he would soon have to suffer. Perhaps it was this that caused sudden anger to sweep through me. I came to my feet, and although I tried to control my face I could feel my jaw tightening and my eyes narrowing.

"Don't call me stupid!" I exclaimed. "Look at me! I'm unharmed. I'm free. I have nothing to fear. But I do have something to tell you that will greatly distress you, and I *hate* having to do it. Now, will you stop bawling at me and telling me what to do and just *listen* for a moment, damn it! There! Now you've made *me* swear, and I've never done that before! You ought to be *ashamed* of yourself!"

I was panting by the time I had finished. Luke gazed at me open-mouthed for several seconds. Then he looked about him, rubbed a hand over his face, turned to the door and closed it, and came back to stand rather rigidly by the fireplace, looking at me with something close to apprehension.

"I'm sorry, Meg," he said quietly. "It's just that I've been so worried about you since this morning. What is it you have to tell me?"

My anger vanished, and I felt utterly miserable as I said, "Luke, I'm so sorry, but you have been completely deceived. This morning I was at Somerset House, where I saw a true copy of my father's will. The person who will inherit the Glencullen fortune if I die before reaching twenty-one is not John Lafayette. It is Adrian Webb. John Lafayette's name is not mentioned in the will."

Luke said, "But—"

That was all. For long seconds he stared blankly at me, and I could almost see his mind slowly working out all that followed from the solitary but undeniable fact that my father's will named Adrian Webb to administer the Glencullen fortune if I failed to live to the age of twenty-one. I saw realization dawn on him that Adrian Webb had produced a false copy and had attributed his own villainies to John Lafayette, that it must have been Adrian Webb who was responsible for Sid Buller's attempt upon me and for the murder of Harry Tasker.

Then, suddenly and brutally, came the knowledge that he, Luke Bowman, had taken me from a place of safety and delivered me into the hands of the man who sought my death. My heart ached for Luke as I saw the blood drain from his face and the horror darken his eyes. "Oh dear God Almighty," he whispered. "What have I done?" He turned, rested his elbows on the mantelpiece, pressed the heels of his hands to his eyes, and said hoarsely, "Tell me, Meg. Tell me the whole of it."

I moved to stand beside him and spoke quietly as I began to relate all that I had learned of Adrian Webb, of my parents, and of John Lafayette in the past twenty-four hours. My story took a full five minutes in the telling, and he did not once interrupt. When at last I came to an end there was silence in the room for a while. Then he turned from the mantelpiece, sank down on the edge of a low armchair, leaned forward with his elbows on his knees, and held his head in his hands.

"Oh, sweet Jesus," he said in a strange voice. "I could have sent you to your death."

I said, "Don't dwell on it, Luke. I'm safe now. Please don't dwell on it and feel bad." I moved to kneel beside him and put my arms about him. At once he started to resist, but I gave him a hard shake and said sharply, "Don't push me away, Luke Bowman! Just for once don't push me away!" I think my words startled him into acquiescence, for he seemed to go limp in my arms, and I slipped an arm around his neck and held his head against my shoulder.

"Listen to me, Luke," I whispered. "You were deceived by a man who is a master of deceit. I was equally taken in by him. By good fortune and good friends I've been brought safely out of danger, so all's well. But you are my first and dearest friend, Luke. You know I don't blame you, and I shall grieve so deeply if you suffer agonies of remorse. Please put it all behind you now. Are you listening? Try to remember that I'm your funny little aborigine girl, your golden urchin, and that we brought each other safely out of the bush when we might both have died, and that I shall never forget all that you and Rosemary did for me. Do you hear me, Luke?"

He gave a great sigh, then very gently disengaged himself and stood up, reaching down a hand to help me to my feet. "Yes, I hear you, Mitji," he said quietly. "I can't put what I've done behind me quite as easily as that, but I hear you, and I'm grateful for your kindness." A sudden spasm twisted his face, and he stepped back. "I'll be going now. There's something I have to do."

He turned to the door, but I plucked up my skirt and fairly raced past him to reach the door first, turning with my back to it, arms spread. "What is it you have to do?" I demanded, and I could feel the alley-cat glare creeping into my face.

He stared at me from eyes like polished blue stones and said in a flat voice, "I'm going to find Webb." His face was almost as white as Markie's albino features, and the rage in him so murderous that I was terrified.

"No!" I cried. "I won't have it, Luke! You'll end up in prison, or worse!"

"I won't complain," he said grimly. His hands shot out, caught me by the arms, and lifted me aside before I could resist. He jerked the door open, then stopped short as he found himself confronting Eliza with no more than half an arm's length between them. She smiled at him, then suddenly kicked him hard on the shin, and as he gasped and staggered off balance she gave him a push that sent him sprawling. Next moment she had stepped into the room, closed the door, and turned the key.

"I thought as much," she said amiably. "We're off to break Adrian Webb's neck, are we? Well, I'm not against the basic idea, mind you, but I don't like my friends being hanged, and neither does Meg, so just simmer down, sonny-boy. Oh, and don't give me any trouble, will you? I've been very restrained with you so far."

Luke lay propped on an elbow, a hand clasped to his shin, staring up at her. Then he gave a brief harsh laugh, and the fury seemed to drain out of him. He got slowly to his feet, his shoulders slumped a little in weary resignation. "Hello, Eliza," he said. "I was never quite able to see you as a vicar's wife."

"Will you laugh if I tell you I'm a vicar's daughter?"

Luke ran a hand through his thick golden hair. "Meg told me. And I don't much feel like laughing about anything at the moment, Eliza."

"I don't suppose you do." She stepped forward, reached up, and took his face between her hands, looking into his eyes. "You made a terrible mistake, and it hurts. It's also given you a bad attack of wounded pride. Well, swallow it, Luke. Just take your medicine and forget it. Nobody blames you, least of all Meg, and we don't want you rushing off and making another mistake." She gave his head a little shake. "Are you going to stay away from Webb like a good boy?"

"All right, Eliza. I promise."

"Don't promise me, promise Meg." She twisted his head to face me, and let him go.

He looked at my feet and said, "I promise, Red."

Eliza lifted an eyebrow at the name he used, but made no comment. She turned to unlock the door and said, "I'm glad that's settled. Now bring Luke through to the terrace, Meg. Simon and Markie are waiting to see him."

THE NEXT HOUR WAS NOT AN EASY ONE. LUKE WAS INTRO-duced to Markie Lafayette and apologized with bitter self-re-crimination for what he had done; both Simon and Markie sought to reassure him, but I had lived under the same roof as Luke for almost three years and I knew how deeply ashamed he must be feeling. It would take time before he could be at peace with himself again.

We sat in the sunshine on the terrace, taking tea, talking of what had happened and what Adrian Webb might do now. I said very little myself, for I could think only of Luke, and I was trying to hide what I felt at being so close to him yet unable to touch him. I had held him in my arms for a few moments in the morning room and was glad that at least I would have those moments to remember. With my primitive upbringing I found it hard to think of Luke in a proper and civilized manner. Instead I found myself swept by sudden surges of yearning to have him possess me, to take joy of him and give him joy in return.

I emerged from a reverie to hear Markie saying, "In a month's time I shall be going to the Cape Colony on business, and I very much hope that Meg will consent to accompany me, together with Simon and Eliza. If she has no wish to, then she can remain here and of course Simon and Eliza will remain also, but I do feel it would be wise if she were to be removed from harm's way for a few months while my agents try to ascertain what Adrian Webb's next move may be." He paused and looked at me. "Would you like to make the trip, my dear? If I am to cease being a recluse elsewhere as I have begun to do here, then I shall need your help."

I had a fleeting and foolish hope that Luke would ask me to come and stay on his estate in Somerset, but he did not speak, and after a moment or two I smiled and said, "Yes, I shall be glad to go with you, Markie."

He turned to Luke. "I seem to be acquiring something of a family, Mr. Bowman. If you would care to join our expedition to the Cape you would be most welcome. I'm sure you have a manager to cope with your farming responsibilities in Somerset, and you might even find some business opportunities to interest you in southern Africa. I shall book passages in the next day or two on a liner calling at Freetown, and there we shall transfer to a smaller ship, a private yacht, in fact, of about nine hundred tons with just half a dozen quite pleasant passenger cabins. She is called the *Caragh*."

I was surprised, and said, "My mother's name again? Is it your own ship?"

He nodded. "It is, Meg. I have substantial shipbuilding interests, and I think there may be a future for this type of yacht. The *Caragh* is not to be compared with the royal yacht, which is three times the tonnage, but it is of a design that has much to attract the wealthy private owner."

Simon said, "Why will it be in Freetown?"

"Because it is at present navigating and mapping sections of the Skeleton Coast for me, dear boy, one of the most inaccessible regions in the entire world, but an area where diamonds are said to abound. There was no point in bringing the ship to England to pick us up when we can so easily take passage to Freetown on a liner." The white face and reddish eyes turned toward Luke. "What do you say, Mr. Bowman? I'm sure we would all be glad to have your company."

I clenched my hands in sudden hope, but Luke said impassively, "You're most kind, Mr. Lafayette, especially in view of the trouble I've caused you, but I must remain in England. There are matters I have to attend to." He looked at me. "Don't worry, Meg. I won't go near Adrian Webb."

I managed to smile. "Well, that's all right then."

He took out his watch, then got to his feet. "I have to leave you now, or I shall be too late to catch the last train out of Paddington to get me home."

We all rose, and Markie said with a whimsical smile, "I wish I had suggested in my wire that you should come prepared to stay overnight, Mr. Bowman, but I doubt that you would have paused to pack a bag. However, I do hope we shall see you again before we leave, for as Meg says, you are her first and oldest friend. Should you change your mind about accompanying us to the Cape, please don't hesitate to let me know."

"Thank you again. You've been more than kind." Luke shook hands with Markie and Simon, bowed over Eliza's hand, then turned to me and said, "Good-bye, Meg. I seem fated to cause you trouble, but you know I meant well."

"Of course I do." I could not say the word good-bye, and I said, "God bless you, Luke."

The others seemed to be waiting for him to make some gesture of farewell to me, but he simply turned and said, "Well, if you'll excuse me . . ."

Markie said, "I have a carriage waiting for you in the drive, my dear fellow. I'll come and see you safely aboard."

They went in together by the French windows. Simon shook his head wonderingly and said, "What on earth is the matter with the man? He rushes up here to save you, goes berserk about Adrian Webb's doings, then acts as if you were no more than a slight acquaintance."

I said, "Don't be silly. It's just that old friends have no need to make a fuss of each other."

Eliza asked, "Why did he call you Red while we were in the morning room?" Before I could answer she went on, "Well, I realize it's because of your hair, but I didn't know he called you that."

"It's a pet name," I said. "That's why it's silly for anyone to say he treats me as he would a slight acquaintance."

Simon made a mock bow and said, "I'm sorry. Don't take offense."

Eliza looked out thoughtfully over the lawns. "You can say what you like," she murmured, "but there's a demon eating that man. I don't know the nature of the demon, but I'd be intrigued to see if I could help banish it for him."

I felt a sudden fierce thrust of anger and jealousy, but in a few seconds it was gone as common sense returned and I realized sadly that Eliza was in no way my rival. She knew nothing of what I felt for Luke, and in any event I could not have a rival, because I had no claim on Luke.

Simon was looking at Eliza with an uneasy air. "I trust you don't plan to set your cap for Luke Bowman," he said.

A faint smile touched her lips as she continued to gaze into the distance. "Given the chance, why not?" she said. "As you've often pointed out, Simon dear, we are both free agents."

IN THE DAYS THAT FOLLOWED I SETTLED INTO LIFE AT CARAGH happily enough, except for the empty corner of my heart that only Luke could ever fill. I obtained his address from Markie and wrote to him in Somerset, saying how glad I had been to see him again and that he was not to blame himself for having been deceived by Adrian Webb. I made it a cheerful and friendly letter, writing in much the same way as I had always written in my diary, but I had no reply from him.

With Simon and Eliza in the house, and Markie emerging from his seclusion, I had the feeling that Caragh was coming to life after years of standing like a great silent tomb. We all set ourselves to coax and encourage Markie without pressing him too hard, but Eliza was easily the most adept at this. I often found them talking together, laughing, strolling in the grounds, playing chess, or arguing some point of literary or philosophical opinion, for during her vicarage years Eliza had been educated to a high standard and was possessed of a very lively mind. It was she who persuaded him to accompany us to a London theater to see a play called *The Master Builder* by Mr. Ibsen.

Markie was nervous at first, and as we expected there were some who stared as we stood talking in the foyer before the play and during the intermission, but Eliza soon found a way to counter this. "If we see anyone staring, Meg," she said, "we'll both stare back as hard as we can."

This we did with much success, for we found that people quickly looked away when we turned our united gaze upon them. The evening was a special occasion for me, as it was the first time I had ever seen a play, and I was entranced by the wonder of it.

I did not write to Aunt Becky again, for Adrian Webb had told her that I was returning to Clairmont, and in any event there was nothing to be said. But I was sad, because I knew my silence would seem unkind, and I felt sorry for her and for Albert; they had both been fond of me, as I had been of them.

Two weeks after my arrival at Caragh a letter came for Markie from his solicitor to say that the inquiry agency employed to keep track of Adrian Webb's activities had reported his departure for America. According to their informant he expected to be away for two or three months on important business in several different cities.

"I'm puzzled," said Markie as we sat at breakfast. "His firm has one or two clients in the United States with interests here in England, but I wouldn't have thought he had enough business over there to merit being away for so long. However, the fellow *is* away, and so much the worse. I would rather have him where we can keep an eye on him, and I shall certainly try to arrange for an American agency to take over the task."

He brooded for a moment, then went on, "It's possible that Webb may have decided to take no action against Meg for the time being. After all, he has well over two years before she becomes twenty-one, and he may wish to make us believe he has abandoned any intention to harm her. On the other hand, we must not permit ourselves to have a false sense of security. Never forget that Adrian Webb may have left instructions with one or another of his underworld hirelings to bring about Meg's death.''

He looked at me. ''I speak bluntly, my dear, to remind us all of the brutal fact that this is what Adrian Webb must achieve if he is not to face ruin and disgrace, for if you come into your inheritance he will no longer be able to conceal the extent of his misappropriation.''

Eliza said pensively, ''I have a feeling about Adrian Webb. I think he has been driven into a corner and will react like a wild creature. I don't believe he will use another Sid Buller or another hireling of the kind who murdered Harry Tasker. I think Adrian Webb will trust nobody but himself from now on.''

I shivered, recalling how he had beamed fondly upon me like a benign Mr. Pickwick.

Simon said quietly, ''I trust Eliza's feelings. She's a clever judge of a man.'' He looked at Markie. ''When you first gave us the job of investigating Webb she spent a week acting as a maid at the club where he usually gambles, and there's no better time to study a man than when he's under stress.''

Markie nodded slowly. ''If Eliza is right, then with Webb away Meg will be in no immediate danger, but please let us not bank on that.''

Twelve days later we sailed from Southampton on the liner *Penrith*, bound for Hong Kong by the Cape route. To my shame and annoyance I was the only one of our party to be smitten by seasickness, and for me the Bay of Biscay was a nightmare. But by the time we reached Lisbon, our first port of call, I had found my sea legs and was enjoying the voyage. From Lisbon we sailed to Madeira and were able to spend part of a day on this mountainous island of flowers before continuing down the coast of Africa to Freetown.

It was during this part of the voyage that Simon asked Markie if we would be exploring some part of the Skeleton Coast on our way south to the Cape. The evening was warm with a slight but pleasant breeze, and we were sitting on deck in the twilight after dinner, the two men smoking cigars.

"Good Lord no, my dear boy," said Markie. "We shall not be going within miles of the coast. Do you know anything about that area?"

"Nothing at all. I've heard a few wild stories about the masts of ancient wrecks standing out of the sand half a mile from the sea, but those are just sailors' stories."

In the darkness I saw Markie shake his head. "Not so. Very little is known of the Kaokoveld, as that coast is properly called, but it does move, and it moves seaward. There *are* ancient wrecks to be seen, half buried in desert sand, for the sea has claimed many victims along that five hundred miles of rock and reef. There is a vicious current called the Benguela current, which drags ships in toward the shore. Most losses came in the days of sail, of course. A steamship such as the *Caragh* is not endangered by the current, and Captain Lester is a very fine sailor, but when I sent him to map the coastline I gave orders that it was to be done at long range by telescope, approaching no closer than a mile, for that is the most treacherous coast in the world. We shall be keeping a full five miles clear of it on our way south."

I said, "Why do you want it mapped, Markie?"

He laughed. "Curiosity, my dear. At the moment the whole area is a barren waste. There are no people, no roads, no rivers or railways, and the coast is a tangle of reefs and rock and sand dunes, with no port or harbor until you reach Walvis Bay at the southern end of the Kaokoveld. But if the land does bear diamonds—and many men have died from that belief—then one day a way will be found to explore and exploit the area. It will not happen in my time, of that I'm sure, but I would like to contribute some small knowledge of the coast to brave men of a future generation who will seek ways to penetrate it from the sea."

Eliza reached out and put a hand on his arm. "You're a fraud," she said. "You pretend to be interested in the diamonds, if there are any, but the truth is you just want to make it possible for men to go where they have never been before. I think that's an admirable motive. You're a romantic, Markie Lafayette, that's what you are.''

He exhaled cigar smoke with a rueful sigh. ''You flatter me, Eliza. I'm rich enough to afford admirable motives, so there's really nothing to admire in what I do.''

This set them off on one of their philosophical arguments in which I rapidly lost my way, for although I had once rather vainly thought I was quite well read, I had recently discovered that I knew nothing of the abstruse and abstract matters that Markie and Eliza sometimes discussed. It was difficult to reconcile this Eliza with the vicar's runaway daughter, the failed actress, and the adventurer's companion who could deal so competently with such as the drunkard at the service in Lawton, or even with Luke Bowman in a fury. I only knew that the more I learned of Eliza the more I liked her.

Simon himself was well up to joining in such discussions, but usually did so only to tease Eliza by making a point that was sure to provoke her. On this occasion I felt it would spoil the evening if he took part, so I asked if he would take a stroll around the deck with me, and at once he rose and offered his arm. For a few minutes we talked easily, but then, as we came to a darker part of the deck, he slipped his arm about my waist and pressed me to him. At once I pulled away and turned to face him, angry and upset.

''Don't ever do that again, Simon,'' I said. ''Not ever.''

He tossed his cigar over the rail, and I thought I saw genuine puzzlement on his face as he looked down at me. ''Why not, Meg?''

''Because you belong to Eliza.''

''Belong? No I don't.''

''Then I'm ashamed of you, because you take all her loyalty for granted and you give her none in return. You want all she gives of herself, but you take no responsibility for her. You're a selfish man, Simon.''

"Ah! Now I see the alley-cat glare I've heard about." His voice was cold and angry. "What the devil gives you the right to criticize me?"

"You gave me the right. You asked why I forbade you to put your arm round me like that, so I've told you." I put out a hand and caught his arm. "Simon, please," I went on quickly, "let this be an end of it. I don't want us to quarrel, but please respect my feelings. I see things quite differently from you, and I'm not . . . available to you in the slightest way, because Eliza is my friend. That's quite apart from anything else."

He dipped his head a little to peer at me. "What else, Meg?" This was a question I did not intend to answer. "Oh, I don't know—just anything else," I said irritably. "Now for heaven's sake let's both forget this last minute or so and go on strolling together."

He sighed, then smiled and offered his arm again. "All right, Meg. We'll do that."

Three days later we came to the port of Freetown, a hot and humid place with tendrils of mist lying over the land and a scent that made my nostrils twitch with unease. As we entered the harbor I was standing with Markie, who pointed to a white-painted ship with a single funnel moored at one of the quays. It was small compared with the *Penrith*, but it had an elegant line and a feminine look that appealed to me at once.

"There's the *Caragh*," said Markie. "Isn't she beautiful?"

I nodded agreement and took his hand in mine for a moment, thinking how much my mother must have meant to this man whose affliction had driven him into seclusion for so much of his life. For the next few minutes, as a tug maneuvered us alongside a quay, we watched two men in white shirts and trousers on the bridge of the *Caragh* who were watching us in turn.

"Captain Lester and his first mate, Mr. Sullivan," said Markie. "Both very efficient, and the same can be said for the engineers. I imagine they'll have steam up and be ready to sail as soon as we've transferred from the *Penrith*."

We were at the quay now, and I moved to the rail as men

prepared to lower the gangway. Next moment I gave a gasp of astonishment and cried, "Markie! Look!"

There on the quayside, in shirt sleeves and with a panama hat pushed back on his head, was Luke Bowman, hands on hips, gazing up at me. "Luke!" I called, waving joyously. "Luke!"

Beside me, Markie said, "Good God, what on earth is he doing here?" With the words, Eliza and Simon came strolling across the deck to join us. I heard her laugh in surprise, and Simon said something, but I did not register what it was, for I was too preoccupied with schooling myself to be calm so that nobody would guess my feelings. Two minutes later Luke was with us, but apart from a brief general greeting he said nothing until we had moved away from the crowd gathering near the top of the gangway and found a quiet spot on deck.

"I sailed on a cargo ship two days after you left," he said without preamble, "but we came direct to Freetown so I was able to reach here before you."

Markie said, "This is a pleasant surprise for us, Mr. Bowman, but I think you must have some very serious reason for intercepting us."

Luke nodded. "After putting Meg in danger by my own stupidity I decided to have close watch kept on Adrian Webb myself. It was reported to me that he had left for America, as no doubt it was reported to you, but I wasn't quite satisfied. He sailed on the *Bostonian*, and his passage was booked to New York, but I made inquiries of the shipping line and discovered that he disembarked at the first port of call, Cherbourg."

There was a silence. Markie took off his dark glasses, screwing up his eyes against the sunlight, and began to clean the lenses with a silk handkerchief. "I've no doubt you have tried to trace Webb's movements after disembarking," he said.

"I sent a man to do so," Luke answered. "I couldn't go myself because you had already sailed and I had to find a passage that would bring me here before you. But I arranged for my agent to telegraph me here, and on my arrival I found a wire awaiting me to say that Webb simply seems to have disappeared.

There has been no sign of him since he disembarked at Cherbourg.''

Eliza said, "You've had more time to think about this than we have, Luke. What do you imagine he's up to?"

Luke shook his head with a troubled air. "Two possibilities, it seems to me. He may have decided he can't hope to dispose of Meg and that eventually the truth will come out, so he's bolted after laying hands on as much money as possible. But I don't believe Webb is a man to give up like that. He has enormous confidence in his own cleverness and ability. I think he knows you're taking Meg to the Cape Colony, and he's gone out there ahead of you with the intention of seeking an opportunity to bring about her death, probably by his own hand. He knows Meg is protected now, so he'll no longer be prepared to rely on hirelings to do his bloody work for him."

Simon said quietly, "Eliza had the same feelings, but that was instinct. You've made it logical." He glanced at Markie. "So do we continue, or shall Eliza and I return to England with Meg?"

Luke and I started to speak at the same moment; then he stopped and gestured for me to continue. I said, "If I go back, then sooner or later Adrian Webb will also return, but we can't know when that will be or how he will strike. I would much rather we let things come to a head now. Let us go on to the Cape, please, Markie. I'm well protected by Simon and Eliza, and when Adrian Webb shows his hand they'll catch him. Then it will all be over and done with, because we shall have proof at last."

I saw Markie look at Simon and receive a brief nod. Then he looked at Luke. "Mr. Bowman?"

"Meg has just said what I was about to say myself. You'll allow me to change my mind and accompany you to the Cape, Mr. Lafayette?"

Markie put his dark glasses on and smiled. "We shall be delighted," he said.

I stood torn between joy and apprehension. To have Luke

near me was wonderful, but I knew it would also bring me pain and heartache, and I thought I was probably being very stupid to look forward so eagerly to the coming days.

FIFTEEN

I LOVED THE *CARAGH*. SHE WAS A DEAR LITTLE SHIP, AND IF I had been describing her to my friend Nicole at Clairmont I would have said she was *mignonne*. A darling.

We were introduced to Captain Lester and his five officers, also to three men of the crew who would serve as stewards and waiters during the voyage. Captain Lester had engaged two local girls as a maid each for Eliza and for me, but the girls had simply failed to appear that morning as arranged. This kind of unreliability was quite usual in African ports, Captain Lester told us wryly, and Markie was full of apologies, but Eliza and I decided we would prefer to look after ourselves and were pleased not to be bothered by maids.

When I had unpacked in my little cabin I went out on deck to see what was happening, for I never tired of watching all the comings and goings on the quayside or in the harbor of a big port such as Freetown. Simon was by the rail, and he greeted me with a smile and a nod of his head toward something below. "Look at this pair, Meg," he said. "Markie shouldn't worry about his appearance compared with the fellow down there."

I moved to the rail beside Simon. Some last-minute stores were piled on the quay for loading into the afterhold, and two of the crew were in some kind of dispute there. One was a tiny lascar wearing sandals, a dark blue shirt, short frayed trousers reaching only to his knees, and a cap set backward on his head. The other was tall and lumbering, wearing a gray shirt and calico trousers. He had a brown face like an Arab and a two-inch growth of untrimmed beard reaching around his chin from ear to ear, but his head was completely bald and he wore a patch over one eye.

The small man seemed to be shouting instructions to the other about one of the crates, but the big man looked baffled and uncomprehending. The lascar turned with a gesture of despair, looking up, and I saw a thin dark face with tattoo marks on the cheeks. Our eyes met, and I felt a shiver pass through me despite the heat, as if a dark and menacing presentiment had touched some hidden depth in my mind. For a moment my vision blurred, and I scented death. Then I heard Simon's voice, and at once all was normal again, the little lascar turning to his companion with fresh exhortations. I had never had such an experience before, and I was angry with myself for being affected by formless imaginings.

"I'm sorry. What did you say, Simon?" I asked.

He laughed. "You were daydreaming for a moment, Meg. I just said I think the bearded one may be simple, poor devil. He keeps making signs but doesn't appear to speak. I wonder why he makes such a spectacle of himself by shaving his skull? With that beard it makes him look as if he's got his head on upside down."

A voice behind us said, "That's what the lower deck thought, sir." We turned to find Mr. Sullivan, the first mate, standing there. He touched his hand to the peak of his cap in a salute to me and went on, "They're mostly lascars with a smattering of English, and they've christened him Chin-up—for the reason you just suggested, I fancy."

"He's no lascar, surely?" said Simon.

"No, sir. The papers he carries from the last ship he sailed on show that he's Portuguese. The little fellow is a lascar, from Java, I believe. We were lucky to get them."

Simon lifted an eyebrow. "Lucky?"

"We had two lascars quit the ship when we docked here, sir, and an Algerian galley hand is missing. They've probably all signed on for another ship, and we had to replace them. The captain was already upset about not having maids for your ladies. Piroo, that's the little one, is a ship's carpenter." He smiled. "They're still called that, even though ships are mainly of steel today. Chin-up replaces the galley hand and also has to help with any odd jobs that need doing. We have to talk to him by signs, because nobody else speaks Portuguese."

Mr. Sullivan took out his watch and glanced at it. "Piroo seems to be finding things difficult, so if you'll excuse me I'll go down and try to sort out their problem." He smiled and saluted again, then moved off toward the gangway. I stood watching Piroo as he tried to convey something to his slow-witted companion, and I found myself with ears pricked and nostrils flared as if seeking the source of whatever emanation had come to me from the quayside a moment ago; but it was not repeated, and as Mr. Sullivan appeared below I decided that I had simply passed through one of those freakish moments people jokingly describe as having someone walk over their grave.

The sea was choppy, and we passed through a storm soon after sailing from Freetown, but though the ponderous pitching and rolling of the big liner in the Bay of Biscay had made me seasick I found myself quite enjoying the quick movements of the little *Caragh*, and the rough sea had no ill effects upon me. There was a happy atmosphere aboard, perhaps because my friends were all aware that I was safely out of Adrian Webb's reach, and so for the next twelve days until we reached Cape Town we would have no need to be on our guard.

As I had expected, I was glad to be with Luke but was sometimes close to tears from the longing within me, especially as he seemed much happier and more at ease in Eliza's company than in mine. Sometimes I envied her so greatly that I almost hated her, but I had to acknowledge that she did not appear to be setting her cap for Luke, as Simon had once suggested. It was more a case of Luke seeking her company.

On our fourth night at sea I lay in my cabin wondering if I was being a fool. Rosemary had begged me to make her a promise I had so far been unable to keep. Could I now go to Luke and tell him that she had asked me to marry him and take care of him? Could I say, "Luke, I want to keep that promise because I love you with all my heart. I expect we shall sometimes be cross with each other as we have in the past, but it wasn't very often and it never lasted. We were always good friends, working happily together, and I shall be a loving and devoted wife. . . ." I tried the words silently in my head and cringed with embarrassment, knowing I could never find the courage to give voice to my feelings.

Next morning I found that the latch on my cabin door would not work properly. A spring inside appeared to have broken, and the tongue remained withdrawn. I told Mr. Sullivan of this at breakfast, and he said he would arrange for it to be repaired. Later that morning when I went to the cabin to fetch a book I found Piroo, the little lascar, on his knees by the door with a bag of tools, working on the dismantled lock.

He still wore his cap, and now he touched a finger to it politely and said, "Mo'ning, missy. I fix yo' lock."

I thanked him and went into the cabin for my book, noting that although he had a powerful scent it carried no aura of badness and I did not feel the instinctive alarm I had felt on first seeing him. As I was about to leave a sudden thought struck me, and I paused. Later I realized it was not a thought to be proud of, for it sprang entirely from a longing to show off, to attract Luke's attention, and perhaps to make him remember a time when we had been very close together, with our lives in each other's hands, but I was not conscious of this at the time. I easily deceived myself into feeling that what I had in mind might be entertaining for my friends.

"You are Piroo?" I said to the lascar.

He looked surprised but rather pleased. "Yes, missy. Piroo. Ship carpenter."

Speaking slowly and clearly I said, "Do you have pieces of wood in your workshop?"

"Wood?" He nodded vigorously. "Yes, missy. Much pieces."

"May I see what you have? I would like you to make something for me."

He beamed. "I make. Piroo very good carpenter." He held a screwdriver like a pencil and made motions as if sketching. "You make picture what you want."

"Very well, Piroo. Thank you. I will speak to the captain to ask his permission."

Piroo's workshop was little more than a large cupboard in the bowels of the ship, but he had a bench set up on the lower deck aft where he could work in daylight. When he showed me his stock of timber I saw almost at once a piece ideally suited to my purpose, part of a broken oar with the blade intact, giving a slight natural curve. Later that day I stood by Piroo's bench for well over an hour while he worked to my instructions with saw and spokeshave, accomplishing in a very short time what it would have taken Yuma or any of my tribe several days to achieve.

Markie and his guests all wanted to know what I was about, but I banned them from the lower deck, refusing to answer any questions until the task was done and I held in my hands a most splendid boomerang, big as a fighting boomerang but so beautifully balanced that I knew I could make it do all the tricks of the comeback boomerangs I had played with as a child. The two ends of the blade were twisted very slightly in opposite directions from the center, just as I had directed, to give the boomerang what the people of my tribe had always believed to be a magical power.

Piroo was baffled, for he had no idea what it was he had made, and after asking the captain's permission I invited Piroo to join us on the upper deck so that he could see what I was about to do. When I appeared there before my friends, holding the boomerang, the secret was out. Markie chuckled and took off his glasses. Eliza exclaimed in surprise. Simon immediately wanted to examine the boomerang, while Luke laughed and said, "From a moving ship? You must be even better than I remember, Red."

I was smitten by sudden panic at his words, for it was only now that I realized I was making a pathetic attempt to show off a useless skill, and that if I failed to throw with great accuracy, the boomerang would be lost in the sea and I would look a complete fool. But when I took it back from Simon the fear passed, for by the feel and balance I knew this was a perfect weapon and would obey me.

From the bridge Captain Lester and Mr. Sullivan watched with open curiosity as I asked for a tarpaulin to be brought and suspended amidships on a line slung fore and aft just forward of the saloon. When this was done I stood for a while sensing the wind, judging the speed of the ship and weighing the boomerang in my hand until it felt part of me. Then I swung my arm and threw. The curved weapon soared out over the port bow, spinning vertically at first before turning gracefully to the horizontal and rising as it sped ahead of the *Caragh* in a wide circle, out to starboard, hovering, then slanting back to swoop in over the starboard beam and strike the heavy tarpaulin behind me only a foot or two above the deck.

After a moment's silence there came cries of surprise and astonishment. Piroo chirped excitedly in his own tongue, Captain Lester called down, "Amazing, Miss Gaynor!" Luke grinned and winked at me, Simon and Markie applauded, and I felt suddenly foolish and embarrassed. I need not have, for in the next hour I had to demonstrate my skill a dozen times, and as I grew more used to the boomerang I was able to throw it so that it would make one or two circles at the zenith of its flight before returning.

When at last I called a halt, Simon took Piroo off to make another boomerang from my pattern, saying he could not rest till he had tried his hand at throwing. Eliza began a game of

hess with Markie, and Luke came to sit with me on a swing
eat under an awning.

"That took me back a few years, Mitji," he said.

I nodded, dabbing perspiration from my brow, and said, "I'm
ot really dressed for it, though." With these words a sudden
nemory came to me, and I laughed despite the accompanying
ang that it brought. "We had our first argument before we
ould understand a word each other said, Luke. It was only two
ays after I found you, and you wanted me to put on one of your
hirts. Remember?"

His face changed, and he frowned down at the deck. "I don't
ink about the past," he said tersely.

I was bewildered. "But you just said seeing me with the
oomerang took you back—" I broke off. "Oh, you mean be-
ause of Rosemary. I'm sorry, Luke."

"Never mind." He got to his feet as if suddenly restless and
noved across to watch the game of chess, while I sat smiling
nd wondering if it would be better to shut myself in my cabin
nd cry, or to grit my teeth and pretend I was dabbing my brow
vhen I dealt with the tears that threatened to brim from my eyes.

That afternoon, after I had tested Simon's boomerang and
old him as much as I could about how to throw it, he sent it
pinning out over the rail and watched disconsolately as it made
half-hearted curve before slanting down into the sea, to the
ccompaniment of some insincere commiseration and sincere
musement from those watching, in particular from Eliza.

At dinner that evening Captain Lester spoke to Markie of my
erformance in a way that invited some explanation, but Mark-
's bland reply did nothing to satisfy the captain's curiosity, and
e was too polite to ask a direct question. Next day I gave the
oomerang to Piroo, not wanting to use it again. I felt that in
ome way I had upset Luke by reminding him of the past, but I
vas puzzled that he had seemed unusually friendly until I spoke
f when we had first met in the desert and he had tried to make
he wear a shirt.

Two days later I had a truly frightening nightmare. In my

dream I was making my way through the rocky maze that m
tribe had called The-place-of-too-many-ways, and I lay down i
a sandy hollow to sleep. A sound disturbed me, and I opene
my eyes to see a hideous creature standing over me, a manlik
thing but with a single eye in the middle of its forehead, like th
one-eyed cannibal giant I had read about in the Greek legend
called Cyclops.

I tried to come to my feet and run, but my limbs would n
obey me. I tried to scream, but my jaw was locked and I wa
voiceless. In utter terror I was aware of the creature lifting m
in its arms, turning, padding away from where I had lain whil
I hung limp and helpless in its grasp. The scent of the creatur
holding me was so malignant that I felt myself swept by a frenz
of fear, yet still my body refused to obey the desperate urging
of my mind. Then came a lurching sensation, as if the creatur
had stumbled, and as I fell the dream blurred to become a haz
kind of reality, for I was dimly aware that I lay on the deck o
the *Caragh*, huddled against some part of the superstructure, a
arm and a thigh bruised by my falling. From somewhere nearb
I heard a shout, but I hardly knew whether I was sleeping o
waking as I tried to get to my feet, for my limbs were still leade
and without strength, and when I tried to cry out only a whispe
came from my throat.

Next moment a man was kneeling over me, saying anxiously
"Miss Gaynor! Miss Gaynor, are you all right?" As my visio
cleared a little I found myself looking up into the face of M
Barry, the second mate, and I broke into muted sobs of relie
He asked no further question, only took off his jacket, wrappe
it about my shoulders, and tried to help me stand. But my leg
refused to support me, and with a murmured apology he scoope
me up in his arms.

I realized now that it was the darkest hour of the night, that
was wearing only my nightdress, and that Mr. Barry must b
the officer on watch. I heard him call to the helmsman on th
bridge, "Hold your present course," then my mind blurre
again, and when next I opened my eyes I was lying on the bun

in my cabin with Simon bending over me and Eliza standing beside him, both in dressing gowns. With an effort I whispered, "What happened?"

Eliza took my hand and said, "We think you must have walked in your sleep, Meg dear. The officer on the bridge heard a noise and found you collapsed on the deck just outside the main door from the cabins."

"I . . . had a nightmare," I croaked, shuddering with nausea, for the scent of the creature seemed strong in my nostrils even though I was awake now.

Luke's voice said, "Is she hurt, Simon?" and as my eyes focused I saw that Luke and Markie were in the doorway of the little cabin, also in dressing gowns.

Simon bent over me, pushing an eyelid up with his thumb and peering closely at my eye. "Probably bruised," he said absently. "Eliza can have a look at her once we're out of the way, but . . ."

After a little silence Markie said, "But what?"

Simon straightened up. "Have you eaten or drunk anything different from the rest of us in the last few hours, Meg?"

I shook my head, thankful to feel a little strength returning. "No . . . I don't think so."

"Eaten or drunk anything at all since dinner?"

"No. Except a glass of water from the flask there before going to bed."

He picked up the flask with the tumbler inverted over it. "This is empty. You drank it all?"

"Don't . . . think so. I feel very strange. Everything hazy."

Simon leaned against the cabin bulkhead and sighed, looking at Luke and Markie. "In my youth I spent a year at medical school before they threw me out," he said, "so I picked up a few rudiments of the profession, but you hardly need that to tell you Meg isn't her usual healthy self. You've traveled much of the world, Luke. Take a look at her pupils. I'll wager you've seen opium smokers in Hong Kong with eyes like that."

Luke came forward and bent to look closely into my eyes. I

forced a smile for him and said, "I'm sorry to disturb every-body. I'll be all right soon."

He straightened up and said, "You mean she's drugged? How the devil could that happen? Are you saying one of *us* is respon-sible?"

Simon made an impatient gesture. "Of course not. For God's sake, let's not begin to suspect one another again. Frankly I don't see how *anyone* could be responsible. Perhaps Meg's car-afe of water was tainted, and this is some kind of stomach upset. Or perhaps there's been a leakage of toxic but odorless fumes into this cabin from the engine room. I don't know." He made a baffled gesture.

Luke ran a hand through his hair. "Nothing is odorless to Meg," he said doubtfully.

With a brisk air Eliza said, "Well, thank you, gentlemen. If you will all kindly leave us now, I'll first have a look at Meg to deal with any scrapes or bruises, and then I shall take her to my cabin for the night until we can be assured there are no fumes here. Simon, wait outside till I call, then you can come and carry this mattress and bedding to my cabin. I'll sleep very well on the floor."

I tried to protest, but in my feeble state I was no match for Eliza, and ten minutes later I lay in her bunk, my bruises dabbed liberally with arnica from a small medical box she carried. She tucked me in, stroked my brow, kissed me good night, then put out the light and got into her makeshift bed on the cabin deck. I was greatly touched by her solicitude and said, "Thank you, Eliza. You're so kind to me."

"Only up to a point," she said cheerfully. "After tonight we'll take turns at sleeping on the floor, but I'll not have you sleep alone again." Before my sluggish mind could frame a question she went on, "Meg, in your early years you had to develop very sharp senses and a strong instinct. Forgetting ap-pearances for the moment, is there any one of us you . . . well, feel uneasy about? Perhaps don't quite trust? I really mean any of us. Markie or Luke, Simon or . . . me?"

I lay trying to read my own instinct, and after a few moments I said, "I trust you all, Eliza."

In the darkness I heard her sigh. "Perhaps your instinct doesn't work very well with civilized people," she said. "After all, you trusted Adrian Webb. I do hope you're right this time, Meg dear."

WHEN I ROSE NEXT MORNING THE PUPILS OF MY EYES WERE normal and I felt much more natural, especially once I had eaten breakfast and walked round the deck for half an hour, but it was not until evening that I was fully myself again. Mr. Barry had reported the incident to Captain Lester, and there was puzzled speculation as to whether tainted water could have caused me to have a nightmare, to walk in my sleep, and to be so strongly affected that I had no power over my body. The chief engineer assured us that his engines produced no toxic fumes, and that in any event no fumes of any kind could penetrate from the engine room to the cabins. After a time I became embarrassed by so much discussion, and pleaded for the subject to be dropped.

It was an hour after dusk the next evening, as we sat in the dining room toward the end of dinner, that disaster struck. For most of us it began so quietly that we were unaware of anything amiss. A little shudder passed through the *Caragh*, lasting only for a moment, and then we were sailing on smoothly again, but Captain Lester was on his feet instantly, muttering an apology as he hurried out. Seconds later I heard an alarm bell ringing loudly, voices shouting, and running feet.

We exchanged glances and were rising from our seats when Mr. Barry appeared, his face paler than usual. "We have struck an unknown object which has damaged the hull," he said. "The extent of the damage is not yet known, but Captain Lester has given precautionary orders. You ladies and gentlemen must please go quickly to your cabins and put on warm clothing, then assemble by the port lifeboat amidships and put on your life jackets.''

For a moment I found it impossible to believe that danger was upon us, but then cold reality struck home and I realized that this tiny floating home, which I had so much taken for granted, was a mere speck, a damaged speck, on the huge and uncaring sea. We were in the Atlantic Ocean, miles from land, and if the ship foundered we would be reduced to drifting in a frail lifeboat, praying to be found before slow death overtook us. With this realization came another, equally chilling—that in the eight days since we had left Freetown I had seen no sign of any other ship.

Fear pierced me like a knife, and I did not dare to speak, for I knew my teeth would chatter. When I looked about me I saw only the impassive faces of people absorbing shock, and I hoped my own face masked the fear that possessed me. Then Markie said quietly, ''Let us do as the captain has ordered. A handbag each for the ladies, nothing more. Provisions and water will be more important than anything else if worse comes to worst.''

It was quite dark when we assembled on deck a few minutes later, but at least I had my fears under control by then, perhaps because a sense of unreality had again descended upon me. Markie stood with his arm about my shoulders, and we all kept peering into the darkness, speaking very little, trying to assess if the *Caragh* was lower in the water now as she sailed on at slow speed, trying to interpret the occasional shouts and the faintly heard voice of the captain on the bridge calling down the voice tube to the engine room.

Then, abruptly, the ship leaned to port, and we clutched at rails and stanchions to keep our balance. There came a bellowing of orders and a rush of feet as British and lascar seamen came running to swing our lifeboat out on its davits.

Mr. Sullivan appeared, a lantern in his hand, addressing Markie. ''She's done for, Mr. Lafayette,'' he said grimly. ''She's torn her bottom open, and the chief engineer says she'll go down in the next few minutes. Please get your party into the lifeboat quickly, sir. I'll be joining you on the captain's orders with Mr. Barry and a few seamen. The sooner we're launched, the sooner the men can get the rest of the boats away.''

Markie said politely, ''Thank you, Mr. Sullivan. We won't delay you.'' Next moment I was plucked from the deck by Luke and swung over the side into the hanging lifeboat. Eliza came tumbling in beside me, the men followed, then came Mr. Sullivan, Mr. Barry, and several deckhands as Mr. Sullivan called their names. I saw little Piroo clamber aboard with a long canvas bag slung across his shoulders, then the big man they called Chin-up was there, dropping several canvas sacks of what I guessed was food into the boat before climbing in himself.

Mr. Sullivan shouted, ''Lower away!'' The pulleys creaked, the lifeboat slid down, swinging well clear of the hull because of the *Caragh's* list to port. We hit the sea with a jolting impact. Another order was bellowed, the lines were cast off, I saw oars appear, heard the clatter as they were set in rowlocks, and moments later we were fifty yards clear of the still-moving *Caragh* with six men heaving on the oars.

Mr. Barry was lighting a lantern in the bow. I sat in the stern between Luke and Markie, facing Simon and Eliza. Mr. Sullivan was at the tiller between us, and when we were two hundred yards from the ship he called, ''Way 'nough!'' The men rested on their oars, and every eye turned to the lights of the *Caragh*. It was impossible to discern what was happening there, but I could make out pinpoints of light from a few moving lanterns, and I knew that the rest of the crew must be struggling to launch the other lifeboats. Nobody spoke as we saw first one small light and then another move away from the *Caragh*. A third followed, but then, with shocking swiftness, the bows of the little ship lifted in silhouette against the sky. For a moment she hung poised, motionless; then the dark sea, a formless monster infinitely huge, swallowed her in a single gulp.

It was like watching the death of a living thing, and I think we were all smitten by new horror at the sight. Three little lights,

besides our own, now danced on the quiet black waters, Mr.
Sullivan said, "We must try to keep with the others." He lifted
his voice. "Give way together!"

The men began to pull again, but after five minutes the lights
of the other lifeboats were farther away than before. Luke spoke,
the first time any of the passengers had spoken since our lifeboat
had been launched. "You can call upon us to take our turn at
the oars, Mr. Sullivan."

"Thank you, sir." Mr. Sullivan's voice was a little strained.
"I don't think it's time for that yet. We seem to be caught in a
freak current that's carrying us away from the others, and it's
too strong to fight." He lifted his voice again and called "Way
'nough!" The seamen stopped pulling, and on a further command they boated their oars, breathing a little heavily.

The only oarsman I could see clearly was Piroo, on the thwart
nearest to me, for the rest were silhouetted against the glow of
the lamp in the bows. At his feet lay the long canvas bag in
which he had carried his tools when he came to mend the lock
of my cabin, and protruding from one end was something long
and slightly curved. At any other time I might have been amused
or astonished to see that he had added the boomerang he had
made to his collection of tools, but at the moment I was too
shocked and fearful to respond to anything beyond the danger
of our situation.

Markie said quietly, "Do you know what happened, Mr.
Sullivan?"

"Not exactly, sir. There's no doubt we struck some uncharted
object. A rock, perhaps. There's a shoal marked on the charts
four or five miles off the coast, but we were out well beyond that
. . . unless we were carried off course by some treacherous
current."

The sea was calm, the night was still, and Markie did not
have to raise his beautiful mellow voice as he said, "What are
our prospects now?"

Mr. Sullivan hesitated, then said slowly, "I hope that by daylight we shall be able to join the other lifeboats. A number of

ships ply this route to the Cape, and there is a chance of our being sighted sooner or later. Fortunately we are well supplied with food and water, so with care we can endure for many days.''

"Thank you, Mr. Sullivan. That is very encouraging." Markie dropped his voice to a whisper so soft that only we who were close to him could hear. "I notice we have seen no debris from the ship. Does this indicate that we have been caught by the edge of some current that is carrying us away from the place where the ship sank? Away from the other boats?"

Mr. Sullivan answered under his breath. "It does, sir."

"I see. Now, please give your honest opinion, Mr. Sullivan. My guests and I seek no false hopes, and this includes the ladies. Is it possible that our boat was on the very edge of the Benguela current, and has been drawn into it?"

"I fear so, Mr. Lafayette."

"In that case we are probably being carried toward a very dangerous coast where no ship is likely to sight us."

"Yes, sir. But I would rather not alarm the men by speaking of this until we know it to be certain."

"Agreed. You may rely on my guests in that respect. But if your fear proves true, what are our prospects then?"

Mr. Sullivan looked about him, at the sky where stars were now appearing and at the dark sea where no light now showed. "If my fears are well founded, sir," he said softly, "then God help us all. The Skeleton Coast does not bear that name for nothing."

Simon said, "Can we row westward out of the current? We have enough men to row double on four of the oars."

"Oars can never pull us clear, sir. We would need an engine for that. And we don't want to exhaust ourselves to no purpose. If we're to face the reefs and rocks of the Skeleton Coast we shall need all our strength and all possible good fortune to get ashore alive. You asked for the truth, Mr. Lafayette, and I tell you truly if half of us reach dry land alive and unharmed I would count that lucky indeed."

I bit my lip to stop it trembling and heard Eliza clear her throat nervously. Markie said, "And then, Mr. Sullivan? If some of us succeed in reaching dry land?" No answer came, and a full half minute passed before Markie said, "If you please, Mr. Sullivan?"

"Why . . . then, sir," came the slow, whispered reply, "then some of us will be ashore on the Skeleton Coast, and they may well come to envy those who failed."

There was a long silence. Somewhere in the bows two men were murmuring together. Mr. Sullivan drew in a deep breath and seemed to brace himself. "We're alive at the moment," he said aloud, "and I'm sure we shall all do our best in meeting whatever lies ahead. Now, let's have those sacks of food all together here in the stern so we can make a plan for rationing." He lifted his voice a little. "Mr. Barry! We have one food sack here. Have Chin-up heave those other two down to the stern, if you please. All other crew and passengers to remain seated."

There was a garbled conversation from the bows as Mr. Barry conveyed the order to the Portuguese, and moments later the man made his way aft, a large canvas sack clutched in his arms, the thin starlight glinting on his shaven head, the eyepatch standing out as a black triangle above the curve of the thick dark beard.

He stood close to me when he dropped the sack, and as he turned away my mind reeled under a hammer blow of shock even greater than the shock of the *Caragh's* sinking, for of that there had at least been a little warning. For a moment I scarcely knew where I was, for my mind was in chaos, with fragments of comprehension whirling as if in a kaleidoscope before coming together to form a dreadful pattern.

Suddenly I knew that the sailor in Freetown whose place Chinup had taken had not simply failed to report aboard but had been bribed, or injured, or perhaps killed. I knew why I had scented death on the quayside at Freetown, and I knew it had not emanated from Piroo. I knew exactly what Adrian Web' planned, and it was nothing that we had anticipated. I knew why, in my dream, I had imagined the creature that carried me off to be a one-eyed Cyclops. I knew that the water in my carafe had been drugged, and that if the creature had not stumbled and attracted Mr. Barry's attention I would have been dropped quietly overboard. And I knew that Eliza's instinct had been true when she felt that Adrian Webb had been driven into a corner and would react like a wild creature, that he would rely no longer on hirelings and would trust nobody but himself.

All this I knew because my upbringing had given me senses perhaps a quarter as sharp as those of a true aborigine but far sharper than those of my civilized friends. All this I knew because when Chin-up had come within arm's length of me a few moments ago I had caught the unmistakable scent of Adrian Webb himself.

SIXTEEN

I SAT AS IF FROZEN, SICK WITH SHOCK, MY SLOW MIND GRADU-
ally creeping toward a full understanding. Adrian Webb must
have learned of Markie's itinerary for the voyage to the Cape;
there had been no secrecy about booking the passage. He had
pretended to sail for New York, but had left the ship at Cherbourg and disappeared.

A man of different appearance had arrived in Freetown days
before our arrival, perhaps off another cargo ship. This man was
unrecognizable as Adrian Webb. The round Pickwickian face
was completely altered by a beard, an eyepatch, the shaven head,
and the brown-dyed skin. In the well-worn clothes of a seaman
he had watched the *Caragh* dock, had ensured that a galley hand
was missing when the time came to sail, and had contrived to
replace the missing man.

I had seen nothing of him during the voyage from Freetown
but choosing his time, he had one night put a strong sleeping
draft in the carafe of water that stood by the bed in my cabin.
Then, in the dark hours, as I lay in a drugged sleep, he had
carried me from the cabin to drop me overboard. He had stumbled, had let me fall, attracting Mr. Barry's attention, and so
his plan had been ruined. But if he had carried it through, no
hint of suspicion would have attached to him. Everyone would
have been stunned by my disappearance and certain death, but

328

it would have been assumed that I had gone for a stroll on a hot night, as I had done long ago on the voyage from Perth with Simon and Eliza, and that by some mischance I had fallen overboard. At Cape Town the seaman called Chin-up would have disappeared, would perhaps have found a berth on another ship back to England. And in due time Adrian Webb would have reappeared in London, ostensibly returned from America.

The brilliance and ruthlessness of the plan were breathtaking. So was the desperation, for although he had been a considerable athlete, had traveled on hunting expeditions in Africa, and was able to call upon his experience in amateur dramatics, it could not have been easy for Adrian Webb, accustomed to a life of ease, to live for weeks in the role of a deckhand with all that this entailed. Only the greatest desperation could have driven him to such an extremity; but now he was in this lifeboat with us, shipwrecked with us, sitting on a thwart in the bows as we drifted toward the horrors of the Skeleton Coast. I wondered what was passing through his cold and dangerous mind at this moment.

Beside me Luke was saying, "Meg? Meg, are you all right? You're shivering."

I came to myself, shaking my head to clear it, holding his arm and saying slowly, "Oh, Luke." Then I touched Markie's arm and drew both men closer as I whispered, "I—I have something to tell you. Please try to believe me."

THE FIRST LIGHT OF DAWN WAS BEGINNING TO PENETRATE A sea mist that drifted about us, holding visibility down to a few hundred yards. I had told my tale long hours ago, first to Markie and Luke, then to Simon and Eliza. When this was done, Markie had filled in some bewildering gaps for Mr. Sullivan by telling him my true identity and explaining Adrian Webb's purpose.

Luke had believed me from the beginning when I said that Chin-up was Adrian Webb. So had Eliza. Markie and Simon wanted to believe me and were trying to, but found it difficult to convince themselves. Mr. Sullivan was utterly lost, which was not at all surprising, and though his manner remained polite it was clear that he felt I had been mentally affected by the shipwreck and was romancing or having hallucinations.

When the light was strong enough for us to see clearly he lifted his voice and called for Chin-up. The big man made his way astern and squatted just in front of Piroo, facing us. There was no doubt in me, for I knew my nose could not be deceived, but even so I found it hard to recognize Adrian Webb. The beard and the shaven scalp combined to alter the shape of his head, and the eyepatch hid much of what could be seen of his face above the beard.

Mr. Sullivan said brusquely, "I've been told you're an Englishman by the name of Adrian Webb. Is that correct?"

The single eye blinked once, moved for an instant toward me, then stared uncomprehendingly at Mr. Sullivan. "*No comprendo,*" Adrian Webb answered with a guttural grunt.

Luke leaned forward. "You might as well give up, Webb," he said in a tight, hard voice. "Meg knows you. And we all know what you tried to do to her on board ship the other night, you murderous swine."

The single eye gazed blankly at Luke; then the man's big shoulders shrugged and he growled something in a foreign tongue. Mr. Sullivan pushed his cap back on his head with a helpless gesture, then pointed to the bows. "All right, get back to your place," he said. "Back. Comprendo?" He pointed again, and Adrian Webb went clambering back over the thwarts. Mr. Sullivan said quietly, "Can any of you confirm what Miss Gaynor says?"

Markie said uneasily, "I've never set eyes on Adrian Webb myself. Mr. and Mrs. Fordyce have seen him, but not for any length of time. Mr. Bowman has some acquaintance with him, but Miss Gaynor lived in the man's house for several months. I know him well by reputation, and I'm quite certain he is capable of carrying out such a deception, but . . ." He turned to me. "Are you sure, my dear?"

"I'm quite sure, Markie."

Luke said, "I can't recognize the man as Webb, but if Meg says so, then he *is* Webb. I've no doubt I'd know him with the beard shaved off, no eyepatch, and a hat to cover that bald pate—"

"Land to starboard!" The shout came from Mr. Barry in the bows of the lifeboat, and every head turned. For some minutes I had been vaguely aware of a distant sound, but was too distracted to identify it. Now that the morning mist was clearing suddenly, I could see the source of the noise, and my heart turned over with fear. Less than a mile away an endless line of breakers was crashing over the rocks and reefs that hemmed the shore of the Skeleton Coast. Beyond the foam and spray I could see sand dunes, and far beyond the dunes a line of barren hills rose steeply to a ridge.

I heard Mr. Sullivan draw in his breath sharply and mutter, "God Almighty . . . !" He rose from his seat, keeping a hand on the tiller, and bellowed, "Oars ready!" There came a great bustle and clatter as the oars were settled in the rowlocks, and then came the command, "Give way together!" The six men began to pull, and I saw Adrian Webb, on the bow thwart, watching me with his single eye as he leaned forward for the stroke.

The boat came around till it pointed shoreward, and Markie said, "What do you intend, Mr. Sullivan?"

The first mate answered without taking his eyes from the land. "I hope to find a gap in the reefs, sir, a stretch of sandy beach, however small, to get the boat ashore. It won't be smooth going— those breakers will toss us ashore like a cork—but if we strike a reef she'll break up while we're still short of the beach."

"And we cannot hold off from the land?"

"No hope, sir. That being so, it's better to use the oars than to drift. At least we may be able to keep her from turning broadside on. Please see that your guests' life jackets are securely fastened."

For five minutes nobody spoke. Every eye was searching for

any hint of a gap in the tangle of reefs guarding the shore. I felt my heart thumping with apprehension, and found I was clutching Luke's hand. Across the boat, Eliza gave me a wan smile. Now, with the shoreline as a marker, I could judge the strength of the current by the rapidity with which the gap between boat and shore was dwindling.

Suddenly Mr. Barry shouted and pointed. I could see no beach, but there was a small stretch where the line of foam seemed less violent than elsewhere, and the boat altered course a little to steer for it. I felt a sudden impulse to tell Luke that I loved him, but I held my peace. If we were soon to die it would mean nothing to him that a girl who had never been more than a burden to him should declare her love. And if we were to survive it would at best embarrass him and at worst destroy what friendship we had.

The end came quickly. One moment we were moving steadily on fairly calm water, the next we were picked up by a wave that rose majestically beneath us, carrying us forward on its broad crest at a breathtaking speed. Mr. Sullivan was clinging to the tiller, shouting orders. The oarsmen heaved frantically to hold the boat straight. The sea ahead was suddenly sucked back to form a great trough with the boat poised above it, racing forward, and as the trough deepened there emerged from it a line of jagged black rocks like the teeth of a monster.

We almost cleared the reef to reach safer water beyond, but at the last moment the boat lurched and turned. We dropped with dreadful impact, and I saw the timbers beyond Piroo burst apart. Then I was flung sideways, torn from Luke's grasp and engulfed in a maelstrom of turbulent sea, holding my breath, fighting to reach the surface, water pounding down upon me as the wave broke.

When I thought my lungs would burst I suddenly found my head above water and I gulped in air, kicking out frantically to keep myself afloat, thankful for my life jacket, thankful that I had learned to swim. All about me, men and wreckage were being flung this way and that by the furious sea. Something struck the back of my head, leaving me half stunned. My hand felt a spur of smooth rock under the water and I clung to it desperately. Ahead I glimpsed a beach of shingle, perhaps a hundred yards away when the waves reached their farthest point, but only fifty yards away when the breakers retreated. My blurred vision made out a few figures between me and the beach, but I could not identify any of them. I called out "Luke!" but my voice was no more than a whisper.

Fearful of being struck again by debris, I looked to seaward and found new terror. Several figures were in the water beyond me, some struggling, some limp and unconscious, but the horror of it was that they were being sucked out of the little lagoon through a small gap in the reef, dragged helplessly by a vicious current intensified by the narrowness of the gap. I heard despairing cries for help, and in the same moment became aware that my own strength was flagging and that if I lost my grip I, too, would be sucked out by that deadly current.

Moments later a new breaker came thundering over the reef. I was plucked from the rock I held and swept forward, tossed like a piece of driftwood on the wave. Beside me I saw the remains of the lifeboat spinning and rolling, one of its broken timbers missing me by inches. I crashed down on loose shingle, and the breaking wave thundered over me and then began to drag me back, greedily and with fearful strength. I dug my fingers into the shingle, clutching frantically, driving my toes in for extra purchase, but the savage undertow tore at me. I knew I was losing the struggle, knew that if the receding wave dragged me back I would never again reach the beach but would be sucked through the gap in the reef like a fly being swallowed by a trout, then pounded to death against the unforgiving rocks.

I lost my grip on the shingle, but in that same moment a hand clamped on my wrist, a hand attached to a skinny brown arm, and through the veil of water filming my eyes I saw Piroo lying just ahead of me, his other arm hooked into a crevice where the shingle gave way to a patch of rock. "Hold, missy! Hold!" he screamed. I clutched his wrist with my other hand, and we clung desperately together for what seemed an age until the power of the receding wave slackened and we were left sprawled in shallow water.

"Quick, missy, quick!" He was on his feet, tugging at my hand. I struggled up, hampered by my wet skirt, and began to stumble up the beach with him. He threw a glance over his shoulder, and I saw his eyes widen with fear. Turning my head I saw another breaker coming, but this one carried the shattered lifeboat on its crest, and seemed to be hurling it at us as if determined to bring us down.

We moved on, staggering in the loose shingle as we tried to run. Somewhere ahead and to my right a man shouted in alarm, and I thought it was Luke. The noise behind me grew louder, and I flung a glance over my shoulder in the moment that the breaker hurled its burden. There was a brief instant when I saw foam and a broken hull leaping at me. Then came a stunning impact, and I knew no more.

WHEN MY SENSES CAME SLOWLY BACK TO ME I HEARD MARKIE'S voice, then Eliza's. I opened my eyes and looked up at low, heavy cloud. The air was humid, I could hear the crash of breakers a little way off, and I was lying on dry sand with Markie kneeling on one side of me, Eliza on the other.

Markie said, "Oh, thank God."

I lifted my head and winced, for it ached and felt bruised along one side. "Luke?" I said. "Simon?"

"Safe, Meg dear," Eliza said quickly. Her hair hung limply, her clothes were soaked and torn. Markie was in a similar state. He had taken off his jacket, and I saw blood from a grazed forearm spreading pinkly on the wet fabric of his torn shirt. "We were all lucky except you," said Eliza. "The breaker that threw you out of the boat carried all the rest of us in the stern well up into the shallows."

"Piroo," I said muzzily. "He . . . he saved my life. I saw people being . . . sucked out."

"Yes, several men have been lost," Markie said in a flat, weary voice. "We saw the sea take them, poor devils. Piroo is alive, but he has a broken leg below the knee. The wreck that stunned you fell on him."

I sat up, then held a hand to my head until the dizziness had passed. Eliza put her arm about me. "Gently, dear," she said. "Don't rush. Simon has fixed a splint on Piroo's leg, and Mr. Sullivan is directing a search for all salvage that may be washed up from the boat."

My head was clearing now, and I said, "Did Adrian Webb survive?"

Markie nodded. "Yes. He and a steward, young Mercer, are safe. I fear we lost Mr. Barry and the other three seamen."

I pushed damp hair away from my face and said, "We must help to find whatever is washed ashore. It's important."

Eliza restrained me as I tried to rise. "Leave that to the men," she said. "Luke says you must rest, and we all agree."

I shook my head, baffled and suddenly angry. "He's talking rubbish," I said. "I'm not hurt."

Markie said, "Look about you, Meg."

I was on a hummock of sand facing the sea, and now I turned my head to do as he had bidden me. The beach was of shingle mixed with fine sand, and extended to north and south for as far as I could see, broken only by a few rocky outcrops, some hummocks of dry grass, and a scrawny bush or two. The beach was several hundred yards in depth, and then the sand dunes began, reaching to the distant hills, with no sign of life at all, not a tree, not a leaf, not a blade of grass. This was not the outback where I had spent most of my life, but it was akin to that, and though I knew how readily such a land could kill, I felt nothing of the freezing fear I had known in the lifeboat. For me the sea was an unknown enemy, the desert a familiar one.

Eliza still knelt with an arm about me. On my other side Markie squinted painfully into the distance and said, "Mr. Sullivan puts our position as somewhere between one hundred and one hundred and fifty miles from the nearest settlement, a coastal village called Swakopmund, with the port of Walvis Bay some twenty miles beyond. From my own knowledge I can tell you that though some rivers are marked on maps, they are bone dry. Their waters sink into the desert long before they reach the sea. No castaway has ever been rescued from this coast, though many have perished here. Even if it was known that we are here, no rescue could be effected from the sea, and no human help can come from the land. So rest a little, Meg my dear, for Luke says you are our only hope, and we believe him. Without you, we all die.''

IT WAS NOON, AND I SAT CROSS-LEGGED IN A FOLD OF GROUND a quarter of a mile from the others. I could not see the sun overhead, for heavy cloud persisted. Mr. Sullivan had told us that this was normal weather for the Skeleton Coast. I did not like such humidity, but at least it would provide heavy dew to help slake our thirst.

After my first awakening I had slept for an hour, then woken again feeling much recovered. No bodies had been washed ashore, and all the food had been lost, for one sack was not to be found, and the other two had been recovered empty, the food having spilled out in the sea. One metal container of water had been salvaged, together with three oars, some rope, three blankets, a mass of broken timber, and perhaps most precious of all—Piroo's bag of tools. Mr. Sullivan carried a revolver in a holster on his belt under his jacket, but nobody including himself believed it would be of any use in bringing us food, for no game existed here.

Piroo lay with his leg firmly splinted, and when I thanked him for saving my life he managed to grin through his pain and say, "Glad, missy. Glad."

I had not looked at Adrian Webb, but I had thought about him a great deal as I examined what had been salvaged from the wreck. I saw Luke using the pocketknife I had given him as a present long ago, trimming the ends of a makeshift bandage he had put on Markie's grazed arm, and when he had finished I asked him to lend me the knife. Then I said I would return later and walked away inland toward the dunes where I sat now, my damp dress dragging at my legs as I moved.

Once hidden by a hummock of ground, I took off my clothes, cut the legs of my drawers very short and put them on again, cut my petticoat to fall well above my knees and put that on, then hacked my hair off short and settled down to focus my mind on becoming what I had once been. Meg Gaynor, or Moira Glencullen, could never bring her friends to safety across untold miles of this barren land where no castaway had survived before, but for Mitji the aborigine it might be possible.

I sat watching grains of sand move as a tiny beetle emerged briefly and burrowed in again. I flared my nostrils, taking in a medley of scents new and old from all about me. I tuned my ears to listen for desert sounds. Slowly, slowly I stripped from my mind the part of me that was civilized Meg Gaynor, and from the inner depths I brought out the primitive creature who might be capable of cheating the dreaded Skeleton Coast of its prey.

Later I prowled the dunes and the beach, looking for sign, and it was midafternoon when I at last returned to the place on the beach where the others were gathered by the pile of salvaged items, bringing with me my discarded dress, shoes, stockings, and the remains of my petticoat. The clouds had parted now, and I saw that a piece of tarpaulin had been set up on broken timbers to provide shade for Piroo, who lay on a patch of sand some little way off. With him sat Mercer, the young steward who had survived, and Adrian Webb, still maintaining his guise of a seaman.

Luke came to meet me as I approached, showing no sign of surprise at my shorn hair and bare legs. "By the grace of God we have that boomerang Piroo made for you, Mitji," he said. "He kept it with his tools, and I found this in his bag, too. It might be equally useful."

He held out a wooden maul, a squat club with a tapering

handle very much like the throwing club I had used since early childhood. I took it and felt the balance, then said, "This will be of more use than the boomerang. Thank you, Luke."

Together we walked to where the others waited, and I threw my clothes on the pile of salvage. "We must take all things of fabric with us," I said. "They will absorb the heavy dew that falls each night. We shall need that." The others eyed me curiously, as if I had changed and come back to them a different person, which was no less than the truth. Even the way I spoke was different now, for I was thinking in the tongue of my tribe and translating into English. Everybody's clothes were dry now, but torn and stained. The men were unshaven and Eliza's hair was still clogged with sand. Markie had lost his dark glasses and had to keep shading his eyes from the sun. They sat in a little group, watching me as I squatted on my haunches with my short skirt tucked between my legs.

Markie said, "As the senior ship's officer present it is for Mr. Sullivan to command our party, but we have told him of your unique experience in such terrain, Meg, and he will be grateful for your advice."

I looked at Mr. Sullivan and said, "I can find food. By sign and by scent I know there are living creatures here. Some are small and live in the sand and rocks, but I also found spoor of something like a dingo. A dog."

"Jackals," said Markie. "I've heard they roam from the hinterland to the coast."

I nodded. "Where jackals can find food, I can find food. Also, jackals are meat. So are the gulls, and I have seen many of them. Also I found spoor of some much bigger birds. And this." I held out to Markie a tiny pink feather.

He took it, examined it, and said slowly, "Flamingos. I've never heard of them here, but it's possible. So little is known of this coast that anything is possible."

Mr. Sullivan said, "Can you find water for us, Miss Gaynor? I think that will be our greatest need."

I shrugged. "If there is water I will find it. Whether I shall find enough I cannot tell." I moved my head to indicate the line of hills several miles away. "There are elephants beyond the hills. Not now, but sometimes. I caught the scent as the wind came from the land. It is very strong. I remember it from Ceylon."

"Elephants?" The wary look Mr. Sullivan gave me made me wish I had not spoken of them. They did not come down from the hills, so the water they needed would be somewhere inland, and that was of no help to us.

I said, "How sure are you of our position, Mr. Sullivan?"

He hesitated, then said, "I'm sure we're much closer to the southern end of the Skeleton Coast than to the northern end. I believe we should be no more than a hundred and fifty miles from Swakopmund."

"Then we must go south."

"Yes, Miss Gaynor, but the going will be very difficult. Hard rock, soft sand, dry gullies. I doubt that we can make more than fifteen miles in a day."

Luke said, "And Mitji—that is, Miss Gaynor, will have to cover half that distance again if she is to cast about for us seeking food and water."

I said, "I can do that, Luke. But our going will be slower than Mr. Sullivan hoped. Piroo cannot walk."

Mr. Sullivan lowered his voice. "We can't take Piroo. We'll leave him a better than fair share of water, and hope to return for him."

I shook my head. "He will die slowly. You know that."

The officer rubbed a hand wearily over his eyes. "Yes, I know," he said, "but my responsibility is to the whole party. I cannot risk all your lives for one."

I understood him, and I sympathized with him in the grim decision he had made, but I was an aborigine again now, bound by the iron law of exchange. Piroo had saved my life, and I must save his if I could. "You have your duty to do, Mr. Sullivan," I said, "but I stay with Piroo. I can keep him alive for as long as need be, and when his leg has mended we will follow you."

Luke said quietly, "If Mitji stays, I stay." He looked at me. "That's if you can cope with an extra mouth to feed, Mitji."

I nodded, not looking at him, afraid he would see the joy his words gave me. Markie said, "I shudder at the notion of leaving Piroo, and I truly believe we can survive only with Meg's help. Let us make a stretcher, Mr. Sullivan. Two oars cut to length and run through the canvas food sacks will suffice. We can take turns to carry Piroo in pairs."

I crouched, hugging my knees, watching the officer's face as he struggled to make a decision. At last he said, "Very well. We take Piroo. What distance can we hope to cover in a day, Miss Gaynor?"

I thought for a while. Eliza was no weakling, but she had not lived as I had lived, and she was not as strong as a man. Then there was Markie to consider. He was older than the others, and unused to hard exercise. Much would depend on whether the terrain changed and whether I could find sufficient water, but those things were in the lap of the gods. I said, "I think we will cover eight or ten miles each day, Mr. Sullivan."

"Well . . . in that case we should reach Swakopmund in about fifteen days, if I'm right about our position."

"If you are right, yes. If not, it will take longer."

"Longer?" He looked about him and wiped sweat from his face. "With the one container of water we have left, we won't last more than three days unless you find more, Miss Gaynor. Not in this climate."

I said, "It is better that you all call me Mitji from now on, as Luke does. He knows it will help me to think and to act in the ways that are right for what lies ahead."

Mr. Sullivan glanced at Markie as if for permission, then said, "Very well. We shall call you Mitji."

I nodded. "Now, there is something very important." Without moving my head I flicked my eyes to where Piroo lay with the young steward and Adrian Webb sitting beside him. "It is best that you kill Adrian Webb now," I said, "before we start."

For long moments there was utter silence, and I saw shock

and revulsion in every face, even Luke's. "Kill him?" said Mr. Sullivan at last in a low, incredulous voice. "That's monstrous! You can't mean it!"

"I mean it, Mr. Sullivan. There is an evil spirit in the man, and he is a great danger to us all. In my tribe it would be right and proper for the men to kill such a person for the sake of all the tribe."

Markie bowed his head and put a hand to his eyes. Eliza said uncertainly, "Oh, Meg . . ." Simon shook his head. Luke stared, still shocked but with a kind of comprehension. Mr. Sullivan drew in a deep breath and said, "It's out of the question. We're not a tribe, we're civilized people, and we can't possibly kill a man in cold blood."

I swung an arm toward the barren desert. "Look about you, Mr. Sullivan. This is not civilization, and for the moment we *are* a tribe. We shall be a tribe until we reach safety."

Luke said gently, "No, this isn't civilization, Mitji, but we remain civilized people. Your tribe would act according to its beliefs, and we must act according to ours. It's quite simply impossible for us to do as you suggest. If Rosemary were here she would say the same."

My other companions were nodding and murmuring earnest agreement. Mr. Sullivan looked around the little circle and said with relief, "Well, that's settled, thank God. I don't yet know if the man *is* who you say he is."

I shrugged, knowing there was no point in further argument. "Being civilized may prove costly," I said, and glanced at the sky. "Let us decide what to take with us and what to leave. Any tool of Piroo's that can be used for digging is important. The metal bailer is important, and so is any container. I will chop and mash all food together, then cook meatballs. It is better you don't know what it is that you eat."

"I second that," Luke said with grim humor. "Mitji's ingredients are sustaining but not tempting."

The officer got to his feet. "Sustenance will do, Mr. Bowman," he said. "Hunger soon takes care of any fads, as you've no doubt discovered yourself.'' He looked at me as I stood up. "We have two gallons of water, Miss . . . sorry, Mitji. How should we ration it?''

I shook my head. "Don't ration it, Mr. Sullivan. The best place to carry water is in the belly. Let it be shared equally just before we start, and let it be drunk then. It will carry us farther than if we drink in small quantities, and less will be wasted.''

He stared, then gave a doubtful nod. "Everybody else seems to be sure you know what you're about, so we'll do as you say." He forced a smile. "I just hope everybody is right."

IN THE NEXT FIVE DAYS WE JUDGED OURSELVES TO HAVE COVered some fifty miles, and in that time I found water only three times. On each occasion we dug for it in the bone-dry bed of a broad gully that had once been a river in aeons past, and we had to dig to a depth of almost four feet before water began to seep into the hole. Without the adz from Piroo's tool bag and the bailer we used as a shovel we could never have cleared the holes to such a depth.

The water was tinged brown and tasted of iron, but nobody cared. We were able to drink well and to replenish our two-gallon container before the seepage into the holes dwindled to dampness, but I was desperately thankful to have made the finds, and increasingly apprehensive that I might fail in the days ahead. This land was different from the outback I had known, and although my friends thought me remarkable I was worryingly aware that among the people I had grown up with I was considered to have hardly any sense of smell at all.

To provide food gave me less anxiety. There were lizards to be found, some quite large, and the gulls proved easy targets for my throwing club. I knew nothing of obtaining food from the sea, and the breakers were too dangerous for any attempt to fish, but Eliza and the men gathered shellfish to add to our store, and twice we found a dead fish washed up high on the beach.

With knife and club I cut and mashed everything together in the bailer, then wrapped balls of the mince in broad fronds of seaweed and baked them under the hot ashes of a driftwood fire. We were without matches, but that presented no difficulty for me. During the first fourteen years of my life I had made fire without knowing that matches existed.

For most of each day I was on my own. The rest of the party moved along the coast a hundred yards or so from the sea, but I went ahead and cast about between the sea and the dunes half a mile inland, searching for food and water. If I had been traveling alone I would have struck directly inland, for I knew there was much animal life to be found there, creatures with hoofs, creatures with paws. I did not know why they came down through the dunes, or why they seemed to do so only by night, but often I found their spoor and droppings or caught their scent.

On my own I could have found a more roundabout but easier way to our destination, for it was of no importance to me how long such a journey might take, but for the rest of the party this was out of the question, especially as Piroo had to be carried every step of the way.

We traveled only by day, because the terrain was so rough that it would have been dangerous to move in the cooler hours of darkness. Whenever I rejoined the party, usually two or three times each day, Piroo always called an eager greeting to me and thanked me effusively when I took him his share of the food I cooked when we made camp. I guessed somebody had told him that "missy," as he called me, had prevented his being left behind, but I did not know who it was.

Simon had evidently made a good job of splinting Piroo's broken leg, for the swelling had abated and he assured me that he was in little pain now. I was more concerned about Markie, for the ceaseless struggle over loose sand and jumbled rock under the brutal heat of the African sun left him utterly exhausted by the day's end, and his white skin had no natural protection from the sun, so that he was cruelly burned despite all his efforts to screen his head and arms. Even so, he insisted on taking his turn at carrying Piroo's stretcher, rotating every ten minutes with the other five men.

I had no further disagreements with Mr. Sullivan. He was a good leader, and after the first two or three days it was clear that he trusted me to do all that Luke had assured him I would do. I sometimes wished I had as much confidence in myself, but tried never to appear worried when I was with the others. Eliza and Simon gave me great support, for though like everyone else they grew gaunter and wearier as the days went by, they had a way of lifting our spirits with a smile, an encouraging word, or even a wry joke.

The young steward, Mercer, was a dark-haired Cornishman of about my own age. With me he was shy and tended to blush if I spoke to him. Though not a big lad he was strong and wiry, always ready to do more than his share of carrying Piroo, and of a placid nature that made me feel he would endure as well as any through whatever ordeals lay ahead. I was greatly touched by the way he tried to continue his duties in taking care of the ship's passengers, of Eliza and of Markie in particular.

Adrian Webb maintained his role so well that there were moments when I almost wondered if I had been mistaken. He gave no trouble, obeyed Mr. Sullivan's orders, and never spoke except to mumble a word or two in what I supposed was Portuguese, but which could have been Spanish or a concoction made up from a few basic words of either. If it had not been for his scent I would never have dreamed that he was other than the dull-witted foreign seaman he pretended to be.

One thing gave me great joy. When the party halted at dusk and I returned from my afternoon's foraging, I always saw Luke coming to meet me over the last few hundred yards, carrying the bailer in which I would mash our food. His lips were cracked, his face burnt, and his beard was growing, so he was beginning to look much as he had looked on the day I first found him, bu he always greeted me with a smile, and it seemed as if in some strange way he was happy now, despite all the danger and bruta hardship of our situation. Certainly he was friendlier than at any time since he had first taken me from Clairmont, and I was so glad to feel once again that easy warmth I remembered from the early months at Shalimar.

Over the sixth and seventh days Mr. Sullivan reckoned that we covered fifteen or sixteen miles, but in that time I found no water and little food. At dawn on the eighth morning we wrung dew from the clothes and blankets spread to absorb it, and licked droplets from rocks to slake our thirst. I could not forage far that day, for without water in my belly the sun would have killed me, but toward dusk I found a patch of fruit like small and rather shriveled melons, growing on tendrils of a creeper that spread over a patch of white sand between high dunes. There was little sustenance in them, but I decided that if we mixed the pulp with some pounded gull meat we had left they would help to fill our stomachs, and I knew that their growing here must indicate water.

With a few of the melons I walked half a mile to where Mr. Sullivan was making camp, then back with Luke and Simon to gather some more in a blanket and to fill our water container. We found water only three feet down, but the yield was small and we managed to fill the container only three-quarters full. This was disappointing, but at least it gave each one of us more than a pint to drink. With the night's dew this meant we would be able to continue for a little longer.

The next day proved to be a good one. I found water again, knocked down two gulls, dug out a fat lizard, and that night used my boomerang for the first time to good effect. This was at Luke's prompting. We had often heard jackals howling after dark, and on this particular evening, as we ate our meager supper, Luke said, "Suppose we went toward the dunes and lay low somewhere downwind, Mitji? There's a clear sky and a good moon, and we might tempt a jackal to come nosing around. We'll never get close enough to use Mr. Sullivan's pistol, but you might be able to pick up a silhouette and knock one down at long range with your boomerang. Meat to last for days, perhaps. Then you would only have to worry about finding water."

I nodded slowly. The prospect of success was not very great, but I was angry with myself for not making an attempt before. We had sometimes eaten dingoes in the tribe, and jackal meat would be much the same. We could use the remains of a gull as bait, and if we succeeded I could skin and quarter the carcass, cut up the meat, cook and dry it, and be free of worries about food for days to come. Even if we failed there was nothing to lose by the attempt except a few hours' sleep. Luke and I could as well spend the night two or three hundred yards away as lie here with the rest of the party.

"Bring Piroo's adz, Luke," I said.

Half an hour later we left camp and moved cautiously away through the darkness. I was holding Luke's hand to guide him, and that alone made the attempt worthwhile for me. Once we were well clear of the camp I set the bait on a flat slab of rock that rose a little higher than the surrounding beach; then we moved on downwind and lay on our stomachs side by side, looking toward the sea. We did not speak, and I was reminded of the day when I had lain hidden behind a *mangu* of brush with Yuma, waiting for the kangaroo to approach.

An hour passed. Two hours. Somewhere a jackal howled, but I could see nothing. Another hour. The wind was blowing toward us, and suddenly I caught the scent. Lifting my head, I peered across the moonlight-dappled beach. Then I saw it, sixty or seventy yards away, a dark shadow moving across a patch of white sand and up onto the slab of rock.

It halted, silhouetted against the sky, and I touched Luke's shoulder in warning as I rose slowly, slowly to my feet, slipping my right arm free from the strap of my petticoat so that there should be no hindrance to the throw. My arm swung, and Piroo's boomerang spun sweetly away, vanishing into the darkness as it curved out to my right. The jackal's head came up sharply, listening, scenting, and then out of the shadows came the whirling blade, its edge striking like a wooden ax to the side of the creature's head.

I cried, "Run, Luke! Run!" and sprang forward, knowing

that the jackal would only be stunned and fearing that it might quickly recover. With all the strength I could muster I raced on, breath rasping in my throat, Luke panting behind me, but as we drew near I saw that the strike had not been a good one, for already the animal was coming to its feet, shaking its head, and we were still twenty paces away. I stopped, and as Luke came running past me I threw Piroo's maul with a sobbing gasp of effort. It struck as the creature began to move, knocking the jackal down again, and as I ran on I saw Luke spring up onto the slab of rock and strike with the adz to the back of the neck.

I came up beside him and together we sank slowly to our knees, panting like dogs in our weakness from hunger and exhaustion. "Oh dear God," Luke croaked at last, "you did it, Mitji, you did it." He turned and gathered me in his arms, just holding me, his cheek against mine. I longed to turn my head and kiss him, but knew from past experience that even to show affection might suddenly change his mood, so I simply rested my head on his shoulder for a few moments until he let me go and stood up, helping me to my feet.

We returned to the camp in triumph with our trophy, and I suggested to Mr. Sullivan that we should make no attempt to travel next day but should rest instead. I would need several hours to deal with the jackal, and we were all very tired. But we had a full container of water, and a day's rest with meat in our bellies would give us fresh strength to continue our journey.

Mr. Sullivan agreed, and next morning as I started to skin the jackal I was approached by Mercer, the young steward. "Can I see to that for you, Miss Mitji?" he said. "I was a butcher's boy before I went to sea." He gave me a shy grin. "Never butchered a jackal before, but it can't be all that different from a sheep."

"I'm sure it isn't." I handed him the knife with a smile. "Cut the meat up small and don't waste a scrap. I'll make meatballs out of anything that might turn people's stomachs."

"Right, miss."

"I'll go out looking for water again now. I'd like to have a full container when we move off tomorrow."

"Yes, miss. Would you mind starting a fire for me first? You're the only one can do it."

The hole I had dug the day before yielded only a little more water, enough to fill half our container, but when we resumed our journey next morning we were all refreshed and in better heart. I began to feel quite proud of myself for having been able to feed and sustain nine people on this dreaded coast where no castaway had survived before, but my pride was short-lived. The terrain changed, and instead of sand and shingle we had to pick our way over honeycombed rock, split by shallow gullies, where it was horrifyingly easy to stumble and sustain a sprained or broken ankle, especially for those carrying Piroo on his stretcher.

In three days we covered only nine pitiless miles, and I found no water at all. Our container was empty. We kept ourselves alive on heavy dew wrung from clothes or sucked from tiny holes and crevices in rock. By the second day we could no longer swallow food because our throats were too dry. Eliza's shoes were torn to shreds, and she walked with her feet wrapped in strips of blanket. Markie's eyes had suffered so greatly that he could no longer open them for more than a minute at a time during the hours of daylight. This meant he was unable to take his turn with the stretcher, and he begged us to leave him behind. But before any of us could argue the point Eliza simply declared that she would not go on without him, so he was forced to continue. From then on he moved by day with a bandage over his eyes, holding Eliza's hand as she guided his steps.

By the evening of the thirteenth day we were at the end of our tether. The terrain seemed to be improving, but our strength was gone. My companions had blistered faces, sunken cheeks, and cracked lips, and they moved unsteadily on dragging feet. My early life seemed to have given me protection from the sun, for my body had now become dark brown without burning, but otherwise I was in no better shape than my companions, and hope had died within me.

At dusk we stumbled to a halt on a sandy patch amid a cluster of rocks a hundred yards from the sea's edge. Luke and Simon set down the stretcher, and we slumped where we stood, to lie without speaking a word between us, knowing that we could never move again. I must have slept, for it was dark when I roused to a touch on my shoulder. Luke's voice said in a rusty whisper, "Come a little way, Red . . . must talk."

SEVENTEEN

THE NIGHT DEW WAS FALLING. I LICKED SOME FROM MY ARMS and shoulders, sucked some from the petticoat remnants I had spread automatically. Luke took my hand and we moved away toward the sea; then he sat down with his back against a rock and drew me down beside him.

His voice was husky and effortful as he said, "Couldn't let it end without telling you. Without explaining." I heard him try to swallow. "Treated you so harshly, Red. Said such cruel things."

"Cruel?" I whispered. "Oh, Luke, no."

"Yes. Now . . . please try to understand. You know I loved Rosemary?"

"Of course. She was the light of your life." I felt strangely remote, as if I were in a dream, but it was good to be sitting beside Luke and to feel close to him.

He said, "You know she was too ill to . . . to be a wife in all respects?"

"Yes, I realized that from the beginning. You didn't . . . what I used to call lie together."

He was silent for a few moments. Then he said, "Mitji . . . Meg . . . I have a terrible thing to say. You were fifteen, and physically grown-up. I liked you. I respected you. And after a while, a year perhaps, I began to want you. I tried so

350

hard not to.'' His voice shook. "I've never pretended to be a saint. I've traveled far and lived hard, but from the moment I found Rosemary there was never anyone else. I swear to you I never stopped loving her, and you know I never touched you or betrayed what I felt. Just the opposite . . .''

I whispered, "I know . . . I know,'' and marveled at my own stupidity. Luke was a man in the prime of life, cut off from the world in remote Shalimar with a wife he adored but could not take to his bed. Then I had come upon the scene, a plain girl but with a strong young body and no notion of modesty, an earthy creature, glowing with health and happiness, working daily with him, sitting at the table with him, ever present in the home. It was little wonder that his blood had been stirred.

I said, "Oh, Luke, Luke, I'm sorry. It was so unfair to you, and it went on for so long. It must have been a torment. You should have sent me away.''

He gave a croaking laugh. "And broken Rosemary's heart? She was only a few years older than you, Mitji, so you were like a younger sister to her as well as being the child she could never have. I couldn't send you away. But I felt like a traitor, and I was so ashamed. That's why I was often unkind to you, as if you were to blame.''

I felt for his hand, and he did not draw it away from me. "That wasn't often,'' I whispered. "For most of the time you were my kind friend.'' We both spoke slowly, for we were drained of strength and struggling to talk from parched throats.

"I hated myself for wanting you,'' Luke said in a low voice. "You were so young, so very innocent, so warm and friendly, like a happy puppy. I used to dream about you, and almost hate you for that. But I'm still haunted by what I said to you when Rosemary died. You had been so kind, so loving, so good to her, yet only moments after she died I told you to get out of my sight.'' He sighed, and his voice faltered. "You know why? It was because . . . because I felt relief, Meg, relief that it was over, God forgive me."

Even my cruel thirst was forgotten in the pity I felt for the tortured man beside me. I pressed his hand and croaked, "There was nothing to forgive. You devoted your life to Rosemary. No man could have given her more love or cherished her more deeply. But she was suffering, and you knew the end was coming, so it was only human to feel relief when it came, when the ordeal was over. I felt the same, Luke, and I loved her more dearly than anyone in the world."

There was a long silence, and then he said in a faraway voice. "That wasn't all. After you had gone, and I thought I was free, I found it hadn't just been . . . crude male lust you made me feel. I couldn't get you out of my mind, Red. I longed for you daily. Oh, I wanted to hold you in my arms, but there was much more to it than that. I wanted to be with you, to work with you, to see that freckled urchin face across the table from me, to watch you just.. . move, because you're beautiful to watch. Even to see your alley-cat glare when you became indignant. I realized then that I'd been in love with you for a long time, yet I had never loved Rosemary any less." He shook his head. "Can a man really love two women like that? I can only say I did. You were so different, yet I loved you both, and it's never ceased to shame me, Mitji. I've been racked by guilt ever since, trying to put you out of my mind so I could stop feeling a traitor."

Meg . . . Mitji . . . Red. He was using all my names as his mind roamed back over the past. I said, "Luke, please listen. Rosemary didn't simply ask me to take care of you when she was gone. She said you would need me, and she begged me to marry you. I couldn't tell you before, because it seemed you wanted me out of your life as quickly as possible. I'm glad that was really only because you liked me. Do you understand what I'm saying, Luke? Rosemary loved us both, and truly wanted you to marry me. So you see, you'v never been a traitor to her, and there's never been any need for you to feel guilty."

I felt tremors pass through his body as if he were being shaken by dry sobs, and twice he muttered her name in a broken voice. With an effort I got to my knees and turned to put a hand to his cheek. "It's hard to talk," I said in a hoarse whisper, "so I have to tell you simply, Luke. I would have married you because Rosemary asked, and because I was always happy in your company. But it's more than that now. I found I was in love with you the day you took me away from Clairmont. It came to me suddenly, as we sat waiting for the ferry at Calais, and I've been trying to hide it ever since, because I didn't think you liked me much."

After a while he said in a voice I could barely hear, "Oh, Red . . ."

Slowly he embraced me, holding me close. Cracked lips touched cracked lips in a gentle kiss. Then I settled beside him with his arm about me, my mind a dreamlike confusion of gladness that we had found each other and an aching sorrow that for us there was no time left. "Nobody could ever replace Rosemary," I said, or perhaps it was only in my mind that I spoke, "but I would have made you such a loving wife, Luke, my dearest."

The world faded, and I slept. A dream came to me, and in it I was Mitji again, walking through the outback with the *kamil*. Ahead of us was a great lake of fresh water such as I had never seen, and we were pressing toward it because a raging thirst was upon us. The *kamil* broke free to run ahead, and in that moment I scented the water and awoke.

The first hint of light was coming into the sky. I was still propped against the rock with Luke, his arm holding me. My tongue felt swollen in my mouth, and I could not speak. Slowly I sat up. Luke stirred, and I saw his eyes open. He looked at me and his lips moved, but no word emerged. Something was different, something was strange. I could still scent the water of my dream, and it was coming from the

sea. The wind had changed and was bringing me a freshwater
scent from the sea, which was absurd.

But the scent persisted, and I groped for Luke's hand,
making signs for him to come with me. Slowly, unsteadily,
we made our way over smooth rock toward the sea. The salt-
water scent was full and strong, but underlying it there was
still the scent I had caught in my dream.

A narrow inlet, a crevice, split the rocky shore fifty yards
from the sea's edge where the breakers foamed. It was a deep
crevice, for the sea reached right up into it, though there was
dry rock on each side. I could not judge the depth, even
though the water here was very clear, but I stood looking
down into the landward end of the inlet, the narrow end,
while Luke swayed as if in a daze beside me.

There were slender ledges in the rocky side of the inlet
just below me, and the scent was stronger now. I let go of
Luke's hand, turned, and climbed down into the water. It
came breast-high when my feet touched bottom. The remains
of a breaker rippled up the inlet, lifting the water to my chin,
then receded. As it did so, I bent down and drank.

*Fresh water! Brackish but fresh, life-giving water, flowing
deep underground from the hinterland and reaching the sea
here, in this inlet. And each time a breaker receded, the flow
from the hidden stream was unpolluted by seawater for perhaps half a minute until the next wave came.*

I drank again, then lifted my head to Luke, laughing,
crying, beckoning, struggling to speak, to explain. Moments
later he was in the water beside me, dipping his head to drink
at my signal. When he had gulped down several mouthfuls I
held his arm and said, "Not too much too soon." My voice
still sounded rusty, but at least I could speak again.

He nodded, turning to me, taking me by the arms as we
stood there in the growing light, breast-deep in the water.
"Not too much," he echoed hoarsely. "I remember from
before, when you took the water bottle away . . . just after
the first time you kissed me, Mitji, and saved my life."

So Luke, too, remembered how I had given him water from my mouth that day. Now he put his lips gently to mine again, then straightened up, held my face between his hands for a long moment, ran a hand back over my shorn hair, and said, "Red, you're wonderful, and I adore you." He made a sideways movement of his head. "An underground stream?"

I was smiling up at him, almost grinning as I said, "It must be, and it's continuous! Oh, just imagine, Luke! We can rest here and drink our fill for two or three days, getting our strength back before we move on. I'll find enough food for us, and we already have most of that jackal meat left. I might even be able to make an extra water container from the skin. Oh please, hold me and kiss me just once more before we go and tell the others."

Five minutes later I squatted beside a full container of water, supporting Markie Lafayette with an arm about his shoulders while Eliza trickled water from a large shell between his lips. Nearby, his leg still splinted, Piroo drank greedily from the bailer. Luke had taken the others down to the inlet to drink, but Markie was too weak to move.

"Drink some more yourself, Eliza," I said. "I'll see to Markie now."

She lifted her burnt face to me and smiled. "There'll be time enough for me when Markie has drunk as much as you think wise. Poor dear man, he's suffered more than any of us."

Eyes closed, Markie lifted a feeble hand to her shoulder as she bent over him. Slowly he swallowed the water from the shell. His face was a patchwork, with small areas of white skin showing between great scabs where blisters had grown and burst. "Eliza," he whispered, "when Mitji brings us safely home, will you marry me, dear Eliza? Please? I know you are free. . . ."

Strangely I did not feel surprise. Tears welled in Eliza's eyes. She smoothed his snow-white hair back with a gentle hand, then touched her blistered lips to his brow. "Thank you for my first proposal, Markie," she said, "and please give me time to think. Will you ask me again when we reach Walvis Bay?"

TWO DAYS HAD GONE BY, AND WE WERE NEW PEOPLE, FOR we had an endless supply of water, and the jackal meat had filled our bellies, tough and stringy though it was. Now we were planning to move on the fourth day. Before we did so we would drink our fill, and when we left the precious inlet we would carry with us two gallons of water in the container, another gallon in the bailer, and a quart or more in a makeshift bag I had fashioned from the jackal skin in the way we had used possum skins when I lived with the tribe.

Mr. Sullivan had agreed that I should forage for as much food as possible before we left so that we could carry a supply with us, enough for three or four days if possible. This would free me from the anxious task of foraging as we went, and perhaps help the whole party to press on more quickly.

With our strength renewed there was an air of optimism about us now, despite the painfully burnt faces and limbs of my companions. After Markie, it was Adrian Webb who had sustained the worst burns, for the whole of his shaven head was a mass of blisters, with a stubble of hair beginning to appear in patches. He could have prevented the sunburn by covering his skull, but he had not done so, and I knew why. With his head covered he would have lost a strong feature of the disguise that made him Chin-up, and this he dared not do. Throughout the whole journey so far he had continued to play his chosen part, never speaking, obeying orders, accepting his share of food and water, causing no trouble, and never showing a sign of recognition in that single eye when his gaze fell upon me.

Because of our strange circumstances my companions seemed to have left the question of Chin-up's identity to be decided later and simply treated him as they treated Merce

and Piroo, as a seaman and one of our party. There was no
doubt in my own mind, though. I knew this man was Adrian
Webb, and I was very conscious that he might become a
danger to us once we were within sight of safety. I had already given warning, and for the time being I could only
ignore his presence except as Chin-up, while keeping always
in mind that this was the enemy who had for years sought my
death.

On the morning of the third day after my discovery of the
underground stream I set off southward along the coast with
Luke and Simon in search of food. The men kept to the
shore, seeking shellfish and the occasional dead fish that
heavy breakers had battered on the rocks, while I worked my
way up into the dunes, emerging every now and then to keep
pace with my companions and to exchange a wave with Luke.
He was a different man since the night we had sat telling of
our love for each other in the belief that we soon would die.
All the strain that once seemed to afflict him had dissolved
as if by magic. We said nothing to our friends of what had
happened, but neither did we try to hide our feelings for each
other.

During the early morning I tracked down and dug out one
large lizard, three small ones, and a furry burrowing creature
unknown to me. I also collected a number of grubs from a
huge and ancient piece of rotting driftwood and put everything in a bag made from a piece of cambric I had long since
cut from my petticoat for this purpose. I carried my throwing
club, hoping to bring down one or two gulls when I joined
the men on the shore, and I had also brought with me the
boomerang Piroo had made. There was little chance of my
seeing any game that would make a target for the boomerang,
but I would never have forgiven myself if such a chance came
and I had not been able to seize it.

Toward midmorning I was lucky to see a fairly large brown
land bird swoop down to pluck a tiny lizard from the sand,
and I was close enough to throw my club before the bird

could take off, so this made a welcome addition to my bag. I started back to the beach well satisfied, deciding that during the afternoon I would concentrate on gulls. Mercer, the young steward, could pluck and gut the birds for me; then I would mash shellfish, lizards, everything together and make a fire to cook meatballs. If my afternoon's hunting went well, we should be able to set off next morning with enough food to last for several days.

When I emerged from the dunes I saw that Luke and Simon were standing still, shading their eyes to look out to sea. In the last few minutes the mist over the sea had dispersed, the sky was blue, and there on the far horizon was a ship. The trail of smoke it had left showed it to be sailing south down the coast, and it was already well past our position, moving away from us. To see a ship passing by with people living safe and secure aboard brought a strange turmoil of feeling, but I knew it heralded no hope of rescue. Even if the ship had been visible earlier, and we had been able to build a driftwood fire, only by a miracle would anyone aboard have spotted what little smoke we could produce before the ship was out of sight.

I walked on, calling out as I drew near the shore. Both men turned, Luke with a smiling grimace, Simon with a rueful gesture. "Nothing to get excited about," said Simon. "No captain in his senses would risk coming any closer inshore on this coast, even if they spotted us. And if he did risk it he could never get boats ashore to pick us up. Those reefs are murderous."

Luke said cheerfully, "Never mind. That freak aborigine girl will get us safely home, won't you, sweetheart?" He came toward me, carrying a piece of blanket made into a bag that was almost half full of shellfish. Halting in front of me, he gazed at me with smiling eyes for a few moments, then shook his head. "By God, you're as grubby and unkempt and almost as undressed as when I first set eyes on you, Mitji—and as welcome a sight as you were that day."

I loved Luke to talk to me like that, for it told me how close we were, with all misunderstanding behind us. "With that burnt face," I said, "you look like a freak *walypala*. I've brought you some juicy lizards and luscious grubs for lunch. Would you like to see them?"

He winced and put a hand over his eyes. "Spare me, Mitji. Let the ingredients of those vile meatballs ever remain your own secret."

Simon came to join us, carrying his haul of shellfish. "Are you two going to be married?" he said soberly.

"If Mitji will have me." Luke took my hand.

A spark of the old humor touched Simon's eyes. "She's much too good for you, but congratulations anyway, and my warmest good wishes to you, Mitji. We didn't realize you two were in love till just the other day."

I said, "We each thought only one of us was in love till only the other day. Thank you for your good wishes, Simon." I looked to the south, where only a faint drift of smoke showed now. "Let's go back to camp. I might get a gull on the way, but anyway I'll come out again this afternoon."

We started back along the beach, and Simon said quietly, "Markie has asked Eliza to marry him. They've both told me separately. Did you know?"

I said, "I was there, Simon, so I knew. Has it surprised you?"

He passed a hand over the thick stubble of beard that thrust through the sores on his face. "I'm stunned," he said. "Do you—do you think she might accept?"

I felt pity for him, but an underlying anger also. "She might," I said. "He is to ask her again when we reach Walvis Bay."

"Oh dear God," Simon muttered distractedly. "I can't imagine being without Eliza. I just can't imagine it."

"You're the one who's left her free all these years when you could have married her," I said. "Don't complain now, Simon. Did you really expect her to go on giving herself to

you until she grew old and you decided you'd like a younger
woman? Don't you realize what a treasure she is for any man?
I'm truly fond of you, Simon, but as far as Eliza is concerned
I think you've been very foolish."

Luke whistled softly but said nothing. I felt suddenly embarrassed for having spoken so smugly and pompously, even
though my words came from the heart. I said quickly, "Forgive me, Simon. I had no right—"

"Don't," he said roughly. "Don't apologize. It's taken all
this to show me to myself as I am. But . . . can you help me,
Mitji?"

"Help you?"

"Help me not to lose Eliza." He looked at me with despairing eyes. "She's part of me. I mean, all these
years . . ."

I felt for Luke's hand and said in a small voice, "Oh,
Simon, how can I even try to help when it means siding with
you against Markie?"

He rubbed a hand across his eyes in a dazed fashion and
mumbled, "Yes. I didn't think. Of course you can't."

We moved on in silence, and I was glad we were now
drawing near to the cluster of rocks where we had made camp.
The coast turned almost in an easterly direction here for a
short distance, so the shade at this hour was still on the far
side of the rocks, and we could see nobody until we came to
within about seventy paces of the camp. It was just as we
reached this point that we heard a shot.

For a moment we froze, then ran forward only to halt again
as the camp came into view. Of the six figures there, only
one was standing. That was Adrian Webb, and from his pos-
ture it was clear that he held a gun in his hand. Piroo lay on
his stretcher as always, his toolbag beside him. A few yards
away Mr. Sullivan and Mercer were sprawled unmoving on
the ground. To one side, Eliza was on her knees, holding
Markie in a half-sitting position, and even from this distance
we could see a great red stain on his shirtfront. Adrian Webb

was turned away from us but looking back over his shoulder; at sight of us he spun round quickly with the gun held ready.

My heart pounded with shock and fear as I said, "It's Adrian Webb. He means to kill us all. He has to."

From Luke came a hoarse whisper, "Dear God Almighty, he's shot Markie. And you warned us, Mitji."

Simon said tautly, "Only one shot fired so far. He must have clubbed Sullivan and Mercer. Saving ammunition to deal with *us*, and then he can take a cleaver to the rest."

Luke drew in a deep breath and his voice was very cool as he said, "Webb may take a cleaver to Eliza any moment, so we have to act now. Listen, Simon. We separate a little, then we both run at him, offering two moving targets. A revolver is pretty useless at more than ten yards, so one of us should be able to reach him—with luck, and with Mitji's help." He gave me a quick glance. "Choose your moment, my darling. It's us he'll be watching. All right, Simon—*go!*"

They began to run, dropping their bags of shellfish and spreading apart at first, then heading directly for the tall figure with the great black beard who stood waiting to kill them. I let fall my bag and my maul, then slipped the shoulder straps of my petticoat down and freed my arms so that I would not be hampered in the slightest degree. My mouth was dry with fear, and I had to clench my teeth to prevent their chattering. Adrian Webb's head turned first to one approaching figure, then the other, and it was plain that he was coolly gauging his moment to fire. I weighed the boomerang in my hand, then blotted out all thought and simply threw, just as I had thrown a thousand times before, but never with so much at stake.

I threw straight and low and hard, so that the weapon would reach its target with utmost speed, but even as it left my hand I knew I had made a mistake. In my anxiety I had thrown too soon, for unless the boomerang took Adrian Webb full in the face it would do no more than wound him, knock him down perhaps, or send him staggering; and because I had thrown seconds too soon he might well have time to recover from the shock and shoot down Luke or Simon or both before they reached him.

Even as the boomerang went spinning through the air I snatched up the maul and began to run, not with any hope of getting within throwing distance before it was too late, but with the frantic hope that my running figure might prove a further distraction for Adrian Webb. I saw the boomerang rise almost from the ground to strike at chest height, but at the last second Adrian Webb must have glimpsed it, for he half turned, trying to ward it off with the arm of the hand holding the gun.

The thin edge of the whirling blade could well have gashed his arm, for I heard him cry out and saw the gun go spinning away; but he dived after it, sprawling full length, reaching out for the gun with his sound hand, while both Luke and Simon, running desperately in the soft sand, were still yards away. It was then that little Piroo, from his stretcher, rolled over sideways twice and swung his hand at full arm's length to crash a heavy wrench on Adrian Webb's head in the instant that he grasped the fallen gun.

By the time I reached the spot, Luke was easing Piroo into a comfortable position, the little lascar jabbering excitedly. Simon was kneeling over the prone body of Adrian Webb, turning him on his back and feeling for the pulse in his neck. I ran past to where Eliza was cradling Markie and tore open the blood-covered shirt. My heart sank, and I shuddered as I saw the wound, for I knew he had only moments to live. His eyes were closed, and his burnt face was gray between the scabs and blisters now.

"Caragh?" he muttered feebly. "Caragh . . . are you there?" Eliza looked at me with desolate eyes and nodded. I took his hand and said shakily, "Yes, I'm here, Markie dear. I'll look after you. Don't worry now."

"Not worried . . . just sleepy. I found her, Caragh . . . found your little girl. You'll be so proud of her."

I could only speak whatever words came to my mind, and I said, "I'm proud of *you*, Markie. You're such a good, kind man. Such a wonderful friend."

"Love you so much, Caragh . . . always." The voice grew even fainter. "So tired now . . . say good night . . ."

"Good night, Markie dear. Sleep well." I leaned forward and rested my lips against his own poor blistered lips for a moment or two, then knelt holding his hand. He lay quietly in Eliza's arms, his breathing shallow and ragged. Then, with one long, contented sigh, he went limp, and his head slumped onto her breast. Very gently she laid him down. Still kneeling, she turned to me and opened her arms. We held each other, both weeping, and it was a little while before we got to our feet.

Luke bent to cover Markie with a blanket. Simon had just done the same for Adrian Webb. Mr. Sullivan was sitting up now, holding his head in both hands. Mercer lay propped on an elbow, staring dazedly about him. "Adrian Webb is dead," said Simon. "Piroo cracked his skull with that wrench."

"Good," said Eliza in a flat voice. "It's as well Mitji made us bring Piroo along with us." She bent to tear some rags from her tattered petticoat and handed a piece to me. "Here, we'd better see to these sailors, dear." She shuffled toward Mercer on her blanket-wrapped feet. I poured water into the bailer, set it down between us, then knelt by Mr. Sullivan and began to bathe the great bruise swelling on the side of his head.

Simon twirled an eye patch on his finger, then tossed it away. "There was nothing wrong with the fellow's eye," he said.

Eliza gave him an impatient glance. "Of course there wasn't. That thing lying there was Adrian Webb. Quite suddenly he snatched a mallet from Piroo's toolbag and clubbed Mr. Sullivan down. Mercer grappled with him and was clubbed in turn." She slipped an arm around the young steward's shoulder and held the wet rag to his head. "All right, sonny-boy, just take your time. It's all over now, thank God."

Luke said, "You saw it happen, Eliza?"

She looked up at him. "Oh yes. I was a little way off; Markie was nearer. In a flash Webb unbuttoned Mr. Sullivan's holster and pulled the gun out. Then he spoke to Markie in English, in his own voice, thick with hate, and he said something like, 'That Glencullen bitch knows, doesn't she? But I've still beaten you, Lafayette—beaten the lot of you. I'll be the only survivor, fools that you are.' "

Eliza bowed her head and shivered. "He lifted the gun to shoot Markie. I ran forward, calling out, trying to distract him. He turned the gun on me and fired, but Markie jumped in front of me. I caught him as he fell. Then . . . you came."

I soaked my rag again and held it to Mr. Sullivan's head. He said unsteadily, "Thank you, Miss . . . Mitji. It happened just as Mrs. Fordyce said. I couldn't move, but I heard the man speak." He pressed fingers to his eyes. "You warned us he would be dangerous. We should have followed your advice."

I said tiredly, "No, Mr. Sullivan. I was wrong. Mr. Lafayette agreed with you, and he was right." I felt my eyes fill with fresh tears. "Even if he had known what would happen he would never have agreed to kill the man, because Mr. Lafayette was a civilized gentleman, not a savage like Adrian Webb . . . or like me. It cost him his life, but he was ready to pay that price to live as he thought right."

I paused to rub my tears away, then said, "What I don't understand is why Adrian Webb chose this moment to strike. I was sure he would wait until we were in sight of safety."

Eliza said, with a catch in her voice, "We are, Mitji. Didn't you see the ship?"

I looked at her, puzzled. "Yes, we saw it, but they can't have seen us from aboard."

"I know, dear. But Mr. Sullivan explained that the coast

just here runs almost east and west for a little way, so the ship must have been sailing on a southeasterly heading.''

I was trying to grasp the significance of her words when Luke said, "But that means it's angling in toward the coast, and surely no captain would deliberately bring his ship within miles of this death trap."

Mr. Sullivan lifted his head and took the damp rag from me with a murmured word of thanks. "That's quite true, Mr. Bowman," he said. "The only reason a ship would start closing on the coast hereabouts is because it's changing course to approach Walvis Bay."

There was a little silence as his meaning sank in, then Simon said, "You mean . . . we can't have far to go now?"

Mr. Sullivan got slowly to his feet. "From that ship's position and heading, I believe Walvis Bay can be no farther than another thirty miles down the coast, which means we're little more than ten miles from Swakopmund. Unfortunately I made the mistake of saying as much when we sighted the ship, and that was when your Mr. Adrian Webb decided it was time for the slaughter to begin." He looked at the blanket-covered forms on the ground. "I still don't know how you stopped him."

"Mitji and Piroo managed it between them," said Simon, his voice not quite steady. "Mr. Bowman will tell you how." He bent to pick up the adz. "I'll go and start digging a grave."

I WAS BUSY FOR THE REST OF THAT DAY, BUT NOT IN SEEKING food as I had expected, for we were now plentifully supplied with food and water to carry us through the last ten miles or so. Without discussion it was taken for granted that Markie Lafayette was not to share a grave with his murderer. Eliza chose the place for Markie to lie, buried deep in the sand, by a flat rock a long way up the beach, and when we had laid him to rest we spent an hour carrying rocks to build a cairn over the grave.

When this was done I spent three hours with a metal spike and a hammer, cutting an inscription in the soft limestone of the flat rock. The letters were shallow and crudely formed, but I would not allow any of the men to help me in my task. The inscription simply said:

MARKIE LAFAYETTE
BELOVED BY HIS FRIENDS

My hands and wrists ached by the time it was done, and I knew that when we were gone no human eye might ever read that inscription till the end of time; but we would know it was there. I knelt and said a prayer for Markie, then called my companions, and when they had gathered by the grave Mr. Sullivan said a seaman's prayer for him. Eliza had made a little posy from gull feathers and petticoat ribbon, and when she had laid it on the cairn we returned to our camp.

Adrian Webb was buried in the sand at least two hundred yards away, and nobody said a prayer for him. This was un-Christian and uncharitable, but Simon said it was also un-hypocritical and he rather hoped there was a hell, because he would be well content to pay for his own sins if he knew Adrian Webb was paying for his. This was a shameful thought, but I had no doubt we all felt the same way.

At first light next day we set off once more. The terrain improved as we went, and toward late afternoon we came to the tiny settlement at the mouth of the Swakop River. The bed of the river was dry, and Mr. Sullivan told us that its water reached the sea only two or three times a year, but there were wells to support the little community. I had never heard of Swakopmund until after the *Caragh* was wrecked, but during the last few hours of our approach Mr. Sullivan explained that it lay on the coast of South West Africa, an area recently annexed by Germany, but that Walvis Bay, twenty miles farther south on the Kuiseb River, was a British enclave.

The handful of Germans in charge of the natives in Swakopmund were astonished by our arrival. They received us with great kindness, provided food, shelter, and first aid for our hurts, and next morning took us by boat down the coast to Walvis Bay in a following wind that allowed us to make the journey in little more than four hours.

Our arrival there caused even greater astonishment, for it transpired that the other lifeboats from the *Caragh* had been sighted and picked up by a cargo ship after only two days at sea, and the crew had been brought direct to Walvis Bay. Some of the men had joined other ships and left, but Captain Lester was still there awaiting passage to England. It was naturally believed that we had long since died, either at sea or on the dreaded Skeleton Coast, and everybody was baffled as to how we had survived and made such a journey.

At my earnest request, nothing was said of the part I had played in this, for I had no wish to be regarded as a curiosity. Mr. Sullivan reported the whole truth to Captain Lester, but apart from that we made Simon our spokesman, and if it had not been for our sorrow over Markie's death we would have been hard put to stifle laughter as we listened to the amazing fantasies woven by Simon's practiced tongue, stories of our castaway experiences that would have put Robinson Crusoe to shame and were never meant to be believed.

Piroo was taken into the tiny mission hospital, and my other companions were given creams and lotions to ease their sunburn. There was a telegraph connection to Cape Town, which enabled Luke to send messages for onward transmission to London and to arrange for clothes, money, and letters of credit to be sent from Cape Town on a ship that was to call in ten days' time en route for Southampton. He also reserved cabins on this ship for our journey home.

Before we left, Luke made Piroo rich with a gift of two hundred pounds. I visited the little carpenter two or three times during our stay, and on the last occasion I returned his boomerang, which gave him great delight. Those were strange, quiet days after our long ordeal. Sometimes I felt overwhelmed by sadness for Markie, and at other times I was filled with joy because Luke was with me, because Luke loved me and wanted me, because I knew and understood why he had sometimes been so cold and unfriendly in the past, and because now, with boundless gratitude and happiness, I could keep my promise to Rosemary, who had been everything to me.

When we were alone together we talked of the future. He asked if I would like to return to Australia when we were married, but I said I wished to live on his farm in Somerset and give him some fine babies, at which he laughed helplessly, kissed me again, and said there was nobody like a freak aborigine girl for calling a spade a spade.

There came a day when we stood on the quayside in our ill-fitting clothes, borrowed or secondhand, watching the approach of the ship that would take us to England. I stood with my arm through Eliza's, many thoughts filling my mind as I recalled how greatly our lives had been interwoven since that first day when I had seen her as Mrs. Fordyce, the preacher's wife. I wondered what thoughts were in her own mind now, and was glad her sunburn was healing well, so that her beautiful face would not be scarred.

Luke and Simon stood behind us on the quay and had been silent for several minutes. No doubt each one of us was busy with memories of all that had passed in the last few weeks. Then Simon cleared his throat and said almost hesitantly, "Eliza . . ."

She did not turn, but said, "Yes, Simon?"

"If Markie had lived, you could have become a very rich lady as his wife."

I saw the corner of her mouth twitch in a brief sad smile as she said, "Yes."

"And I believe you could have been very happy together, Eliza."

"Yes, I'm sure we could, Simon."

"He wouldn't have been such a fool as to take you for granted, or fail to realize how much you meant to him."

"No, I don't suppose he would."

"I liked Markie even when he was simply the man in the dark room," said Simon reflectively. "Then later, when we came to know him, I was proud to be his friend. But when saw his courage during those days on the Skeleton Coast I admired him beyond measure. I'm truly sad to have lost a friend, and I shall always remember that he died for you, Eliza. All I can say now is . . . would you consider marrying a selfish fool without much money instead?''

Eliza did not stir. I saw her eyes close for a few moments; then she opened them again to gaze out over the bay. ''I might, Simon,'' she said at last in a gentle voice. ''Ask me again when we're home.''

EIGHTEEN

AUNT BECKY DABBED HER EYES WITH A HANDKERCHIEF AND said, "It was very kind of you to come, dear."

Two months had gone by since our return to England, and I was sitting in her drawing room in my new coat and flat-crowned toque. Luke was waiting in a carriage outside. Aunt Becky looked ten years older. Her eyes were sunken and haunted.

"I just came to reassure you," I said. "The mortgages on both houses have been cleared, and if you sell the manor house at Eastbourne you'll be able to manage very well with the boys' schooling and—and everything."

She wept again, and I longed for this ordeal to be over. When she had recovered a little she said tremulously, "I know what he did, Meg. The solicitor told me. It was all in a statement from those sailors and Mr. Fordyce. He stole a lot of your money and he tried to kill you." She shook her head despairingly. "I didn't know him at all. I simply didn't *know* him."

I said, "Please don't distress yourself. Most of my father's northern estates are intact, and in any event I don't need the money. I shall be marrying Mr. Bowman next month, and apart from that I've been told by solicitors that a large fortune has been left to me by Mr. Lafayette."

Markie had also bequeathed handsome legacies to Simon and Eliza, but that was of no interest to Aunt Becky. "I just wanted to tell you," I went on, "that you need not worry about legal actions or losing the houses." Then I summoned up my best powers of hypocrisy and added, "I'm sorry your husband died."

She blinked at me with red-rimmed eyes. "Sorry? Oh, don't be, dear. Don't be sorry. I was *glad* when they told me, even before I knew what he had done, shooting that poor man out there in the desert."

Startled, I said, "You were glad?"

She leaned forward, and her voice became a whisper. "Because of the confession, dear. The confession. They won't take any action now, of course, because he's dead."

I said gently, "What confession, Aunt Becky?"

"The man in prison. He was dying, and he wanted to clear his conscience, so he made this confession and they wrote it down. That was just after *he* went to America. Well, he only pretended to go there really, of course."

Aunt Becky's account was very confusing, but I realized that *he* was her husband, Adrian Webb, whose name she did not want to speak. "What was the confession about?" I asked.

Her eyes closed and she rocked as if in agony. "About my father, dear. This brute of a man confessed that he—he *killed* him in the stable. Hit him with a club that had a horseshoe nailed to it, so it appeared that my poor dear Papa had been kicked by the horse. The man's confession said *he* made him do it. As a solicitor, *he* learned something bad about this man, you see. That's how he made him do it, but he gave him some money, too."

I sat stunned for long seconds, recalling how Markie had voiced suspicions about the way Aunt Becky's father had died. Then I said, "You mean your husband arranged for your father to be . . . murdered?"

"Yes, dear! So that *he* could inherit the property—through me, of course." She covered her face. "Oh, the wicked, wicked man. I shudder to think I was married to him." Slowly she drew her hands away, leaving her cheeks streaked with tears. "I'm trying so hard to get in touch with dear Papa," she said pitifully.

"I thought that now I know the truth he might have found it easier to reach me through Mrs. Cruikshank, but we've had no success."

I felt desperately sorry for her, but I had done all that was in my power to help her, and now I wanted to be free of any link with Adrian Webb. "Perhaps it takes time for such things to have an effect on departed spirits," I said vaguely, "but I'm sure you must find great comfort in the séances, Aunt Becky."

On the last words I rose, gathering up my gloves and handbag. "Please excuse me now. I have Mr. Bowman waiting outside with a carriage."

"Yes, of course, dear." She jumped to her feet and moved with me to the door of the room. "You mustn't keep your fiancé waiting. I do hope you will be very happy, and I'm deeply sorry for all the tribulation you've suffered. What was the name of that poor man *he* murdered in the desert?"

We were crossing the hall now, and I said, "That was Mr. Lafayette, the gentleman who protected me, Aunt Becky."

"I'll see if Mrs. Cruikshank can get in touch with Mr. Lafayette, dear," she said confidingly. "He *might* be able to help her get through to my dear papa. Is there any message you would like her to give Mr. Lafayette if she can find him?"

A brusque reply rose to my lips. I did not know whether it was possible for the living to speak with the dead, but I hoped and prayed that Markie's spirit had found peace in being freed from the affliction he had borne during his life on earth, and did not want that peace disturbed. With an effort I held back the words I would have said. Aunt Becky was a pathetic figure now, widow of a murderer and perhaps with many shapeless troubles to come, for her young son Edward appeared to be a replica of his father.

She was waiting eagerly for my reply now, so I said, "Perhaps Mrs. Cruikshank could simply give him my love and gratitude."

"Yes, dear, yes. I'll tell her." Aunt Becky was at the front door with me now. "It's only a hope, you know. Mrs. Cruikshank may not be able to make contact. She can only try."

"Yes, I understand."

"Where are you going now, dear? I'll let you know what happens."

"Well, until I marry I'm staying with Simon and Eliza Fordyce at a house they've taken in Portman Square, but I—I really don't want to know what happens."

Her face fell. "Oh, well . . . it's entirely up to you, Meg."

"Thank you, Aunt Becky. I'll say good-bye now."

"Good-bye, dear."

I kissed her cheek and heard the front door close as I walked down the steps, thankful that the visit was behind me now. A few paces along the pavement Luke stood waiting, leaning on his cane, raising his hat as I approached. There was no sign of the carriage. I took his arm and said, "What happened to the growler?"

"I sent it away," he replied airily. "I thought we might walk back to Portman Square through Hyde Park, because then I can enjoy having all the men we pass look at me with envy."

"Flattery," I said as we began to walk. "You always told me I was plain."

"I lied, Red. I lied."

"Well, we'll see. There, that man didn't look at all envious."

"Fools don't count, my darling."

I laughed. "Oh, Luke, I do so long to be married to you."

"Ladies are not supposed to long."

"I know, but I'm a savage."

He sighed. "Ah, Red. I carry so many pictures of you in my mind. There's that first moment in the outback when I opened my eyes to see your dirty freckled face as you gave me water, and another moment days later when you were so ill, your whole body smothered in spots, but you kept on and on until you collapsed, trying to bring this strange *walypala* to safety."

We crossed the road into the park, and I said, "Tell me other moments, Luke."

"Oh . . . there was one in those early days at Shalimar when we were working together, you in your secondhand boots and shapeless dungarees, but so happy and grateful for everything, pitiful though it was. And you were ready to go and hunt down the sorcerer who was making Rosemary ill, even though you were terrified of his magic. You were going to bring him down with your boomerang, and then run very fast and kill him with your spear."

I had almost forgotten the incident, and though it came back to me now, I remembered it as if the girl Luke spoke of had been a stranger to me. I said, "I know it seems quite awful to a civilized person, but it wouldn't have been at all shocking to my tribe, and I would have dared anything for Rosemary."

"I know, my sweetheart. In my mind I have pictures of her teaching you, and you struggling so hard to learn from your books. I have pictures of you giggling together in the kitchen about something, and of you taking such care of Rosemary at the end."

We walked on in silence for a little while. Then he gave a soft laugh and said, "There are sad pictures and happy pictures and funny pictures. I can see you now, when you returned from fetching that map of the gold mine and I caught you unawares in your—your outback undress. Great big green eyes round with indignation as you ran to cover yourself with a bit of petticoat."

He pressed my hand holding his arm. "There was never an ounce of guile in you, Red, and you were just the same when I came for you at Clairmont—and found myself stunned to discover a beautiful young lady in place of the ragamuffin I'd fallen in love with. That's another picture I carry with me. There are so many, but some of the most vivid are of moments on that godforsaken journey down the Skeleton Coast, when you were Mitji again, and keeping us all alive."

I gave a loud, unladylike sigh of content. "Oh, you do say such lovely encouraging things, Luke. But what about my alley-cat glare?"

He grinned. "Oh, that's what I'm marrying you for. It's one of my favorite bits of you."

I laughed, and we walked on, emerging from the park at

Cumberland Gate. No man looked with envy at Luke, but that neither surprised nor troubled me. "*Mitjiquin*," I said.

He looked down at me, puzzled. "Queen Victoria? What about her?"

"No, not Queen Victoria! I told you ages ago and you've forgotten. *Mitjiquin* is a very powerful magic word I was taught by an apprentice sorcerer, and I can use it to bring about my heart's desire."

"Well, there's a lucky girl. May I know what your heart's desire is at the moment, Miss Glencullen?"

I copied his formal style. "By all means, Mr. Bowman, though I fear you will think me a shameless hussy. However, I make only modest wishes, and at this moment my heart's desire is simply to take a cab and arrive home at Portman Square with all possible speed, so that we may have the privacy to kiss each other, perhaps several times."

"Ah!" He held my hand tightly, looking up and down the road, and his face fell. "Not a cab in sight," he said. "This is sheer persecution."

"*Mitjiquin!*" I repeated firmly, then burst into surprised laughter as a hansom came clattering around the corner toward us.

"Witchcraft," Luke breathed wonderingly. "Red, you're unique." And he lifted his cane to hail the cab.

The *Choice* for Bestsellers also offers a handsome and sturdy book rack for your prized novels at $9.95 each. Write to:

The Choice for Bestsellers
120 Brighton Road
P.O. Box 5092
Clifton, NJ 07015-5092
Attn: Customer Service Group